KT-420-324

WITHDRAWN FROM
BROMLEY LIBRARIES

To renew, find us online at:
https://prism.librarymanagementcloud.co.uk/bromley
Please note: Items from the adult library may also
accrue overdue charges when borrowed on
children's tickets.

Also by Maya Blake

The Sicilian's Banished Bride
The Commanding Italian's Challenge
The Greek's Hidden Vows
Reclaimed for His Royal Bed

Ghana's Most Eligible Billionaires

Bound by Her Rival's Baby

Also by Caitlin Crews

The Sicilian's Forgotten Wife
The Bride He Stole for Christmas

Pregnant Princesses collection

The Scandal That Made Her His Queen

The Lost Princess Scandal miniseries

Crowning His Lost Princess

Discover more at millsandboon.co.uk.

A VOW TO CLAIM HIS HIDDEN SON

MAYA BLAKE

RECLAIMING HIS RUINED PRINCESS

CAITLIN CREWS

MILLS & BOON

First Published in Great Britain 2022
by Mills & Boon, an imprint of HarperCollins*Publishers* Ltd,
1 London Bridge Street, London, SE1 9GF

www.harpercollins.co.uk

HarperCollins*Publishers*
1st Floor, Watermarque Building,
Ringsend Road, Dublin 4, Ireland

A Vow to Claim His Hidden Son © 2022 Maya Blake

Reclaiming His Ruined Princess © 2022 Caitlin Crews

ISBN: 978-0-263-30081-9

05/22

MIX
Paper from
responsible sources
FSC® C007454

A VOW TO CLAIM HIS HIDDEN SON

MAYA BLAKE

MILLS & BOON

To Mansa, my gorgeous baby sis. This one is for you!

PROLOGUE

SOMEONE WAS HACKING *his bank.*

Again.

If Ekow Quayson hadn't been so infuriated at the ease with which the hacker had infiltrated his formidable internet firewall, he would've been impressed. But his sense of humour had left the building after the third breach.

'How the hell is this still happening?' he barked into the phone. 'Correct me if I'm wrong, but don't I pay you astronomical sums to ensure this sort of thing doesn't happen?'

He didn't need to be in the same room to know that his cyber security team were shaking in their boots. He hadn't yet taken the final step of firing them after weeks…no, *months*…of the cat-and-mouse game this hacker was playing with him only because they were the best—*supposedly*—on the market.

'Sir, they're using a very sophisticated system. One we haven't seen before. But we're attempting to—'

'Stop attempting and get it done! You're cyber security experts. It's your job to make sure no system, sophisticated or otherwise, messes with my bank. You're failing. Fix it. Now.'

'Yes, sir. Our counterparts in South Africa are working on the issue right now. That's where we pinpointed the last few attacks. We should… It'll be taken care of within the next few hours.'

Ekow froze in his chair. 'Did you say South Africa?' he asked, choosing to ignore the false confidence his security chief had layered on his response. They were all skating on thin ice, and he wouldn't hesitate to fire them if the breach wasn't sorted this time.

'Yes, sir. We're moments away from tracking the hacker down.'

Ekow barely heard the response as his fingers curled into a fist on his desk and a curious roiling started inside him.

South Africa.

He knew he was giving too much power to a geographical location, but the slow, unrelenting knots tightening in his gut mocked that knowledge.

South Africa… Specifically Cape Town…

The place he'd met *her.*

By his very strict record, he should've forgotten her by now. Moved on to the next available woman as he did every few months. It was the way he preferred things. It ensured mutual enjoyment without inviting notions of permanence. Since he'd turned thirty, two years ago, it was as if he had switched on an unknown beacon to the opposite sex, urging them not to take seriously his 'just fun, nothing heavy' edict when it came to relationships.

Every single one had eventually discovered he'd meant it, of course. Because he'd sworn off entanglements of any sort except the very transient kind. And if those brief liaisons with the opposite sex had only got briefer and less enjoyable in the last few years it was no one's business but his own.

When life had taught you that emotional connections led to disappointment and devastation, you learned the very real lesson that keeping your emotions out of things was the best way forward.

He'd learned that truth up close.

First by observing his father's patently biased relationship with Ekow's eldest brother, Fiifi. And then by watching that same brother with the woman he'd lived for and eventually died with.

Fiifi's relationship with Esi had been a melodramatic tragedy to challenge the most epic historical love saga—starting with her being forbidden fruit because their families were sworn enemies, then swerving into the volatile nature of their relationship. He'd never seen two people so right and yet so wrong for each other, their highs and lows a dizzying spectacle he'd watched from a safe and highly sceptical distance.

Of course it had been heartbreaking but almost karmic to witness it end dramatically in a car crash on Fiifi's twenty-fifth birthday, with a lovers' row after a night of ferocious celebration. A shocking tragedy that had rocked both families.

And then there was Ekow's relationship with his father. Or, more accurately, the distinct *lack* of one.

He'd known all that sixteen months ago, during his business trip to South Africa. Yet none of those warnings had made a blind bit of difference while he'd been with her.

Because she left you.

Was he so shallow to let a rejection affect him for this long? Aggravate him this intensely? Or was it something else? Something about *her*?

Evangeline.

Was it because she'd never told him her full name, perhaps? That he wasn't even sure if the first name she had given him was correct? Even while he'd been cynically confident he wouldn't be ensnared by her air of mystique—deliberate, he suspected—he'd ended up yearning to know every single thing about her...

Impatient with his train of thought, he gritted his teeth and surged to his feet. He hadn't thought about her in weeks. And he had more pressing matters to deal with than a woman he was sure would've turned out to be just as ordinary as the rest of them.

'I want a report in the next four hours of who is toying with my security. Fail me and you will be terminated,' he grated into the phone.

Control reinstated, Ekow ended the call and resumed his work day, dismissing the mystery woman from his mind with the same ruthless efficiency with which he ran his family bank.

The report arrived in two hours.

Another hour later and he had the right people in place to track down his hacker.

But some problems required the personal touch, and so Ekow found himself reaching for the phone one final time, and summoning his pilot to ready his jet— destination Cape Town.

He'd deal with this problem once and for all in the only way he knew how—with Quayson power and might.

And if he was heading to the same city as Evangeline, the woman who'd given herself to him in ways that still stopped his breath and then disappeared without a trace, what did it matter?

CHAPTER ONE

'JONAH, DID YOU hear me? I said dinner is—'

Evangeline Annan froze in the doorway of her brother's room, mild dread seizing her as she watched him scramble around the tiny desk in his room before facing her, his thin-lipped, now-permanent scowl fully in place.

'How many times do I have to tell you to knock before you come in?' he demanded, belligerent even while attempting to wipe the look of guilt from his face.

Evangeline pursed her lips, the worry gnawing at her insides intensifying. 'The door was already open—and, no, that wasn't a suggestion that you lock it from now on. You're fifteen, and the rules—'

'I know what the rules are! "No locking doors in this house,"' he parroted in a voice on the cusp of breaking.

He finally straightened and she felt a pang of mingled pride and sadness. Pride because she'd had a hand in raising this boy who now towered over her, and had succeeded in keeping him alive despite the dire challenges they'd faced. Sadness because her mother hadn't lived to see the man he would eventually become. *If* whatever secrets he was keeping from her didn't land him in worse trouble than the one-week school suspension he'd already incurred in the last academic year.

'What's going on?' she forced out, despite her senses screaming at her to leave it alone.

She'd been a teenager once, and knew that surging hormones, anxiety and finding one's place in the world didn't always make for good bedfellows. Add the death of their mother two years ago, after a long, debilitating and costly illness, and then the very real threat of losing the only home he'd ever known, and it was no wonder her brother had retreated into himself.

Despite all that, though, her baby brother had been extra closed-off in recent months, and while they hadn't been super-close because of their twelve-year age difference, the changes in him felt like night and day, and her sense that there was something wrong wouldn't let up.

On cue, he rolled his eyes. 'There's nothing wrong. Quit the mother hen routine, would you, sis?' he admonished, with a hard bite that hit her in the raw.

He brushed past her on his way to the tiny dining room in the tiny house they shared in Woodstock, on the outskirts of Cape Town city. She knew he'd wolf down his food and dash back into his room within minutes, leaving her torn between giving him his space and attempting further communication.

She followed on slower feet, wondering whether there was another reason for his belligerence.

The thought pulled her focus in a different direction. She bit her lip and glanced towards the closed door of her bedroom. As she'd come to expect, her heart flipped over with awe, love, and the lingering dose of anxiety that constituted being a mother.

Especially a mother to a child whose father had denied every trace of his existence.

Her heart lurched. She breathed through the pang of

disquiet and churning emotions dwelling on the man who'd fathered her baby triggered.

This wasn't about her beloved seven-month-old son and the circumstances surrounding his conception and birth.

This was about Jonah.

Entering the dining room, she glanced at her brother. Was he resentful of his new nephew? Resentful that he no longer had Evangeline all to himself?

She shook her head.

No. Jonah adored his nephew.

But it had been just them against the world for so long. They'd been through hell and back, fighting to stay together, fighting to keep the roof over their heads while looking after their sick mother.

That sort of experience should've bonded them, shouldn't it?

'Jonah, whatever is going on, you know you can talk to me, don't you?'

'Sure. Whatever,' he grunted around a mouthful of tuna pasta bake, almost bringing a smile to her face.

But immediately worry wiped it away. 'Are you in trouble?' She mentally crossed her fingers, her breath held, as first outrage and then impatience weaved over his face. 'Because if you're hiding something from me that you shouldn't—'

'You mean like you hid your pregnancy from me for months? Because if anyone knows about keeping secrets it's you, right?' he threw back at her.

They both froze in the ensuing silence, and for a moment remorse flashed in his eyes. Then he brazened it out, shrugging as he went back to eating.

Evangeline swallowed, her fingers curling over the back of the chair across from him. It wasn't the first time her brother had brought this matter up, but it didn't lessen the pain.

'I've told you why I didn't tell you when it happened,' she replied, her lips barely moving.

'Oh, yes—you didn't want to worry me. Because I'm just a useless child, right?'

She sighed. 'Of course not. I mean, okay…yes, you are a child, but that wasn't why.'

'Okay, then, here's your chance. You didn't tell me you were knocked up until you were almost four months pregnant with Leo. Are you going to tell me who the father is or that another secret too?' he asked, one eyebrow raised cockily.

In moments like these, when she got a snapshot of the man he would become even while remnants of his boyishness lingered, she wanted to freeze time, hold the picture in place for ever.

His protectiveness would've been adorable if he hadn't been staring at her with aggrieved hurt.

It was her job to protect him, not the other way around. Which was why she'd used bulky sweaters and loose clothing to keep her pregnancy secret for as long as possible. It had also helped that she hadn't really started to show until well into her second trimester.

'It doesn't matter who he is—'

'Why do you keep saying that? Of course it matters! It'll matter to Leo when he's old enough. Remind me again—which one of us constantly demanded to know who our fathers were before Mum got sick and used that as an excuse not to tell us? You wanted to know, so why is this different?'

'Look, this is nothing to do—' She stopped herself, but knew she'd already said enough when his features tightened.

He scraped back his chair and rose. 'It's nothing to do with me? Well, then, what I do in my spare time is nothing to do with *you* either!'

'Jonah…'

Her conciliatory tone fell on deaf ears as he stalked down the hallway and disappeared into his room.

A quick glance showed he'd eaten every scrap of his meal, and again she would've smiled had the distance between them not seemed so impassable.

Rounding the table, she picked up his empty plate and took it into the kitchen. His accusation stung, but how could she tell him about that weekend?

How could she tell him she'd made a huge error of judgement and landed herself exactly where she'd sworn she'd never be, after witnessing the turmoil and strife her mother had gone through as a single parent? Witnessing the doors closed to her once her family circumstances were discovered…?

According to her mother, she'd been a manager in a small hotel when she'd met and had a brief affair with a businessman, resulting in Evangeline's birth. Then, twelve years later, history had repeated itself and Jonah had been born.

Even on her deathbed her Ghanaian-born mother had refused to tell her and Jonah who their fathers were, citing everything from memory loss to an insistence that Eva and Jonah were better off not knowing.

All Eva had known for certain from her own skin tone and hair was that her father was white. For years she'd been hurt, and then furious with her mother for not divulging her father's identity.

Now, having had her own child, she was still furious, but she had a thin, grudging understanding as to why her mother might have chosen to stay silent. Because if Eva's circumstances were any indication…

With another sigh, she placed her own dinner in the fridge and left the kitchen, her appetite gone.

At the end of the hallway she turned her bedroom door handle slowly and peeked into the room, her heart melting when she saw her son sprawled on his back, his chubby arms and legs spread wide as he slept in his crib.

She'd loved Leo even before she'd seen his tiny feet kick on the ultrasound image at her second prenatal check-up. She had painstakingly taken care of her health in the nine months she'd carried him. And she'd fallen head over heels all over again the moment he'd been placed in her arms.

She'd known then she'd fight to her last breath to protect him from harm or heartache. She didn't care that he was the product of a one-weekend stand. That, like her mother, she'd turned a blind eye to the flashing warning signs telling her she was getting in over her head in waters she'd never swum in. That the kind of overwhelming passion and desire surging through her that weekend was the kind to leave an indelible mark on her.

And, good heavens, had it ever?

Shutting the door, she trudged her way past the kitchen and into the covered porch overlooking the small garden. She took a deep breath, hoping the slightly humid Cape Town air would disperse the memories.

But, no… They came thick and fast.

Those unnerving few months of uncertainty as to whether Pieter, her boss at the accounting firm where she'd worked, was actually covertly harassing her sexually or—as he'd sardonically stated when she'd mentioned it—it was all in her head.

Then had come his surprise invitation to dinner one

Friday after work, to discuss her recent appraisal and a possible promotion. It had followed straight on the heels of her visit to HR, incidentally—which should've cemented her suspicions.

She'd been euphoric that her hard work was being recognised, that she might soon earn enough to afford to pay a few outstanding bills, buy new clothes and educational supplies for Jonah, perhaps eventually move him to a good school, where his computing genius would be better harnessed.

Evangeline had been overwhelmed when Pieter had taken her to the Quayson Cape Town Hotel—*the* most stunningly iconic and luxurious hotel in the city— where A-listers and royalty were rumoured to stay within its sublime spaces.

She hadn't realised just how wrong she'd been until it was too late and all her hopes had crashed and burned at the feet of her lecherous boss and his wandering hands. It had driven her to the bar, straight after she'd thrown her drink in his face and unceremoniously quit on the spot.

Reality had crashed hard on her within minutes. Even in those incandescent moments after she'd walked away she'd known she'd played right into his hands. That by not staying and fighting she'd done herself and her feminist values a disservice.

Newly jobless, and disappointed in herself for her erratic behaviour, she'd been on the point of angry, frustrated and increasingly anxious tears when she'd hopped onto a bar stool and ordered a stiff rum and Coke. The need to drown her sorrows had made her swallow half the contents at once, grimacing as the bracing liquor seared her throat on its way down.

And then she'd looked up.

Evangeline hated to invoke clichés, but when the most beautiful man you'd ever seen was staring at you when you were feeling at your worst, and his eyes were promising delivery from the depths of the despair you'd blindly tumbled into, you could excuse yourself a cliché or three.

Granted, she'd probably been a touch tipsy, seeing as she wasn't a regular drinker and hadn't eaten all day, naively anticipating the dinner her now *ex*-boss had promised her. The drink had gone straight to her head, doing its job of finding an outlet for said despair.

She'd stared at the drop-dead hot stranger, who'd managed to perch on a stool at the far end of bar as if he owned every man, woman and stick of furniture in sight.

Of course she'd discovered later that his family did indeed own the hotel, along with many more awe-inspiring, successful business ventures.

Unfortunately she hadn't been brazen enough to step down from the stool and sashay her way over to him in that sexy and sultry way she'd seen in the risqué movies she liked to watch. Instead, her fingers had tightened on her glass, the exquisitely carved crystal digging into her flesh, and her every heartbeat had pounded loudly in her ears as he'd returned her brazen stare.

A type of heat she'd never experienced had invaded her system, announcing boldly that she was in the throes of sexual desire. That the stranger at the end of the bar wanted her. And that she wanted him back. *Badly.*

The shocking realisation had shot through her, potent and bewildering enough to whip her focus away from him before he witnessed just how he affected her.

For several seconds she'd stared into her drink, wondering if it was the alcohol having this unusual effect on her. When she'd concluded that the rum definitely didn't help, and that she needed to stop drowning her sorrows and leave, she'd pushed the glass away, her shaky legs thankfully holding her up when she'd slid off the stool.

There had been three exits from the bar—one through the restaurant she'd just come from, another leading to the spectacular atrium and reception area, and a third leading directly onto a quiet side street.

Evangeline had told herself she'd chosen the third door because it was the one nearest to the bus stop for the bus she needed to take her home, not because it would take her past the handsome stranger. Or because it would give her one last glimpse of him before she stepped out into the rainy July evening.

She'd been quietly stunned when her hips had seemed to sway of their own accord, her spine straightening, shoulders squaring and her chin lifting as she made her way down the length of the bar.

She'd been fiercely glad she was wearing her most chic black wraparound dress with its deep V-neck design, its skirt skimming just above her knees, and matching black heels. And that she'd touched up her make-up just before leaving work and her usual flyaway hair was pinned in a neat chignon.

Her professional life might have just been detonated, but at least she could take pride in her appearance. Especially in the presence of the viscerally masculine man who…*dear God*…looked even better up close.

The deep awareness spiralling through her had almost made her stumble. Exhaling in relief when she hadn't, she'd tightened her fingers on her handbag, dragged her gaze from the perfect symmetry of his face, and was forcing herself to take one more step away from him when he spoke.

'Are you really going to let this moment pass?'

Those rumbled words, directed at her but spoken without lifting his gaze from his glass, sounded as if he was mildly offended she hadn't stopped, perhaps come on to him—probably something women had been doing since he hit puberty. They had stopped her dead in her tracks.

'Excuse me?' She hadn't stuttered, for which she'd been immensely grateful, considering the edges of her vision were mildly fuzzy and her heart was beating much too fast.

He'd cracked a ghost of a smile—which, impossibly, had made him even more compelling. 'Is this a run-of-the-mill thing for you, then?' he'd rasped, his eyes scouring her face in a vivid, captivating scrutiny that had made her heart beat even faster, before returning his gaze to his glass.

'Is what?'

The sentence had sounded grammatically off in her brain, but she'd shrugged inwardly. She would toss that into the disastrous dumpster fire this whole evening had turned into—along with her professional life.

His nostrils had flared a little then, as if he wasn't sure whether to be amused or irritated with her. 'Invoking this level of...*stimulation* everywhere you go?'

Evangeline had licked her lips, the stressed word firing up a blaze in her blood and transmitting far too enthusiastically to her groin. It had been as if she was caught in some mysterious sexual vortex, one only he could free her from. And in that moment, when something close to traitorous relief had coursed through her because *he'd* been the one to make her stop, and she was only being well-mannered enough to stop and respond when someone spoke to her, she wasn't entirely sure she wanted to be free.

'I don't… I don't think you can hold me responsible for…for whatever it is you're feeling.'

'Ah, but I do.'

She'd summoned a light laugh—from where, she didn't know. 'Does that pick-up line work with anyone? At all?'

He'd raised his head again then, speared her with a soulful gaze so deep and incisive and all-consuming she'd gasped. If she'd been compelled before, she was completely enthralled in that moment. Looking away had felt like sacrilege—as if she would miss something pure and vital and fundamental, a once-in-a-lifetime phenomenon, if she so much as blinked.

'Forget about anyone else,' he'd rasped, those eyes fixed on her face with such ferocity she'd felt it all the way to her soul. 'Ask yourself why you're still standing there if you're unaffected.'

She'd sucked in an audible breath—because she *had* been affected. Some entity had taken her over, keeping her rooted to the spot, trapped in his electrifying orbit. 'I was just on my way home,' she said. 'And *you* addressed *me*,' she tagged on, proud and grateful to be able to proffer that fact.

He'd scrutinised her face again, as if digging for some truth beneath her skin. 'Yes, I did. And you haven't answered me yet.'

Are you going to let this moment pass?

She should have let it pass. But the lifesaving *yes* had remained locked in her throat. And then he'd risen to his feet, and she'd compounded her circumstances by swallowing the word down.

Well over six feet, with shoulders that blocked out

everything else—including her common sense—he had been truly overwhelming. In an almost melodramatic way that made her wonder why he was talking to her, an ordinary girl with an ordinary, if challenging, life.

When he'd wheeled away to address the bartender, Evangeline had reminded herself to breathe.

'Inform the maître d' that I'll take my usual table, and set another place for my guest.' As the bartender had sauntered off to do his bidding he'd turned back to her. 'You *are* staying for dinner, aren't you?'

It had been a sultry invitation and a dare.

A promise of unspeakable pleasure and a warning.

She should've heeded the danger and stepped away from the temptation.

'Only judging by the short and…*interesting* time you spent in the dining room, you've yet to have dinner,' he'd added, one silky eyebrow rising in amused query.

Heat had crept into her face. 'You…you saw me?'

'I think everyone on the ground floor saw you,' he replied. 'It was quite the performance.'

But she didn't care about anyone else. Just *him*. Every racing thought—and there were many in those charged minutes—circled back to him.

While the tipsiness had receded enough for her to make a cogent decision, she'd been getting steadily intoxicated on other things.

His presence. His face. His voice.

The sublime body packed into a bespoke suit.

She'd been about to fall in with his wish, and with whatever else he wanted besides, when a sliver of common sense had arrived, along with a reminder of why she'd been at the bar in the first place. Why she needed to head home to plan for what came next.

He'd followed the glance she'd cast over her shoulder. 'If you're worried about your companion, don't be.'

'He is…*was* my boss. He made a pass at me and I… Well, you saw what I did.'

The glint in his eyes before his jaw clenched tight had been almost…*admiring.* 'Rest assured that I've had him thrown out with a firm recommendation never again to grace this hotel with his dubious presence.'

Evangeline suspected now that *that* was the moment she'd decided to throw caution to the wind. The enigmatic stranger had taken care of one problem without even knowing her name. He'd made her feel better and hadn't mentioned it until she'd needed that tiny little win.

'So what's it going to be?'

The low, unbridled intensity in his voice had sent shivers through her body. And before she could talk herself out of it, she'd responded, 'I'll stay.'

The dark satisfaction gleaming in his eyes should've been further warning that she was playing way out of her league. But, as if he'd known that somewhere inside she was quaking with uncertainty, he'd slowly stepped forward, making her almost swallow her tongue at the sight of his sheer masculinity as he'd held out his arm.

And waited.

Jonah had been away for the weekend at school camp, the only thing awaiting her at home the cold, stark reality of the abrupt ending of a job she'd loved and the shock she was certain she was suffering.

She hadn't been ready to face it. Tomorrow would be soon enough to work out how she'd afford rent and food for her and Jonah once her meagre savings ran out.

So she'd slid her arm into the breathtaking stranger's and let him lead her out of the bar.

They'd been shown into a private dining room—a cosy, stylish space, dripping with the sort of high-quality tasteful decor she only saw on TV shows and in glossy magazines.

But soon enough everything—the superb food, the excellent wine, even the conversation which had contained far too many intoxicating subtexts—had receded from her consciousness.

She'd been wholly and utterly captivated by him.

And it'd seemed like the most profound, transcendent unfolding of a dream when he'd asked her to spend the weekend with him and she'd said...*yes*...

Evangeline squeezed her eyes shut, fighting memories that even now had the power to move a peculiar blend of bewilderment and lust through her body. To turn her nipples diamond-hard and punch heat into her pelvis. To make her clench her fists and drop her head against the windowpane as ravenous need clawed through her. To quietly infuriate her with the knowledge that there'd been no man before or since him. Hell, even the mere thought of dating made distaste sour her mouth.

Because once she'd snapped out of the hypnosis he'd cast upon her a few weeks later, she had been confronted with the harsh reality that he'd left her with an indelible reminder.

Her lips twisted.

And it had just been a small taster of what tangling with Ekow Quayson had in store for her.

Jonah wanted to know who the father of her baby was. But Evangeline knew how headstrong her brother was. Knew he wouldn't rest until he'd forced Ekow to acknowledge Leo the way Jonah's own father hadn't ever acknowledged *his* existence.

She intended to protect Leo from that with every bone in her body.

Because her own attempt to do the same for her son had reaped disastrous results.

Reaffirming to herself that she'd done the right thing by not telling her brother, and that whatever strain there was between them would be overcome in due course, she headed back to the kitchen. She needed to eat, to keep herself healthy. She'd be no use to her family or the treasured clients she'd managed to secure for her small but growing online accounting business if she made herself sick.

She'd just hit the one-minute button on the microwave to warm up her food when she saw the headlights swinging into her small drive.

It wasn't late, but she wasn't expecting anyone. Definitely no one who'd call in after eight p.m.

Evangeline reassured herself that the jump of dread in her stomach didn't mean anything. It was most likely a driver who'd taken a wrong turn.

Still, trepidation wove through her body as she went towards her front door, swallowing as a second, and then a third set of headlights pierced the darkness.

Her neighbourhood was low-income, and most of her neighbours used public transport, just as she did—although her mother's old jalopy functioned from time to time when needed.

The few who owned cars definitely didn't have vehicles gleaming with expensive chrome work, like the ones she spotted when she peeked through the curtains.

She jumped as firm footsteps sounded on the paved path leading to her front door. Her gaze flitted to Jonah's door, and she experienced a peculiar dart of gratitude that he was out of sight.

Taking a deep breath, she pulled open the door before her unwanted visitor could knock and disturb the household.

The breath was snatched clean out of her lungs when her gaze surged up...and up...and collided with the dark brown, piercingly intense eyes of the very man she'd spent the best part of the last half-hour striving to push out of her mind.

Evangeline was aware her mouth was gaping, her eyes probably wide and horrified as she stared at Ekow Quayson.

'Wh-what are you doing here? And how do you know where I live?' She'd moved since her one and only attempt to reach him fifteen months ago. And she most definitely hadn't been given the chance even to state her full name to him, never mind offer anything close to a phone number or an address for him to reach her.

A scathing dressing down about how 'women like her' were the lowest form of life, followed by a hastily scrawled cheque shoved at her from across a massive teak desk and a stark warning never to set foot in the city of her birth again, were all she'd received from the designated member of his family sent to do his dirty work.

Altogether, her audience with Ekow Quayson's father had taken less than five minutes. But it had left her reeling long afterwards.

And she'd heeded the warning, because in the clear light of day, after that heady weekend, she'd seen who she was dealing with. Known the veritable powerhouse of the family she'd entangled herself with.

'Evangeline.'

The sharp rasp of her name sharpened her focus. Staring at him, she got the feeling he was just as stunned as she was. That whatever he'd expected when he'd marched up to her front door it hadn't been her. But he quickly mastered his expression, leaving her wondering if she'd imagined it.

But if he hadn't then what or who *had* he been expecting?

Her heart leapt into her throat and she quickly glanced over her shoulder, the premonition in her gut expanding. It couldn't be Jonah. *Please, God, no.* 'What do you want, Mr Quayson?' she demanded, far more sharply than she'd intended.

His features clenched with displeasure. 'Hardly the way to greet me after all this time, is it?' he mocked with icy arrogance.

Her own anger trailed through her unease. All this time after the way his father had treated her? After Ekow's own complete silence over his son?

'You think you deserve the red carpet? How very like a rich man to believe the world owes him courtesy simply because of the number of zeros in his bank account.'

One eyebrow slowly rose, his eyes narrowing on her face as he stepped closer. 'I suggest you think twice on the tack you want to take with me. Perhaps you haven't yet seen who else I've brought with me?' he breathed, warning stamped into every syllable.

The fact that it took a monumental effort to drag her far too avid gaze from his face—even more arresting then the last time she'd seen it—past those mile-wide shoulders and the streamlined body draped in a sharp bespoke suit that screamed its birthplace of Milan further irritated her.

But she managed it—only to feel the cold hand of dread tightening its hold on her insides.

'Wh-why have you brought the police with you?'

Unlike the first time they'd met, when her voice had held admirably, her words shook. And she hated every second of that weakness. Hated this man's lasting ability to shake the ground beneath her feet so effortlessly.

First with pleasure, then with debilitating cruelty.

'The chief inspector is a friend. He was kind enough to accompany me here. In case of any…unpleasantness.'

He'd stated the position of authority to further rile her. Evangeline knew that. But despite her best efforts her insides did shake, and she felt her palms growing clammy.

'Do you bring the police to visit all your past acquaintances?' she asked, striving for a tone of casual dismissal which surprisingly held.

The slight flare of his nostrils said she'd hit her mark. But she was too riled to derive any satisfaction from it.

'When they attempt to cause me this level of aggravation, yes,' he returned, in a low, rumbling voice, sending shivers dancing over her skin.

'What are you talking about?'

He didn't answer immediately. He conducted a lazy but thorough scrutiny of her body, reversing her shivers into tiny little sparks of fireworks.

She knew her body hadn't changed that much after childbirth, except maybe in slightly thicker hips and a fuller bust. But she felt as if every inch of her skin had reawakened under his regard.

'Do you live alone?' he continued in his distant thunder voice, and this time there was an edge to his demand that sped up her already racing heart.

'Why?'

His eyes flicked over her shoulder and it was all she could do not to follow his gaze down the hall. 'Because otherwise it seems I've travelled a few thousand miles to discover that *you* are behind the problems I'm having. For the sake of our past...*connection* I'm willing to hold off the handcuffs and hear you out. So invite me in, Evangeline.'

Memories of pleasurable restraints made of expensive silk ties threatened to crater her thoughts. She furiously shook them away.

'Not until you tell me what you think I've done to lead you to my door. And most definitely not until you send the police away. I'd rather not have a conversation with you while the authorities hang out in my front garden.'

His lips twisted. 'If you're worried about police scrutiny then you shouldn't have hacked into my bank, should you?'

Her shocked gasp dropped into the space between them. 'What? I have no idea what you're—' She snapped her mouth shut far too late.

His sizzling gaze fixed on her face, his eyes slowly narrowing at her unguarded response. 'Then I'll ask you again. Do you live alone, Evangeline?'

She opened her mouth just as the door down the hall opened. And she couldn't quite hide her soft groan of despair as understanding finally dawned.

Before her, Ekow's face turned tight with fury and censure, as if the discovery that she didn't live alone was a black mark against her. He continued to glare at her as footsteps drew closer.

'What's going on?'

Jonah's voice, unmistakably that of a still-growing boy, drew Ekow's sharp gaze over her shoulder. She saw the wheels turning in his head. Watched his formidable censure begin to recede.

'Eva...?'

The less confident demand from Jonah finally made her turn.

His terrified gaze was fixed on the police cars crouched on their driveway, but it was the guilt on his face when his gaze darted to the police inspector now stepping out of his car which sealed her fears.

'Jonah? What have you done?'

He didn't answer her. She watched him gulp, then gather the jagged edges of his courage before turning his focus on Ekow, animosity brimming in his eyes.

'Jonah!'

She barely registered Ekow turning away from her, taking a few steps to murmur to the police inspector. The older man levelled a reproving gaze on Evangeline for several seconds before, nodding, he returned to his vehicle.

The breath she took didn't quite stem the alarm flaring inside her as Jonah shrugged, shoved his hands deep into his pockets and attempted not to look relieved at the sight of the departing police officers.

'Do not take the absence of the authorities to mean my presence here is benign, Evangeline. One simple phone call can reverse that.'

Evangeline swung back to him. 'No! I... You don't need to do that.'

He nodded, his eyes resting on her face in blatant expectation until she cleared her throat and said, 'Come in.'

The moment Ekow Quayson stepped into her house, her sanctuary, she regretted inviting him in. Not because she dreaded what was to come—and she did— but because she knew she'd never be able to step into her living room again without recalling his towering presence there. Without seeing him stride past her, his sharp eyes taking in every item of furniture and personal knick-knack before, brimming with disapproval, he turned to her.

'Firstly, you will tell me who this is,' he said, nudging his chin at Jonah. 'And then you'll tell me which one of you is responsible for the breaches in my bank's security. And make no mistake: before I leave here, whoever is responsible will be held accountable.'

CHAPTER TWO

EKOW HADN'T BEEN altogether surprised when the woman who'd taken up far too much space in his brain lately had materialised in front of him.

He'd accepted even before he'd boarded his plane that at some point during his trip to Cape Town he would track her down and pinpoint exactly why she intrigued him so much before walking away.

Of course he hadn't expected to meet her under *these* circumstances. The name his investigation had thrown up was Jonah Annan.

But what really stunned him as he stood in the depressingly tiny living room containing shabby furniture, Evangeline and a glowering teenager, was the rush of hunger, the hard thumping in his chest he realised with alarm was an elevated heartbeat. And the sense of... *anticipation* topping it all off.

The equally unsettling thoughts following fast on the heels of those initial reactions further alarmed him. Sixteen months was a long time between liaisons. The idea that Evangeline, whose surname he now knew was Annan—a Ghanaian name, which absurdly pleased him—could be attached to another man perturbed him.

His gaze darted to her hand, but the punch of relief at seeing her bare fingers was fleeting. The lack of a wedding ring didn't mean much these days. Someone in this house could have a claim on her.

Even confronted with this teenage boy whose features suggested a familial bond, he couldn't quite stem the unnerving sensation. He looked too old to be her son, but that didn't mean she didn't have a significant other on the scene.

'This is Jonah, my younger brother,' she offered eventually.

And just like that Ekow's attention was re-captivated. Just like on the evening in the hotel bar. Just like every second he'd spent with her from then on.

But he couldn't let himself be swayed by the crushed ice and caramel voice that promised sweetness and yet held dangerous edges that could cut a man deep. It was merely one more tool in her alluring arsenal.

He remembered vividly how their weekend had ended.

He turned his attention to the boy. 'Do you know who I am, Jonah?'

The boy shrugged, and a look passed between the siblings. He watched Eva's eyes widen in surprise, while the boy's lips pursed.

'I'll take that as a yes, shall I?' Ekow said, then turned to her. 'Unless you're an accomplished actress, your surprise when I mentioned my bank's security being hacked tells me you know nothing about this?'

A flash of fury was quickly smothered by alarm. 'Of course not. Do you think I'd condone such a thing?'

Ekow's jaw clenched tight before he answered. 'I have no idea what you'd condone. Our getting to know one another was cut rather short, if I recall accurately,' he stated.

She sucked in a quick breath, sending her brother a

fleeting look before glaring at him. When she didn't reply, Ekow let loose a grim smile. 'Or am I not supposed to mention that we know one another?'

Instead of responding, Ekow watched her turn to her brother.

'Is what he's saying true?' she asked. 'Have you been tampering with his bank?'

Jonah snorted. 'I don't *tamper*.' He spat out the word as if it offended him.

'Answer the question, Jonah.' Her gentle tone had attained a ring of steel Ekow would've found impressive had he not still been reeling from seeing this woman in the flesh, sixteen months after she'd left his bed. After he'd been dealt a blow to his ego he wasn't sure he'd quite recovered from.

The young boy shrugged again—a reaction Ekow was recognising was his go-to crutch. 'Answer your sister,' he commanded.

Jonah froze, before his face turned rigid with mutiny. 'So what if I poked around your firewall occasionally? It's not as if I did anything bad. If anything, you should be thanking me for exposing the weaknesses in your system—'

'Jonah!'

'Trust me, you'll be showing me exactly that and more before we're done here,' Ekow announced briskly.

Eva rounded on him, alarm flaring in her eyes. 'What's that supposed to mean?'

'It means now I know I've got the right address and the culprit, you and I are going to talk about reparation. And make no mistake. The penalty will be steep. Your brother is going to walk my team through exactly how he breached my security.'

'Are you saying they don't know? You mean all your

billions couldn't buy you adequate protection?' the boy taunted with a smirk, earning himself another fierce glare from his sister.

'That's enough, Jonah,' she said, firmly enough to make him deflate a little.

'Your sister and I need to talk. Excuse us,' Ekow said.

Jonah drew out his obedience for a handful of seconds. Then, with another speaking look at his sister, he started to walk away. Halfway down the hall, he spun around. 'Aren't you even going to ask me why I did it?'

Beside him, Evangeline tensed, then swallowed, as if she was attempting to stem the nerves evidently eating at her. Ekow redirected his gaze to her brother, assessing the teenager's face and his neat but threadbare clothing before he replied, 'You don't look the "hacktivist" type, so I'm going to assume you were just bored.'

The expression that shrouded the boy's face was one decades older than his teenage years. It spoke of a fierce protectiveness buried under all the bravado and acidic fury. And Ekow realised instantly that he was wrong. Whatever had fuelled the young man's desire to toy with his cyber security, it hadn't been done out of boredom but something powerful.

Ekow frowned inwardly. His motive seemed almost...*personal*. Meaning what, exactly?

He focused as Jonah fully faced him, dislike blazing in his eyes. 'Guys like you always assume stuff like that. No, sir, I did it because—'

'It doesn't matter why he did it,' Eva interrupted hurriedly, physically placing herself between them.

Ekow felt a pang of irritation. He was many things, but he wasn't an ogre who went around terrorising women or children. If anything, these two should be begging his forgiveness for their transgressions, not making him feel he was in the wrong for finally tracking down the source of the breaches in his bank.

'I'm sure he's sorry and will work with you on whatever reparations are needed. Won't you, Jonah?' she encouraged pointedly.

Another look passed between them. Ekow swallowed a growl at the increasing certainty that he was missing vital information.

With another careless shrug, the boy sauntered off without answering, walked through a doorway into what Ekow assumed was his bedroom and slammed the door behind him.

Ekow watched Eva stare at the closed door for several seconds, her face a picture of frustration and worry. Her gaze shifted to the second door at the end of the corridor and she swallowed. Then, hastily diverting her gaze, she faced him.

And Ekow felt the punch of lust all over again.

Impossibly, the time between their last meeting and this had added layers of allure to her beauty. Her sultry eyes held mysteries he wanted to uncover. Her unpainted lips seemed even fuller than before, and he was struck with a ravenous hunger to take them, to hear that moan he remembered in his dreams echo in real life.

As for her body...

She might be wearing a pair of worn denim cut-offs and a simple spaghetti-strap top, but the denim clung to her curves, her full hips and rounded buttocks, and her full breasts reminded him of every second he'd spent exploring the silky richness of her skin, discovering which caress made her gasp, which location to linger on with his lips to make her moan.

The high scarlet gloss she'd worn on her fingernails that night might be non-existent now, but he recalled how arousing it had been to feel them digging into his back as he'd taken her again and again. Her scream of pleasure when she'd found her release.

Ekow wasn't aware he was moving towards her until her nostrils quivered and her eyes widened.

'Wh-why are you looking at me like that?' she rasped.

He had pushed his hands into his pockets, much as Jonah had done minutes ago, to stop himself from reaching out to touch her. Reacquainting himself with the cushiony softness of her plump lips.

'Why did you sneak out of my bed before I got the chance to learn your full name?' he grated, and then froze.

The words had surprised him almost as much as they evidently did her, but once the question was spoken he knew the answer was one he'd been seeking for sixteen months.

Her beautiful eyes widened even further. '*That's* what you want to talk about? I thought you were here because—'

'We'll get to your brother's transgressions and your role in them in due course. Tell me why.'

'I don't owe you an explanation—and what do you mean by my role in them? I had no idea he was doing… whatever it is you think he's done.'

'Which either means you're shockingly inattentive or you just wilfully turned a blind eye to what was happening under your own roof.'

'How dare you!'

Just as he remembered from the incident in his restaurant at their first meeting, her fiery animation drew him like a vivid beacon. Her spark made him want to step closer, experience her heat. Singe himself raw with it.

Ekow accepted then that whatever else had brought him to Cape Town, the allure and mystery of Evangeline Annan would be an added bonus he would unravel before he returned to Accra.

But first things first... 'I dare because his actions have cost me a couple of million dollars in security investigation fees.'

She gasped. 'I...that's not possible.'

'Are you calling me a liar, Eva?'

Her lips pursed. 'If you think I'm just going to take your word for it, then, no, I'm not going to. I'll need proof of what you're accusing Jonah of.'

'Even though he just as good as admitted it?'

She sent a fleeting glance over her shoulder, then squared both those gorgeous shoulders. 'Like you said, he's a teenager. Maybe he tinkered around a time or two on your bank's website, but that doesn't—'

'He's been doing it for eight months, Evangeline,' he corrected, fresh irritation storming through him.

She gasped. 'No...'

'Yes. And he did much more than tinker. Shutting down my systems for a few hours and sending pictures of picnicking cats to all my board members isn't a laughing matter.'

A look of deeper trepidation settled on her face. 'He didn't do anything more...banking specific, did he?'

'Are you asking me whether he stole money from my bank?'

She froze for several seconds, then exhaled shakily. 'Did he?'

'Fortunately for him, no, he didn't.'

Her shoulders sagged in relief.

Ekow's lips thinned. 'Don't break out in thankful

song yet, sweetheart. He's still committed multiple cybercrimes—both here in South Africa and in Ghana.'

'Is that why you've come here? To cart my fifteen-year-old brother off to jail?'

He'd most definitely come because he wanted to get to the root of a problem which should've been dealt with months ago if the cyber thief hadn't been so slippery. But discovering Eva's connection to the boy threw a different light on things. The sense that something else was going on with Jonah, at least. Perhaps with them both.

'I haven't made up my mind yet.'

'I won't have you toying with him. Or me,' she warned, her beautiful chin tilted up in fierce defiance.

'Not even if accommodating me might earn you a path to my better, more lenient nature?'

Suspicion filled her eyes. 'Accommodating you in what way?' she demanded.

He delivered a mirthless smile. 'Not in the way you think. I've never needed to seek sexual favours in return for co-operation or anything else. I believe that was your ex-boss's remit?'

The suspicion drained from her eyes but there remained a fire deep within the dark hazel depths that echoed the one burning low but insistent inside him, triggering a pulse of satisfaction.

'Then what *do* you mean?'

'You can start by telling me why your brother would target me and my bank in this way. Because, whether you want to admit it or not, this feels personal. What are you two hiding from me?'

In the time between Ekow's unwanted arrival on her doorstep and learning of Jonah's online activities Eva had asked herself the same question.

Unfortunately, and alarmingly, everything pointed to her brother having taken it upon himself to punish Ekow Quayson. His comments at the dinner table finally made sense.

While she'd been thinking she was protecting him by not enlightening him about the inauspicious period surrounding Leo's conception, birth and what had happened during her visit to Ghana afterwards, Jonah had been smarting at being kept in the dark. And he'd taken matters into his own hands.

Her brother had always been a whizz kid with computers. She knew in her bones that he'd gone snooping and discovered the truth—or at least enough of it—and attempted to dish out his own retribution.

A small part of her was fiercely proud of his protectiveness. But the major part knew this was a big problem.

Eight months...

She barely stopped herself from shutting her eyes in despair. The formidable man in front of her would still be there when she opened them. His scent would still fill her nostrils, his intoxicating good looks would threaten to blind her despite the fact that with every second that passed without him even asking about his son pain was biting into her chest like steel barbs.

How could she stand there cataloguing his every breathtaking feature when he was the epitome of everything she despised in men? In her book, there was nothing worse than a man who didn't own up to his responsibilities.

Over the years, even though her mother had never admitted it, Eva knew she'd attempted to reach Jonah's father. She'd seen the returned letters and overheard phone calls which had driven her mother to heartbreak-

ing tears in the middle of the night when she'd thought
her children were asleep.

Jonah had always been sensitive, and Eva suspected
her brother had discovered his own father had rejected
the chance to know him. The same course Ekow Quayson had instructed his father to take on his behalf over
their son.

Hell, he hadn't even been man enough to tell her to
her face that he was rejecting her offer for him to know
and love his own flesh and blood. No. He'd left the task
to his brutally unforgiving father.

She shivered at the recollection, then welcomed the
burn of anger the memory stirred inside her.

'Is that distaste filling your face supposed to mean
something to me?' Ekow demanded in a low, deep
faintly mocking tone.

Her mouth twisted. Of course her reaction would
bounce like water off his formidable shoulders. He was
well-insulated by his wealth, power and effortlessly
perfect good looks. Men like him felt they only needed
to lift a finger to have their problems disposed of. No
doubt he'd inherited that trait from his father.

'I'm surprised you chose to come here yourself.
Don't men like you have endless minions to solve problems like this for them?'

'You're changing the subject. And you know that
will only raise my suspicions, don't you? As for at-
tending to this myself—you should be thankful I did.
A subordinate would've been instructed to let the authorities handle this matter and your brother would be
in handcuffs by now.'

Something vital quaked inside her but she refused
to back down. 'Are you...will you give me your word
that you won't involve them?'

He tilted his head to one side, a sardonic look shrouding his face. 'You've been in equal measures belligerent, defiant and downright hostile. Why should I do you any favours, Evangeline?'

Dear God, but the way he said her name made treacherously sinful thoughts invade what should be a clear-cut discussion.

Eva admonished herself for that unfortunate reaction and cleared her throat. 'You want to know why Jonah is interested in you? The weekend you and I were…together…he was supposed to be at school camp. But he didn't like it there and he'd been trying to reach me—to ask me to come and get him. When I didn't answer my phone he decided to take matters into his own hands. He ran away and came home early. But I wasn't at home.'

He frowned. 'That was why you left without waking me?'

It wasn't entirely why. She'd already been halfway out the door when she'd received the call from a worried camp supervisor. 'Partly.'

His eyes narrowed. 'We're going to be better acquainted before this issue between us is resolved, so I should mention that I don't like half-answers. What's the other reason that had you leaving my bed at the crack of dawn?'

'Why don't you come out and state what's really bothering you?' she asked him.

He half smiled. 'What makes you think I'm bothered?'

'The way I left you? Isn't that why you're questioning me like this? Because I took away your power over the situation by not staying until you'd formally dismissed me after the weekend was over? I imagine not many women leave without fawning endlessly over you.'

'You imagine correctly,' he replied, without an ounce of self-doubt. 'So why *did* you leave?'

His persistent questioning was the last thing she'd expected. After all, he wasn't a man who needed to preen to get attention. He wasn't a man who had to boast about his masculine beauty and his raw physical prowess.

Every square inch of Ekow Quayson screamed power and authority. Every streamlined muscle had been designed to command the female gaze, so he could glory in having won the genetic lottery that had sculpted a perfect man, who only needed to enter a room to control it. Only to look at a woman to have her in the palm of his hand.

That first night she'd resisted in the final moments between leaving the dining room and going upstairs with him. Lord, had she resisted.

Granted, the event with her boss which had immediately preceded their meeting had inured her somewhat to the raw potency that had hit her the moment she'd laid eyes on Ekow Quayson at the bar of Quayson Cape Town—the sublimely luxurious, six-star hotel she'd discovered, somewhere between her second and third drink, was part of the worldwide hotel conglomerate operated by his family. But still it had only been a matter of time before her resistance had crumbled to nothing.

Before she'd convinced herself that not all men were like her disgusting newly ex-boss. Or the two men who'd sired her and her brother, then left her mother to face the hardships of being a single parent on her own.

Before she'd acted so completely out of character that she still reeled in recollection nearly a year and a half later.

Now she forced an unruffled shrug, despite her stomach churning with fresh warning that things weren't what they seemed. 'I thought I'd spare us both the unnecessary morning-after awkwardness,' she said lightly. Only to feel her heart flip over in alarm when his jaw tightened and something resembling displeasure shimmered in his eyes before he grappled it down.

Was she mistaken?

Had he, contrary to his very thinly veiled warning for her not to take their weekend as anything above face value, not been thrilled that she'd left his penthouse suite in the early hours of Monday morning while he'd been fast asleep, their sexual antics having worn them both out so completely it had taken huge willpower to force herself to leave?

'Impatient to get on with the rest of your life, were you? I find that hard to believe. Our time together wasn't as forgettable as you pretend—was it, Eva?'

The question held traces of conceit—as if, no matter her response, he'd already made up his mind about their time together and his belief cemented his place as an unforgettable entity in her past…one she'd never be free of.

She pursed her lips, determined not to give him the satisfaction he craved. Because, even without the living, breathing reminder of their encounter currently fast asleep down the hall, Eva knew she would never have forgotten him. Their coming together had been a visceral, earth-shattering event. At least for her.

As for Ekow… He hadn't seemed to dislike it either. Not that she was about to claim any sexual expertise. After all, she'd been a virgin before she'd taken his hand and boarded the lift up to his penthouse that Friday night.

She'd come down to earth a far too enlightened woman. A woman who knew the true depths of physical intimacy… Who knew the touch of a sublime, masterful lover… Who knew she would never be the same… A woman who hadn't been able to bring herself to seek that kind of intimacy elsewhere since.

Perhaps if she hadn't discovered weeks later that she was carrying Leo she would've resented Ekow for ruining all other relationships for her. But her life had taken a drastic turn, leaving her with no option but to focus on the one treasure that mattered.

Her child.

The child she needed to put above all this pointless reminiscing…

'Whether it was forgettable or not, I left on my own terms. That's all the answer you need, isn't it?'

A grim smile cracked across his face. 'No. I never take things at face value or I wouldn't even be here in the first place.'

Another layer of unwanted panic slid into place inside her. 'What's that supposed to mean?'

'It means someone wanted my attention and they made their presence known by interfering with the smooth running of my bank. Tell me the truth. Did your brother act under your instruction?'

She frowned. 'Why would I do something like that?'

He shrugged. 'Perhaps it was your brother acting on his own. The question is why? I don't believe it's his idle curiosity about who you were with that weekend.'

She waved a hand, attempting to render the whole argument inconsequential. 'He's a teenager. They all want attention in some form or another, even though it's the absolute last thing they'll admit to wanting. You're a young, successful billionaire—he's probably convinced he can emulate you in some way. I don't think you should take it too seriously.'

For some reason her response sent another of those mysterious shadows across his face. And, just as before, it was gone almost as soon as it arrived. 'His supposed hero-worship has cost my bank a lot of time and resources—so, no, I'm not simply going to overlook it and walk away.'

'He's a fifteen-year-old boy. What exactly do you hope you'll achieve?'

'At the very least I will impress on him that this kind of course of action might land him in jail, or worse.'

For a fleeting second Eva wanted to confess she wanted to do that too. She hadn't exactly mastered the art of tough love—not when it came to her beloved sibling—and look where it had got them. But then she reminded herself of the ruthless power of the Quaysons. Of what their patriarch had threatened her with when she'd dared to do the right thing. She couldn't expose Jonah to that sort of treatment.

'My investigation has revealed that you operate an online accountancy business from your home,' he said, changing tack.

'Yes, what of it?' she answered briskly, determined not to show how nervous his questions made her.

'You deal with people's private finances while your brother is a prolific hacker?'

His words were so dry Eva imagined the smallest spark would start a blaze.

'I'm sure I don't need to draw you a picture.'

He didn't, and that fact had crossed her mind more than once since he'd turned up. Her freelance business was still fledgling. She treasured the flexibility it gave her to raise Leo while earning an income to keep the roof over her family's head. All it would take was for word to get out about Jonah's activities and everything she'd worked so hard for would be jeopardised.

But she was damned if she'd give Ekow the satisfaction of admitting her alarm. 'Are you remotely near making a point?' she asked. 'Or should I take what you say as the threat it clearly is?'

Those far too sumptuous lips twisted, as if she amused him. As if all this turmoil he was causing was a trifling inconvenience and he was simply taking time out of his busy day to deal with it.

But it wasn't, though, was it?

He'd boarded his private jet and flown all the way here to deal with this matter. And there was a watchful tension about him, a careful examination of each word she spoke, each look, each tiny movement of her body.

She already knew how powerful he and his family were. Unless she took control of this she'd find herself back in the same place she'd been fifteen months ago, when she'd faced down another Quayson and been unequivocally vanquished.

Looking at Ekow now, she saw the visceral resemblance to the older Quayson, and the alarm snaking through her grew more potent. More vicious.

Surprise flashed through his eyes, and she might've thought it genuine if she hadn't had an unforgettable play-by-play of his rejection of their son in her mind.

'Threaten *you*? So far my issue is with your brother. Why should you and I be enemies?'

She shook her head to dispel its spinning. 'You're joking, right?'

His eyes narrowed. 'Why would I be?'

A waterfall of ice doused her anger, replacing it with deep, deep dread. All along she'd thought his absence from Leo's life was deliberate. That her news had been received with the heavy scepticism and rejection she'd feared, and received confirmation of when she'd made the trip to Accra. But what if—?

'Eva?'

She forced herself to focus on the present. She knew the truth about him, whatever reason he had for wanting to play dumb right now. The son he'd rejected was truly better off without him if he couldn't even be bothered to enquire after him.

Was this how her mother had felt? Why she'd been so bitter and disillusioned for most of Eva's life?

She pushed the thought away.

She needed to handle the matter in front of her and be done with him—hopefully once and for all. 'I'm not sure how your family operates, but to me if you have an issue with my brother, then you have an issue with me.'

That infernal smile made an appearance, although this time it didn't quite reach his eyes. 'My family isn't without its challenges, but I can't say we've ever resorted to trespassing where we're not wanted or dabbled in cybercrime.'

Her shivering intensified. She truly wanted to believe this was all some giant misunderstanding. But the very real presence of the authorities he'd brought to her front door told her she couldn't wish reality away.

Thank God she lived on a quiet street. It was dark enough for most of her nosy neighbours to have missed this event. If she was lucky.

'It sounds like your brother is more than a handful,' he said into the tense silence.

'I'd thank you not to disparage—'

'It's a frank observation. Take offence if you like, but it won't diminish the truth.'

His words seared her with their honesty. She'd known for a while that she was burying her head in the sand where Jonah was concerned. Nevertheless, hearing it from this man, who'd shirked his chance at fatherhood, struck her as a little too raw, rousing her anger to fiery proportions.

'With respect, your observations mean less than nothing to me. Jonah is my problem, not yours.'

His face hardened, a granite ruthlessness settling over his features. 'That's where you're wrong. He put himself in my crosshairs by messing with my bank. He's now *my* problem.'

'Fine. Go on, then. What hoops do we have to jump through so you can be satisfied?'

For an age, he just stared at her.

Eva felt her skin tightening as apprehension and some emotion she didn't want to entertain slithered through her. It was far too reminiscent of that first time, when he'd stared back at her from across the bar as if he already knew all her secrets. As if her every desire was his to command and satisfy at his leisure.

'Have dinner with me,' he said abruptly.

Her shocked exhalation was the only sound in the room following his demand. Then, 'What?'

He cast a fleeting glance around the room, his eyes lingering on the dining table she hadn't quite finished clearing. 'It's late tonight. It looks like you've already eaten. I have meetings all day, but I'm free to discuss this tomorrow night. We can have dinner while we do.'

He expected her to sit down and break bread with him after what he'd done to her? Evangeline would've laughed hysterically at his sheer gall had his utterly despicable behaviour not felt so searingly personal. So reminiscent of her mother's heartbreak. Of the fear and uncertainty Eva herself had felt after returning from Accra with his father's threats ringing in her ears and her tail between her legs.

'No, Mr Quayson. My answer is, *hell*, no.'

CHAPTER THREE

SHE WAS DOING it again. Openly displaying the dismissiveness that said she didn't care whether they remained talking or he disappeared in a puff of smoke.

In truth, it was what had intrigued Ekow at their first meeting, when she'd stood up from the bar and walked past him with every intention of leaving.

Sure, she'd had many highly admirable physical attributes which had also caught his attention. But her mild disdain—when everyone else he met went out of their way to ingratiate themselves with him—while she'd been in the process of walking out after that singularly electric connection between them… Yes, it had left him flummoxed.

For the first time he'd *enjoyed* a woman playing hard to get, relished being a true hunter instead of a man whose prey fell willingly into his clutches.

And, yes, it had also produced in him a welcome edge which had cut through his jaded senses, triggered a sharp hunger in him, a man used to feasting whenever he desired.

Put simply, Evangeline's unique blend of innocence and passion had been a refreshing, addictive novelty. And then, just as quickly as he'd tasted her desire, he'd known one night wouldn't be enough. And had been surprisingly thrilled when she'd agreed to spend the weekend with him.

Had it all been a carefully orchestrated set of events to bring him here, to this moment? In his experience, women who gravitated towards men with billionaire status were willing to go above and beyond to achieve their goals.

But if she wasn't playing a part, he could—

What? Talk her into picking up where they'd left off? Or, more accurately, where she'd left *him*? Stunned, surprisingly dejected, and a little irritated at both feelings. Or was it because he'd woken up craving more of her and having to let that hunger go unsatisfied wasn't an occurrence he'd appreciated?

The sting to his pride had cut deeper than he wanted to admit. And hurt it still did. He was damned if he would grant her the chance to stage a repeat act.

Wouldn't payback be sweet if *he* did the leaving this time? Left her wanting more? It wasn't as if the hunger was one-sided. He'd seen the same flare of awareness in her eyes when she'd opened her front door.

Contrary to Eva's words, she wasn't quite over their torrid weekend together. They had unfinished business. She'd robbed him of something by stealing out of his bed before he'd finished things on his terms.

The more the idea settled in his brain, the more palatable it grew.

It was better than living in limbo.

Limbo was where his father had left him for most of his life. And even in death his old man had ensured his youngest son was left with questions which would haunt him for the rest of his life.

Had he ever done anything to make his father proud, or was he truly the inconsequential 'spare', only useful for the duties no one else in the family had wanted to take on? Even after he'd clawed his way up from lowly intern to managing Africa's largest private bank after his father had stepped down it had only been because the old man was being forced to relinquish control after suffering a series of grave health issues, not because he'd deemed Ekow worthy of the position.

And on his last day on earth he'd asked not for Ekow but for his second son, Atu. His father had hung on until his brother's plane had landed from Malta, then sent Ekow to fetch the heir apparent. It was Atu and his mother who'd been by their father's side when he passed away. Joseph Quayson hadn't even bothered to hang around to bid his youngest son farewell.

A week later he'd discovered he hadn't been worthy of a mention in his father's will either. All his assets had been left to his wife and his second son.

Ekow had been ready to fight to retain control of the bank he'd given his life to, but luckily neither Atu nor his mother had dared to stand in his way.

Some days, though, victory felt hollow, and he despised himself for *still* needing his dead father's endorsement…

He gritted his teeth against the surge of dark, tormenting memories. These days he fought not to dwell on his father unless it was absolutely necessary.

'Hell, no?'

He echoed her answer, steeping himself in the present. Regardless of the ideas he was tossing around in his head about Eva, Jonah had effortlessly breached his bank's firewalls—the last skirmish as recently as last night. *That* was as unacceptable as her answer.

'By all means we can have a discussion about Jonah

and what he can do to make things right. But I won't be having it over a cosy dinner, as if we're friends.'

He frowned inwardly at her acerbic tone, then shrugged it off. She could protest all she wanted, but *he* was the wronged party.

'You misunderstand. This isn't a social engagement. We'll be sitting down to discuss the best way forward. I'm a busy man. Come Monday, I'll be flying back to Accra. By then, one of two things will have happened. I will have handed this matter over to the authorities— an outcome I suspect you don't want—or we will have reached an agreement on how to handle this issue privately, between us. Which option would you prefer?'

Her expression indicated she preferred neither. That she wished him as far away from here as was humanly possible. Which also grated. No woman had ever been this conclusively dismissive of him. Usually they fell over themselves for a second date with him.

But not Evangeline.

She'd folded her arms, and her stunning face was set in mutinous lines resembling the expression her brother had flaunted a short while ago. 'Very well. But if I decide to eat with you dinner will be at a place of my choosing,' she stated eventually, her snappish tone disencouraging further disagreement.

'Because…?' he asked anyway, intrigued despite himself at her sheer temerity.

'Because you're about to suggest we dine at your hotel—am I right?'

Since it was the truth, he didn't deny it. 'The Quayson Hotel boasts the best restaurants and chefs in the city. I fail to see what you have against it.'

Her lashes swept down and he felt a moment's satisfaction in a sea of disgruntlement. She wasn't making the demand because she hated the idea of dining with him at the Quayson Hotel. She was doing so because she wasn't quite as indifferent to the memories plaguing him as she wanted him to think.

'Ah...you don't want to be reminded of how uninhibitedly passionate you were with me there that night? Is that it?'

He'd expected her to deny it, coyly or otherwise, like most women who attempted to project one emotion when they felt another. To his surprise, she lifted her stubborn, beautiful chin.

'No, I don't. It was a night I prefer not to remember at all.'

Anger now played second fiddle to another, far superior emotion—the unnerving punch of rejection, chilling and achingly familiar. He told himself it didn't compare to the sensation he'd had to live with growing up, to the endless times his needs had been batted aside by his father. But, alas, there it was, eating its insidious way inside him, reminding him far too efficiently that he'd never been good enough. Never worthy of the care and attention his eldest brother had enjoyed, and even his second brother Atu to some extent. Because, despite their head-butting, hadn't his father been desolate in the weeks after Atu had upped sticks and relocated to the other side of the world, citing his inability to live with their merciless father?

And hadn't he, Ekow, the one left behind, been to all intents and purposes invisible to his father?

Perhaps under different circumstances he would've granted Eva's wish. But a cloying need not to be dragged back into that desolate swamp of indifferent dismissal he'd been subjected to far too often in his life hardened his decision.

'Unfortunately for you, I hold all the cards here, Miss Annan. You will come where I wish and stay for as long I wish. And my wish is that you join me for dinner at the Quayson Hotel.'

Her eyes flared with alarm, sparking the merest twinge of guilt. But it was gone the next instant, and stony defiance was etched into her expression as she returned his stare.

'If throwing your weight about is what strokes your ego enough to get this situation resolved, then so be it.'

He welcomed the spark of triumph that washed away the stench of dejection and allowed himself a smile. 'My ego is perfectly robust and healthy. I'll inform you if it needs tending. I'll pick you up at seven p.m.'

Something resembling angry relief crossed her face. It was peculiar enough to slow his steps to the door. 'And just in case you're thinking of making a run for it, don't bother. I have people watching this house.'

Her head whipped towards the window, then returned to him, her face flushed with her wrath. 'You're not serious!'

Ekow crossed his arms. 'Try spending months wondering who's toying with your bank's security systems and making a fool out of you, and you'll know just how serious I am.'

She batted his words away with an elegant hand. 'I'll be here. I'm not afraid of you, Mr Quayson. Definitely not enough to uproot my life just to hide from you. I didn't do it sixteen months ago and I won't do it now.'

He opened his mouth to demand to know what she was talking about, but she strode past him—and, damn it, he was too distracted by the sway of her hips and the delicious bounce of her rounded buttocks to form the words before she opened her front door.

Hand on the doorframe, she glared at him. 'As for having someone toy with your life—believe me, I know what that feels like. Goodbye, Mr Quayson.'

'Not goodbye, sweet Eva. It's good*night*.'

Her luscious lips firmed and that hard punch of temptation returned, rushing lustful heat through his system. His tongue thickened with the need to taste her. It was all he could do to stride forward, walk out into the sultry Cape Town heat to his town car. And he barely registered the journey, his thoughts playing back over his encounter with Eva.

Sixteen months ago he'd needed a release valve for the thick layer of discontentment cloaking his every interaction. Eva had been it for him. Her sinful curves had literally stopped his breath when he'd seen her stalking out of the restaurant, fury enlivening her magnificent, expressive face.

The evening had unfolded in a way far beyond his expectations. Discontentment had been washed away by raw, mindless sex with a woman whose occasional displays of innocence had perfectly blended with her unbridled passion.

So much so, he'd even contemplated extending what he'd intended to be a two-day affair. He'd planned to ply her with a lavish breakfast on Monday…give her a few more pertinent details beyond his name and his connection to the Quayson Hotel Group and the Quayson conglomerate at large.

He'd decided right before he'd succumbed to sleep that he did, in fact, deserve a vacation.

In the wider professional arena he'd earned accolades, respect, and a bank balance he couldn't spend in several lifetimes. All while dealing with an increasingly ungrateful and ever more indifferent father.

Taking a week, maybe two, out of his busy schedule to unwind in South Africa hadn't sounded like the worst idea in the world. Especially when the woman he intended to spend that time with had dramatically quit her job and sent her wholly undeserving boss packing. Making her a free agent.

The last thing he'd expected was to wake up alone, with no sign of the woman who'd electrified his world.

Ekow slid a contemplative finger over his bottom lip as he eased back in his seat. He hadn't been able to banish her from his mind as he'd wished, but no matter... He'd risen to his enviable position in life because he knew when to grasp opportunities when the timing was right.

And he couldn't help but welcome the one just presented to him.

'You're going out? Let me guess... With *him*?'

Eva flinched at her brother's acerbic tone. She didn't need to look up from changing Leo's nappy to know he was seriously ticked off.

She exhaled before she answered. 'Yes, I'm going out. Yolanda will be here in half an hour,' she said. 'I'll try not to be late.'

'I don't need a babysitter,' he grumbled, sauntering into the room as she tickled her son's rounded stomach and revelled in his unfettered laughter. 'Why are you going out with him?'

She glanced at him, fighting her irritation. All day she'd tried to get him to discuss why he'd targeted Quayson Bank's security systems. All she'd received were grunts and sullen silences. 'Why do you think? This problem isn't going to go away just because you refuse to talk about it, Jonah.'

He stiffened, then shrugged. 'What's there to say? I messed about with his bank's firewall.'

'You could start by telling me why you did it!'

'You know why,' he tossed back, his face darkening with anger. 'He knocked you up and left you to fend for yourself, just like Mom had to! Someone needed to teach him a lesson. Someone needs to teach them *all* a lesson.'

Her heart dropped. Having her suspicions confirmed chilled her to the bone. 'Jonah, it's not up to you to take matters into your own hands like that.'

'Yeah? Why not? You weren't going to do anything. You were just going to let him get away with it. Let him live his life and do it all over again to some other woman like your father and mine did!'

Leo whimpered, his beautiful hazel eyes growing wider as he picked up on the tension in the air. She picked him up, brushed a kiss on his cheek as she bounced him in her arms.

'That's enough,' she directed at Jonah, keeping her voice even so her son didn't get even more distressed. 'First of all, my battles are mine to fight—not yours. You don't know the whole story—and, no, I'm not going to tell you, so don't even ask. All I'm concerned about is you and Leo. That you're both healthy and happy and safe. You bringing the authorities to our door risked that, and I wish you hadn't done it.'

His lips twisted but he kept silent.

'Promise me you won't do anything like that ever again,' she pressed.

For an age, he remained mutinously silent. Then he met her gaze. 'I won't mess with his bank if he does the right thing by you.'

She buried her face in her son's curly hair and

squeezed her eyes shut, her heart fracturing a little bit more. She knew if she told Jonah the full story he'd be even more livid.

Somewhere along the line, he'd developed a rigid sense of right and wrong. To him there were no grey areas. She loved him for that, but also despaired a little at his complete intransigence.

'I don't need anything from him,' she said eventually. He frowned and opened his mouth, but she beat him to it, holding a babbling Leo out to him. 'Here, look after your nephew. I need to get dressed.'

He eyed the dress on the bed as he took Leo from her. With money being tight, and Eva not needing to dress every day for the office anymore, her work wardrobe had essentially stayed the same in the last few years. But, as much as she wanted to, she didn't think she'd make the right impression by turning up at the Quayson Hotel in cut-off jeans, a boat-necked sweater and ballet flats.

The black dress she'd worn the night she'd met Ekow remained her most stylish and timeless dress and, while it evoked memories she'd rather not dwell on, it fitted the bill for tonight.

'You're going to dinner with him to discuss me. Shouldn't I be there? To…you know…defend myself?' Despite his belligerence, Jonah cracked a smile when Leo grabbed his cheek.

'I think you've done quite enough, don't you?' Her tone was a little sharp, but she didn't regret it. She'd been far too soft with him. She hardened her heart against the hurt look he cast her.

His lips pursed. 'If he hurts you again…'

Her anger melted away. Going to him, she engulfed both her adored boys in a bear hug, kissing one chubby cheek, then a leaner one. 'He won't. I won't let him. I promise.'

Jonah regarded her for several seconds and then, nodding, he left the room with Leo.

Forty minutes later she was reciting those words to herself as she kissed her baby, said goodbye to her friend and neighbour Yolanda, and shut her front door behind her.

Earlier this afternoon she'd left a message at the hotel to say she would meet Ekow at the restaurant. She'd deliberately not spoken to him directly because she'd feared he would object and turn up at her house anyway. She didn't think she could abide another evening of him invading her space while actively ignoring the son he'd never once acknowledged.

Besides, making her own way there would ensure she approached this evening on her own terms.

The small car she'd inherited from her mother was old, but it still ran well—thanks to Yolanda's husband's mechanical skills and insistence on a free yearly service. About to unlock it, she paused when powerful headlights cut across her front lawn.

Frozen, Eva stared at the luxury town car idling several feet away. Her heart leapt into her throat when the back door opened and Ekow alighted with a suave grace that screamed his class and pedigree. Straightening to his full, towering length, he let his gaze rake leisurely over her.

'What are you doing here?' She ignored the breathlessness in her voice and attempted her fiercest glare.

He looked from her to her car, dismissing it with faint distaste. 'I said I would pick you up.'

'And I left a message saying I would meet you there.

I'm sure your staff are competent enough to have delivered it.'

His lips thinned. 'They did. I ignored it. Because you're not going on your own. Especially not in a death trap. Is that rust-bucket even roadworthy?' he sneered.

'There's nothing wrong with my car. It runs perfectly fine.'

'But you won't be using it tonight.'

He waved a hand her towards the sleek town car. She remained where she was, and slowly his face hardened.

'I insist.'

Only the reminder that she needed to keep him onside if she hoped to gain leniency for Jonah kept her from shoving his insistence in his face. As he'd stated last night, he held the cards. For now.

Dropping her keys back into her clutch, she strutted to the car on heels that felt a little alien since she hadn't worn them in months, and she was entirely too conscious of how much her hips swayed, how her hem brushed her thighs. How she couldn't catch a full breath because of the traitorous awakening occurring inside her at the first whiff of his masculine scent.

What the hell was wrong with her?

She watched him wave away the driver and reach forward to open the door himself. As he straightened he turned his head and their gazes collided.

Evangeline gave a soft gasp at the fire blazing in his eyes. Whatever else was going on, Ekow remained an intensely passionate man, unafraid to show when he found a woman attractive.

And he found her attractive.

No. She was just the tool he'd used to scratch an itch sixteen months ago. One he'd been content to forget despite the life they'd created between them.

She would walk through the flames of hell before she succumbed to even a fraction of what had happened in those forty-eight hours of madness.

If not for her own sake, for the sake of her precious son. For her brother.

She willed rejection into her body, forcing icy coldness into her eyes as she returned his stare.

Slowly, the fire died in his eyes, and the sensual lips she recalled devouring far too vividly thinned into a flat line.

'Get in the car, Eva,' he grated, pulling the door wide open. 'I'm quite eager to understand why you keep directing such hostility at me with those beautiful eyes.'

Her fingers tightened around her clutch as bewildered anger washed away the icy chill. 'I don't understand *you*. In what world do you think it's acceptable to expect me to be civil towards you when you've rejected your own—?'

A child's distressed cry ripped through the evening air, making them both turn around.

Her heart leapt, then dropped sharply, leaving her choking back her own distress. Leo was at that frustratingly adorable age when he rejected everyone and actively threw himself into his mother's arms whenever she was within eyesight.

And her son, having caught sight of her from the front door, was now straining towards her, his plump arms insistently outstretched.

Her gaze shifted to her brother, who stood defiantly on the front porch, his angry gaze fixed on Ekow while he held his nephew.

She squeezed her eyes shut for a calming second.

Jonah knew exactly what he was doing. He might have half-heartedly given his word that he wouldn't meddle any more in Ekow's professional business, but he'd still found a way to force him to acknowledge his son.

Beside her, Ekow froze, his eyes widening as he took in the scene.

Eva's heart leapt into her throat as she watched him set eyes on his son for the first time. Watched him stare. And stare. *And stare.*

His head whipped towards her, and there was shock she didn't believe for one second flashing in his eyes. 'Is there something you want to tell me, Eva?'

Her insides quivered at the granite-hard demand.

'No,' she said, through lips numb with the pain she'd hoped would've healed by now but apparently lay just beneath the surface, waiting to surge up, to remind her not only of the rejection Leo has suffered but her own rejection by the father she'd never met. 'I've wasted enough time trying to do that.'

His eyes narrowed. 'What the hell is that supposed to mean?' he breathed.

Leo cried out again.

Jonah stepped off the porch, his slow strides bringing him closer. She wanted to scream at him to take her baby boy back inside. To guard him against what she knew was coming. But, astonishingly, she couldn't find the words. They remained frozen in her throat as Ekow exhaled sharply.

'Answer me,' he insisted tightly. 'Is that boy your son? Is there a lover lurking in the background I should know about? *Ewuradze*, are you married?'

Those last words were spat out like poison-coated bullets.

Something sharp lanced between her ribs. He wasn't asking about his son. Ekow wanted to know her relationships status. He was offended that she hadn't informed him who was currently sharing her bed.

'Where do you get off, thinking I owe you that sort of personal information?' she threw at him.

Derisive eyes met hers. 'You know very well why you do. Deny it all you want, but the chemistry that gripped us that night at the bar is still present, and I daresay as potent as ever. Clearly whoever fathered this child—if he's yours—is either no longer in the picture or he's not satisfying you the way someone as passionate as you needs to be satisfied.'

'You're right. On both accounts.'

That all-consuming fire leapt in his eyes again, but before his usual very male satisfaction could shine through he studied her a little more intently. He'd obviously gleaned the deeper meaning to her words.

Again, his gaze swung towards Leo, his incisive gaze sweeping over his chubby features. 'How old is the boy, Eva?' he demanded tersely, and she saw a different tension invading his body.

'He's seven months, three weeks and two days old. And don't insult my intelligence by pretending to make calculations.'

'What…?' He stopped, took a slow, chest-filling breath. He reached out a hand, propping it on the hood of the car. 'What are you saying, Eva? And before you think to toy with me, know that my patience is in serious deficit.'

'I'm saying I got the message loud and clear. My son hasn't been your business since he was conceived. And he's absolutely not your business now.'

A stunning transformation came over his face as he absorbed her meaning. 'What you're saying…that means…'

He staggered one step backwards and it was a sight

to behold. Such a pillar of a man seemingly floored by the truth.

Eva wanted to laugh, to mock and dismiss him just as callously as he'd dismissed her, after she'd spent a sizeable chunk of her precious savings to buy a ticket to Accra to inform him about his impending fatherhood, only to have her efforts thrown back in her face and topped off with threats.

She didn't laugh. Because the reality was nowhere near humorous.

Had he hoped she would temper her words? Perhaps give him a pass so he could deign to acknowledge her somewhere down the line?

She glanced away from him to Leo, the most treasured thing in her life. Jonah, perhaps sensing his impetuousness was causing more ripples than he'd imagined, had stopped in the middle of the lawn and was attempting to calm Leo, who was still holding out his arms, insisting on the love and attention from his mother that was his due.

Unable to deny him, she went over and lifted him into her arms. 'It's okay, my darling. Mommy's here.'

He immediately stopped whimpering, an adorable toothless smile breaking out as he played with the chunky colourful necklace she wore with her dress.

Behind her, Ekow's presence loomed large, and even though he kept his distance she could feel every scrap of his focus fixed on her.

'Give me a proper answer. Now, Eva,' he muttered tersely after a minute had passed.

She shook her head. 'I'm not doing this. Not out here.'

She strode past a wide-eyed Jonah and re-entered her house, achingly aware of Ekow half a step behind.

Yolanda hastily stepped back from the window, and Eva cringed at the thought that the older woman must have overheard a good chunk of their conversation.

'Is everything okay?' her friend asked.

Before she could answer, Ekow strode into the living room and stopped, his eyes narrowing on her neighbour.

'I need to talk to Eva. Leave us. Please,' he tagged on tersely, his wide-legged stance stating that he wouldn't be moving anywhere anytime soon.

Yolanda's eyes widened, then shifted to Eva, one eyebrow raised in question. Swallowing her irritation at Ekow, as he obliviously tapped out a message on his phone, she smiled at her friend. 'It's fine. Thanks for your help tonight, Yo.'

'No problem.' Her gaze shifted to Jonah, who lingered in the doorway. 'Do you want to come home with me, Jonah? I'm sure Eric wouldn't mind a sleepover,' she said, referring to her son, who was in the same class as Jonah.

For once, her brother looked uncertain, almost contrite as his gaze searched Eva's. 'It's all right. You can go,' she encouraged him.

He gave a nod, rushed to his room, and emerged seconds later with his treasured backpack. Without looking at Ekow, he darted out through the front door.

'I'll call you tomorrow,' Eva said to Yolanda.

'You'd better,' her friend murmured under her breath, her expression rife with curiosity as Eva walked her to the door.

Eva whirled on Ekow as soon as she'd shut the door behind her friend, trying not to dwell on the fact that she was alone with him. 'I'd thank you not to order people about in my home.'

Her words bounced off him, and his broad shoulders

lifted in a shrug. 'Feel free to call her back. Let us air our dirty laundry in public, shall we?'

She pursed her lips, seething that he'd called her bluff. 'Let's get this over with,' she said.

But instead of peppering her with the questions brimming in his eyes, he pivoted away from her, putting the width of the small room between them. Then, in a repeat of his stance outside, he leaned forward and gripped the back of the sofa until his knuckles were tight, his bones straining against his dark skin.

For an eternity he stared at Leo, his expression a mixture of shock, awe and bewilderment. 'Is this boy mine?' he finally rasped, his voice like burning gravel.

Something seismic and esoteric shook through her. Perhaps because, despite the callous repudiation she'd suffered at his father's hand, Eva had always held this moment in her heart. Perhaps she'd even placed herself in Leo's shoes, imagined what it would be like to be handed the essential answer to a puzzle, after years of wondering and hoping and yearning over her own father.

'His name is Leo. And you know damn well he's yours. You've known for the better part of a year and a half. So, here's what *I* want to know. Why are you pretending otherwise?'

CHAPTER FOUR

EKOW COULDN'T TAKE his eyes off the child.

He couldn't breathe.

Hell, he was absolutely certain that had he not been gripping the back of the shabby sofa he would've crumpled to the ground.

His child.

His *son*.

One plump cheek was nestled against his mother's chest as he valiantly fought to stay awake and adorably lost the battle. Within a minute, sleep finally overtook him, and his long lashes spread out in half-moon fans. His hair was thick and curly and, courtesy of his mother's mixed heritage, his skin was a soft, dark caramel.

He was...beautiful. Perfect.

Incredible, really, that something so flawless belonged to him.

And he'd had no idea...

Knowing he couldn't disturb the child was the only reason why a torrent of questions stayed locked in Ekow's throat. Why he wasn't bellowing his fury at her outrageous lies.

'He's mine.' Those two words shifted something inside him. Settled a path forward with such clarity that it staggered him all over again.

Ekow had never asked for a role other than the one he'd carved for himself in his dysfunctional family. To make such a demand from the father who'd sired him just to have a son to boast about, and then treated him like an unwanted visitor, would've been as futile and painful as bashing his head against a rock. Far too quickly as a child, he'd learned to rely on no one but himself.

But now he'd been presented with this everything he'd deemed essential faded into insignificance.

Was this…love?

He had no idea. That emotion was alien to him. It had been non-existent in his father. And his mother had been too absorbed in being the perfect wife, too cowed by her overbearing husband, to display any emotion which didn't mirror her spouse's. Perhaps recently, since his father's death, his mother had shown some signs of affection. Unfortunately, any capacity he had to be receptive had been eroded under his father's demanding and cruel boot.

Recently, though, his brother Atu had married. And when Amelie had given birth, shortly after they were married, Atu had been curiously overcome as he'd proclaimed fatherhood as a life-changing experience.

But, while Ekow took his duties as uncle and godfather seriously, his devotion had always felt…removed. He hadn't understood Atu's vow to burn the world to the ground should any harm befall his wife, his daughter, or their baby son.

Right now, in this moment, he knew what his brother meant. Being confronted with his flesh and blood had already altered the trajectory of his life.

But what he found incomprehensible was that *he hadn't known.*

'All this time you kept me in the dark.' The stark words fell from his lips wreathed in quiet fury and bewilderment. He couldn't shake the thought that he could've gone years, decades, perhaps even his entire life, without knowing his son existed.

And that was unacceptable.

Eva's eyes had widened at the low growl erupting unbidden from his throat. Now she had the audacity to take a step back, as if *he* was the dangerous one here. As if *he* had committed this unconscionable transgression.

She opened her mouth, most likely to spew more lies. But her gaze dropped to the baby. *His baby.*

'I need to put him to bed. We can continue this when I'm done.'

She started to turn away, and a sharp, desperate yearning pierced his heart. 'Wait.'

The word was quiet, but forceful enough to make an impact. She froze.

Ekow dragged in a long, sustaining breath. Released his hold on the weathered sofa. Drew himself up to his full height. On ludicrously shaky legs, he crossed the room to where she cradled the precious bundle who bore his DNA.

He didn't care that the hand he lifted towards his son shook uncontrollably. That another guttural sound rose in his chest as he touched his son's warm, satin-smooth cheek for the first time.

Up close, he was even more beautiful, and his features, now he was examining them closely, bore the unmistakable Quayson stamp. He didn't need a paternity test to prove this boy was his.

He trailed his hand over his child's silky curls, his tiny shoulders and one tightly furled fist. When it opened to curl around his finger, the sound in his throat erupted in a hoarse, unintelligible sound, unleashing a longing he fought to contain.

Eva's gaze raked his face, and whatever she read there made her nostrils quiver momentarily. Then she gathered herself, sending him another censorious look. He would get to the bottom of that look. Get to the bottom of this whole elaborate ruse of hers to keep what was his from him. Her absurd allegation that he'd known and denied his child's existence.

The reality that he was a father continued to shake through him as he watched her stride down the hall, fighting to stay still when everything inside him clamoured for another glimpse, another touch of his son.

He paced the living room, his unseeing gaze darting over the cheap furniture, the worn carpet and tired curtains.

Evangeline had had his baby, kept it from him, for whatever reason, and chosen to live in a low-income neighbourhood, scraping a living out of a business that was barely breaking even, instead of in the lap of luxury as the mother of his child.

Why?

When she returned ten minutes later, the question erupted out of him.

'Why hide him from me all this time? I could've given you a much better life than you're living right now. Because money is what all this is about, right?'

She stilled in the small archway framing the hallway. In the reflected light her voluptuous body was thrown into relief, punching fresh lust into the tumultuous emotions churning through him.

'You think this is about *money*?' she spat out with disgust. 'I don't want your money. I never did.'

His mouth twisted. 'You're going to have to do better

than that. And why did you imply that I already knew I was a father?'

Her small fists curled. 'It wasn't an implication. It was the truth.'

He shook his head, certain he was hallucinating. 'Do you deny your brother targeted my bank to lure me here?'

For a long second she didn't answer. Then she shrugged. 'No, I don't deny it. But until last night I had no idea what he was doing.'

'You expect me to believe this *truth*, too?' He didn't bother to soften his derision.

An angry flush rushed to her face. 'I don't care what you believe.'

'Yes, you do. At least enough to put on that dress. What were you hoping, Eva? That I would be so bowled over by seeing you in that dress again I'd turn to putty in your hands? Or was it more the memory of my sliding it off your body and indulging in the delights underneath that you hoped would sway me into your way of thinking?'

Her eyes widened. 'What are you—?'

'Because I'll confess it almost worked.'

He confessed that truth tightly. Seeing her when he'd pulled up outside, the dress still clinging in all the right places, had ramped up his temperature to almost lethal proportions.

He'd spent all day debating how best to proceed with Evangeline and her troublesome brother. He'd concluded that the boy didn't belong behind bars. His clearly prodigious talents were better off being nurtured in the right way, under strict supervision.

He'd smugly envisaged how he would convey his magnanimous decision to Eva…perhaps thaw the ice wall she'd erected between them. Hell, he'd even imagined a second performance of their scorching night together—a way to draw a firm line beneath what he still considered unfinished business.

Not for a wild and stunning second had he imagined *this*…

'You think I put on this dress for *you*?' she scoffed.

He ignored his sharp at her tone and raised mocking eyebrows. 'Why else?'

'Did your ego not get out of your way long enough for you to consider that this might be my favourite dress? That I like it, and it's mine, and I can wear it whenever I damn well please? Or do you think the world revolves around your greatness?'

'Look me in the eye and say it didn't once cross your mind.' He modulated his voice in the way that usually confounded his business opponents. His brother had termed it his 'oh, hell' voice.

Ekow favoured it when he wanted to cut through the BS. And, while this issue needed to take a back seat to the more important one of the son he'd been kept in the dark about, he needed to establish a baseline of control. That control included shattering Eva's subterfuge. And what better way to shatter it than to get her to admit her true intentions in wearing the dress?

This time he knew the heat flooding her face wasn't born of fury. It was a live wire of awareness. Perhaps even arousal.

A lethal cocktail of sensations churned through the air, leaving them locked in battle for an eternity before she shook her head. 'This is insane,' she rasped, but he caught the huskiness in her voice, saw the outline of her nipples as she strode forward. 'Do you want to discuss Leo or keep making absurd observations?'

Hearing his son's name sharpened his focus. 'Ah, yes. You insist your brother acted on his own. And that somehow I knew I had a son but denied his existence?'

'Somehow? You know exactly how. Your father was an effective emissary, believe me.'

Every cell in his body froze. 'My *father*? What are you talking about? What has he got to do with this?' he demanded through lips numb with a foreboding he didn't welcome.

She pressed her fingers into her temples before spearing him with another contemptuous look. 'Please, spare me the shocked innocence! I'd say you sent him to do your dirty work, but after meeting him I imagine no one sends your father to do anything. He probably always offers to dispatch another one of your discarded affairs on your behalf. I get it.'

His insides clenched tighter. He felt icier. 'Be careful who you're disparaging, Eva.'

The silky warning drew a sharp inhalation from her, but to his surprise her chin remained at the defiant angle he'd first seen when he'd watched her toss a drink in her boss's deplorable face.

'You've called me a liar more than once in my own home and now you're warning me about the way *I* treat *you*?'

He slashed a dismissive hand through the air. 'What you're saying never happened. At least own your poor decisions.'

Fire flashed through her eyes and her small, slim hands curled into fists again. 'You don't believe me? Feel free to ask your father.'

He'd thought his insides couldn't get colder, the sensation in his chest more desolate. 'That would be quite impossible since he's no longer alive.'

She stilled, her eyes widening before she swallowed and looked away from him. 'I... I didn't know that. My condolences.'

He stiffened at the gentleness in her voice. It went nowhere towards absolving her of the immutable crime of keeping his son from him.

Almost compelled, he returned his gaze to the door at the end of the hall behind which his handsome son slept. And, yes, he was smug about *that*—because he and Eva had created something beautiful, something extraordinary.

Something he'd been denied.

He opened his mouth but she put up a hand. And, *Yesu*, that regal action was commanding enough to do the job of silencing him—a feat very few people would dare attempt.

'Your father may no longer be in a position to corroborate what I'm saying, but I have proof of my visit.'

His heart hammered and lurched, driving discomfort through his body. Even now, some three decades into the abject knowledge that his father had never favoured him, some part of him still lived in denial.

But if what Eva was saying was true, then his father had...

No.

It was unconscionable to believe his father would've taken such conclusive steps to deny a Quayson the right to claim his own flesh and blood. Or had Ekow been deemed unimportant enough even to run such a conversation past him?

He shook off the dark shadows attempting to pull him deeper into the quiet despair he'd lived with for decades. 'Show it to me,' he said, his voice an alien sound.

Muted hurt flashed across her face. Her lashes swept

down and she exhaled slowly, then crossed to the clutch she'd dropped on the coffee table when they'd come indoors.

Ice and dread and fury churned in a lethal cocktail through his gut as he watched her flick through her phone. Her movement was too purposeful to be a bluff, but what else could it be?

Having found whatever she was looking for, she held out her phone. 'See for yourself,' she dared him.

Teeth gritted, he stared down at the screen. At the electronic airline ticket and booking confirmation for a hotel in Accra a handful of weeks after their weekend together.

Ekow couldn't clearly define the sensations shifting through him. He suppressed what felt like relief and reached for cold, hard logic. 'This just shows you travelled to Accra. Your surname is Ghanaian, so I'm assuming at least one of your parents is West African. Your father?'

This time her anguish wasn't muted. It was visceral and thick. And it lasted more than a few seconds. She visibly swallowed before she gathered herself. 'My parentage is none of your business. If you don't believe this, use whatever means you used to track me down. I'm sure there's some footage somewhere that shows I visited the Quayson Hotel in Accra and met with your father exactly when I say I did.'

The churning intensified. Her words were easily verifiable. She wouldn't be so foolish as to risk him calling her bluff. Which meant—

The doorbell sounded, cutting across the unthinkable, unacceptable conclusion his brain wanted to make. He didn't...*couldn't* believe his own father would have done such a thing. Eva had to be lying.

And yet as he trailed her to the door—because he suspected he knew who had rung the bell—he couldn't shake the knot of dread thickening in his gut.

He paused behind her when she opened the door and frowned at the man on the doorstep. 'Can I help you?' she asked.

'He's here for me,' Ekow interjected, then addressed the man. 'Did you do as I asked?'

'Of course, sir.'

Ekow took the bags he held out. 'Thank you, Samson. Return to the hotel. I'll let you know when I need you.'

'Yes, sir. Goodnight, sir.'

Ekow shut the door and found the mother of his son glaring at him.

'What is this? And who was that man?'

'Samson is my driver.' He held up the bags. 'And this isn't quite the meal I intended us to have, but it's dinner, nonetheless. We'll need the fuel, I suspect, since we've barely broached the surface of everything you need to tell me.'

'What *I* need to tell *you*? What makes you think—?'

'Enough, Eva!' He deposited the takeout boxes on her dining table and swivelled to face her. 'We're going to eat, and then you're going to take me through everything that's occurred from the moment you stole out of my bed till now.'

Her chin tilted higher. 'Eat if you must. I've lost my appetite.'

Ekow exhaled long and slow. Had it been anyone else, Eva might have imagined he was at the end of his rope. But then he locked eyes with her and silently reminded her that he was a formidable tycoon who could crush her on a whim.

'My son is seven months old. Are you still breast-feeding him?' he asked, his voice thickening curiously as his gaze dropped to her chest and rose back to her face.

Unwelcome heat engulfing her, she nodded.

'Correct me if I'm wrong, but doesn't that mean you should keep regular eating habits?'

'My eating habits were absolutely fine before you turned up on my doorstep, Mr Quayson. And my son is perfectly healthy.'

'I'm happy to hear it. Why don't we ensure it stays that way?'

The rigidity edging the question said he wouldn't be moved from his intention. Fighting irritation, and the misguided notion that he cared anything about her, she went into the kitchen to retrieve cutlery and clean plates, telling herself she'd planned to eat with him to-night anyway.

But that was *before* he'd called her integrity into question.

Before he'd looked her in the eyes and called her a liar.

Sure, nothing had changed. Nothing except Ekow Quayson's absurd assertion that he hadn't known his son existed.

She jumped when firm hands closed over her own. 'What are you doing?' she demanded. 'Let me—'

'Your fists are clenched around the cutlery, Eva. I don't want you to hurt yourself,' he said gruffly, calmly prising the utensils from her hands and laying them neatly on the table. 'We haven't reached the blood-shed-ding part of the evening yet, I don't believe.'

'You think this is funny?'

His face grew granite-hard. 'Believe me, I don't find a single moment of this situation humorous,' he replied, before reaching for the first takeout bag.

Considering the enormity of their situation, it was surreal to watch him laying out the food boxes on the table. It was most definitely the wrong time to recall he'd insisted on feeding her the night they'd met too, as if that aspect of caretaking really was important to him.

Bitterness seared her. Too bad that feeding her was the extent of his nurturing. Too bad that when she'd needed him to show the same level of caring on discovering she was pregnant with his child he'd declined, sending his father to do his dirty bidding...

About to insist he not bother with the food, she held her tongue. Because, for all his arrogance and austere pronouncements, for a fraction of a second Ekow Quayson had seemed...floored by Leo's existence.

There remained a tightness around his eyes, harsh lines bracketing his lips, and the stiff way he held his body looked as if he was bracing himself for something monumental.

For good or ill, she forced herself to consider, for a fraction of a second, if he'd been truly in the dark as he claimed.

'Evangeline.'

His firm, insistent voice said that whatever she believed might not matter. The expressions she'd imagined she'd seen were nowhere in sight when she refocused on him.

He'd pulled out a chair, was waiting for her to take it. Fighting a compulsion she couldn't seem to dismiss, she approached the table. She'd been too riled up to spot the logo on the food boxes before. Now, seeing the veritable feast spread out on her table, she couldn't miss it.

Of course he'd ordered from one of the most exclusive restaurants in Cape Town. She hadn't even known the restaurant did take-out. Perhaps they only did it for powerful billionaires.

She pushed away the nonsensical thought when it threatened to produce a touch of hysteria. If he wanted to throw a layer of civility over this situation she'd go along with it. She mustn't forget Jonah's situation hadn't been resolved either.

So she sat down, striving not to be affected by his proximity, not to inhale the stimulating blend of oak and earth and man pulsing from his skin. Not to watch the hypnotic way he moved when he rounded the table to open the boxes from where the intensely aromatic fragrances emanated.

Eva hated her sudden surge of hunger. The resurgence of the appetite she'd loftily denied.

'You'll have to help me out,' he said stiffly. 'I don't know what nursing mothers are allowed to eat.'

'Unless you're serving fugu, or some super-exotic delicacy, most foods are fine. It's what I drink that I have to watch.'

He nodded curtly, then started to dish out portions with streamlined efficiency. A minute later he set down a plate heaped with mouthwatering linguine and lobster rolled in a creamy sauce, delicate stalks of asparagus, and tapioca chips.

'No pufferfish in sight.'

With that dry delivery, he served himself, then pulled out the adjacent chair.

He ate in silence, his movements precise and unhurried, as if he had all the time in the world. As if the battle they both sensed hovering on the horizon like an impending storm didn't exist.

Determined not to be the first to break the silence, Eva ate enough to reassure herself that Leo's next feed would be unhindered.

When she placed her cutlery down Ekow's gaze sliced to her half-finished plate, then rose to meet hers. Perhaps her challenge was clear enough. Perhaps he, too, was picking his fights. He set his own tableware down and pierced her with fierce brown eyes.

'When did you find out you were pregnant?' he lobbed at her, his voice tight with bridled emotions.

'A month after I…after we were together. We used protection. I didn't have any reason to think it would fail.'

'Clearly it did. I believe that's what the disclaimer warning on the condom box is for,' he stated in a bone-dry voice.

She stiffened. 'I hope you don't think I helped it along somehow.'

'Did you?' he returned, brooding eyes fixed on her.

'No,' she said, just as coldly. 'You might not believe me, but I detest women who trick men like that.'

'Why wouldn't I believe you?'

His father's harsh words rang in her ears. 'You're a very wealthy man. Isn't that the first conclusion you'd draw? That any woman you sleep with might want to take a nine-month shortcut to wealth and prestige?'

'The women I sleep with know the rules going in. You were an…anomaly.'

'You mean I was a nobody, with no clue to how your sophisticated world works?'

A muscle rippled in his jaw. 'Don't put words in my

mouth, Eva. I don't make a habit of picking up women at bars. And I don't think you do the same with men.'

Tight-lipped, she gave a shake of her head.

'So our situation was unique from the start. And I want to know why there's a month's gap between discovering you were pregnant and your arrival in Accra.'

The tension in his voice bewildered her. Then her eyes widened with enlightenment. 'Why? Did you think I was trying to find another solution?'

His shrug was stiff. 'We've agreed our situation was exceptional. If you'd chosen a different path, no one would've been any the wiser.'

'I wanted my baby the second I knew I was pregnant! Leo wasn't planned but he was wanted. Very much.'

He searched her face with such intensity that Eva had to fight not to squirm. Then he nodded, and despite her ruffled emotions something eased inside her.

'It took me two months to reach out to you because I was busy looking for another job. I had bills to pay and a brother to look after. I couldn't just jump on a plane. And you might not be aware of this, but apparently you can't just pick up the phone and ask to speak to the billionaire banker you happened to spend the night with.'

'Two nights,' he returned huskily. 'We spent two nights together.'

Heat spiralled through her as his eyes dropped to her mouth and lingered for far too long. Clearing her throat, she continued. 'When I managed to track you down, I called you. Several times. I didn't get farther than Reception because I refused to give a reason for my call. When I realised only a face-to-face meeting would work, I went to Accra.'

His tension increased, and his eyes were no longer

burning with that all-consuming heat. 'Where you purportedly met my father.'

'Would you like me to describe his office to you? Would that make you believe me or is there some particular reason you're insisting on clinging to the belief that I'm lying?' Something about his heightened tension pushed another possibility at her. 'Or is this something else? Something you don't want to accept because believing me would mean shining a different, unwanted light on the situation?'

Cruel rejection hardened his face. But she sensed she was right. He didn't want to accept her explanation because the alternative was unthinkable.

'You say you met my father. What did he say to you?'

She forced a shrug. 'The usual things men like you say to women like me, I'm guessing. He called my character into question, quizzed me about dates and, like you, claimed I was lying. When I showed him my ultrasound photo he said the child I was carrying could be anyone's.' She took a shallow, non-sustaining breath. 'Then he dismissed me with a threat never to contact you or anyone in your family again.'

She kept her gaze fixed over his shoulder, afraid he'd read every moment of the anguish she'd suffered in her eyes if she looked at him.

His eyes narrowed into vicious slits. 'That's not all. If you're hiding something from me I'll find out. I always do.'

She swallowed her alarm, asking herself why she hadn't mentioned that final thing. 'Is that a threat?'

'No. It's a statement of fact.'

In that moment Eva wanted to scream every brutal word his father had spoken to her in his office. She wanted to jump up, march into her bedroom and retrieve the final act of her humiliation.

The cheque Joseph Quayson had scrawled his signature on and thrown across his desk at her.

Money for her silence. Money so she would never utter his son's name in connection with her *spawn*.

But she'd vowed never to relive those intensely humiliating moments ever again.

She was startled when he surged to his feet, going to the window she'd stared out of only last night as she'd recalled their first meeting. For an age he remained there, a pillar of seething emotions, one hand braced on his nape.

Then he snapped around, his face a hard, determined mask. 'I now know of my son's existence. That's the most important thing here.'

'If that's your roundabout way of saying you don't believe me, be a man and say it.'

Fury flashed across his face. 'You don't want to test me right now, Eva. I want my son. I intend to have him in my life. The only thing I want to discuss now is how to make it happen.'

Alarm shuddered through her. 'You can't just throw down demands and expect me to fall in line.'

A tic appeared at his temple. He shoved his hands into his pockets and rocked back on his heels. 'I've been ignorant of my son's existence for the better part of a year and half so, yes, my speed will be blistering.'

She watched him stride towards her, ferocious intent in every frame of his body.

'You have until morning, Eva. You want me to believe you intended me to be in our son's life from the moment you found out you were pregnant? This is your chance to prove it.'

'By doing what? Interrupting my life and his at your whim?'

If anything, he turned stonier. 'You think this is a whim?'

She swallowed. 'You claim you've only just learned you're a father. Perhaps you should take some time—'

'Absolutely not. He's mine. I'm not denying either myself or him another second without each another.'

Her heart plummeted to her feet. 'What does that mean?'

He dropped his head a little closer to hers, as if he didn't want her to miss his next words. 'It means you and Leo are coming back to Ghana with me.'

Eva reared back, taking several steps away from him. 'What? Are you out of your mind? We're not going anywhere—'

'Do you really want to become embroiled in an international custody battle with me?' he enquired, his voice silky yet deadly. 'Because that wouldn't be my first option, if I were you.'

'You talk about options, but what you're giving me is an ultimatum.'

He shrugged, her accusation bouncing off him. 'Call it what you will. Those are my terms. For you and our son, at least. We're yet to deal with your brother. His situation will require a different plan.'

She felt a dart of shame, because she'd forgotten about Jonah in the aftermath of Ekow's bombshells. 'What's that supposed to mean? What plan?'

'It means he might need special guidance.'

Her eyes narrowed. 'If that's billionaire-speak for some sort of juvenile detention, be warned that I'll fight you with everything I have!'

One corner of his mouth twisted but the rest of his

face remained a tyrannical mask, without an ounce of give. 'Your devotion is admirable. But coddling him isn't the answer, and deep down I think you know it.'

She inhaled sharply. 'He's been through enough.'

'And he's used whatever that was as an excuse to get away with murder. What he needs is structure.'

'And, let me guess, you're going to provide it?' she scoffed, despite a part of her grudgingly accepting that he was right.

He shrugged. 'The level of skill your brother has shown is…exemplary. That kind of genius needs careful harnessing. Agree to my plan and he'll receive the expert guidance he's lacking.'

She knew better than to snatch the carrot he dangled, and yet… 'If I agree, how long do you expect Leo and me to stay in Ghana for?'

'The first few years of his life at the very least. More if we decide he would be better off with us remaining a unit rather than apart.'

Astonishment made her gape for several seconds before she collected herself. 'Excuse me? Did you say the first few *years*? I'm not sure what sort of guests you invite to your home to visit for years, but I don't intend to be one of them.'

Intense eyes rested mockingly on her, and Eva was sure a snort left his throat before he strolled forward to stand before her.

'You misunderstand, my dear. You're not coming to Accra for a visit. You and our son are coming to live with me. He's going to take my name and his place as my rightful heir. And you, Evangeline, are going to live under my roof as my wife.'

CHAPTER FIVE

SLEEP ON IT.

Those had been Ekow's words before striding out of her house as if he hadn't turned her world upside down.

Her mild hysteria had resurged, ready to break free at the smallest pressure. Perhaps he'd noticed and timed his exit accordingly.

Needless to say, she hadn't slept.

She'd still been staring at the ceiling when Leo had woken up just before sunrise. It had been a relief to leap into the routine of feeding, bathing and setting him up for the day. And she had unashamedly doubled the normal forty-five-minute routine, simply so she could postpone thinking about the seismic change Ekow expected her to make on his say-so.

She'd grasped Yolanda's offer to drive Jonah to school with both hands, had even summoned a smile to put her friend at ease when she'd stopped by to collect Jonah's school things.

Eva knew she'd have to explain herself at some point, but how could she when even *she* didn't know what direction her life was headed?

While Leo contentedly played in his playpen Eva sat at the dining table, cradling a cup of fast-cooling coffee.

She and Ekow had created a son between them, but

when it came right down to it, they barely knew each other. While marriage for the sake of their son sounded like a worthwhile sacrifice, was she doing him a disservice by even contemplating it?

Questions continued to tumble through her head.

An hour later, after despatching a client's paperwork, she typed Ekow's name into an online search engine.

After his father's treatment of her in Accra, she'd vowed never to waste another minute on him. But with one click thousands of hits exploded onto the screen.

The Quayson brothers had been deemed supremely eligible bachelors long before the oldest brother had died in a tragic car crash. Now the middle brother, Atu, was married and off the market, Ekow was considered an even more exclusive catch.

Though she knew it was a dangerous path, she couldn't stop herself from reading story after story about his past liaisons, the lengths some of those women had gone to in order to bag a billionaire.

Thirty minutes later, overwhelmed with information, she shut her laptop with more force than necessary, and knotted her hands in her lap as she pursed her lips.

No wonder he'd been sceptical about everything she'd told him. Even just a few minutes in Eva had discovered three separate stories about women who'd tried to lay paternity claims on him.

Rising from the chair with a dash of impatience, she dumped her cold coffee in the sink, then stood frozen, staring at her garden.

Was this why his father had denounced her claim right off the bat? She hadn't given him any evidence, after all. It hadn't even occurred to her that she might need it.

But it didn't excuse his threats and his humiliating her.

Compelled, she went to her bedside table, pulled open the drawer and, after rifling through her documents, pulled out the cheque Joseph Quayson had contemptuously tossed at her that day in his office.

Even after all this time, the zeros on the cheque still boggled her mind.

She should've destroyed it a long time ago. She knew that. She'd questioned herself before and after Leo's birth, but deep down she knew why she hadn't.

It was an effective reminder of her shockingly innocent belief that she was doing the right thing and therefore the father of her child would do the same.

Staring at the cheque, she took comfort in knowing she hadn't let herself be bought off with money. Throughout all her challenges, she'd retained her integrity.

Placing the cheque back in the drawer, she returned resolutely to her laptop.

It had been hard, but she had found the best of all worlds. She got to watch her son grow happy and healthy while building her business from home. She didn't need to change any of it.

Eva let that conviction settle deep inside her as the hours ticked relentlessly towards evening. She was showered and dressed in comfortable clothes, leggings and a light sweater, with Leo propped on her hip and Jonah tucked away in his room doing his homework, when she answered Ekow's knock.

His laser gaze fastened onto her, conducting a searing head-to-toe scrutiny before swinging to Leo, where it stayed with the same fascination and yearning she'd glimpsed yesterday. Eva released a breath at that look, not even knowing she'd craved this particular reassurance until just now.

Stepping back from the doorway, she let him in. Minutes later she watched his gaze cloud over as she gave him her answer.

'No?'

She wanted to laugh at his incredulous disbelief.

'That's my answer. No, thank you. I won't marry you. What you're offering sounds more like a prison sentence.'

His eyebrows rose. 'A prison sentence? In a prison where your every need is catered for? Where our son will thrive with the best life has to offer?'

Prideful affront hardened her spine. 'You speak as if I'm bringing him up in a gutter.'

He braced his hands on lean hips. 'You're attempting to do your best. I'll give you that. But I'm confident we'll do better together.'

She hated the way he cut her off at the knees, infusing his every argument with statements that made it sound as if he really cared about the son he'd claimed not to know about.

'Why don't you give it a chance?' he pressed.

She couldn't let the lofty dreams she'd had for herself with her own father play out in her son. But then hadn't she scraped together money she could ill afford to buy an airline ticket just so her son would know his father? Was she really prepared to deny him, then put them both through a custody battle she might not win?

Ekow watched steadily, waiting her out, as if simply standing there looking gorgeous and heartrendingly virile would change her mind. After a handful of minutes he slowly sauntered towards her, stopping a foot away.

But he wasn't staring at her.

His gaze was fixed once again on Leo. And it occurred to her that he was seeing him truly awake for the first time. Their son was babbling a mile a minute, his avid gaze swinging between her and his father.

Her heart stopped when he held out one chubby hand to Ekow. Without hesitation, Ekow offered him his hand. Leo eagerly wrapped his fingers around two of his father's and then, to her surprise, started straining towards him.

Ekow's gaze shifted with lightning speed to hers and then returned to fix on his son. 'May I hold him?' The question was gruff, low, infused with feelings and emotions she wasn't quite ready to name.

A lump rising into her throat, she nodded.

Large, secure hands wrapped around Leo's tiny body, and with easy strength Ekow took control of her son.

For a flash in time, panic rose inside her. She understood for the first time that she wasn't in complete control. She'd named Ekow on Leo's birth certificate, which gave him the right to fight for access.

Whether she agreed to marry him or not ultimately didn't matter. He had lawyers, money, power. As much as she loathed to admit it, were she in his shoes she would use whatever she had at her disposal to ensure she was a part of her son's life.

She watched, a bereft feeling widening in her gut, as father and son moved towards the window overlooking the back garden. Ekow murmured low and unintelligible things to his son and Leo answered with enthusiastic babbling.

Part of her wanted Leo to protest, so she could swoop in and reclaim her precious baby, but he simply stared at his father with an avidness that struck her in the chest. Leo might be too young to comprehend his connection with the man holding him, but that would change very quickly.

Would he blame her for the path she was choosing just as she'd secretly blamed her mother for the choices she'd made?

The weight of her decision dropped on her, shaking through her as Ekow pivoted and slowly retraced his steps back to her.

When he stopped in front of her he didn't hand Leo back. In fact, his arms seemed to have been made to cradle his son, and she felt his ease with Leo striking her deep inside. She recalled that Atu's wife had young children, making Ekow an uncle. A few thousand miles away there was an extended family her son didn't know yet.

Deep in her bones she knew Ekow wouldn't give up his son, regardless of the answer she'd just given him.

'Do you know what I did this afternoon?' he asked.

His casual question threw her. 'No,' she answered warily.

'I visited Jonah's school.'

Anger sparked to life inside her. 'You did what?'

A smile quirked one corner of his mouth. 'I wanted to see the environment he was being educated in.'

'You had no right,' she replied hotly.

'Take it easy. I didn't interrupt his studies or ask to see his school records. What I did was assess things for myself. Do you want to know my conclusion?'

She pursed her lips and didn't answer. She knew what he was doing. What she'd been attempting to do herself but hadn't so far because of her financial constraints. Because scholarships for the kind of school Jonah needed were like gold dust.

Ekow answered anyway. 'Your brother is wasted in that place. I think you know it.'

'You seem to think you have all the answers.'

'I do,' he delivered arrogantly. 'I spoke to the heads of two schools renowned for their nurturing of prodigious talents like Jonah's. With the right incentives, both are prepared to take him immediately.'

Eva gasped. 'What gives you the right to make decisions about Jonah without consulting me?'

'No decision has been made yet. But if you think I'm going to sit around twiddling my thumbs while you make up your mind one way or the other, you're wrong.'

'You think packing my brother off to some school is going to make me fall in line with what you want?'

'No. For starters we won't be doing anything your brother doesn't want for himself.'

She frowned. 'What's that supposed to mean?'

'I told you I'd researched him before I arrived here. Part of that research showed me where his interests lie. He probably hasn't told you about it because he knows there are stumbling blocks in the way of what he wants.'

'And you think you know what Jonah wants?'

He smiled, and while it wasn't cruel, it wasn't kind either. 'Did you know he wants to attend a boarding school in Switzerland? A school especially renowned for harnessing Silicon Valley prodigies?'

Her guilt intensified, and her gaze strayed down the hallway to her brother's closed door.

'His second choice is an equally excellent choice, right here in South Africa. The third choice is in Dubai. I know you've applied for scholarships and been refused on the Dubai school. I can make all three accept him. Just say the word.'

'Really? You would…?' She stopped herself from

snatching at his offer. Reminded herself that it came at a price.

'Yes. I would,' he confirmed anyway.

His utter confidence shook through her. With a click of his fingers he could change her brother's life.

'All of this is conditional, isn't it?' she said.

'Of course it is,' he stated briskly, as if she were a little bit slow. 'You care about your brother. He needs more help than you're able to provide him right now. The quicker you face that, the quicker we can get on to more pressing matters.'

'You mean like you not taking no for an answer?'

He looked down at Leo for a long moment before lifting his head. 'He's mine. I won't leave him behind. With your brother where he needs to be, you'll have one less thing to worry about.'

'And you don't get that one of the other things I worry about is you?' Eva immediately cringed at the telling phrase. When his eyes narrowed, she knew she'd given herself away. Yes, she was afraid of giving in to him. As much as she wanted to deny it, that live wire of sexual chemistry was alive and kicking between them. The more she remained in his orbit, the weaker her defenceless grew.

'State your concerns and I'll be happy to address them.'

Eva wrapped her arms around herself, as if that would stop the unwanted zings from firing through her system. She needed to concentrate on a more grounded argument for not wanting to go ahead with this.

I won't leave him behind.

His words echoed through her brain, growing louder by the second.

She didn't need debate to know he meant every word.

'We could live together, without marriage, for a year or two.'

The words tumbled out of her mouth before her brain recognised what she was saying. But it didn't matter because he was already shaking his head.

'No. I want my son secure and untroubled for his formative years at the very least. He needs stability and I intend to give him that. It's marriage or nothing, Evangeline.'

'What if we can't stand each other?' she threw out wildly, attempting to ignore the way her heart leapt. 'What if we start this absurd union and end up at each other's throats within months?'

As if he couldn't help himself, he returned his gaze to Leo. For an age, he remained silent, and then, 'For our son's sake, I'll attempt to curb whatever habits you find unacceptable. I'll even accommodate whatever characteristics you possess that you think are demonic enough to drive me away,' he said wryly.

'Just like that?'

His gaze raced up then, to spear hers in an intractable hold. 'Do you not think he's worth it?' he asked.

For the second time Ekow had cut her off at the knees. Because the answer was so clear, so inexorable, she could only reply one way. 'Yes, he is.'

Triumph blazed in his eyes and he gave a brisk nod. 'So we're agreed. We will marry.'

It wasn't a question. It was a statement of undertaking that he expected her to agree to.

The foundations of her world shook. She'd all but agreed to hand over her life to him for the foreseeable future. To uproot her life for the son she loved.

'For our son's sake. For Jonah's sake,' Ekow's deep voice compelled, sensing her wavering.

But was she forgetting herself in all of this? Somewhere in all the parenthood books she'd read whilst pregnant with Leo there had been an insistence on self-care. She would turn her life inside out for Leo, but wasn't *she* also worth a little consideration? What exactly would marriage to a dynamic billionaire entail for her? Despite his father having passed away, how was she to know how other members of his family would treat her?

'Evangeline…'

There was a dangerous pitch to his voice, demanding an answer. But it was hard for her to accept what he was offering.

She shook her head. 'Marriage for an undefined time is a…a big undertaking.' His nostrils flared, but before he could open his mouth she continued. 'You've set out your conditions. I have some of my own.'

'Let's hear them,' he growled.

The first searing objection was one she didn't want to voice. It would give her away. Would lay bare the path of her thoughts. But Eva decided she couldn't *not* speak it. 'I don't want… I think it would be best if we live in separate residences.'

His eyes narrowed. 'Excuse me?' His voice positively sizzled with displeasure.

'For the sake of propriety.'

'You must have missed the part where I said you would be staying under my roof.'

His scornful tone shuddered through her. But she held her ground. Lifted her chin. 'I won't be sleeping with you. And the last thing I want is for us to be in a position where we have to tolerate each other's… activities.'

His face clenched into an icy mask. 'You intend to have lovers whilst married to me?'

'No,' she protested hotly. 'But I assumed... I thought... I don't know what to think. About you.'

'What exactly does that mean?'

She shrugged. 'You're a man. With needs. I'm not foolish enough to think that you have plans of remaining celibate for however long we're married.'

His lips twisted. 'How very stoic of you to embrace nun-hood while labelling me a Lothario.'

'Am I wrong?' she demanded, a touch desperately.

His jaw clenched. 'Yes. And make no mistake. There will be no lovers for you or for me. You're wrong if you think either of us will last a month without giving in to what comes naturally. But I'm willing to wait you out.'

Heat climbed into her face, then rushed in the opposite direction to pool low in her belly. 'You'll be waiting a very long time,' she stated, with more confidence than she felt.

His languid gaze slid over her, conducting a slow, torturous journey from her head to foot and back again to settle on her mouth. 'We'll see. And to return to your suggestion—no. There will be no separate residences. You'll live in my house, sleep in my bed. To our son and to every member of our families this marriage will appear real. Only the two of us will know the truth.'

He was a formidable man to face down, but she was no shrinking violet. She had no intention of sharing his bed again, of giving her body to him.

Once—with her being a virgin—it had been an earth-shaking experience, after which her life had altered irreparably. Now, within twenty-four hours of him resurfacing, he'd set it on a different course entirely. Again. Giving him more ground, losing control around him, was a sure-fire way to invite disaster.

'Are we agreed, Evangeline?'

She took a deep breath. Everything was blurring around her but the figure of father and son standing before her. That was the image she needed to hold in her mind. She was doing this for Leo. Giving him the stability, the love, the freedom of growing up without the question marks she been unlucky enough to have. She needed to hold that as her divining rod. And the bonus was that Jonah would receive the advantages he deserved.

So why did it feel as if she was pulling out her own soul? As if she was pushing her son and her brother into the light while she left herself in the dark?

It didn't matter, she thought impatiently. The sacrifice would be worth it.

Ekow took another step closer, placing himself within touching distance. Whether it was deliberate or not, it reawakened cravings she didn't want to have. From the moment she'd set eyes on him she'd known he was temptation she should resist. She hadn't been able to resist then, and every second in his presence now was a battle with that temptation.

The compulsion to breathe him in assailed her. She took a deep breath, felt the evocative scent of man and aftershave wind itself inside her, dredging up torrid memories she needed to deny, but couldn't.

It was time to answer him.

She forced herself to meet his gaze, to hold it as

the earth beneath her feet shifted once more. 'Yes. I'll marry you.'

His jaw clenched tight once. His slow exhalation reeked of triumph. But of course he wasn't done. 'The rest, Eva. Let's hear it, so there's no misunderstanding between us,' he commanded.

'I will live under your roof. But I won't sleep in your bed. That is my offer. Take it or leave it. Give your family whatever excuse you need to, but it won't happen.'

For another long spell he simply stared at her. Then he shrugged. 'Accepted. We'll marry within the month.'

Shock spiralled through her. 'What?'

She wasn't sure whether to be upset at how easily he'd accepted the 'no sleeping together' clause, as if it didn't matter, or to be glad he hadn't argued the point. But, more than that, the idea of disassembling her life in a matter of weeks triggered panic.

'I can't marry you in one month.'

'Why the hell not?' he growled.

'Because I have obligations here in Cape Town. Clients. And Jonah has school.'

'We'll inform the school he'll be leaving immediately. If you agree, of course. I think it's best we get him into one of the other schools as soon as possible, don't you?'

She bit her lip. He was right, but she was reluctant to admit it. 'I'll talk to him.'

He glanced down the hall and raised an eyebrow, clearly expecting her to fall in line again. Before she could answer one way or the other the door to Jonah's bedroom opened and he walked out, freezing when they turned to face him.

'What?'

She approached him, nerves eating at her. 'Come in. I have some news.'

She'd expected him to object, to throw Ekow more of those hostile looks he'd subjected him to yesterday. But with each word she spoke his eyes widened, and when she was done he gave a short, shocked laugh.

'Are you serious? I get to go to that awesome school in Switzerland?'

'If that's your preference, yes,' Ekow said. 'With some conditions, of course.'

Again, she expected Jonah to protest, but he just nodded. 'Yeah, sure. Whatever.'

Eva's eyes widened. 'You're not upset about leaving here? Leaving home?'

His gaze met hers. 'That's the best school in the world for computing, sis. And Cape Town...' He shrugged again. 'It reminds me too much of Mum. I think we both need to move on from all that...don't you?' he mumbled.

Tears prickled her eyes. She tried to speak around the lump in the throat. When she failed, she merely nodded.

He turned back to Ekow. 'Do you mean it? You're not just going to ghost Leo and Eva again, are you?'

'I hardly...' Ekow cleared his throat. 'I mean it,' he confirmed. 'But I need reassurance from you as well. If you step out of line there will be consequences.'

A long, steady look passed between the man she'd agreed to marry and her brother. Then Jonah nodded. At Ekow's echoing nod, her brother turned and grinned at her.

It struck her then that it had been a while since she'd

seen a true smile from him. It grated a little that Ekow was the reason for it, but she smothered the feeling.

'Okay, can I go now?'

At her nod, Jonah strolled to the fridge and grabbed a bottle of fizzy soda before disappearing back to his room.

When they were alone again, Ekow's eyes locked on hers. 'Say it again, Eva.'

She took a deep breath. 'I'll marry you.'

CHAPTER SIX

Two weeks later

EVANGELINE MADE TWO discoveries in the fortnight following her agreement to become Ekow Quayson's wife.

One, that money and power ruled the world. Or, in her case, whether a wedding was staged for convenience or whether it was between two people head over heels for each other, it didn't change the juggernaut of over-the-top planning, over-the-top lavishness, and a determination to make it the most talked-about wedding of the decade once that intention was birthed. In fact, it took on a life of its own, and it was impossible to stop it.

Two, that somewhere along the line she'd buried any desire or dreams of a fairy tale wedding with a floaty white dress, a tasteful tiara and a veil. Had shoved away any fantasies of giggling bridesmaids and a champagne-fuelled, dancing-in-a-limo hen night, followed by a luxury spa day, in favour of cold, hard reality.

Years of watching her mother struggle and fall sick, years of caring for her while ensuring Jonah was safe and healthy, had eroded all fanciful thoughts of happy-ever-after. She'd stoically carved a different vision for herself. One which didn't include a laundry list of what she wanted for her own purportedly dream wedding.

And even faced with unrelenting reality and a future mother-in-law with an unlimited budget, Evangeline discovered she still couldn't summon up enthusiasm for her wedding. Because it was a *sham*.

Which brought her to the third problem. Her lack of enthusiasm didn't thrill her future husband or mother-in-law.

It had started with a strained conversation when Ekow had briskly informed her that the guest list had topped a thousand.

Her shocked laughter at the number had elicited a clenched-jaw reaction, and their conversation must've reached his mother too, because Evangeline had been informed stiffly over breakfast the next morning that the list had been trimmed to an immovable seven hundred and fifty.

Evangeline's flippant shrug hadn't gone down well.

Naana Quayson had left the breakfast table with an affronted sniff to seek the company of her new grandson, while Ekow had levelled a narrow-eyed stare at her before refocusing on the *Financial Times* he was reading.

Evangeline had returned to her Iberian ham, boiled egg and toast, stoically chewing before washing it down with coffee.

And if the stiffness between them hadn't yet dissipated… Well, she blamed everything on the speed with which her life had been turned inside out. The faster she tried to acclimatise to her new life the more surreal it seemed.

Hell, most mornings she expected to open her eyes and find herself back in her old bed in Cape Town, staring at the faint brown rain stains on the ceiling, not tucked away in the master suite of a grand mansion sitting over a small hill in the gated enclave known as Quayson Hills.

Within two days of arrival she'd discovered that the prime real estate within the ultra-exclusive location was mostly inhabited by a Quayson uncle, third cousin or great-aunt. She literally couldn't walk down the street without bumping into someone connected by blood to her future husband.

Besides the Quayson clan, only the very *crème de la crème* of the highest social echelon were invited to live within the enclave. Each jaw-dropping mansion was more stunning than the last, but of course Quayson House, holding pride of place atop its own hill, further shattered any illusions that this was going to be in any way a 'normal' if convenient marriage.

If there were two bright spots to be celebrated in the organised chaos that had ensued once she'd stepped off the private jet at Kotoka International Airport, one was that Leo had been accepted wholeheartedly into the Quayson clan. Her baby couldn't be more loved if she'd made a wish upon a thousand stars and had every one of them come true. And the other was that Jonah was ensconced in his new boarding school in Switzerland and already loving it.

Did it break her heart a little that she'd gone from seeing him every day to talking to him only a handful of times on the phone? Yes. But she'd forced herself to see the big picture. At least where her brother was concerned.

More and more, though, she was wondering why a wedding was even necessary, considering Leo's rousing acceptance by the Quayson family...

Which was far less than *she* had received.

Where her son had been gushed over, Evangeline had

been met with a tight-lipped coolness and daring probes as to which Annan family she hailed from.

Her evasiveness hadn't earned her any brownie points. But then how could she tell them she didn't know? That their assumption of her surname being her father's was wrong? How could she say that her mother had given both her children her name because she'd never married and had refused to divulge any details of the men who had fathered her children? That she had very little to no knowledge of her Ghanaian heritage because her mother had made South Africa her home and proceeded to forget all about her birthplace?

It was none of their business, Evangeline had assured herself. But somewhere deep inside the cold knot of loneliness had tightened. Along with the shame, the dejection and rejection. She couldn't proudly say she hailed from the royalty-adjacent Saltpond Annans, or the renowned Cape Coast Annans, or even the Takoradi Annans, because her mother had refused to talk about her family.

It didn't matter, she'd stressed to herself, after yet another mild probing over arrangements for the traditional 'knocking' ceremony.

Ekow's mother's new desire to stretch out the nuptials for several weeks was what had finally roused Evangeline enough to hunt down her future husband, three Saturdays after her arrival. Thinking she'd have to call or text to have a conversation with him, since he worked long hours at his bank even at the weekends, she'd been stunned when the house staff had directed her outside.

Evangeline had found him lounging beside the immense swimming pool, with the son she'd thought was still taking his early-afternoon nap busy exploring a selection of the wonderful new toys his father and his many relatives had showered him with. Evangeline couldn't take more than a few steps in the immense house without tripping over yet another gift delivered by a family relation or a friend with an impressive pedigree.

Her child—the newly discovered Quayson—had become something of a celebrity.

'I didn't know Leo was awake,' she'd said.

She hadn't meant it to sound like an accusation, but the notion that she hadn't known the whereabouts of her own child had rubbed her the wrong way, despite Leo looking exceedingly content, sitting on a fluffy blanket surrounded by protective cushions, with wide umbrellas shading his delicate skin from the harsh sun.

Ekow had lifted his gaze from where it had been fixed on his son. Although his eyes had been shielded by a pair of designer shades, she'd known he was staring at her because her skin had grown hot, awareness shooting through her like low-level fireworks.

'I was nearby when he woke up. I asked the staff not to disturb you.'

'It's not a disturbance to look after my own son.' This time the bite in her tone had been undisguised.

Leo had looked up from the bright orange toy he was rattling and beamed at her. His unabashed joy had calmed her roiling senses.

Ekow's nostrils had flared slightly before he'd surged upright. 'Accepted. But you should work your way into being okay with me spending time with my son without your express permission, Eva,' he'd said.

Her heart had thumped hard once, and the feeling of not being in control any more had swelled inside her.

'I thought he was sleeping. I wasn't expecting to find him awake and out here with you.'

'So you were looking for me?'

The barest hint of smugness in his tone had made her hands curl.

'Maybe now you're reassured our son's fine, you can sit down and can tell me why you were looking for me when I understand there are wedding matters for you to discuss with my mother. Albeit reluctantly, I'm told.'

She had paused, bristling at this indication that his mother had discussed her with him. Then, 'That's what I want to talk to you about.'

Not missing her clear irritation, he'd plucked off his sunglasses and speared her with narrowed eyes as she'd taken the lounger next to him. Then wished she hadn't when she'd become acutely aware of the powerful play of muscle in his hair-dusted thighs, the impressive outline of his manhood barely disguised by the swim shorts, and his far too mouth-watering torso so close she could have reached out and stroked his warm skin.

Her gaze had fallen on the strong arms braced on his knees and she'd fought to ignore the stronger fireworks shooting off inside her.

'You *could* drum up some enthusiasm for your own wedding,' he'd stated, a touch of chill in his tone.

Evangeline had aimed her gaze at a spot on the curve between his neck and shoulder, hoping it would be less disrupting to her senses, only to recall how it had felt to bury her face in that very spot, sinking her teeth into his firm skin as he surged deep and hard and utterly blissfully inside her.

Focus!

'It's difficult to conjure up enthusiasm for several hundred people I've never met before,' she'd replied.

'My mother invited you to make a list of your own, I believe.'

The smile she had attempted in the name of civility had felt dry and tight. 'And I told her it wasn't necessary.'

He'd studied her for a few more seconds. 'You know that only invites more questions, don't you? Especially with someone as inquisitive as my mother?'

Evangeline *had* noticed that the mistress of the house positively thrived on knowing everyone's business. Her attachment to the smartphone which trilled and pinged with endless phone calls and text messages easily rivalled Jonah's attachment to his electronic gadgets.

'Does it matter who I do or don't invite? You've got what you wanted. You've secured your son as you wished.'

When he had remained thin-lipped and displeased, she'd continued.

'It's not too late to change your mind, you know.' Why her insides had quivered as she'd spoken those words she'd refused to examine. 'We can call this off, come to a new arrangement—'

'No. There will be no calling it off. You've gone to great lengths to assure me that you're going a certain way, that your word is to be believed. Don't try and go another way now or you'll disappoint us both. Our agreement stands. And that includes the part where you strive to act as if this marriage is real. I may not care what people think generally, but I'd rather not be forced to deny that you're doing this wholly against your will,' he delivered acerbically.

That had been yesterday.

He'd invited her to join him and their son there at the pool, albeit with a cool voice and even cooler eyes.

But the invitation had been tested immediately when another house staff member had stepped out to inform her she was needed by the wedding planner.

Ekow had stared at her with one eyebrow raised.

She'd stiffly declined his invitation.

And the well-oiled wheels of their wedding plans had continued to spin.

The grounds of Quayson House had been transformed, and despite her determination to remain grounded, untouched and removed, a small corner of Evangeline's heart had been affected by the magic being created around her.

On one side of the estate white pavilions had been erected by expert craftsmen, and a processional path had been created, leading to a large platform upon which she'd stand and make her vows to Ekow.

On the other side, the more traditional set-up for the morning 'knocking' ceremony before the afternoon wedding was also taking shape.

But the last thing she could afford was to be sucked into it.

She'd effectively given up years of her life for her son's happiness. While she would have given her very life for him, didn't she deserve to retain her sanity, her soul, her heart for herself? Didn't she need to safeguard herself from the husband and the family who had already judged her and found her lacking?

Now she stood on top of a small round dais set up in her room by the wedding gown designer. And again she felt that touch of magic she knew she should resist. Because the dress seemed plucked from a discarded dream—a fantasy she'd dismissed before she'd grown out of playdates and tutus.

Tasteful, demure but stylish, it was a perfect medley of lace and silk, with delicately embroidered butterflies stitched into the lightest chiffon neckline, long sleeves, and a waterfall train that sprang from a slit at the back of the pencil skirt.

While full skirts and elaborate trains on wedding dresses had their place, they weren't for her. This classy design, with its equally unfussy veil hanging from a simple diamond-encrusted hair comb, suited her perfectly.

'This one,' she muttered.

The designer exchanged startled looks with the wedding co-ordinator. 'Do you want to try any of the others? We have two dozen more...*classic* gowns for you to—'

'This one,' she said more firmly. If she had to find a little bit of enjoyment through this ordeal, she'd find it in this.

Matching shoes were presented for her to choose from. She was in the middle of selecting a kitten-heeled satin pair when Ekow's mother walked in.

She had a presence that rivalled her son's. Despite her advancing years, her dark mahogany skin glowed with vitality and her greying hair was styled with such expertise it was difficult to imagine her not wearing the same style in her youth. The few lines around her eyes and mouth were mitigated by light, delicate make-up, and on her tall, slim frame she wore a soft purple kaftan with a stunning embroidered detail that drew the eye to the dark gold necklace gracing her throat.

Eyes the same shade as Ekow's glanced around her as she stopped in the middle of the room. 'How are we getting on? Have we tried any dresses on yet?'

Eva gritted her teeth when she directed the question to the staff instead of her.

'A choice has been made, Mrs Quayson,' the designer said, pointing to the gown Evangeline had chosen.

Naana Quayson's eyes widened, before her face darkened with a frown. 'This? I don't remember this being in the selection.'

'Your son added two dresses this morning,' the designer said. 'This is one of them.'

Evangeline gasped softly.

Ekow had chosen her gown.

Just as she hadn't spent time imagining a fairy tale wedding, she hadn't expended any energy on silly wedding traditions. She didn't mind that he'd seen the dress before she walked down the aisle. But she did mind that he might read something into her choosing one of the dresses he'd selected.

How had he even known?

'I'm not sure where he got the idea to add those. They don't make any sort of statement. No, I don't think that one would be suitable at—'

'I like the dress,' Eva interjected. 'That's my choice.'

'How can you know without trying any of the others?' Naana replied haughtily.

'I know,' Eva insisted. 'And I'm sure there are things we can be doing other than wasting an hour or two on gowns when I've already made up my mind?'

Silence descended in the room.

'At least you're taking an interest, finally,' Naana said after several seconds, her tone starchy with disapproval. 'If you're sure that's the dress you want, we'll move on. Do you feel up to picking a bouquet arrangement?'

She didn't, but with Ekow's admonition echoing in her head she had no choice but to nod. 'Of course. Lead the way.'

Three nights later, in bed after another hectic day of wedding activities, Eva admitted that perhaps getting involved wasn't so bad. That she might even grow to like some of the Ghanaian traditions her mother had told her about, and others she'd discovered on her own.

Since Eva had no older relatives of her own, Ekow's brother had offered to stand in as her representative for the knocking ceremony—a process that involved a representative member of her fiancé's family literally knocking on her family's door and asking to be allowed in to seek her hand in marriage. Using a Quayson shouldn't have been allowed, since it was essentially a conflict of interest, but it seemed both brothers were happy to flout tradition for the sake of marrying the women they'd chosen.

She'd smiled and chuckled in all the right places, but had stopped herself from correcting the mistaken assumption that Ekow had allowed this because he desired her, when Atu's wife, Amelie, had amusingly retold the story of how her husband had gate-crashed her own knocking ceremony and asked for her hand in marriage when, traditionally, it was left to the elders of the family to do so.

The reminder that she'd agreed to this marriage appearing real had echoed at the back of Eva's mind during the afternoon tea her future sister-in-law had arranged for them, and she'd mostly smiled as the young, beautiful and self-assured woman had relayed anecdotes about her own wedding.

Eva had felt a little ashamed for her pang of jealousy at seeing Atu and Amelie so evidently in love, and had instead dwelt on their mutual adoration of their daughter Amaya and young son, Kobi.

That was an emotion she knew well, echoing her cherished feeling for her own son. A feeling she was sure Ekow too shared, if his apparently complete obsession with Leo was any testament.

Their marriage would be another matter entirely, of course…

Leo's distressed cry pulled her out of her rumination, and away from the even more dangerous thought that she might not mind her wedding ceremony after all. Might even relax her guard for a few hours and attempt to enjoy it…

Another cry launched her out of bed.

The nursery adjoined her suite, a vast space she was fairly sure was bigger than her entire Cape Town house. Crossing the room, she suppressed the frisson of worry feathering over her skin. Leo was a good baby. He'd started sleeping almost through the night a few weeks ago. Now, at just past midnight, he should've been fast asleep. But when she reached him his face was creased in misery and his plump arms and legs were punching the air in unhappiness.

'Hey, sweetheart. Hush…' she crooned as she lifted him and cradled him close.

'What's wrong?'

The question was gruff and tight.

She spun to find Ekow framed in the doorway, a frown clenched between his brows. A pair of silk pyjama bottoms rode low on his hips and she quickly averted her gaze before he caught her gaping at his topless perfection.

'What are you doing up?' she asked, then cringed at the inane comment.

'I wasn't asleep. I heard him crying through the monitor.'

Of course he had a monitor in his bedroom. Just as he'd had baby carriers installed in all the vehicles in his fleet of that weren't sports cars. His level of devotion was admirable. And yet she couldn't help her lingering anxiety.

Her breath snagged in her throat as he prowled towards them, his gaze on fixed his whimpering, squirming son. Telling herself she didn't want him to look at her at all, she watched him smooth a long, gentle finger down Leo's cheek.

'What's up, champ?' he asked, his voice low and rumbling.

His scent hit her nostrils when she finally took a breath, and it was all she could do not to groan at the delicious, decadent scent of earth and spice.

'I think he's teething,' she offered, desperate to focus on Leo, to strengthen the walls of her crumbling resistance against his father.

Of course her suggestion swiftly redirected Ekow's focus to her. Her gaze met his a second before his eyes lanced over her, immediately drawing her attention to the thin, short nightdress she wore. And the tiny thong she wore beneath it.

Eva barely heard him when he said, 'He's the right age for that.' But she couldn't hold back her surprise.

'You know what age he should be teething?'

A wry, tense smile whispered over his lips before disappearing. 'I've missed enough of my son's life. I'm determined I won't miss any more.'

She wasn't sure whether there was blame in his tone or whether the chill of his words was directed at something...someone else. But needing to focus on Leo, she chose to let it go.

'What can I do?' he said, after another tense moment had passed.

Again, she suppressed her astonishment. But she had

no yardstick to judge this initial phase of fatherhood by, did she? She didn't know if this was the obsession before indifference, or if Ekow truly intended to be invested in every aspect of his son's life.

She nodded towards the bathroom. 'There's some teething powder in the cabinet. If you don't mind...?'

He was already striding across the room.

Rather than stand there gaping at the hypnotic ripple of muscle in his back as he moved, she headed for the rocking chair set beneath a window overlooking the garden. Perching on it, she bounced Leo on her knees. But his agitation merely increased, and one small fist was wedged between his tiny lips as he tried to alleviate his distress.

Ekow returned with the medication and crouched in front of them. 'May I?'

It was as if a large rock blocked Eva's throat at the gruff question. Pressing her lips together, she nodded haltingly, reminding herself again that it had only been a few weeks. True fatherhood meant holding on when things got tough. It meant going the distance through thick or thin. And yet watching Ekow gently tending to their son made a peculiar knot melt inside her.

It was almost a relief when Leo protested loudly again. It meant she could direct her focus to him. Not wonder at the depths of Ekow's emotions. Not wonder if he would even make the first year of their agreement. If she and Leo would find themselves on their own sooner rather than later, like her mother had.

'Evangeline?'

His steady focus and firm tone said he'd been trying to get her attention for a while. Clearing her throat, she flicked a glance at him. Nope. His proximity was still an issue, with that maddening slope of neck into shoulder making her fingers itch to caress the spot.

'Hmm?'

'I asked if you had any other ideas?'

She nodded briskly. 'Yes.'

Without elaborating further, she repositioned Leo and started to lower one spaghetti strap of her nightdress. Then nerves hit her. Her hips had thickened during pregnancy, and her breasts had also grown larger. Elsewhere on her body, a few veins and stretch marks charted the path of her pregnancy.

'It's a natural act. You don't need to be shy around me.'

Despite the heat invading her system, she shrugged. 'I'm not.'

His gaze dropped to her chest, and the charged look that triggered this insane chemical reaction between them sparked to life.

'Do you want me to leave?' he asked, his voice even thicker than before.

Perhaps she was foolish to be pleased by her effect on him. Because surely she was either playing with fire or inviting a situation she would regret later? But she mildly stunned herself by slowly shaking her head.

'No, you don't need to leave.'

Then she lowered her strap.

Supremely conscious of Ekow's eyes on her as she fed Leo, it was a miracle that she managed not to squirm. Or revel in the heady sensation his undiluted attention triggered in her.

CHAPTER SEVEN

HE DIDN'T TAKE his eyes off her even when Leo kicked out one foot. Ekow caught it, and the sight of her son's small foot in his father's large palm threatened to dissolve that knot inside her completely.

To alleviate the feeling, she bent low and dropped a kiss on her baby's head.

'He's beautiful,' Ekow said, a note of quiet awe in his voice.

'I'm a little terrified he's going to get egotistical with the amount of compliments showered on him these past weeks.'

Ekow nodded gravely. 'I can see how that might become a problem. We'll ensure it's limited to just one compliment a day, then.'

For some absurd reason Eva had the maddest urge to smile—to laugh, even. 'Yes, I think that would suffice.'

One corner of his mouth quirked, and she was fiercely reminded of the night they'd met. Of their easy conversation over dinner while deep and turbulent undercurrents of sexual promise had meandered between them. He'd literally charmed the clothes off her body, and she'd been more than willing to let him.

Before she could be drawn deeper into memory's dangerous quagmire, Leo lost interest in being fed and gave another wail. Straightening her nightie, she bounced him against her shoulder. But after five minutes with no success in calming him Ekow glanced at her.

'We should take him for a drive. I've heard it's a good way to help agitated babies sleep.'

She nodded. 'It works. I've done it a few times when he wouldn't settle.'

One eyebrow cocked sardonically. 'In that rust bucket you called a car?'

She lamented the demise of the car Ekow's people had disposed of, along with whatever else she'd left behind in Cape Town, but she lifted her chin. 'She served me well. And I won't have a bad word said against her.'

He stood, held up his hands in mock surrender and took a melodramatic step back. Eva wanted to smile again. She disguised the urge by burying her face in her son's neck—a move that was rewarded with another irritated cry.

'I'll get dressed,' Ekow said, pivoting on his heel to return to his suite.

For a moment she sat there, wondering if it was too late to salvage the foolish melting sensation in her belly. Wondering how quickly she could kill the fizz starting inside her at the thought of taking a drive with Ekow. At the thought of being alone with him after the mad circus she'd lived in since her arrival in his stratosphere.

It wouldn't mean anything other than a means to soothe their distraught son.

He would be back to being the domineering banker who'd invaded her habitat with a clutch of law enforcement officers a little over three weeks ago.

Repeating that to herself, she quickly changed Leo's nappy, placed him in his crib, and returned to her room to dress.

She threw on a short floral dress, added low-heeled platform mules and tidied her hair. A glide of lip gloss and she was ready.

She returned to fetch Leo, and was about to pick up his baby bag when Ekow appeared.

He was dressed in hip-hugging jeans and a pristine white polo shirt that made his dark skin glow. Again she diverted her gaze, before she swallowed her tongue, but when he started towards her, to take Leo into his arms, Eva couldn't stop her eyes from returning to him. From watching the entirely too masculine swagger, the unrepressed confidence and the sheer aura of his personality.

'Ready?' he asked, after he'd reached for the bag to take that too.

Eva concluded that all these aberrant feelings were hormonal—probably post-partum. Not because at far too many points after Leo's birth she'd wished that she wasn't undertaking the monumental task of parenting alone. That she wouldn't end up like her mother, utterly resentful of the absence of the men who'd fathered her two children and too bitter to share their details with said children.

'Yes,' she replied.

In silence they went downstairs, via a wide, sweeping staircase, then through the marble-floored hallway and past a pristine, magazine-shoot-ready kitchen and into a garage housing more cars than she could take in in a single glance.

She'd accepted mere days into her arrival that in some aspects her life had changed for ever. It turned out billionaires couldn't just step out on a whim without a multitude of bodyguards in attendance. So she wasn't surprised in the least when four burly men appeared from another door attached to the garage and climbed into sleek black SUVs.

Eva cautioned herself not to be disappointed that this wasn't a cute family of three out for a late-night drive. But she couldn't hide the resurgence of the blasted fizz inside her when Ekow headed towards another, sleeker SUV.

As if he knew he was going on his own personal adventure Leo had quieted a little, his curious eyes rounded as he took in his surroundings.

Ekow opened and held the door for her, then settled Leo in his car seat.

The roads were quiet, a contrast to the incessant traffic which clogged them during the day, and their ride was smooth as they left the city behind. Eva didn't mind the silence. She was too busy trying not to glance at Ekow's capable hands on the steering wheel and the way the muscles in his thighs played beneath the streetlights when he changed gear. Hell, she was too busy using up all her energy in not breathing too deeply, because she felt as if his scent was pulling her closer with each inhalation, inviting her into that sinful space where his essence resided.

'Think it's working?'

She jumped, petrified she'd spoken her feelings aloud. 'What?'

His head turned, his gaze slashing through the dim interior to lock on hers. 'He's quiet. I think the drive's working.'

His son. Of course.

Eva exhaled shakily. They'd just started winding their way up the snake-like roads into the Aburi mountains. She knew that in minutes they'd be treated to spectacular views from the top.

She craned her neck and watched Leo succumb to sleep, his long lashes brushing the tops of his cheeks. 'Yes, it is,' she murmured.

Ekow nodded. 'Good.'

The soporific sensation was threatening to burrow into her when he pulled up to a vantage point at the side of the road. Eva ignored the other two SUVs pulling up on either side of them as Ekow stepped out, left the engine running, and rounded the hood to her side.

She let him help her out and they walked to the edge of the lookout. The air smelled infinitely cleaner and richer, and she took a long, deep breath, her gaze on the twinkling lights that looked magical...near enough to reach out and touch.

Aburi was set into the mountains north-east of Accra, and at this time of night, with a clear starlit sky above, the city was a breathtaking multi-hued carpet of bright lights.

'The view is better from up there,' Ekow said after several minutes.

Eva followed his gaze to where he pointed, but all she could see was a dark surge of trees and rocks marching up the side of the mountain. 'Where?'

'Come. I'll show you.'

He led her back to the car, taking care not to jostle it and wake Leo.

They travelled even higher. After ten minutes, he stopped in front of high security gates and a wall that soared at least twenty feet high.

He entered a code and electronic gates slid smoothly open, displaying a long, palm-lined, white-stone-paved drive. Strategically placed lights illuminated rolling green grass on either side of the drive, but her gaze was drawn to the large stone-clad building set into the side of the mountain.

The house was smaller than Quayson House but no less grand for it. Every square foot of the outside screamed moneyed elegance which she discovered was repeated on the inside, with a warm cream theme in marble, and furniture and art chosen as if in invitation to enjoy a slower pace, a chance to linger and admire, to lounge and indulge. The sumptuous sofas were made for sprawling, unlike the stately formality of the decor at Quayson House.

With each room they silently walked through, with Ekow effortlessly carrying the sleeping Leo in his car seat, Eva fell in love with the house.

'You own this house?' she murmured.

'Yes.'

She wasn't sure why that both delighted and alarmed her. While she didn't like the sensation of being pulled deeper into Ekow's web of power and influence, she found she didn't particularly mind this silken strand tugging at her. Which was a little disconcerting, considering her determination to stay aloof.

Because she didn't want to risk Leo waking, she remained silent until Ekow set him down in a fully furnished nursery, the sight of which drew two dozen questions, then stepped out and noiselessly shut the door.

'Did you plan to bring us here?'

His lips tightened, then he shrugged. 'Only to show you the view I promised. Shall we?' He waved a hand at the grand staircase leading to the upper floors.

Beautifully carved wooden doors she suspected led to bedrooms were dotted along one long corridor, interspersed with richly woven rugs made traditionally by loom-crafting artisans. At the end of the hall French doors opened out onto the large terrace she'd seen from outside.

Eva's breath caught when she stepped out, her feet compelled to take her to the iron railing.

The view had been breathtaking from a few hundred feet below, but up higher it was beyond magnificent. Perhaps it was made more so by the exclusive location, the feeling that she was being treated to a special, unique view from Ekow's private terrace.

'I'd forgotten how beautiful it is up here in the mountains,' she murmured, unable to tear her gaze from the view.

'When was the last time you visited?'

She tried not to stiffen at the question, despite her words having thrown the door wide open for his speculation. But she knew the tension seizing her stemmed from her reluctance to discuss her mother, not his curiosity. 'You mean before I came here last year, to tell you I was pregnant with our son?'

She sensed him stiffen too, and tiny pangs of guilt and shame pierced her. The ride through the winding hills had been beautiful and serene. She didn't want to wreck it with tension.

When he remained silent, she sighed. 'I last visited when I was twenty-one. I don't remember much of our visits before then. They were always spur-of-the- moment and short when I younger.'

He frowned. 'Why?'

Her back tightened some more. She'd never made a secret of the fact that she and Jonah were each other's only family, as far as she knew. Would he pity her?

She shook her head to dissipate her thoughts. 'I think my mother missed her homeland, but something here made her unhappy. We'd arrive excited but she'd get sad within a couple of days. The trips were always cut short and she never told me why.'

'So you came back when you were old enough to experience it for yourself?'

She nodded. 'I toured Aburi and the rest of the Eastern Region in my first week, and the rest of the country in the four weeks after that.'

'What happened to her?' His voice was a low, even rumble. Filled more with curiosity than interrogation.

Eva tightened her gut against the tug of pain. 'She had a chronic disease—COPD. It worsened over the last six years. She died two years ago.'

Silence reigned for several moments before his hand brushed the back of hers. 'I'm sorry.' The words were gruff...sounded unused. As if he didn't know grief. But hadn't his father died recently?

Eva opened her mouth, perhaps to utter one of the automatic replies to the sympathies people offered in this situation, despite the risk of shattering this somewhat mellow couple of hours they'd enjoyed.

But he beat her to it with another question. 'And your father?'

The hole in her heart where the questions and heartache surrounding her parentage resided squeezed painfully. 'Is not a subject I like to talk about.'

Somehow the hand brushing the back of her hand had found her wrist. Caught in a light hold, it nevertheless snagged her attention, soothing, but making her intensely aware of his warm touch as his fingers caressed her pulse.

'Not to anyone else, maybe. But I'd like to think I have special dispensation as your husband.'

The throb of possessiveness in his voice made her

heart skip several beats. 'We're not married yet,' she pointed out, a touch too breathlessly.

He shrugged. 'That's just semantics. I already consider you mine.'

She should've been outraged by that—and she was, somewhere in the murky soup of her emotions, she assured herself. But the subject lying between them like an undetonated bomb wouldn't let her dwell on the currents of electricity zipping beneath her skin.

Hyper-aware of the thumb caressing her inner wrist, she tried to focus on the carpet of lights before her, to lose herself in the view while she chose her words. But in the end it all came tumbling out.

'I don't know my father. Have never met him. For as long as I can remember I've yearned to know. But my mother wouldn't tell me anything. He was in her past, as far as she was concerned, and whatever happened between them was enough for her to cut him out of her life. And mine,' she added, with a layer of bitterness in her words.

'Did you ever try to find him?'

Anguish burned like acid in her heart and seared her throat with tears. She blinked rapidly to dispel it. 'I wouldn't know where to start. I don't have a name. She didn't even give me that.'

That infernal thumb traced her pulse again and her breath shuddered out.

'Maybe she was trying to save you from heartache,' he said, and she caught a note of perplexity in his voice. As if even while he could make the deduction the act was still alien to him. While she fought the knot in her throat, he added, 'Or disappointment.'

This time the note was definitive. Blisteringly so.

And it was formed from a tight bundle of bitterness and quiet rage.

It was enough to make her forget her turbulent emotions and turn to him just as he faced her. 'Telling myself that doesn't help,' she said.

His jaw rippled with that same twist of emotion. 'Sometimes nothing helps. The only thing you can do is forget. Or seek escape.'

She gasped. 'You have the world at your beck and call. Why would you need escape?'

'Beds of roses generally have thorns, Evangeline. And some wound deeper than others.'

'What do you mean?'

His strain intensified, and for several seconds he turned away, presenting her with an austere profile. Still, she saw flickers of charged emotion cross his face, so that when he glanced at her again her stomach was clenched in anxiety.

'I mean having two parents present doesn't automatically guarantee a happy bond. You met my father. I probably know the answer, but what were your impressions of him?

Memory tore open in her mind, stinging her anew. 'Not great,' she said tightly.

His lips tightened, his face a bleak mask. 'So at the very least you know he wasn't an…easy man to deal with.'

She licked her lips. 'I thought perhaps he was protecting you from me. Are you saying…?'

'I'm saying that being a Quayson son was…*is* a lot to live up to. And in his eyes I didn't live up to expectations. Neither of his remaining sons did.'

'He played favourites with his sons?'

'Blatantly and without remorse,' he admitted, his

tone an arid desert. 'He lived for only one person—his firstborn son.'

The raw confession drew a gasp from her, and her insides grew soft with compassion for him. 'Ekow…'

He shook his head. 'This isn't my way to win your sympathy. It's a way for you to weigh the balance of what you think you've been deprived of with the possibility that you might be better off. If your mother cared for you, perhaps you should be content with having one parent's love instead of none at all.'

She bit her lip, hearing his words, feeling them touch her, but unable to dismiss the coiled pain and loss at not knowing. Would she spend the rest of her life feeling this way?

Torn by her thoughts, by the weird sense of solidarity she felt with him at his painful admission, she turned blindly to him when he stepped close.

'Enough. I don't want to ruin this view and this peace with this subject. Not when I want something else more…'

Her gaze rose. Locked with his. 'What…?' The question was barely a whisper. She stopped breathing as he raised her wrist to his lips and brushed a kiss across it.

'This…'

His free hand slipped around her nape, his thumb trailing down her jaw before tilting her head up to meet his hungry, burning gaze.

Evangeline had more than ample time to pull away, to step back. To nudge a *no* from the jumble of words clogged in her throat. But she did none of those things.

Because she wanted him to kiss her. Wanted to feel his lips on hers. To wipe away the troubling memories she'd dredged up.

She wanted to *feel*.

To feel the way she had that weekend with him in Cape Town. The way she hadn't felt *since*. Because, as she'd feared when she'd stealthily dragged her clothes on at dawn, fearful of waking him and yet almost willing him to rouse and stop her from leaving, Ekow Quayson might have ruined her for any other man.

The thought shook through her anew, convincing her that testing out the theory was prudent. Essential, even. So when he bent lower, his nostrils flaring as he inhaled, she gave a tight, needy moan...

And surged up to meet his decadent lips.

She'd imagined it would be as intoxicating as the first time she'd kissed him. But, no. Ekow was like a fine wine from the renowned Stellenbosch region of western South Africa. He'd matured with time. And like the perfect vintage he swept through her, lowered her inhibitions and invited her in for a third, fourth, *fifth* taste.

Beneath the mesmerising night sky she swayed closer, winding her arms around his neck, revelling in his throaty hum of approval as he drew her even tighter to the steel and flesh masterpiece that was his warm body.

His lips parted hers, deepening the kiss, and every cell in her body seemed to rouse, to strain towards the pleasure only he had been able to deliver.

'You taste even better than I remember,' he rasped, in between nipping her bottom lip and then laving it with his tongue. Repeatedly. Making her shudder. Making her nipples pucker and her breasts ache.

'You remember?' she asked, then immediately regretted it. It made her sound much too needy. Too gauche.

To her surprise and pleasure he murmured again, one hand boldly cupping her breast, moulding, caressing.

'I remember,' he stated thickly. 'You've stayed a vivid memory, Evangeline.'

She ached to explore that statement. But he was toying with her nipple. And she was losing her mind. Which was why she barely registered it when he wrapped one strong arm around her waist and lifted her off her feet, plastering her against the wall beside the French doors seconds later.

One taut thigh slid between hers, and she whimpered when he pressed firmly at the apex of her thighs. His tongue stroked and teased hers, driving her fever higher, making her yearn for him to explore her in other, needier places.

'I definitely haven't forgotten how deliciously responsive you are,' he rasped, his mouth leaving hers to explore the highly sensitive column of her throat.

It was a stronger, more desperate shudder which shook a thread of sanity free. Which dragged open eyes she didn't remember shutting. The ferocious blaze in his eyes nearly undid her.

She was grateful for the breeze that whispered over her skin. And when his head started to descend again she held on to the thread and turned her head. His sinful lips landed on her cheek, began to chart another chaotic path down her neck.

'I… I think that's enough.'

He froze, then one corner of his lips quirked. 'It not nearly enough, sweetheart,' he muttered hoarsely. 'Not for me anyway.'

A moment later she realised his meaning, her breath snagging all over again as his engorged shaft pressed against her belly.

Then he was stepping back, placing cool air between them, and she immediately regretted it. To her eternal relief she didn't reach for him, beg him to disregard her protest and continue. She turned unseeingly for the hallway, not stopping until she stood in the doorway leading to where Ekow had left their sleeping son.

He was still fast asleep and she bit her lip, reluctant to disturb him. But they needed to leave this peaceful, magical place that was seeping under her defences, laying fertile soil for dreams she had no right to harbour.

'Here, let me,' Ekow murmured low behind her.

A quick glance showed lingering after-effects of their passionate tussle—mostly in the bank of fire in his eyes. But he was back under control. When she gave a jerky nod he lifted the carrier smoothly, his easy strength barely rocking it.

Minutes later they were back in the SUV, with the house growing smaller in the rear-view mirror.

'You're either beating yourself up about wanting what happened up there or convincing yourself you didn't want it in the first place. Both are wasted efforts,' he drawled when they were halfway down the mountain.

'You're a mind-reader now?' she whispered heatedly.

He shrugged. 'I don't need to be. You give yourself away far too easily, Eva.'

She turned away, literally, from the unwanted truth, staring out of the window as the lights of the city—and her wedding—grew closer.

The smooth ride must have lulled her into a doze. The next thing she knew she was being lowered into her own bed. She roused herself with a start, staring into Ekow's dark brown eyes. 'Leo…?'

He pressed her down. 'Is fine. He's already in his crib. Transferring him was a delicate operation, but I managed it. Just about.'

What did it say about her that she'd been completely oblivious to all of it?

Ekow sighed as he straightened, his gaze hardening at whatever he read in her face. 'I'm sensing a theme here. I guess I'll need to wean you off this "me against the world" mentality you have.'

'It's not a mentality if it's true.'

For endless moments he stared at her. The passionate, attentive man she'd tangled with a short hour ago was gone. The eyes raking her were still heated, but the fire was nowhere near as ferocious. Or warming.

And it felt decidedly less so when he took another step back.

'I'm going to be busy the next few days. I'll see you at the altar.'

'What if I don't make it there?' she threw defiantly at him, attempting to claw back the ground she hadn't even been aware she'd lost to him.

He didn't so much as blink in response. 'You will,' he stated with enviable assurance. 'Unfortunately for you, angel, you won't get rid of me that easily. Sleep well.'

His voice held enough sardonicism to tell her that neither of them would sleep well after the state they'd left things in. After their earth-shaking kiss.

But she managed to stop her runaway tongue from inciting further emotional wreckage. It'd done quite enough for one night.

So she watched him leave, his magnetising presence taking every essence of her being with him as he shut the door calmly behind him.

To alleviate the sudden loss, Eva dragged a pillow close, hugged it as she tried to calm her roiling senses. But one fundamental reality kept echoing in her head.

They might have set out settle their distraught son,

but what she'd just proved to herself was that when it came to her emotions around the man who had fathered her child, things were far from settled.

Hell, they were even more volatile than she'd thought.

CHAPTER EIGHT

EVA HADN'T IMAGINED her wedding day.

So of course she hadn't entertained the idea of being nervous to the point of nausea. Or of accommodating butterflies the size of small birds in her belly from the moment the veil was placed on her head and the exquisite bouquet, the stem of which was wrapped in ribbons of colourful Kente cloth, was placed in her hand.

All around her a contingent of Quayson females were dressed to the nines. The traditional Ghanaian wear of the rich and boldly coloured *kaba* and *slit*, with elaborate matching headdresses, was interspersed with westernised wedding attire, while stunning jewellery and accessories provided bursts of colour. It was almost too overwhelming to take in.

She wallowed in a momentary well of sadness that neither her mother nor Jonah was here before she shook it off. While not entirely sure what her mother would have made of this, Eva wanted to believe she would've given her blessing.

Breathing through the swell of anxiety, she followed the procession of cutely dressed flower girls and page boys, whose attire followed the theme of blending traditional attire with tiny tulle gowns and tuxedos, to the terrace of Ekow's home, beyond which the sprawling, immaculately landscaped garden now seating several hundred guests awaited her arrival.

Clamping her hand around the bouquet to stop the shaking, she deliberately kept her gaze low to avoid searching out her soon-to-be husband.

True to his word, he'd absented himself from the mansion in the last few days. If she hadn't known better, Evangeline would've thought he was avoiding her. But it was more as if after their ride into the mountains, seeing the magical view from his house and *that kiss*, he'd been content to retreat with her bluff called, knowing she wouldn't…*couldn't* do anything but honour their agreement.

It had worked, hadn't it?

Hadn't she spent countless hours weighing the wisdom of reneging on her agreement against every emotional advantage she could give Leo by going through with this wedding?

And what about your own advantage?

Eva shook her head, unwilling to admit that their kiss replayed far too frequently in her mind, and that the other challenge Ekow had thrown her—about how she would want more from their marriage, specifically things of the carnal kind—had interrupted her thoughts way too much for her liking.

But… She pursed her lips. She'd been completely fine without sex before she met him. She'd be completely fine for however long this marriage lasted.

Liar.

Enough.

Time to get this show on the road.

She'd chosen to walk down the aisle on her own, a decision and a last grasp at independence no amount of disapproving looks from Ekow's mother or the clicking tongues of his various aunts and cousins could sway her from.

Still, stepping out into the blinding sunlight and being confronted with a multitude of curious eyes, Eva wished for a moment she'd insisted Jonah be here at her side. Or accepted Atu's offer to escort her.

Beneath the short veil, she lifted her chin. She could do this. She'd given birth alone, despite being terrified of what the future would bring for her and her son.

The strains of music played by a renowned Ghanaian cellist said to have played at the last English royal wedding signalled the start of the wedding, and she made her practised progress in time with the hiplife tune.

Eva was thankful for the shield of her veil as her gaze avoided the altar and instead searched through the crowd until she found Leo.

He was dressed in the cutest tuxedo, the dark grey colour matching his father's. She'd expected him to be fussing but, surprising her again, he remained calm, taking in everything with wide-eyed interest. Currently perched on his grandmother's lap, he occasionally glanced at the father he was now bonding with at a rate of knots. Eva would have been jealous if she hadn't been so pleased for her son.

In fact, walking down the aisle, surrounded by people she didn't know but who were kin to her son, she finally accepted that she'd done the right thing. He would never feel lonely or overwhelmed at making the choices she'd had to make when her mother's health had started to fail. He would always have support.

A different kind of lump wedged in her throat—the mingled pride and dismay that came from putting another's needs above one's own—and repeatedly caught her in the chest.

Finally she let her gaze be compelled to the figure at the altar. The one she'd been avoiding because she knew she wasn't anywhere near prepared. Perhaps never would be.

Despite clenching her gut against it, the punch still arrived, and his magnificent form and impressive presence instantly blocked out everything else.

Because Ekow in a morning suit, his designer stubble expertly trimmed and his entire focus on her, was more than enough to interrupt the steady, practised glide of her feet.

His gaze was blatantly possessive. Feverishly fixed on her in a way that roused every dormant sexual cell into rude life.

I already consider you mine.

Telling herself he didn't own her was pitifully inadequate. Because his gaze announced differently. He might have accepted her 'no sex' clause as part of this convenient marriage, but he didn't intend to remain detached. At least not in public.

Those words throbbed in time to her heartbeat. In time to the intensity in his eyes. And no amount of telling herself it was all for show could stop the trembling that seized her then and continued through their vows, through the glide of his ring onto her finger, and especially through the feeling, as he repeated his promise to her, that she was taking a road from which there would be no return.

Eva took solace in counting the hours. In knowing that within twenty-four hours things would go back to being relatively normal.

Ekow would return to the challenging demands of running Quayson Bank and she would be left to bring up her son in peace. Or as peacefully as her disapproving mother-in-law would allow.

She was still reassuring herself about that when, her hand tucked into her new husband's, they arrived at the grand salon in Quayson House, where the reception was being held.

The new gold band weighed heavy on her finger. She knew the nugget it had been formed from had been mined from his family's gold mine a decade ago and set aside for this occasion because her mother-in-law had informed her of it, with a lofty sniff that had suggested Evangeline should fall to her knees and be overawed.

She'd settled on a serene smile instead.

Several long banquet tables groaning under the weight of exquisite food were positioned around the room. Mouthwatering jollof rice, rice and beans, *kpekple* with king crab. All beautifully complemented with various rich sauces and meats roasting on a dozen spits, and exclusively labelled spirits flowing alongside the locally brewed *asana* and palm wine.

Evangeline had a vague notion that had this been a common social gathering she would've enjoyed herself. But it wasn't. She was a stranger here—and not a particularly wanted one.

As she discovered when she excused herself an hour into the reception to visit the powder room and met the cool eyes of the woman there, poised in front of the mirror.

Tall, statuesque, she wore a stunning purple outfit that made her flawless skin glow. She approached Eva on high heels, the gentle flare of her hips and her endless legs announcing her supermodel status. From a sleek purse she pulled a tube of lipstick, but made no move to refresh her make-up. Instead, she speared

Evangeline with a look that was a cross between pity and envy.

'Well played, sis.'

'Excuse me?'

The woman launched a tight smile through the mirror. 'You've achieved what many women would give a limb for. You've landed the last eligible Quayson. Be careful, though, that you're not playing out of your league. The Quayson men are notoriously hard to please.'

Eva opened her mouth to tell her she hadn't set out to *land* anyone. That claiming his son and heir was her new husband's main goal, and she'd merely been swept along in his unstoppable endeavour. But Ekow's warning that this marriage was to appear real echoed in her head and stilled her tongue. So she summoned another serene smile, and rose above it.

'Thanks for the warning. I hope you enjoy the rest of my wedding.'

She sailed out with her head held high, thankful that her simple, elegant dress made walking much easier than one of the fuller, more elaborate gowns Ekow's mother had been pushing on her would have.

Ekow's gaze zeroed in on her the moment she stepped back into the room, and it was like a flash of lightning through her system, making her shakier still by the time she arrived at the chair he'd pulled out for her.

'You should eat something,' he murmured in her ear as she took her seat.

The very thought of it made her stomach roil. 'I'm not very hungry,' she said, reaching for her glass of mineral water.

'I thought wedding nerves were supposed to occur *before* the ceremony, not after?'

She shrugged. 'Maybe I'm an exception to all the rules.'

Expecting a mocking response, she was stunned when his face grew circumspect. 'Perhaps you are,' he concurred with a rasp that sent a frisson of something dancing over her. 'You walking down the aisle on your own certainly flouted a rule. But I find that not knowing what to expect from you next is…interesting.'

She bit her tongue against asking if that was a good or a bad thing. She didn't want to know. But the heated gleam in his eyes which remained whether they were talking about the weather or debating the wisdom of a fiery kiss called her a liar.

She wanted him to be interested.

Eva swallowed against the foolish notion as he continued to watch her, continued to assess her like a juicy deal he was seriously contemplating landing.

The atmosphere grew thick, the steady rise and fall of his chest mocking the rapid agitation of hers.

Beyond her peripheral vision his older brother and best man stood and made a speech Eva barely heard, drawing applause she absently smiled at as Ekow's gaze clung to hers, asking questions she wasn't ready to answer.

Then the first dance was announced.

The mild panic in her midriff grew as he rose to his feet and held out a large, forthright hand to her.

They'd touched exactly three times since she'd met him at the altar. When he'd placed the ring on her finger, when he had been invited to kiss the bride and he'd taken hold of her, drawing her to him and placing a firm but short kiss on her lips that had nevertheless set her whole body tingling. And when they'd walked down the aisle after exchanging their vows.

The rest of the time he'd been courteous but physically distant.

And now she was supposed to sail into his arms, pretend she was ecstatic...

She took his hand, unable to disguise its tremble, an action he took note of, if the slight tightening of his own fingers was a sign.

'If you get any stiffer you'll break into little pieces, dear wife,' he murmured, close enough for her to feel his breath on the shell of her ear. Close enough to make her shiver when his lip brushed the top of her ear.

'It's hard to relax when a thousand eyes are watching you.'

'They stare because you look exquisite,' he stated, with a lofty arrogance which should've set her teeth on edge but only made something vital inside her melt, then catch fire, as if it wanted to compete with the smouldering look in his eyes. 'They stare because they envy you,' he added, his hands gently guiding her across the grand salon floor to the strains of another Hip Life masterpiece from the cellist. 'And if it bothers you, then know that you only need to be concerned with *my* eyes.'

But your eyes are the worst... They make me...yearn.

She kept the response inside, of course. Because none of that was part of their deal. 'Thanks for the compliment. But it won't surprise you to know I can't wait for all this to be over.'

His hands tightened momentarily around her waist, then eased just as quickly. But the sharpness in his eyes intensified. He watched her for several seconds before he gave a short nod, with a look of annoyingly supreme understanding in his eyes. 'You're understandably overwhelmed. It will pass soon enough, once we're on our way.'

She jerked slightly in his arms. 'On our way where?'

Although his face stayed carefully neutral she saw a glint of displeasure in his eyes. 'I had one of my assistants email you our itinerary. Should I be concerned that you didn't look at it?'

'I've been too busy to check my personal emails. And excuse me if I've not brushed up on the etiquette of being married to billionaires who communicate with their wives through assistants and emails. I prefer face-to-face communication myself.'

For some reason that made his lips twitch. 'Are we having our first marital fight, Evangeline? When we haven't even finished our first dance yet?'

His reference to their union didn't stem the rising tide of panic. Nor did the dangerous quirking of his lips in amusement.

'It's not much of a fight when one party seems infinitely amused, is it?' she asked.

'Perhaps amusement is one option.'

Something about the timbre of his tone unfurled another flare of heat inside her. 'And another is what, exactly?'

He stepped back, took her hand and swung her around, before expertly catching her in his arms again. 'Scandalise you by kissing that sassy mouth until neither of us can see straight,' he said, almost conversationally.

She tightened her defences against what his suave moves and his words did to her. 'You have my thanks for not choosing the less sensible option, then.'

His smile this time looked strained up close. 'Being

sensible is the last thing on my mind when I think about kissing you, wife.'

Before she could respond, the music slowed to a melodic end. She forced a smile at the rapturous applause and let him lead her off the dance floor.

When he was promptly claimed by a small crowd of relatives and friends Eva almost breathed sigh of relief, and then the wedding co-ordinator discreetly approached, asking whether she would like anything special packed, she was reminded her that she hadn't discovered where they were going.

She was tempted to ask the wedding co-ordinator, but what would it say about her if she confessed she had no clue what her own husband had planned?

Responding that, no, she didn't want anything special, she made her way back to the table, where a flagging Leo was doing his best to stay awake. The middle-aged nanny, who'd started watching him whenever Eva had been required for wedding preparations, looked up and smiled.

'He's just had his bottle. I was about to go and get him ready for your trip, Mrs Quayson.'

Eva started, something desperately needy catching in her midriff at the new form of address. 'Please, call me Eva.'

The woman smiled again and nodded, before her gaze swung over her shoulder. Eva didn't need to look to know Ekow was close. Her very skin fired up at his proximity. Eva placed a lingering kiss on her son's head, then stepped back and watched, feeling something moving deep in her chest, as Ekow drew close and did the same.

Once they were alone, Ekow turned to her. 'Almost time to say our goodbyes.'

She'd been feverishly counting the hours and minutes before. Now, hearing the throb of...*something* in his voice, she wished she could stop time.

'You didn't tell me where we're going.'

He stepped close, caught up her hand and, uncaring of the avid eyes fixed on them, brushed his lips over her knuckles. 'We're going on our honeymoon, Evangeline. Where else?'

Paris and Cape Verde were the eventual destinations for her honeymoon, Eva found out two hours later when, after finding herself alone for a scant five minutes when the stylist left her to change, she frantically searched her emails.

But first they were travelling by helicopter to a private resort in Axim, where they'd spend the night, before returning to Accra and heading for Paris.

The forty-five-minute flight saw them land on the edge of a breathtaking beach just as the sun was setting on golden thatch-roofed chalets and winding pathways.

'What is this place? It's stunning,' she gushed as Ekow helped her into a sleek little tender, handed Leo over, and aided the nanny.

He smiled, her response obviously pleasing him. 'It's a set of ten eco-lodges. Three, including the one we're using, are set on their own islands.'

Their island was no bigger than a tennis court, but the chalet looked directly onto a serene beach with swaying palm trees and golden sand. 'How did I not know about this place? I scoured information on hundreds of places to stay when I visited the last time,' she said from the balcony, after she'd helped the nanny put Leo to bed.

Ekow came towards her, handing her a glass of fruit

punch. Like her, he'd changed into less formal clothes, and his open-necked shirt was being caressed by the setting sun, giving her mouthwatering glimpses of his strong throat.

'It's only a year old. I only knew about it because Atu's was dying to get his hands on it.'

She frowned. 'And he didn't succeed? That's unlike him…' She'd only known her brother-in-law a short time, but the Quayson fortitude was as alive and present in him as it was in his younger brother.

Ekow strolled away and returned with a platter of seafood, pointedly holding it out to her. Perhaps it was the ocean air, or her magnificent surroundings, but her appetite suddenly roared back. She took a bite of grilled prawn and melon and moaned under her breath.

Ekow's smile widened, his eyes heating up. 'He tried. I beat him to the punch.'

Her eyes widened. 'You own this place?'

'Not any more.' Reaching into his back pocket, he drew out a thick folded piece of paper. 'It's yours now. My wedding present to you.'

She nearly dropped her glass. 'I… What? I can't—'

His fingers brushed her lips, freezing her words. 'You can. You will. I'm not taking it back.'

'But… I didn't get you anything.'

A fierce light gleamed in his eyes. 'You've given me Leo. But if you're offering more…'

The husky rasp in his voice had her stepping back, afraid of the spark of her own yearning. 'No. I said… We agreed…'

His lips twisted. 'And I gave us a month before we succumbed. Well, here we are. Let's see how we do, hmm?'

That clear intent lingered for the rest of the evening

as they ate, drank, and pointedly steered away from lustful subjects; even as they changed into their night-clothes and headed for the one, albeit large and sump-tuous, bed in the chalet.

As she and her new husband slid into bed, then lay staring at the ceiling on this their wedding night, thick ropes of sensuality slowly coiled around them and, al-most inevitably, reminding her of their weekend in Cape Town. Reminding her that Ekow was the only man she'd slept with.

The only man, she suspected alarmingly, she'd ever want to sleep with.

Because everything had gone like clockwork so far, Eva didn't doubt their transition from Axim back to Quay-son House before they headed to the airport would hap-pen at the allotted time.

Dressed in a sleeveless cream silk jumpsuit with a waist-length African print cape of a similar colour-scheme tossed over it, she fixed her hair and caught up her bag.

Several suitcases were packed, ready to be stowed in the SUVs heading for the airport. The nanny ap-proached her in the hallway with Leo in her arms and Ekow's mother next to them.

Naana Quayson's gaze was cool, approaching chill-ing. Eva still had no idea why the older woman disliked her, save the glaring fact that she wasn't the woman Mrs Quayson had chosen, and had apparently spent considerable time and effort matchmaking for her re-maining single son.

Short of actually saying what she'd considered tell-ing the beautiful stranger in the powder room yesterday, all she could do was smile. 'Everything went perfectly yesterday. Thank you.'

Ekow's mother looked momentarily stunned, as if she hadn't expected the courtesy. But that smallest hint of warmth soon disappeared, leaving the coolness Eva had come to expect.

'My son deserves the best, so that's exactly what I delivered. I don't need thanks from *you* for that.'

As usual, the warm, joyous weight of Leo lifted Eva's spirits, and she pressed a kiss to his cheek before she looked at her mother-in-law. 'Well, we're a family now, so what you do for him, you do for me.'

The moment the words spilled from her mouth she knew she'd taken the wrong tack. But of course she couldn't take them back.

Naana Quayson's face tightened further, disdain crossing her face before, glancing at the silent nanny, she replaced it with neutrality. 'Enjoy your honeymoon,' she said stiffly.

The unspoken *while it lasts* lingered in the air, following Eva downstairs and into the first of the fleet of SUVs waiting to whisk them to the airport.

For the first ten minutes Eva stared at the passing scenery, letting father and son entertain each other.

'Something troubling you? Or is the silent treatment for crimes I'm unaware of?' asked Ekow.

Her intention of staying silent lasted only a nanosecond. 'I'm not sure who hates me more—your mother, or all the women out there who'd hoped to become the last Mrs Quayson.'

He stiffened, turning to face her. 'Did she say something to you?' he bit out.

Eva shrugged. 'Words weren't necessary.'

His jaw gritted for a moment before he relaxed. 'Letting go isn't easy for her, I suspect. No doubt you'll feel the same about our son?'

'Or maybe it isn't that at all,' she blurted. 'She clearly thinks you've made a mistake. That seems to be the general consensus, doesn't it?' Eva hadn't realised how much that chafed until the words fell between them.

'The "general consensus" is irrelevant. And none of those women are the mother of my child,' he responded tightly.

Just like that a chill swept over her, icing over every ember she'd been foolish enough to leave flaming 'Of course. How can I forget my unique position?'

'If you want me to say otherwise then you're going to be disappointed.' He exhaled noisily, then his gaze probed hers deeper in the dim interior. 'Do you want more, Evangeline? Is that what this is about? Because if it is, you only have to—'

'It isn't.'

Her voice had emerged firmly enough to fool even her. Was that a flash of disappointment in his eyes? She couldn't tell because his lashes swept down, then away, his focus once more on Leo.

'Then what are we arguing about?'

The chafing turned into a deep burn, eating away at the edges of her heart. 'Nothing at all.'

Nothing at all.

Ekow was more disturbed by those three words than he cared to admit.

For reasons he was at a loss to name, Evangeline was disrupting his previously exemplary thought processes.

Take those few moments during his wedding, for example, when he'd entertained the same idea he'd had that first night last month, after seeing her again.

He'd forgotten himself. Forgotten the infernal agreement he'd made with his new wife not to claim her in the most intimate way.

Seeing her walk down the aisle towards him in the classy yet deeply sensual dress he'd chosen and she'd picked for herself, he'd been thrown back to their first meeting. And to their evening in Aburi, when he'd kissed her. When he'd felt a strange peace with her he'd never felt with another.

More than her ethereal beauty and the memory of the sex and the passion, it had been seeing her turn up at all. Yes, he'd called her bluff after that trip. How could he not have? He'd stared into the face of rejection so many times with his father, he'd learned the deep art of the poker face. He'd learned to face up to the possibility of loss and rejection before it came, rather than wait to be gutted by it when he least expected it.

Eva rose to a challenge, he'd learned. So he'd dared her to turn up at the altar.

Watching her stride down alone and yet fiercely proud, he'd once again toyed with the idea of...*more*.

Now he knew that idea wasn't a viable one.

She didn't seem to want what every other woman before her had craved—power, money, prestige, and not necessarily in that order. All she truly cared about was her brother and their son.

He stared at his beautiful boy, the child he now believed she'd intended to tell him about all along, and wondered if there was a way to alter things between them.

As they pulled up to the Quayson private jet he glanced at the woman who now bore his name. Considered the possibility that she really wasn't like most women. That she'd set out simply to do the right thing and wanted nothing from him.

Nothing at all...

Just like his father?

He gritted his jaw, displeased by his thoughts circling back to the one person he didn't want to think about today.

Ekow ignored the taunting inner voice and stepped out, unbuckling his son before taking control of his carrier.

When Eva stepped out, her eyes widening on his jet, he felt a punch of satisfaction. It was a mildly fatuous thought, but if, like with her wedding gift, he could dazzle her a little more, perhaps she might see her way to...

What?

Forgetting every accusation he'd thrown at her in Cape Town?

And then what?

Dazzle her some more? Coax her into his bed? Sex for the sake of it?

When he would've given a resounding *yes* somewhere in the not so distant past, now Ekow's insides twisted at the idea, a hollow feeling chasing fast on its heels.

That thought of *more* he'd entertained punched harder, insisting on recognition he couldn't give it.

He glanced down at Eva as he led her and their son towards his plane.

Or could he?

CHAPTER NINE

Eva landed in Paris with a different man.

Where there'd been distance before, there was none now. Ekow even took her hand as they stepped off the plane at Paris Charles de Gaulle Airport, and didn't release it as they got into another SUV that took them to the heart of the city.

She wanted to ask him what he was playing at, but the words stuck in her throat. The idea that she didn't want to know because she *liked* it was all too real as they were transferred from the vehicle to a penthouse suite.

The grand hotel on Avenue George V, part of the Quayson Hotel Group, oozed jaw-dropping elegance and luxury. From the centuries-old chandeliers to the sparkling marble floors and the courteous butlers and smiling staff, Evangeline was quietly awed by it all.

When Ekow caressed her wrist her objections stuck in her throat as they were shown to a multi-level three-bedroom penthouse, with a master suite some distance from the other two, she started to believe she was in trouble. The views alone were mesmerising—the Eiffel Tower so close she could almost reach out and touch it.

With Leo quickly settled in his crib, and the nanny tucked away in her own room, she found herself alone in the living room, her gaze on the stunning view. But she knew the moment Ekow walked into the room.

Her gaze, utterly compelled, swung to follow his stride across the plush pale gold carpet.

'Are you tired?' he asked.

She shook her head. 'Sleeping on the plane was probably not a good idea. I'm wide awake now.'

He shrugged. 'I've arranged for dinner here in the suite. Or we could go out if you prefer?'

She glanced out of the window, the sight too magnificent and inviting to be denied. 'I'd like to go out, if you don't mind?'

He shook his head. 'Of course not. That, too, is already arranged.'

She glanced down at the clothes she'd worn to travel. 'I'll go and change.'

Walking into the suite she believed was to be hers, she stopped at the sight of the bare dressing room. Turning, she approached the open doorway of the master suite.

Ekow, with the same intent of changing, had removed his shirt and was in the process of toeing off his shoes when she entered the room. The sight of his naked torso froze her in place, her mouth drying as she stared at his chest, at the ripple of his abs as he reached for his belt.

One eyebrow quirked when he saw her.

'I... I think my suitcases have been put here by mistake.'

A tic throbbed in his jaw. 'It wasn't a mistake. I didn't correct the assumption made by the staff that we're sharing a suite since we're newly married. The question is, do you want to fight about it now or later, after dinner?' he asked sardonically.

She raised her chin but couldn't dismiss the waves of

heat rolling through her at the sight of his hard-packed body. 'My things will need to be moved, but I don't want to fight. Not right now, anyway.'

'Good. Neither do I. Your clothes are in there.'

Eva bit her lip, realising she wasn't blasé enough to stride across the room to the dressing room when there was a half-naked man, albeit her own husband, within touching distance.

But other than changing her mind and going out to dinner in the jumpsuit she'd travelled in, she had no choice but to head to the dressing room, striding dangerously close to his mind-bending perfection. While he watched her all the way.

The smooth efficiency of the staff was evident in the already unpacked and tidily put away clothes.

Plucking a neat little cerise number off its hangar, she quickly gathered the accessories she needed. And then stopped. The idea of scurrying away to dress out of sight when they already had an established agreement irritated her.

The faint sounds of the shower made up her mind for her.

Quickly undressing, she pulled on the thigh-skimming wraparound dress, trying not to imagine Ekow next door, water cascading down his chiselled body.

She slid her feet into silver diamante strapless heels and added the accessories she'd selected. While she hadn't asked for it, she was grateful for the new wardrobe included with her wedding apparel, although the labels on the dresses and accessories made her jaw drop.

Eva didn't think there'd ever come a time when she'd got used to the staggering wealth attached to the man she'd married. Perhaps it was a good thing, since this marriage came with a use-by date anyway.

She ignored the way her stomach dipped, and concentrated on refreshing her make-up before Ekow emerged from the bathroom. She'd just tucked her phone and lipstick into her silver clutch bag when he entered the dressing room.

The towel wrapped around his waist rode low enough to make her tongue swell in her mouth, the sudden rush of craving stinging her core.

He either didn't notice her reaction, or he didn't care that he was half naked in her presence as he strode across the room to his side of the dressing area.

Realising she was still gaping at him after several seconds, Eva whirled around and headed for the door.

'Evangeline...'

The husky utterance of her full name stopped her in her tracks.

She glanced over her shoulder, almost too terrified to look at his body again. 'Yes?'

'You look breathtaking,' he said thickly, his gaze conducting a searing head-to-toe scrutiny before meeting her eyes.

Eva swallowed. The thick lust in the air threatened to suffocate her but she was sure she would die happy. All the more reason to get out of there—fast.

'I... Thank you.'

He gave an arrogant half-smile and continued to look deep into her eyes for another few moments before he turned away and started to drop his towel.

She fled.

By the time he joined her in the living room fifteen minutes later, she'd managed to get herself under some semblance of control.

'I've just checked on Leo. He's sleeping soundly. He shouldn't wake up before morning.'

Eva knew she was rambling, attempting to cover up the electricity zinging between them, but she couldn't help herself. She had to dissipate it somehow before it swallowed her whole.

Her attempt to do was reduced to ash when he threaded his fingers through hers. Her resistance died even before she'd taken her next breath. Whatever was happening here was greater than her willpower could sustain.

And, really, what was the harm in letting him hold her hand? They were in the most romantic city in the world, and it *was* technically their honeymoon.

Ignoring the voice cautioning her about treading on dangerous ground, Eva followed him into the lift.

They walked a few streets to the restaurant he'd chosen, with Eva doing her best to ignore the bodyguards trailing behind them. Perhaps someday she would accept the fact that her husband didn't go anywhere without serious security, but she suspected it would be a long while yet.

Her husband.

He was behaving in every sense like a real husband would, smiling at her across the dining table set in an intimate corner of a restaurant discreetly announcing its double Michelin star status with a plaque beside the door.

He ordered premium exquisite canapés which he shared with her. She chose a lobster bisque which he sampled shamelessly, his smouldering eyes faintly amused when she expressed outrage.

Eva knew she was sinking deeper into the quagmire, risking an emotional attachment she couldn't afford and heading towards the same mistake she'd made last time.

But…no…

That weekend had brought her Leo, the one thing in the universe she loved above everything else.

'You're pensive. Something wrong with the food? Or the company?' he asked, his amusement edged with something more serious now. More circumspect.

'I'm remembering that sitting down to eat with you comes with a price,' she divulged, before she could stop herself.

His face hardened a touch. 'A price that has never been forced on you.'

She shook her head. 'No.'

Because it was the truth. Whatever she'd done up to this point had been done with her eyes wide open. It was unfair to blame him for any of it. Sure, some of the choices had been less favourable than others, but she'd always had a choice.

Just as she had a choice in whatever was happening now…?

When her attempt to shrug away the question didn't make it go, Eva decided to embrace it. She accepted it when they were finished eating and Ekow led her down a few more streets, then descended steps leading to a promenade that wound alongside the Seine.

Her heart tumbled when she saw his hardened expression hadn't disappeared. But she walked with him in silence, taking in the magnificent city at night and attempting to calm her own agitation.

'You were right,' he stated heavily.

Her heart tumbled a little further, straining towards her toes. 'About what?'

'My father. Your visit. All of it.'

Eva felt something sharp catch in her throat. She swallowed three times before she could speak. 'You looked into it?' She wasn't sure whether she was disappointed or elated at the vindication. Because his revelation meant he hadn't believed her in the first place.

He nodded, having no idea he was deepening whatever this peculiar feeling was rushing through her. 'I couldn't not.'

Eva darted another glance at him. The timbre of his voice was urging her to see things from his perspective. 'You didn't do it because you didn't believe me, did you? You did it for your own reasons?' she surmised.

He didn't answer for an age, his bleak profile turned away, his dark eyes watching a fully lit riverboat slide slowly through the waves, throwing sparkling lights on the murky water. 'Yes,' he eventually admitted.

'Why?'

The gaze that met hers was full of expressions too dark to decipher. 'Because I needed further proof of what I've always known. That I was a mere pawn in whatever game he was playing.'

She gasped. 'Surely that's not true?'

'Why? Because a parent would never do that?'

She opened her mouth to say yes, then closed it. She had no comparison except with her own mother, and even in her most desolate moments her mother had stayed loving to her and Jonah. She'd given them all the support she could, and besides her withholding her father's identity from her it had been enough.

Was Ekow right? *Had* she had it better than some—perhaps even him, despite his wealth, power and prestige—and not appreciated it?

He gave a grim smile, perhaps intuiting her thoughts, and then his gaze once more veered off into the distance, as if meeting hers was too much. As if he was putting distance between them again.

He shrugged. 'Maybe that's not entirely right. My

eldest brother wasn't a pawn. He was the rook my father pinned all his hopes on.'

Her heart twisted. 'Your brother...the one who died?'

Ekow gave her another grim nod. 'Yes, he died. Atu had no interest in replacing him. And I...'

'You wanted to be more than a pawn. You wanted to be useful. You wanted the regard every child deserves from its parents.'

He turned sharply to her, his eyes narrowing on her face. 'I just wanted not to be invisible. Nothing more, nothing less. Not to feel as if I didn't matter. Sometimes I'd wonder why he'd wanted more than one child, when it was clear he couldn't find it in himself to...' He paused, his jaw clenching.

'Did you talk to him about it? I know pushing for answers doesn't always work...' she gave a dry laugh, recalling own vain efforts '...but maybe...' She trailed off when he shook his head.

'We didn't have that sort of relationship. Whatever paternal emotions he had were reserved for his golden boy. For the longest time I wondered if that was how it was meant to be. But then I discovered that my cousins and friends had siblings who were all treated equally, so I thought...' Again he stopped.

'You thought it was your fault?' she murmured.

His eyes probed hers. After several tense seconds he sighed. 'How could I not?'

She nodded. 'I thought the same too, when my mother refused to tell me about my father. I thought perhaps I'd done something to make him not want to know me.'

He reached for her hand, a resolute look in his eyes. 'This is why we won't give Leo a moment's doubt about how much he's wanted—yes?'

Her throat clogged and she grappled with an urge to throw her arms around him, to show him every gratifying emotion she felt at his loving their son as much as she did.

'Yes,' she answered hoarsely.

His free hand rose to her face, his knuckles tracing her cheek. She watched as the dull embers in his eyes slowly roused to life. 'My father had no right to deny me my child. No right to treat you the way he did. For that, I'm sorry.'

A tight knot—one that'd been clenched for endlessly long months—eased. When she could speak past the lump in her throat, she asked, 'Why did he do it?'

The question had plagued her for weeks, until she'd been forced to put it out of my mind for the sake of her sanity and caring for the baby she'd carried.

'Probably because he was distrusting and sceptical, and believed money was the answer to everything,' Ekow said. 'I'm surprised he didn't try to buy you off. He'd done so many times before, with others.'

She winced, her heart plummeting. She opened her mouth to tell him he had, that she'd kept the cheque as a reminder. But looking into his eyes, seeing the anguish his father had caused, Eva couldn't find it in her heart to pile on more heartache. Perhaps someday soon she'd tell him, when things weren't so raw.

Ignoring the warning echoing at the back of her mind, she focused as he continued.

'He was a powerful and influential man with rigid views. He wanted to rule over every inch of our lives. A possible grandchild he didn't know about was out of his control. He acted the only way he knew how, by making sure the problem went away.'

She didn't understand Ekow's father's motives for

what he'd done but, God help her, she couldn't help the aching of her heart for the painful childhood Ekow had experienced.

'What about your mother? Didn't she do anything?'

'She was equally under his thumb.' He shrugged. 'Or perhaps she found her own peace in being a compliant wife. I've never stopped to analyse it.'

Eva frowned, certain there was more to it. 'But your relationship with her...?'

'Is better than it used to be. But it'll never be what I want it to be. I know that now.'

'What does that mean?'

He shook his head. 'It means I'm more interested in the family I have now. The family you and I are in the process of creating.'

Her heart lurched. 'But we aren't—'

'But we could be,' he pressed, cupping her shoulders to draw her close enough so she could see the determination in his face. 'You want me. I know you're not contrary enough to deny it.'

She raised an eyebrow, despite her heart banging against her ribs hard enough to drown out the sounds of the city. 'Is that a bluff or a double bluff?'

The smile she'd expected didn't materialise, and his eyes continued to burn into hers. 'Eva...' Again, there were questions and promises in those eyes, warnings and passion. 'Don't condemn us both to celibacy when it doesn't have to be that way.'

Both. Her heart leapt, because at the back of her mind she had always wondered if his words to her that day in Cape Town had been mere talk. But she needed to be sure.

'You mean you don't intend to...?' She licked her

lips, stifling a moan when his gaze dropped to linger on her tingling flesh.

'No, I don't. There is no honour in infidelity.'

This moment. This cataclysmic moment when a handful of words could shift her foundations permanently. Underpinning them with fragile hope and whispers of dreams that might not come true but dreams she couldn't pull herself away from.

'Tell me you want this too,' he insisted fervently.

Her lips parted before she could stop herself, but thankfully the words failed to emerge. Because she needed a moment. Several moments.

To see past the magic of the city and the overwhelming presence of Ekow to the truth in her heart.

To accept that she wanted this. That she'd always wanted this.

Neither her son nor her brother featured in this decision. It was hers alone. Hers to claim. Hers to keep.

For as long as it lasted?

She pushed away that final question. Looked up into the eyes of her husband of one day and said, 'Yes.'

For an age, he simply stared at her. Then he nodded. 'Yes.'

She was thankful he didn't ask for reaffirmation. Not because she wouldn't have given it, but because she was impatient to get to the heart of her needs.

He drew one strong arm around her, binding her waist with his other arm, plastering her against his lithe body. She sighed, her body a willing vessel, all too eager to strain up onto her tiptoes, eager for the kiss he gifted her a moment later.

The kiss, right there on the banks of the Seine, was the stuff of magic. The way his lips claimed hers, his tongue stroking deep inside her mouth, to fulfil every passionate fantasy she'd ever had, was enough to rob her of thought.

Eva didn't care that they were in public and were probably a spectacle for indulgent smiles or scandalised whispers. Wrapping her arms around his waist, she pulled him closer, holding on for dear life as he swept her away, mind and soul.

She swayed when he pulled back, his eyes burning flames of passion as he captured her hand with his. 'We're returning to the hotel. Now,' he stated gruffly.

She nodded eagerly. Let him pull her along as they rushed back to the penthouse.

Eva gave a laugh of delight when he swung her into his arms on the threshold. 'We've already done away with enough traditions to bother with any more, don't you think?'

He shrugged, leaning down to brush his lips over hers. 'I don't indulge because it's tradition. I do it because I want to.'

Unable to help herself, she reached up and framed one taut cheek in her hand. 'What else do you intend to indulge in?' she asked saucily.

His smile was all red-blooded male arrogance. 'Patience, wife. You'll find out soon enough.'

Their laughter died, whittled away under the force of their lust as he set her down next to the immense emperor-sized bed.

Memories of their first time invaded her brain, plaguing her with doubts, making tremors surge from her toes upwards through her body. The first time she'd been a virgin. This time would be different. She'd given birth to his child and her body had changed. Both memorable events were enough to make her wonder…

'It'll be even better,' he murmured deeply, that uncanny ability of his to read her mind striking again. 'Because you're even more beautiful now than you were then. And you've borne my son.'

Tears stung the backs of her eyes and she rapidly blinked them away. If she knew nothing else, she knew Ekow loved his son—had already moved mountains for him. But Eva found she needed an untouchable place created for just herself. A moment in time she could call her own without the title of *mother* overshadowing it.

'But I take you as my wife. When I'm deep inside you, it'll be because I desire you as badly tonight as I did the first time we met.'

His intuition was eerily uncanny, and she would've been a little bit frightened had he not reached for the ties that secured her dress. With one firm tug the dress fell open, displaying the lace and satin lingerie set that formed part of her wedding trousseau.

Eva hadn't expected the evening to end this way when she'd put it on a little over three hours ago. But she was fiercely glad she had when his expression altered, a stamp of desire deepening in his face as his gaze scoured her.

'Every inch of you, every curve, is exquisite,' he breathed, his nostrils flaring as he leaned in close and inhaled her scent. 'I can't wait to be inside you.'

His words had the desired effect.

She swayed towards him, uncaring about being too eager. She couldn't stop. Ekow Quayson possessed the ability to tap into her deepest sexual desires, effortlessly stoking the flames until she feared she would lose her mind.

'Please… Kiss me.'

'All in good time, wife,' he growled.

He took his time to slide her sleeves down her shoulders and arms, inciting tiny fireworks with each glide. By the time the material pooled at her feet Eva could barely stand.

Large hands grasped her waist, easily spanning it. In the next moment he'd yanked her close, plastering her almost naked body to his clothed one.

Bypassing her mouth, he trailed his lips down the side of her neck, gliding his tongue over her fluttering pulse, down her collarbone to the valley between her breasts, still cupped by her bra.

His kisses trailed over her skin, making her breasts go heavy and the peaks diamond-hard. Between kisses he murmured words of praise, drawing moans from deep in her throat as she fought to stay on her own two feet.

When he had done with torturing her, he straightened, his gaze burning into hers as he nudged her backwards onto the bed.

Eva propped herself up on her elbows, watched him step back and start to unbutton his shirt. She licked her lips, her hunger threatening to completely overwhelm her.

When her thighs twitched, he smiled. But it was a strained smile, the evidence of his own arousal framed thickly behind his fly.

Shirt discarded, he trailed his gaze feverishly over her body as he unbuttoned his trousers and slowly eased his zip over his erection.

At his unguarded flinch, she felt more dampness pool at her core, the blatant evidence of his state turning her on.

'You like that?' he asked in response to her helpless moan. 'You enjoy seeing your effect on me?'

'Yes,' she replied, unable to act coy. He did that to her, this man.

Moments later he was gloriously naked, coming closer, prowling over her on the bed. Staring deep into her eyes, he slid one hand behind her back and effortlessly snapped open her bra.

His nostrils flared as her breasts spilled free. His thick groan was music to her ears. And then all sense of time and place disappeared as he dropped his head and captured one nipple between his lips.

Arching her back, Eva silently pleaded for more. He delivered. His hands, lips, teeth and tongue pleasuring her in ways she'd imagined would remain only fevered memories shaped by their first time together.

By the time he pulled her panties free she was hopelessly wet, aching and needy, ready to plead for mercy.

No plea was needed, because Ekow was equally driven, hunger stamped in his every movement as he reached for the foil packet inside the bedside drawer.

With far too sexy movements, he sheathed himself. Then dropping back off the bed, he stood at the side. Gloriously male, unashamedly aroused, he grasped her behind the knees and firmly parted her.

At the sight of her damp core, he groaned again, his breath escaping in harsh pants has he tugged her body downwards. 'Watch me, wife. Watch me make you mine.'

The primitive throb in his words drove her further towards the edge. Barely able to hold herself up, Eva angled her gaze downward.

'Tell me to take you.'

'Please,' she whispered urgently. 'I need you.'

Satisfaction washed over his face. His grip tightened, the capable hands holding her still as he notched himself against her heated entrance. Then, with his gaze equally riveted on where they were almost joined, he thrust inside her with one slow, relentless drive.

Her long moan bled into his thick, utterly male grunt, and the outward sounds of their coming together quickened the lust between them.

With each thrust Eva felt her resistance eroding, the dreams and fantasies she'd forced herself to stop spinning unfurling, taking on a life of their own—one which involved the man who possessed her so completely. The only man capable of driving her to these frenzied heights where only bliss resided.

When his gaze shot up, commanding hers to his, she was helpless to resist. So, with their gazes locked on one another, her lips parted on a cry that went on for ever, his relentless pounding finally pushed her over the edge into unrivalled pleasure.

Eva was vaguely aware that she moaned his name, clutched his sweat-slicked shoulders a little too tightly, but she couldn't find the strength to ringfence the torrent of emotions he'd unleashed in her.

However, she took solace in his own undoing as he gave a rough shout of pleasure before his own release tumbled him over the edge.

For endless minutes she clung to him as their bodies cooled and their breaths steadied. When self-awareness began to creep in she tried to hold it at bay, to revel in this moment for a few seconds longer. Only for it to be compounded when she gave a helpless protest as he pulled out of her, leaving her empty.

Watching him walk away towards the bathroom didn't alleviate the bereft feeling inside her. Unbidden, her gaze drifted towards the pillows. Then to the clothes on the floor.

They'd been in such a rush that they hadn't discussed what happened after this. Did she return to her bed? Did she want to?

No on both accounts, her heart screamed. But then wasn't it her heart she was risking by staying?

'You're staying right here,' Ekow's deep voice said from the bathroom doorway. His eyes dared her to countermand his command.

She'd grown far too vulnerable, far too raw in the aftermath of lovemaking, and the sight of him returning, godlike, his eyes burning with the residue of passion, dissolved the last of her resistance.

Her breath caught as he dropped to his knees beside the bed. When he caught one ankle between his hands, she realised that they'd made love without taking off her shoes. For some absurd reason, that drew laughter from her throat.

His gaze dashed up to meet hers, a ghost of a smile quirking his lips. 'Is this an interesting preference I should note?' he asked.

She shrugged. 'I wouldn't know. I've only ever been with you, so I guess we'll have to find out together.'

He stiffened, his eyes widening, locking on hers. 'What did you say?' he rasped, his voice raw and uneven.

Eva straightened, attempting to pull her heel out of his grasp, but he held on. 'You heard me.'

His stark astonishment would've made her laugh if she hadn't sensed his mounting tension.

'You were a virgin the first time we had sex?'

She squirmed beneath the fierceness of his gaze. 'Yes, I was. And before you give me a speech about not telling you, it was my choice.'

A flash of displeasure rushed over his face before he exhaled loudly. 'Nevertheless, I wish I had known.'

She tilted her head. 'Why? What would you have done differently?'

The question seemed to take him by surprise. 'I don't know,' he replied. 'Virgins are not my thing. Not until you, apparently.'

She told herself not to feel in any way special, but her heart refused to listen. It attempted to sing as he rose, discarded her shoes, and placed her in the middle of the bed.

Sliding in beside her, he pulled her close.

Utterly unable to help herself, Eva curled a hand on his chest, pillowed her cheek on one shoulder and let a little bit of that dream seep in.

She'd been a virgin.

He hadn't even noticed.

A vein of disgust slid through him, cutting through the primitive satisfaction swelling in his chest.

As she moved against him, her eyelids beginning to drift shut, his brain scrambled to recall every detail of their first time together.

Had he been gentle? Or had he fallen on her like a ravenous monster? Dear God, had he hurt her?

He remembered her pleasure, her eager hands reaching for him as they'd done tonight, her nails digging into his back.

Her sweet, insane snugness.

He wanted to be satisfied that he'd pleased her enough to take away the discomfort of her first time, but a frown slowly crept across his face as he replayed her words.

Why had she kept it a secret? Had she been afraid it

would alter the way he felt about her? How *did* he feel about her?

His frown deepened, spikes of apprehension running alongside the primitive possessiveness.

So many emotions.

He silently shook his head. How very effortlessly she seemed to trigger them. Trigger *him*. And he'd asked for all of it.

He'd discovered a new emotion—the tireless love a father could have for his son—and now he was eager to experience more. When all he'd ever seen before were the extremes of love.

His brother Fiifi had been violently in love with Amelie's sister, while his father had channelled what little he'd felt towards one son, to the complete abandonment of the other two.

Ekow had vowed never to be like his father, but what safeguards did he have in place to avoid turning out like his brother? Especially if he let all these messy emotions in?

Sex for the sake of it, he decided grimly. It had never failed in the past. Why would it fail him now?

It wouldn't, he concluded. The wild possessiveness he'd felt for Evangeline just now was because he'd been her first. It would pass.

As would this insane rush that flowed between them every time they so much as looked at each other. In the end all that would remain was sex for the sake of it.

And their son.

He was fine with that.

And he'd repeat that to himself until he believed it.

CHAPTER TEN

CAPE VERDE. As magical as Paris.

Eva hadn't been at all surprised to discover that Ekow owned a sprawling villa on the northernmost point of the island.

Over the past two weeks she'd discovered a lot about her husband.

He despised mushrooms. He spoke fluent Portuguese, alongside a handful of other languages—a talent she'd discovered she enjoyed when he used it in the bedroom.

Best of all, he made love as if was born to do it.

Eva was mildly stunned that she hadn't lost her vocal cords by now, with the amount of screaming she'd done during their honeymoon.

It was almost as if he wanted to prove something to her—to show her that, now she'd agreed to it, when they made love each lovemaking would be more mind-blowing than the last. To show her that beyond their son they had new common ground.

But the growing well of disquiet that had plagued these past few days was growing as the days ticked down to their return to Accra. Because with every moment spent in his presence she felt her foundations crumbling. Felt the reasons why this couldn't be a real marriage being eroded. The thought that she might be left vulnerable piled dismay on the anxiety. Because nothing had changed besides adding mind-blowing sex into the equation. Every scrap of love Ekow possessed was reserved for Leo—his reason for marrying her. While she feared she was in danger of being unable to contain her emotions to just Leo.

The growing alarm, and the need to stop herself from making the foolish mistake of falling for her husband, made her track him down to his study. The door was ajar. She paused in the doorway, her breath catching as she watched him finish a call.

His gaze found hers before travelling the length of her body, heating up with each second.

When the call ended he sprawled back in his seat, his eyes still fixed on her in a blatant declaration that said sex wasn't far from his mind. 'Is there something I can help you with, Eva?' he drawled.

She entered and shut the door behind her, clearing her throat to dissipate the sex-drenched atmosphere. 'Yes. It's about Quayson House. I feel as if I'm in a fishbowl there.'

One eyebrow slowly lifted, a brooding look entering his eyes. 'Hardly.'

'I know it's a mansion and all that. But you grew up there. You're fine with endless streams of staff running around and people visiting each other at the drop of a hat. You're used to it. I'm not. Put yourself in my shoes for a moment.'

'So you want to move?'

She sucked in a deep breath. 'Yes.'

'Are you planning to take me for half of what I own too, or going the whole hog and claiming everything while you're at it?'

There was amusement in his tone, but there was the bite of something else too.

She lifted her chin, feeling pride and hurt like twin arrows, seeking a bullseye within her. 'Neither. You can rest easy. You have nothing that I want.'

He regarded her steadily, his gaze growing more mocking by the second. 'Really? Nothing at all?'

Heat filled her face, and the memory of screaming his name and begging for more of his searing brand of possession ricocheted through her mind. 'You know what I mean.'

His face tightened. 'Perhaps. But for the sake of clarity you should spell it out.'

She took a deep breath that didn't quite reach her lungs because of the curious snag of pain beneath her ribcage. 'The house in Aburi. I'd like to live there full-time with Leo.'

His face tightened. 'Somehow we seem to find ourselves back to debating separate residences. Anyone would think you can't stand the sight of your husband. But we both know that's not quite true, is it?'

'Yes... No... Can we stay on point, please?'

He gave an eloquent shrug, drawing her much too avid gaze to the sleek symmetry of his body. 'That's the great thing about multitasking, sweet wife. We can discuss the subject of you attempting to live under a separate roof *and* sex. All at once. Would you like me to prove to you how eager you are for the latter beneath all that bluster?'

For embarrassingly long seconds she was stymied by the need to say *yes*. To kick the vital subject of moving residence and common sense to the kerb, stride over and slide into his lap.

She'd run her hand over the designer stubble that

called to her fingers, cup his nape and drag his mouth to meet hers. She'd savour those velvety lips for moan-making minutes before letting her tongue tangle with his…

A slow-motion replay of doing just that held her mind motionless for a handful of seconds. Only the slow, smug smile sliding across his lips roused her from her erotic musings.

'The only subject I wish to discuss right now is the Aburi house and my moving into it.'

For an age, he stared at her. Then he nodded. 'If that is what you want.'

Before she could take a breath that was puzzlingly wrapped in disappointment, he added, 'But you won't be living there on your own. I take your point that Quayson House place might be overwhelming for you, but where my wife and son go, I go. No negotiation.'

When disappointment immediately turned into an illicit thrill at his words Eva knew she was in trouble. 'Okay…thanks.'

She turned to leave.

'Angel?'

She curbed the punch of pleasure that hit her somewhere in the chest at the nickname.

'Why do you call me that?' she demanded. Exasperation erupted out of her, because she was genuinely alarmed by how much she loved his special abbreviation of her name.

'Because it suits you. I'm not naive enough to think angels are benign beings. You project being a peacemaker and nurturer when it suits you. But I also know you have claws you're not afraid to show when you feel the need to.'

Foolishly intrigued, she retraced her steps. 'And you like that?'

An entirely too arrogant smile crossed his sensual lips, drawing her attention to the delicious curve, reminding her how desperate she'd been to taste them last night.

'Have I not shown you yet how much? Perhaps you need a refresher?'

That she considered his raspy invitation for more than a fraction of a second told her how far gone she was. He watched her gaze flicker over the furniture in his office, his smile growing more smug as her breath caught. As images tumbled through her mind that drew her nipples into sharp points and made her panties damp.

God, she really needed to get herself under control around him. But why the urgency? Why not enjoy the sensuality he'd repeatedly promised and had more than delivered?

Where was the harm?

The question triggered a kernel of self-preservation she needed to hang onto. A warning that she risked more than falling prey to sexual decadence.

That she risked her heart.

His smile started to dim, and a displeased circumspection entered his eyes. 'I see the overthinking is starting again...'

'Someone has to do it. Did you want to talk to me about something else?'

'Yes. One of your clients.'

Her eyes widened at the name he tossed out. 'What about them?'

'They're a subsidiary of a business I own.'

Her heart caught for a different reason. 'So?'

'So I've been vetting your work. And I've made a decision about it.'

She settled her hands on her hips. 'You couldn't interview me, like anyone else? And what do you mean, you've made a decision?'

He took in her stance, his lips quirking again. 'Would you have accepted a position offered by me without overthinking that too?'

'I guess now we'll never know.' She turned to walk out, a larger kernel of hurt lodged in her midriff.

'Evangeline.' The firm bite of her name made her pause. 'I reached out to your previous employer.' When she froze, he shook his head. 'No, not the one you decorated with your drink the night we met. The director of that company, who was disappointed to see you go. He spoke of your work in glowing terms. So has everyone else you've worked for on a freelance basis since.'

She glanced over her shoulder. 'I know the quality of my work.'

'Then you won't think I'm practising nepotism when I offer you a position. And neither will anyone else.'

'Do you really care what anyone thinks?'

He gave a supremely arrogant shrug. 'Not especially. But I know you do.'

Why did that snag at something vital inside her? Why did it threaten to melt all the hardened edges she needed to keep around him? She should be annoyed he'd gone behind her back, but instead she felt…oddly treasured… What did that say about her?

He pushed a file towards her and she brushed the question away, a little too eager to sidestep it.

'What is this?' she asked.

He nudged his square chin at her. 'Take a look. Let me know if anything in there interests you.'

The list of his business interests was jaw-dropping.

And within each one were positions that made the professional in her silently moan in envy. If she hadn't quit her job she'd be in one of these positions by now.

But then if she hadn't quit her job she wouldn't have walked into the Quayson Hotel bar. Wouldn't have met Ekow Quayson. Wouldn't have had her son...

She glanced up to find his far too perceptive eyes fixed on her. She lowered her gaze again, before he could read the direction of her thoughts.

Not all the positions were available, of course. But there were enough to tempt her. Especially the one at the Accra headquarters of Quayson Bank.

Again she stifled the voice questioning her true motive behind considering that particular position. So what if Ekow worked in the same building? They'd probably hardly ever see each other...

'The suspense is killing me,' he murmured. 'Would you like me to choose for you?'

'I'm completely capable, thank you.'

His mouth twitched but he said nothing. Merely sprawled back in his chair, a mogul completely at home in his billion-dollar playground.

Her gaze zeroed in on the position where her husband would be close by. Impatient with analysing why she should refuse something she wanted, she closed the file. 'I'd like to interview for the senior accountant position in the PR department at the bank.'

The gleam deepening in his eyes indicated that she'd chosen as he'd expected. Perhaps as he'd intended.

Enough.

'Done. But I want something in return.'

'What?'

'Lunch with me when we're both in the building. Every day.'

It was the last thing she'd expected him to say, and something far too excitable tugged inside her. *Again.* 'I... Why?'

His gaze raked over her in a slow, leisurely perusal that left her even more breathless. 'Do I need a reason to have lunch with my wife?'

'I... No, but...'

He raised an eyebrow. 'But?'

She pressed her lips together, alarm rising once more as she felt the erosion of her resistance and disregarded it anyway. 'Fine. If I'm not busy.'

He rose slowly to his feet, his large body completely absorbing every frame of her attention. She'd seen him in different forms of clothing, but Ekow in a formal suit would always remind her of those electric moments when she'd first set eyes on him. Those hours, then days of madness, when she'd experienced true sexual awakening for the first time.

She stayed in place as he rounded his desk and sauntered towards her. 'You want me to earn your attention? Is that it? I could push for marital privilege...' he taunted, with a smile still playing at his lips.

When he smiled like that she wanted to tell him he could push for anything he wanted. She stemmed the careless response just in time. 'You could... I wouldn't recommend it, though. Do I need to remind you of the last boss who attempted to push me?'

'No—and I would never be that offensive.'

'Good.'

She'd expected a flat refusal to the living in Aburi proposal. An argument at the least. His agreement to that and his offer of a job had shocked her.

Accomplishing his agreement to one and being surprised with the other drew a smile from her as she looked up at him.

He raised an eyebrow. 'I take it you're pleased with the outcome of your visit?'

She affected a careless shrug. 'Maybe.'

He moved closer, and her heartbeat escalated, her skin heating up. 'Something else you want to fight about, wife?'

Another thing she'd learned during their honeymoon was that Ekow loved a challenge. Enjoyed it when she stood up to him. She'd never have believed it of herself, but she had discovered a kinky side to their lovemaking she was growing alarmingly addicted to.

'Maybe you should leave a few items of clothing on the floor, or insist I put on sun cream a hundred times a day like you did yesterday. See how that works out for you.'

He gave a low, husky laugh as he closed the distance between them. Her breathing went haywire.

'I could do that…or I could go straight to the thing I most enjoy about you.'

She stepped back as he towered over her—not because she was afraid of him, but because she knew he would follow. True enough, he mock-prowled after her across his study, then pinned her against a perfect space between two tall bookshelves.

Eva could barely breathe past the anticipation and hunger spiralling through her. He reached for the tie that secured her midriff-baring top, tugging it open to reveal the bikini she wore underneath.

'Leo—'

'Is asleep—or you would've brought him with you.

Besides, I heard you singing him to sleep via the monitor.' He jerked his head over his shoulder. 'So nice try.'

'I do my best,' she replied tartly, unable to stop the smile curving her lips.

His gaze raked over her face, his own amusement disappearing. 'You're beautiful,' he rasped thickly.

His words literally made her sag at the knees, and she was thankful she was propped up against the wall. When he reached for the button to her tiny denim shorts she let the last of her resistance fall away.

She was naked within seconds.

For the sake of equality, she reached for his clothes, her eager hands sending more than one button flying off his shirt as she dragged it down his tightly muscled biceps.

Their fever continued to grow, until at last he surged inside her, his grunt of pure male satisfaction melding with her cries, her body opening up to his complete possession.

Another thing she'd discovered about her husband was his seemingly endless stamina. Repeatedly he sent her to the edge, only to withdraw, letting her hunger build and build, before cupping her breast, squeezing her nipples between thumb and forefinger and growling in her ear, 'Come for me, Angel.'

As if responding to a Pavlovian trigger, her climax hit her with full force, bliss washing over her until she was gladly drowning, her body screaming with pleasure as her husband possessed her.

He barely gave her time to catch her breath before he was spinning her around, pushing her chest into the wall and thrusting inside her from behind.

'Sweet heaven, I can't get enough of you,' he growled.

Those echoes of bewilderment in his voice had grown increasingly stronger in the past few days—just as hers had built since that night in Paris. Eva knew they were teetering on a dangerous edge. Or perhaps she had already tipped over. She'd refused to listen to the alarm bells growing steadily louder, and she knew her heart was involved somewhere in there.

How could it not be?

From their first meeting she'd known those hours spent with Ekow were too good to be true. The distance she'd created this time, with their agreement, was the buffer she'd needed not to lose her heart.

But then Paris had happened.

Just like their nights together the first time, she'd let herself be drawn deeper, allowed the fantasy to linger a little longer. Soon the chemistry would fade, she knew. Ekow would go back to his life, and she would be left with the same craving she'd endured before the reality of her pregnancy had shifted her focus.

Only this time it would be ten times worse. Because she'd have to endure living under the same roof as Ekow, being confronted with the very thing she couldn't have.

'Angel?'

Her heart lurched, that name on his lips creating its own set of problems. 'Eva,' she insisted.

Against her neck, she felt him smile. 'Angel,' he repeated.

She shook her head, blind panic swirling inside her. 'I have to go.'

'Where's the fire?' he murmured as his lips continued to wreak havoc on her senses.

'Give us time… I'm sure we'll find it.'

When she glanced over her shoulder she saw a faint

frown had creased his eyebrows. Knowing he was about to demand an explanation, she hurriedly tugged on her shorts and top.

'Um…thank you for agreeing to the Aburi thing. And for the job offer.'

He continued to watch her with those piercing eyes as he pulled his own clothes back on.

Afraid he would see through her to the heart of her fears, she hurried out of the door.

In the shower, minutes later, she braced her hands on the wall, a multitude of questions cascading over her. When she couldn't find an answer to a single one, Eva knew that what awaited her was a devastation the likes of which she'd never known.

She objected to him calling her Angel only because each time he murmured the name in bed, or tossed it out casually across the breakfast table, she feared she was falling in love with her husband.

Perhaps she already had.

Her husband who had only married her to secure his son.

He'd given her no promises other than sex. He'd delivered on that promise in the last two weeks. *And nothing else.*

Her heart squeezed as she faced the hard truth. She'd been too hasty in getting excited about Ekow wanting to live with her and Leo. Surely he would grow bored with living in Aburi after a few months. And then what?

They were married now. There was no escaping him. But she could keep him at arm's length. Take steps to avoid further devastation before it completely annihilated her.

She turned off the shower, the decision weighing

heavily on her heart. By the time she was dressed again she'd accepted it was the only solution.

She had to resist her husband at all costs—before she fell deeper into the hell that was loving a man who didn't love her back.

Something had changed.

One minute his wife had been crying out in ecstasy in his arms, and the next she'd been freezing him out.

At least she hadn't given him the clichéd excuse of having a headache when he'd tried to pull her into his arms in bed last night. She'd simply speared him with those chocolate-brown eyes and shaken her head. 'Not tonight.'

Call him arrogant, but Ekow knew it wasn't because she'd suddenly developed an aversion to him. He'd seen the desire lurking in the backs of her eyes, read the familiar signs of arousal in her body.

But he'd accepted her rejection, nonetheless.

Then he'd lain there for the rest of the night with panic growing in his gut.

Something was wrong. Something had happened after that searing sex against the wall. Had he been too rough on her? Too demanding?

He frowned.

The woman he'd come to know in the last six weeks wouldn't have hesitated to put him straight had he stepped out of line. She'd been right there for an intensely satisfying ride. Right until the very end, when she hadn't been able to get away fast enough.

His gaze flicked to the bedroom door on his private jet, as it had done repeatedly since they'd taken off from Cape Verde three hours ago. He wanted to storm in, demand to know what was going on. But she had the buffer of their son between them, and the last thing he wanted was to disturb Leo's sleep.

There would be time enough, he reassured himself, settling back to work he could barely concentrate on. The past few weeks had shown him he'd been right to take this path. They were compatible in so many areas of their lives.

So what if love wasn't involved?

That dip in his chest occurred again, mocking the statement, urging him to re-examine his belief.

He shook his head, denying it. Sex was all it was.

Sex and all the other things that made him think about her when she wasn't in his presence...crave her even more when she was.

His frown intensified.

That description skated far too close to what Fiifi had said he'd felt with Amelie's sister, Esi. What Atu had described to him one drunken night when he'd been parted from his wife—a rare occurrence that had seen his brother track Ekow down to help alleviate the purportedly agonising feeling of missing his wife.

Ekow had scoffed then. He wasn't scoffing now.

What did that mean?

He jerked to his feet, striding in the opposite direction to the cockpit.

Five minutes later he sensed he was irritating his pilots with his relentless questions and retreated back to his work.

He *wasn't* developing feelings for his wife. He sure as hell wouldn't let himself stray to either extreme side of emotional spectrum that had plagued his father and his brother—rejection or obsession.

He simply wouldn't allow it.

He was simply experiencing the adverse effects of being far too long absent from his desk. A return home to normality would put everything back in its proper place.

CHAPTER ELEVEN

THE DAYS FOLLOWING their return home cemented Eva's conviction that moving to Aburi was her only option.

Her mother-in-law's cool reception of her had turn into frost.

It would all have been so much of a cliché had she not been living it.

Even more alarmingly, Ekow hadn't put up a fight when she'd chosen to stay in her own suite on the night of their return and the following nights.

Yes, she'd intended to keep him at arm's length. But was it already over?

Her heart squeezed, adamantly opposed to her rare reluctance to fight this particular battle. What was the point of fighting when she knew she'd lose?

A week after their return, she entered the living room after putting Leo to bed for his afternoon nap, to find her mother-in-law waiting there for her.

'Ekow tells me you're moving to the Aburi villa.'

Her heart clenched. 'Yes,' she replied.

Naana Quayson's eyes narrowed. 'Why?'

'I don't think that's any of your business,' she retorted briskly.

Her mother-in-law rose from where she had been seated, the Queen of the residence, wherever she invited herself. 'He's perfectly happy here. Why would you want to change that?'

'He may be—but I'm not.'

'Marriage is not about just doing what you want, young lady. Marriage is about accommodating your husband's every need.'

Alarm, heartache and fear bubbled up inside her and she slowly balled her hands and shoved them into the pockets of her sundress. 'And I thought marriage was about compromising, doing everything in your power to make *each other* happy—not just one party.'

The older woman's face tightened. 'Be careful—'

'Of what?' She tipped up her chin in defiance. 'I seem to be getting warnings every time I turn around. I'm not forcing your son to do anything he doesn't want,' she said, but then felt a tug deep inside.

Had she pushed Ekow? Was that the reason for his withdrawal?

She shook her head.

It didn't matter now. She was leaving before she did the unthinkable and blurted out her love to a man who only wanted sex and a mother for his child.

'I'm sorry our decision is not to your liking. You're more than welcome to visit any time you want—with advance warning, of course.'

She turned on her heel, ignoring her mother-in-law's shocked face as she walked out. They hadn't discussed a date for their move to the mountains, but as she hurried down the hall Eva decided this was as good a day as any.

Locating the housekeeper, she instructed her to start packing her belongings.

Three hours later she was in another of those SUVs that seemed to miraculously cut through the heaviest of Accra traffic.

She was minutes away from the villa when her phone rang. Tentatively she answered.

'I'm informed that you're packed and heading for the mountains. Care to tell me what the hurry is?' Ekow said, frost edging his voice.

'Care to tell me why it has to be later rather than now?'

He remained silent for several seconds. 'My mother is on her way to see me, I understand. Is there anything I need to know before she arrives?'

Eva let out a harsh laugh, startling her son. She reached out to soothe him as she answered. 'She's your mother. The privilege of dealing with her is yours.'

She hung up before he could reply, feeling a slash of shame for using the unpleasantness between his mother and her as a tool to put further distance between them.

But hadn't that distance been there all along? Temporarily cloaked with sex?

She shook her head in a wild bid to end her chaotic thoughts.

The truth was she was in love with Ekow.

The only thing that would stop the wrenching inside her chest was knowing it was reciprocated.

And it wasn't.

So she concentrated on Leo, shamelessly basking in his joyous existence. And as she let herself into the villa, as the memories of her last time there washed over her, she kept him close, pouring all the love she couldn't give his father into him.

In the following two weeks Ekow visited just once, to ensure that Leo was safely installed in his new home and healthy and happy.

And Eva resigned herself to the endless days of devastation that lay ahead of her.

* * *

He wasn't a coward.

But the evidence was irrefutable. Possibly marriage-ending.

Somewhere in his eagerness to secure his son and Evangeline to him, he'd abandoned the sixth sense he'd felt in Cape Town that Eva was hiding something from him.

Now, with his every breath he wanted to shoot the messenger—even if that messenger was his mother.

The chequebook stub from his parents' private account had been the fatal clue. His father hadn't bothered to hide his actions.

A cheque for one million dollars, written out to Evangeline Annan.

Ekow didn't doubt his father had been testing the woman who'd claimed to be carrying his child.

She'd failed. And she'd kept it from him.

He'd mentioned his father's habit of paying off 'nuisances' in Paris *and she'd said nothing*.

He wasn't a coward.

But he couldn't bring himself to storm up the mountain to confront her.

What could she say to redeem herself? Or, worse, what if she told him it had all been about money? Hadn't he bankrolled her brother to get him out of trouble and set him up on a path to success?

Sure, she'd left the Quayson Hills mansion, but with her new surname she could command the prestige and the power she'd claimed she didn't want anywhere in the world.

He hadn't demanded she sign a prenup. He wasn't perturbed at the thought that she might demand whatever she wanted from him. He had powerful lawyers to deal with that if need be.

But it was undeniable that the longer she stayed in the marriage the more clout she would have against him later. Perhaps she'd even attempt to take Leo from him.

He surged to his feet, striding to the window and back again as he'd done repeatedly since his mother had dropped the bombshell.

Had he read Eva so spectacularly wrong? The beautiful, laughing, vibrant woman who'd burrowed deep under his skin? Had those excuses he'd given himself about it all being about sex been so much hot air?

He wasn't a coward.

When he strode to his desk one last time and snatched up the phone to call his pilot, he told himself it was because of his son.

But even before he boarded the helicopter to fly to the mountains he knew it was because of *her*.

It had always been fundamentally because of her.

He'd gone to South Africa hoping he might see her again. He'd grabbed the chance to secure her to him in marriage the moment he'd discovered the existence of his son.

It had always been about her.

The used chequebook burned his chest as he alighted from the chopper twenty minutes later.

She was waiting on the terrace, a vision in white, her beauty so devastatingly breathtaking he felt something shake inside him, triggering a searing hunger which confirmed once and for all that what he felt for this woman was more, *much more* than he'd ever anticipated.

She raised her chin as he drew closer, those arms

wrapped around herself in fierce defence. 'I didn't know you were coming.'

'Do I need an invitation to visit my own home?'

Her lips pressed together, and it was all he could do not to catch her in his arms and kiss those lips, demand a warmer welcome than the frostiness she was throwing at him.

'Where is Leo?'

Her eyes flashed at him. 'He's perfectly fine. He's had his evening bath and is playing in his crib. The nanny is with him.'

He nodded. 'We need to talk.'

Her eyes widened, and for a moment he fooled himself into thinking he saw alarm in there. The same alarm snaking through him at the thought of losing her, at the thought that there might not be a surmountable explanation for what she'd done. Because he wasn't sure he could stomach a wife who loved his money but rejected him… He'd had enough rejection to last him a lifetime.

When she nodded, he struck off down the hallway towards his study. He entered, held the door open for her, then shut it behind them before leaning against it, feeling a searing reluctance to start.

He was far too aware that this conversation might well fracture the fragile foundation of what he'd started building weeks ago.

Yes, at the time he'd loftily imagined sex was the answer to everything.

Her absence had shown him differently.

Shown him enough to stir up a grudging respect for what his brother had felt for Esi, because the no-holds-barred expression he'd in seen Fiifi's eyes the night he had passed away had held what Ekow was feeling now. Fiifi had even been hinting of giving up his place in the Quayson family and company for the woman he loved—a decision that would've caused much more chaos than had already existed in their families. *And he'd have done it because of love.*

'Are you going to talk, or just stand there brooding at me?'

He almost smiled because, even cornered, she was fearless. He straightened, reaching into his pocket as he strolled towards her. 'Would you care to explain this to me?'

Her gaze darted down, then flew back to his in wary alarm. His heart fell.

'Where…? How…?'

'I warned you not to keep secrets from me. I told you I would find out everything you were hiding from me eventually.'

Predictably, her chin notched higher, and she blasted him with a look so fierce he would've burned to a crisp were he a lesser man.

'What else can it be? This was your father's way of buying me off.'

'Which you accepted, of course?'

The faintest tremble seized her lips, before she clamped them together and steadied herself a moment. 'Of course. How else was I to remind myself of the sort of people I was dealing with?'

He frowned. 'What's that supposed to mean?'

'Your father offered me a million dollars to stay away from you—to pretend the child I was carrying wasn't yours. Everyone around you throws around money like confetti…like it'll solve every problem you have. I kept the cheque as a reminder on how *not* to bring up my son. *Your* son.'

An earthquake shook through him. 'You kept the cheque?'

'Did your spies not tell you what happened to the money?' she scoffed.

His jaw gritted. 'The cheque came from my parents' private account. I don't have access to the records. My mother showed this to me."

"Right. I guess now I know why she doesn't like me. And she thinks what, that I must've had some shady characters squirrel it away for when I need it?'

His eyes narrowed. 'It isn't beyond the realm of possibility, especially if you say you kept it.' The burning sensation was too much to contain. 'Dammit, Eva, I thought you were different. That you were above this!' He waved the infernal chequebook between them. 'I opened up to you in Paris. You know how I felt about what my father did. How I felt about his rejection.'

Her eyes were suspiciously wet, but they blazed all the same. 'Well, I thought *you* were different, too. But what have you given me to make me think so, hmm? Fabulous sex? I reckon if I search hard enough I'll find someone else who will—'

A growl left his throat as he felt fear and jealousy congeal inside him. 'You'll have to rid yourself of me first. And I promise you that won't happen without a fight.'

Desolation settled on her face. 'Why? Why would you fight for me when you don't feel anything for me? You're ready to label me a gold-digger when all I was trying to do was stop you from feeling more pain.'

'What?'

'Yes, I could've told you about the cheque earlier. Maybe even in Cape Town. But when you told me your father had a habit of doing that, I thought you'd be devastated to know he'd done it with Leo, too. I just wanted to save you from being hurt further. But no. Everything I do has to contain an ulterior motive, doesn't it?'

The indictment shook through him, intensifying the quaking beneath his feet.

Dear God, he was going about this all wrong.

'You wanted to save me from pain?'

His voice wasn't as steady as he wished, and a terrible fear was taking hold inside him that the loss he'd feared was within seconds of being realised.

She rubbed a shaky hand over her temple. 'I find myself wanting nothing but the best for you. I risked rejection to tell you that you had a son because I believed you should know. I married you because—' She stopped, shook her head. 'More fool me, right?'

He jerked forward. 'No! Don't say that. You're not a fool. God, *I'm* the fool. I've missed what's important, Eva. What's right in front of me.'

'You don't really believe that. Staying away has been easy for you,' she accused, and he caught the trembling in her voice. 'You want to know what happened to the cheque? Stay here.'

Pivoting, she strode to the door and threw it open.

And, of course, because he couldn't stay there, couldn't let her out of his sight because he'd missed her so damn much, he trailed after her, his gaze eating her up as she launched herself up the stairs.

His heart leapt when she strode into his bedroom. Despite telling himself not to read anything into it, he couldn't shake the thought that she'd been sleeping in his bed, perhaps even clutching his pillows at night the way he'd been clinging to hers, pathetically attempting to catch her scent and alleviate the desperate loneliness and hunger inside.

He forced himself to concentrate as she strode out of the dressing room, a piece of paper clutched in her fingers.

'Here's your precious cheque. Take it and get out. I never want to see you again.'

His vision clouded. He fought through it. Took the cheque and tossed it over his shoulder, uncaring where it landed.

'No. Please. Let me make things right. I should've… I suspected you were keeping something from me, and normally I would have been relentless in finding out. But the feeling went away. Because here…' he pressed a hand to his heart '…where it counted, I knew whatever you'd done wasn't something I needed to fear. Forgive me. I… I don't want to lose you.'

'Lose what, exactly? What do you have besides our son?' The agony in her voice tore at her. 'If I packed my bags right now and left, giving you equal rights to our son, would you even miss me?'

'Yes! It would kill me. Tell me what I need to do to make things right,' he pleaded again, holding his hands out to her. 'Please, Eva,' he croaked desperately.

He wasn't a coward. So he laid it all on the line. 'I can't breathe without you. Can't sleep…can't think.'

She laughed. 'And yet you made it so effortlessly easy for us to be apart.'

He frowned. 'Because I thought that was what you wanted.'

Her eyes widened. 'We agreed we would live here. Together.'

'And then you turned away from me. That day we made love in the study something happened, didn't it? Did I do something?'

She whirled away from him, but not before he spotted the sheen of tears in her eyes.

She shook her head. 'It doesn't matter now, does it? I'm a gold-digger who pocketed one million dollars—the mother of your child who you probably imagine is just hanging around for more.'

He stepped around her so he could see her face once again. Now the haze had cleared, he could see how devastatingly wrong he'd been. He just hoped it wasn't too late. 'You rejected a mega mansion in favour of a mountain villa out of sight of the great and the good of Accra. You could've deposited that cheque in your bank account within days of receiving it, but you didn't.'

'That proves nothing.'

He shrugged. 'It proves that what is happening between us isn't about money. I discovered this cheque existed a week ago, but I didn't do anything about it because, again, it wasn't about money. It was about fear. I didn't want to risk you telling me that you wanted to live here on your own. Without me. I couldn't stand the thought of that. I can't stand the thought of being away from you, Eva.'

Slowly she turned around. 'Why? You still haven't given me a good enough reason, Ekow.'

Emotion shook through him and for the first time he welcomed it—good or ill. Because he would walk through flames for this woman. Rip his own heart out if it would make hers beat. For him. For Leo. *For them.*

'Because I love you. That evening at the bar you took my breath away, and you have been taking my breath away ever since.'

He saw her tremble and could barely stop himself from reaching out for her. He stood still, watching her eyes widen with disbelief. And hope?

'You love me?'

'So much. I fooled myself into thinking it was just sex. I invited you to stay with me that weekend because I thought I could work you out of my system. When I woke to find you gone I felt empty. More empty than I had a right to feel after just two nights. But you've never strayed from my mind. The moment I discovered my hacker was in Cape Town I had to be on the plane. Even when I didn't know how to find you, just to be in the same city as you stopped the aching inside. And when you opened the door to me there was no way I could let you get away. I love our son, and I thank the heavens every day for his existence—and not just because he brought me back to you. But you have to know that I was always going to find you, Eva. It was only a matter of time. You're the missing piece I've been looking for all my life. I can live with you not loving me as much as I love you right now, but I can't live with the thought of a permanent separation. Please, Angel.'

He watched another tremor go through her, and inhaled sharply at the look that came over her face.

'That's what did it,' she murmured softly.

'What?'

'You calling me Angel that day in the study in Cape Verde.'

He shook his head. 'But I'd called you that many times before.'

Her arms dropped from their protective stance, and he felt the faintest shred of hope.

'I know. But something about the way you said my name that day scared me a little bit, because I knew I was falling in love with you.'

Hope surged wilder, filling his heart. 'You were?'

'Oh, yes. I've been falling in love with you since that

first moment, Ekow. It was why I fled from you before dawn that weekend. I wanted to stay—so badly. But I didn't know how without risking my heart.'

His own heart turned over. With joy. With awe. With gratitude for the magnitude of the gift she was granting him.

'You will never have to risk your heart with me, my darling. I will treasure it. You have my promise. Always.'

Tears filled her eyes and he finally breached the gap between them, cupping her cheeks before swiping his thumbs beneath her eyelids, wiping away the drops that fell.

'I love you, Eva. I want you to remain my wife, please. Tell me what I need to do and I'll do it.'

'You're already doing it. You're right here, with me, giving me everything I've been yearning for. Please stay?'

'Of course I will. A thousand horses couldn't drag me away.' He paused then, grimacing before looking over his shoulder. 'Please forgive me for that,' he pleaded, nudging his chin at the cheque on the floor.

Without answering, she walked past him and picked up the cheque. Returning to him, she ripped it into a hundred pieces. 'I should've done this a long time ago.'

'Maybe. But maybe it was what we needed to push us into fighting for what our hearts desired.'

She swept back into his arms and he caught her up, his heart filling with true, pure love as he lowered his head and kissed her.

Several minutes later he lifted his head and grimaced at the tears filling her eyes all over again. 'I'd like my feisty wife back, please.'

She laughed. 'Don't worry, she's right here. But

you need to give her a while to bask in this wonderful moment.'

He brushed his lips over hers again, sliding his arms around her waist to pull her even closer. 'Take all the time you need, my love. I'll be right here loving you, loving our son, through thick and thin.'

'Do you think your mother's going to start liking me now?' she joked.

His lips twisted. 'Don't worry. I will leave her in no doubt that any further interference from her will not be welcomed. She will be told, firmly, that you are the woman for me. From now till eternity.'

Her lips trembled, and he kissed her once more simply because he couldn't not.

'I love you, Ekow,' she whispered.

That seismic phenomenon occurred again, and he knew he would experience the magnificent feeling repeatedly with this woman in his life.

'I'll do everything in my power to keep earning that love, Eva.'

'Angel,' she corrected softly. 'I like being your angel.'

'You are. For always,' he promised.

'Always…'

EPILOGUE

One year later

EVANGELINE STOOD NEAR the terrace railing outside her bedroom suite at their Aburi home, making sure to keep out of sight of the trio on the rolling lawn below.

Moments like these were little treasures she furiously hoarded and took out at the end of the day, when she counted her blessings.

Her lips curved in a smile, her heart leaping with joy as an almost-toddler's exuberant shrieks pierced the air, followed by unfettered giggles. Unable to help herself, she peered over the railing to see her son galloping across the grass on chubby legs, hotly pursued by two tall forms as he fled the threat of tickles.

'Are you shamelessly spying again?'

Her husband's low, deep and intensely sexy voice was followed a second later by his strong arms sliding over her hips to band low over her belly.

'I can't help it. It's all so…precious.'

Her voice thickened with emotion and Ekow's arms tightened reflexively for a moment before his head dropped into the crook of her neck.

'Hmm… And you do know Jonah will immediately stop if he catches you watching?' he murmured.

'It's uncool to let me see how much he adores his nephew, apparently,' Eva grumbled good-naturedly, relaxing back into her husband's chest.

In some ways the changes in her brother were nothing short of remarkable. His sullen moods had disappeared, and his enthusiasm for his studies and his outlook on the future were almost effervescent.

The last of Eva's misgivings had been laid to rest when she'd spoken to him in those weeks after he'd started at his new school, and they'd completely disappeared by his first visit home to Aburi. Watching him top his class consistently in the past year had been proud moments for them both.

But he was still a teenager, with strong views on how he needed to act—especially around his sister and the brother-in-law she knew he secretly hero-worshipped.

Hence her covert spying activities on the terrace.

'He's not the only reason you're in stealth mode, though, is it?' Ekow rasped.

Her heart somersaulted, and her throat clogged all over again as her gaze drifted to the other figure trailing behind her brother and son.

The man's all-grey hair and slightly stooped form spoke of his advancing age. When he turned slightly and she caught the indulgent smile he beamed at her son love surged through her anew.

She didn't need to hear his voice to recall the strong Dutch accent. To see shades of him in Leo's face when he laughed.

Henry Rodling.

Her father.

Eva experienced another *pinch me* moment when, sensing her scrutiny, the older man looked up and raised a hand in greeting. Her own hand shook a little as she

returned his wave, an overwhelming sense of blessing and gratitude washing over her at the knowledge
that while she'd been wishing for him, her father had
been yearning for the child her mother had forbidden
him from ever knowing after their brief relationship
had soured.

Like Leo's had been for her, Eva's conception had
come as a surprise to her mother. And to Henry when
she'd eventually informed him. Her father, a low-income earning businessman living in Amsterdam, already supporting a large family consisting of his elderly
parents and three siblings, hadn't been in any position
to support a newborn—a fact which her mother hadn't
taken very well and so had forbidden him from ever
contacting her again.

Henry had felt as if he'd had no choice but to accept
her mother's wishes to stay away. But he had always
meant to find Eva, and had been attempting to do exactly that for the last five years with no success—until
Ekow's stellar investigators had located him. Knowing
that had helped her heal the wounds of abandonment a
little quicker, leaving only budding love and the hope
of a deeper relationship in future.

'I don't know how I'm ever going to thank you for
finding him,' she said to the man who was the reason
for her unfettered happiness, her reason for breathing.
The love of her heart, mind and soul.

'You don't ever need to thank me for making your
happiness my priority. Finding your father is a fraction of what I should give you in return for the treasure
you've given me in yourself, our son and Jonah. In the
love I never believed I'd find that you bless me with
every second of every day.'

Unable to speak for a moment, she reached up and

laid her hand against his cheek, glorying in the taut, warm skin beneath her touch and the kiss he trailed over her palm a moment later.

'But seeing as you're in a generous mood...' he drawled teasingly.

She started to laugh, then slapped her hand over her mouth before the sound travelled to the beloved family she was spying on. But, twisting her head, she let her eyes ask the question, making Ekow's own eyes gleam with sensual intent as he bent his lips to her ear once more.

'I'm very keen to make a withdrawal from the brownie points department...'

Pivoting in his arms, she slid hers around his neck. 'I really didn't think it through before granting you unlimited access, did I?'

He shrugged. 'With the type of interest rates you earn with that deal, you'll never experience a negative return.'

His shameless wink drew more laughter. 'Can we dispense with the banking lingo now, please?'

He sighed. 'And here I was on a roll. But if you're keen to move on, let me interest you in something else...'

Before she could ask what, his head descended, its destination her very willing mouth.

He drew her further back from the railing and into the bedroom as his tongue tangled with hers in a possessiveness that set her heart racing.

Within moments she was breathless, her body primed for the kind of exhilarating excitement only he could deliver. Still, she attempted to halt the dizzying rollercoaster by catching his hand when he tried to release the tie of the silk robe she'd thrown on after her mid-morning swim.

'Wait…we can't… Atu and his family will be here soon.'

'We can,' he countered heatedly against her throat. 'He texted to say they're running late. I texted back and told them to take their time. That means I have you to myself for a whole hour…at least. And I don't intend to waste another second. Now, tell me to show you how much I love you,' he growled thickly.

That tiny obstacle dispensed with, Evangeline sighed and melted into her husband's arms. 'Show me, my love. Please…'

Two hours later…

'Oh, my God, this *red red* is the best I've had in ages!'

Eva smiled indulgently at her sister-in-law, watching as she forked another bite of the addictive, sublime fried ripe plantain and black-eyed beans and smoked tuna stew into her mouth. 'You gush over every dish my housekeeper makes. I'm almost terrified you'll poach her one of these days.'

'Confession: she tried just before you arrived. Sadly for her, Ekow is Gettie's favourite,' Atu relayed in a deep, rumbling voice.

Amelie gasped, turning to glare at her husband. 'I can't believe you just snitched on me!'

'You'll forgive me, because you have a chef I know you'll kill to keep. And he makes amazing *red red*, too.'

Amelie sighed. 'Yes, Mensah is awesome, isn't he? I'll just have to convince Gettie to give me her recipe. It'll go down a treat at the resorts…'

The conversation moved from Gettie the housekeeper's magical talents to the Quayson Hotel Group and its upcoming exciting projects and Ekow tuned out, rising to fetch another bottle of wine from the cooler.

Bottle in hand, he paused, his gaze wandering over the family seated at the large banquet table they'd set out in the shaded terrace overlooking the gardens and swimming pool.

At one end of the table Henry was situated between Ekow's mother and Amelie's mother, and Ekow winced in sympathy at the not-so-low-key grilling the old man was undergoing.

Then his gaze drifted to Jonah.

The boy didn't know it, but Ekow intended to spend the rest of his life in gratitude that the prodigious teenager had hacked his bank and led him back to Evangeline.

A few other cousins, uncles and aunts had also invited themselves along for the Sunday meal, but he didn't mind. The more the merrier.

Then, as if drawn by sweet, compulsive magic, his gaze finally arrived on his wife.

Against the white halter neck dress her golden-brown skin glowed.

Yesu, she couldn't look more beautiful if she tried. He didn't bother to calm his leaping heart. It existed solely for the woman who'd made him whole.

'Counting your blessings again?' Atu murmured from beside him, a trace of good-natured mockery in his voice.

Ekow dragged his gaze from Eva and met his older brother's. '*Our* blessings. Don't think I haven't seen that misty-eyed look you keep sliding to your own wife.'

His brother sighed. 'What can I say? I'm a hopeless sap when it comes to her.'

Ekow sniggered. 'Don't let the board members hear you say that.'

Atu shrugged. 'I'm still ruthless when I need to be, but Amelie has taught me that there's nothing wrong with opening your heart to the ones you love. The rewards are immeasurable.'

Ekow nodded, agreeing wholeheartedly. 'I wish Fiifi was here,' he confessed gruffly, after a moment of silence.

Atu swallowed, his eyes shadowing for a moment before he clasped Ekow's shoulder. 'He is, brother. And so is Esi. They wouldn't miss this for the world.'

A curious lump lodged in Ekow's throat as his gaze locked with Eva's. She hadn't heard their conversation, but the look in her eyes said that she knew his thoughts and his heart. That, like him, she was grateful they'd found the precious miracles they'd searched for their entire lives.

The missing pieces of their souls and a home founded in love.

* * * * *

RECLAIMING HIS RUINED PRINCESS

CAITLIN CREWS

MILLS & BOON

To Jackie, the patron saint of a certain kind of scene.
Consider this an homage.

CHAPTER ONE

AMALIA MONTAIGNE ONLY realized how much she loved her life when it was taken from her.

She supposed there was a lesson in that, little as she enjoyed learning it. She had been raised as the Crown Princess of Ile d'Montagne, a tiny island country in the Mediterranean, with her every move pored over and scrutinized by friend, foe, and paparazzo alike as she learned how to walk in the footsteps of her formidable mother, Queen Esme.

Her main concern throughout her life so far had been the attempt to carve out a space in that fishbowl existence to be *her*. Not the Princess, bound by duty and convention. Not the public figure, owned by anyone and everyone who looked at her. A woman with a real life of her own, however hidden away from view.

But *real life* wasn't easy to come by for a woman in her position. Her single experience with it had ended badly. And as far as she could tell, her mother had abdicated her own real life, such as it was, in service to the crown long ago. All Esme spoke of was her throne, her legacy—not as a mother, but as a queen. If she had private thoughts about anything else, she usually kept them to herself.

Amalia had been determined that *she* would not do

the same. *She* would live up to the expectations placed upon her *as well* as create a place, somewhere in the swirl of duty and honor and obligation, where she could be entirely herself.

She hadn't been succeeding in that objective, but now it no longer mattered. The truth had come out, shocking the world and turning her life—real or otherwise—inside out. Princess Amalia of Ile d'Montagne had been switched at birth. Or, rather, three days after her birth, to be precise—with the daughter of a farmer from Kansas. And the girl who had been raised on that farm, the true blue-blooded heir to the throne Amalia had been training to take over her whole life, had gone and married the head of the rebel faction that had been tormenting the Ile d'Montagne royal family for centuries.

Meaning that not only was Amalia not the Crown Princess, the future of her country and her mother's successor, but the true Princess had returned to claim what was hers with the Montaigne family's sworn enemy—a neat little bloodless, slow-moving coup that would change the little island country forever. It already had.

Not that it mattered to the actual, real life Amalia who was still a headline at the moment. She assumed she wouldn't remain one for long. The fascination with her would pass quickly, she had no doubt, and all that attention would shine on someone else, instead. Probably actual princesses, including the one she had been unwittingly masquerading as all this time. Amalia's name would be trotted out every decade or so to kick up the scandal anew and sell papers, that was all. Especially once Delaney Clark, the true heir, became Queen. And the more obscure Amalia became in the meantime, the more the greedy tabloid consumers would love it.

Can you believe *that* she *was almost a queen?* they

would tut on their morning commutes, or standing in their checkout lines.

The upshot of all this was, for the first time in her life, Amalia could have been anyone at all.

What she felt most keenly, however, was that she was a newly twenty-five-year-old woman who had no idea what to do now that her destiny wasn't mapped out before her, step by step, until death. Now she had nothing to do, for the rest of her life, but be *herself.*

Whoever *that* was.

"Are you ready?"

Amalia smiled at the aide who stood with her in the small hall off the entryway to the palace that the royals used for more private entrances and exits. Paparazzi were expressly forbidden. Both Amalia and the impassive woman beside her were pretending. The aide that it was perfectly normal that the once future Queen was slipping away so ignominiously tonight, with no fanfare and no farewell committee. And Amalia that she was serene about her change in circumstances.

But then, she had no choice but to act serene. It was that or go kicking and screaming, and what would that get her except pity and scorn? Amalia thought she could handle almost anything but pity. She felt lucky, truly, that her mother hadn't offered her any—as she rather thought it might have killed her.

And she was immune to scorn. A life in the gimlet crosshairs of the public eye had made certain of that. But who knew—maybe a heaping of scorn as a private citizen would do her in too.

Best to put a good face on it, she'd decided.

Amalia was doing her best not to think about it all too closely while she was still here. Still in the palace where she'd been raised. The palace she considered her home. Instead, she concentrated on waiting gracefully, because she knew her behavior in these final moments would be dissected and retold, no matter how professional the aide was acting while still in her presence. She folded her hands before her and pressed her tongue to the roof of her mouth to keep her jaw from tightening around her polite smile. She'd used to think of such tricks, used while forever being in public and watched so closely, as making her mother proud.

Though she had to remind herself—yet again—that Queen Esme of Ile d'Montagne was not her mother. No matter the twenty-five years they'd spent together. It was all washed away as if it had never been. A few blood tests were all it had taken to erase their relationship.

It was stunning, really. Breathtaking. Impossible to fully comprehend.

Because at first, the Queen had been defiant. *Shall the throne of Ile d'Montagne be toppled by these grubby upstarts?* Esme had thundered. *Not on my watch.*

If it's a scam, it's masterfully done, Amalia had hedged. *Truly.*

She could remember that moment so clearly. She and the Queen had been taking their morning meal together, as was their long-held custom. They sat together in the Queen's private salon so that Esme could rage about her enemies—almost always the rebels in the mountains, but sometimes the insufficiently reverent European press—and lecture Amalia on topics ranging from Esme's strategy for finding suitable marital prospects for her only child to comprehensive critiques of Amalia's public appearances.

Amalia had learned long ago when to treat these lectures as conversations and when it was better to sit there quietly and listen to Her Majesty deliver a monologue.

'Masterful' is not a word I would apply to the likes of Cayetano Arcieri and his obsessive fever dreams of someday taking my throne, Esme had sniffed that day.

But Cayetano, rebel warlord and thorn in the side of the royal family, had played his hand well. He had married his not-quite-a-farm-girl in secret in his stronghold in the hills. Only once the true Princess had been bound to him forever had he given that fateful interview to a friendly British paper that had been hanging on his every word since university. And in that one, specifically devastating interview, he had dropped—almost as an afterthought—the news that the woman he'd married was, believe it or not, the long-lost daughter of none other than Esme herself.

Esme, who had suffered the sort of pregnancy complications that had necessitated she fly to America, to the only hospital in the world that specialized in that exact syndrome, the better to protect her heir. And because of this, was there at the same time as the other mother—*my real mother,* as Amalia tried to remember to think of her. The nurse who was suspected of having made the mistake and given the real Princess to the wrong mother couldn't defend herself, having died years ago.

Two babies switched in a hospital, Cayetano had said in that interview, with the quiet charm that was a hallmark of his media appearances. In person, Amalia had always found him more off-putting. Much colder and more…warlord-like, which made sense. *Who could imagine such a thing?*

And since Cayetano had spent the better part of his life building up his media relationships in all the right places, making himself the protagonist in the story of Ile d'Montagne instead of the villain Amalia had always believed him to be, his accusation caught fire.

I can't imagine what he's playing at, Esme had seethed the morning after that appearance, slapping her hand on the stack of newspapers before her. *An accusation like this is so easily disproven. What a fool.*

That night Amalia had stood in her rooms, finally alone after a long day forever surrounded by courtiers and aides, fussy ministers and the occasional subject. And she'd thought it sounded lovely to grow up on a farm in a place like Kansas, which she knew chiefly from *The Wizard of Oz*—a film she'd watched at least a hundred times on her own. She'd gazed out of her window, looking out over the sparkle of Ile d'Montagne's royal city with its blue roofs and white buildings by day and gleaming lights by night. And she'd thought, *Wouldn't that be funny, if Mother was the wicked witch after all?*

But she hadn't really thought it could be true. How could she be someone else when there had been battalions of tutors and aides and ministers to make sure she was exactly who she was supposed to be? Always and forever?

Then had come the blood tests—then several repeats of the same blood tests. There had been endless speculation in the press. Amalia had tracked the inconceivable truth through Esme's growing distance. The Queen became too busy in her mornings to break her fast with Amalia. And then, after a while, Amalia had been sent out on a deeply uncomfortable meeting with Delaney Clark, Kansas farm girl turned future queen, to show that the crown accepted reality. And did so with grace and self-deprecating humor, Amalia's specialty.

Amalia had seen Esme alone only once more. The Queen had called her into her formal rooms, where heads of state came to pay their respects and underlings were dressed down for all manner of slights and missteps. Amalia was treated as a member of the latter group and made to stand some distance away. As if they had never been anything to each other.

And the woman she still thought of as her mother had not made the slightest attempt to reach out to her or comfort her in any way. Then again, Esme had not been big on reaching out or offering comfort the past twenty-five years, either. That was not one of her strengths.

You will always be cared for, Esme had told her, stiffly. Maybe that was her version of comfort. *You need have no worries in this life, Amalia. I will guarantee you that. I am deeply cognizant that nothing that has occurred is any way your fault.*

That would be a long game indeed, Amalia had said quietly, her gaze respectfully lowered in the presence of the sovereign, no matter the churn of emotions within her. *Especially if I started said game at three days old.*

Once, Esme would have pounced on a comment like that. That day, when Amalia snuck a look, the Queen's eyes had been cool and she had only smiled that tight smile she mainly used to stop courtiers at ten paces.

It wasn't that Amalia had expected a hug. Esme was not tactile, as she liked to tell dignitaries from effusive countries when they attempted to get too close. Amalia knew better than to hope that might change…but she did anyway.

Nonetheless, Esme had told her frostily, clearly not in any kind of *hugging* mood, *it has been decided that it would be best if you took a step back.*

Of course, Amalia had said, because what else could she say? *I serve at your pleasure. Or do not.*

It was the last time she saw her mother. Because Her Majesty the Queen was always too busy for anyone not deemed essential. And wasn't that a bit of a shock? To discover that after all these years, all she'd given—and more, had given up—she could be hustled away and thrust out of sight so easily?

It wasn't only Esme. When Amalia was feeling charitable, she rather thought that the Queen didn't know quite what to do. What was there to say or do, after all? The reality of those blood tests had to have shaken the proud Queen to the core. Because Esme hadn't noticed that her baby had been replaced. She hadn't noticed that she was raising an imposter. Surely that said more about her than the daughter she was now distancing herself from.

The newspapers certainly thought so.

Amalia went from having two extra mobiles manned entirely by staff—so they could handle the endless influx of calls—to barely needing her own, private mobile at all. Since no one called her. Because no one knew who *she* was. They only knew she wasn't the Princess.

She was used to having parades of men circling around her, jockeying for position because one of them would be chosen—eventually—by the Queen to become the Crown Princess's husband. And would therefore one day be King. Amalia had always found these men irritating, so it was a surprise to discover that she noticed their absence so keenly. Even though Esme had finally narrowed it down to two acceptable suitors in the past year. And while Amalia had really never cared much for those two, both of vague royal blood in one way or another, they had been so solicitous. So generous and thoughtful.

Yet neither one of them had bothered to reach out once the news broke.

It was clarifying.

And perhaps this was a gift, she tried to tell herself as she waited, stuck in limbo until the Queen decided it was time for her to exit quietly. One she would look back on someday with gratitude. Because she had always wondered how much she truly mattered to anyone, taken apart from her bloodline. And now she knew.

Like it or not, she knew.

"Just a few more moments," the aide beside her said now, her fingers on the earpiece she wore. "Then you can be on your way at last."

As if Amalia was setting off on a pleasant holiday. And not being shuffled out the back door in disgrace. That it was none of her own making was neither here nor there.

The palace had planned her exit carefully. The Queen was welcoming Cayetano Arcieri and the new Crown Princess of Ile d'Montagne—his wife, Delaney—with a grand reception now that the two of them had returned to the island after an extended honeymoon. It was the first time an Arcieri had set foot in the ancient palace since the famous feud between his people and Esme's had begun.

No one would pay the slightest attention to Amalia as she faded off into the night. Which was precisely how everyone wanted it.

Amalia was to simply…disappear.

Her Majesty has seen fit to provide you with a most generous situation, her mother's most fearsome minister had told her. He was the one who did the talking, though he'd come into the meeting with a phalanx of palace attorneys to back him up. As if, Amalia had thought, she had been attempting blackmail instead of just...reeling. *The expectation is that you will handle these unforeseen developments with grace.*

My mistake, Amalia had murmured. *I thought the Queen was taking care of me because I have trained my whole life to be a person that I am not. I didn't realize it was a bribe for future good behavior.*

The minister had gazed at her with a certain amount of steely forbearance. *Her Majesty is cognizant of the fact that you might have a number of feelings concerning recent events, Amalia. So do we all.*

Amalia had spent the previous few weeks overseeing the packing up of her things. Which had involved a great deal of thinking about what was actually hers. Because so much of what she considered her own was in fact her mother's. Or the palace's. Or, more properly, belonged to the people of Ile d'Montagne.

People who were not hers.

She tried, very hard, to be fair.

But she also had to bear in mind that she was not moving house, as regular people did all the time, or so she was informed. She was taking what was reasonably hers—and what the Queen, through surrogates, wished to bestow upon her—and shipping it off to a storage facility outside Paris. Because *outside Paris* seemed as good a center of operation as any, because wasn't that what people needed? A home base of some kind? Having never thought beyond Ile d'Montagne, she hardly knew how she was expected to figure out where she ought to live.

Much less how.

Amalia felt certain that she could learn how to do

all those things that were considered normal. Like pay bills. Or…have bills in the first place. And a place for those bills to find her. One thing she had gathered from watching television over the years was that most people were preoccupied with bills. She imagined that she would be too, then.

But she was going to have to figure that out on her own. It was that or have someone teach her, and how could she tell if such a person would have her best interests at heart? She was a suddenly ex-princess with zero street smarts. No one had to tell her that she was ripe for the picking. She imagined there would be all sorts of people lining up to take advantage of her.

Anyway, she found herself less than sympathetic to the notion that the palace staff might have found any of this as difficult as she did.

If I'm understanding you correctly, she'd said dryly, *the concern is that I will fling myself into the sort of antics that I was always expressly forbidden. And in so doing, bring shame upon the House of Montaigne. The only concern of the Queen, as I think we both know.*

That you are not the blood relation of Her Majesty may be well known, the minister had replied. *But I think you know that doesn't matter. You will be scrutinized for the rest of your life. You will be compared to the new Crown Princess. And then, one day, to the new Queen. That may not be fair, but it is reality. There is no virtue in pretending otherwise.*

Wonderful, Amalia had said, with her practiced smile. *At least all these years of training won't be entirely useless. I'll be able to act as appropriately as ever, forever in service to this country which, it turns out, has nothing to do with me at all.*

The minister had surprised her then. He had looked

at her with what she very much thought was genuine compassion.

You have always impressed us all with your grace and character, he said quietly, knocking her smile off her face. *I have every reason to believe that no matter what you do, you'll never change such an essential part of who you are. If I were you, my lady, I would look at this not as a punishment at all. But as freedom.*

That was the word that echoed inside of Amalia tonight. *Freedom.*

Whatever that was.

She nodded at the aide beside her when she was finally given the go-ahead. She smiled the way she always had, serene and easy—a smile she'd practiced for years in the mirror. Then she walked out of the palace and climbed into the waiting car that would sneak her away from everything she knew, down to the docks where a boat waited to take her off of this island and far from Ile d'Montagne. Likely forever.

Amalia couldn't think of a single reason she would ever return. Not when she could only be a sad shadow lurking about the island she had loved, a reminder of so many years of unwitting deception.

But that was all right, she told herself stoutly as she boarded the small yacht that waited for her, far from the royal docks and staffed with the most trustworthy of the Queen's men. Because she was setting sail for *freedom*.

Not that she'd had a great lot of experience with the concept. *Freedom,* her tutors had told her sternly when she was growing up and needed to be more like a queen and less like the bored child she was, *is for others, far less privileged. It is not for you.*

And aside from one golden summer, that had been true.

Amalia didn't stand out on the yacht's deck. She

didn't want to be seen—it would disappoint the Queen and she still cared about that. More than she should. And besides, she didn't want to look back at the island. At the life that had never been hers.

At everything she was losing tonight.

She curled herself up in her stateroom and settled in for the night. Because there, in private, she could indulge herself the way she'd tried so hard not to all these years.

Oh, how she'd tried—and failed.

But tonight there was no one to scold her. No one to remind her of her duty—because she had no more duties. She had the Queen's request to avoid scandals that might reflect badly on Ile d'Montagne, though she was no longer required to honor the Queen's request. She wasn't the Queen's subject. Oh, and she had freedom, whatever that was.

What was that song that suggested it was nothing more than nothing left to lose?

So—for once without the usual guilt—Amalia thought about that summer.

And better yet, him.

Joaquin Vargas.

Even his name made her shiver, across space and time.

She had been twenty and sheltered. Guarded her whole life.

The Crown Princess was always supervised. Never left to her own devices, for fear that any decisions she might make on her own would lead to embarrassment for the palace.

Far too many European royals work out their adolescent drama on the front pages of the tabloids, the palace media manager had told her severely when she was still a girl. *Her Majesty the Queen does not intend for Ile d'Montagne to join these ranks. Do you understand, Your Highness?*

Amalia had understood. How could she not? The contours of the glass bowl she lived in had always been clear to her. And it only took a few unflattering turns on a tabloid cover to understand that there was very little benefit to smashing her face up against that glass. It could leave unsightly marks. It might even cause a commotion. But what it didn't do, ever, was change her circumstances.

The summer of her twentieth year, the rebel faction in the mountains had been louder than usual. And the warlord, Cayetano, was entirely too good at whipping up international sympathy for his cause. It had driven her mother mad.

Maybe that was why it was agreed that the Crown Princess could have a holiday, instead of following her mother around from engagement to engagement as usual.

As long as I do not hear of any yachting about the Côte d'Azur, the Queen had said gravely. *Like some common Hollywood tart.*

And looking back now, Amalia couldn't remember how she'd found Cap Morat. Once thought to have been connected to the Spanish mainland, the island had been a fortress for many ages, then had fallen into disrepair. It had been bought at some point before that summer and transformed into a luxurious hotel experience boasting the height of privacy there in the Balearic Sea.

The palace had rented the whole of the island for the summer, so that her guards could keep themselves to the perimeter—meaning mostly on boats and the odd beach—and Amalia could wander about and pretend she was normal.

As the only guest on the island, she'd made friends with the staff immediately.

But it had been the owner who had captivated her.

Joaquin Vargas. She couldn't remember, now, what she had known about him at the time and what she had learned in the five years since. That he was self-made. That he had come from nothing and only by sheer force of will had he made himself into a myth. A legend. Capable of transforming a rock in the sea and a crumbling old fortress into an opulent retreat for the wealthiest and most famous—and that was but one of the tricks he'd used to cement his position as the darling of the financial world.

Though what she remembered chiefly about him from that very first meeting was the green of his eyes, gleaming with intent and too much fire from a face that seemed cut from stone. And polished to shine.

It was not too sentimental to admit that she had fallen at first sight. It was a fact. One moment she had been who she always was, eating a breakfast out on the patio overlooking the sea. She had been enjoying the touch of the breeze against her face. The song of birds in the trees. She had been trying her best to fully inhabit this freedom she knew would not come again. Amalia had been thinking about her mother's insistence in choosing a husband for her only daughter. And how little interest she had in any of the candidates her mother favored.

Same old, same old.

Then she looked up and Joaquin was there. And nothing that summer was ever the same.

She was never the same.

She shivered again, now, in her comfortable berth in

the boat that took her across the water, heading for that same rock set down in the sea. She drew her soft cashmere wrap tighter around her and tried to take the sort of deep, cleansing breaths that one of the personal trainers she'd worked with over the years always claimed held near-magical properties.

Amalia could admit, privately, here in the privacy of her own head, that there was a part of her that wished that she was running to Joaquin after all this time.

When she knew that if she tried such a thing, he would likely set her on fire as soon as look at her.

That was the choice she'd made. The only choice she could have made, she told herself now as she had then, but that didn't make it any less harsh. Because summer had ended. There had been no possibility Queen Esme would ever accept a self-made Spanish businessman as an appropriate mate for her only heir. No possible way that she would even entertain the conversation.

Amalia had gotten one perfect summer. And that was more than she had ever dared hope she would get. But she and Joaquin had loved each other so well, so deeply, and with such earth-shattering intensity that she had known there was no way he would ever accept the idea that she would *choose* to leave him.

Because she wouldn't—if she had been anyone else. If she had been anything but a crown princess, heiress to a throne and subject to her mother's decrees in all things. She had ended it abruptly, and unkindly. And had fled back to her duties, her responsibilities, her plotted-out life and suitors she hadn't wanted even before she'd met a man like Joaquin.

She sighed as she closed her eyes and remembered. And she could pretend, as she lay in her bunk, that she was returning to those syrupy gold, endlessly sweet days five years ago. She'd pretended exactly that on more occasions than she could count. Joaquin was her secret and she'd kept him tucked away inside her like a precious jewel too dear to expose to the light.

When instead, the truth was that she had rented herself a little villa on the island under a false name, because that might keep the tabloids at bay. And she expected no syrupy sweetness, because she did not expect that she would run into the island's owner at all. Not after the way she'd left him five years ago. This time she merely intended to hide away from the other guests and the whole of the world, until she felt strong enough to face what was happening to her. And perhaps, somewhere in there, able to come up with some kind of plan for the future.

Because hers was no longer plotted out for her, step by step, until her death. Maybe, at some point, she would find such a freedom exhilarating. Until then, she intended to stare at the sea, hide herself away from the intrusion of press and idle speculation, and heal in the only place she'd ever let herself imagine...*what if?*

She might even consider seeking out her real mother at some point, she supposed. A woman with a farm in Kansas, which was as fanciful a location as another planet to Amalia. But first, she supposed, she needed to let go of the mother she'd had in Queen Esme all these years. Distant, difficult. Often demanding. Always formidable.

But still, her mother for a quarter of a century. And Amalia loved her, for all the good it had done her. She still felt too brittle and taken aback to process any of that, but she knew it was coming. Along with a healthy dollop of grief, she imagined.

Because it was one thing to complain about your

life. And another thing to have it snatched away from you with no possibility of ever getting it back. At some point, she expected she would need to mourn what was lost.

But not tonight.

Tonight, she drifted off into sleep and only woke when the boat docked at Cap Morat.

She made herself presentable and then climbed up onto the deck, sighing a bit as the island gleamed there before her, golden and glorious, just as she remembered it. The old fortress rose imposingly, burnished to shine. It was a small island, easily walkable, and she already itched to wander its paths and sit on its rocky cliffs to look out to the endless, beckoning sea. Surely she would find herself here. Surely she would encounter the woman she was meant to be as she left the Princess behind.

A shiver of foreboding worked its way down her neck. Amalia told herself it was the breeze.

It seemed particularly quiet, she thought as she stepped off the boat. She smiled vaguely around her, looking for the hotel staff that she remembered being effortlessly ubiquitous when she'd been here before. Perhaps it was different when there were other guests about.

She walked along the stone path that led from the docks straight toward the grand front entrance of the hotel. Each step was like walking through her memories. She longed to kick off her shoes and let the warm stones kiss her bare feet. She couldn't wait to take down her hair from the ruthless chignon she always wore as Princess Amalia. She wanted to swim in the sea and dry herself on sunbaked stones, letting the salt stay on her skin. She wanted to bask in the sunshine, letting it tan her skin without a single thought as to how that might make her look in endless rounds of photos that her mother had always decreed ought to look timeless.

This place was timeless, so she need not be.

That was what she was thinking when she walked in the grand, open arches that served as doors, yet were always open to the elements, inviting her in. Inside, the hotel lobby was empty. She stopped then, confused. For surely there ought to be staff here, if not down at the docks. There ought to be *someone*. She turned in a circle, taking in the ornate architecture, the high ceilings. The fireplace that seemed to hover in one wall. The fountain that splashed in the center. The sense that somehow, though she stood in an ancient fortress that had been built to keep everything out, it somehow invited in the sun, the sky, the sea.

It was only when she turned the second time that she saw a shadow detach itself from the far wall.

At first she thought she was imagining it. That she was too dizzy from the sunlight that poured down from the ramparts, memory like magic, making her silly.

But he kept coming.

And her body knew him before his name fully formed in her head.

She felt that betraying flush, rolling over her, making her pink…everywhere. Between her legs, there was a kind of keening, an ache so intense it seemed to bloom and spread. It rolled to her breasts, making them feel heavy and tender. It wrapped itself around her, pulling taught.

Still he kept coming.

And she knew this dream. She'd had this dream a thousand times and always woke up, gasping for air and shattered to discover herself alone. Always alone.

She knew this dream, but today it was different.

Because as he drew closer, she drank him in, greedily. It was still him. Still the Joaquin she remembered. It was gloriously, unquestionably him. He was still breathtakingly tall. His body was a symphony of lean muscle, from mouthwateringly wide shoulders to narrow, athletic hips. He wore an obviously, exquisitely bespoke dark suit, yet still managed to look vaguely disreputable. It was the dark hair. Or his jaw, like that of a boxer. It was the way he carried himself, perhaps, as if he was ready and able to handle whatever might come his way. Whether it be bandits or wayward princesses.

She had pored over pictures of him in these last five years. She knew the possessive way his hands splayed on the back of any woman he squired about to this event or that. And could remember how it had felt when it was her. She'd wept over such things in the privacy of her bed in the palace. She'd studied his face in every picture, looking for hints of the Joaquin she'd known. How she'd loved the sculpted lines of him, the angelic cheekbones, the sensual mouth.

But what she had never seen before was the way those green eyes of his blazed a cold fire as he approached.

In her dreams, he never looked at her like that. In her dreams, there was only ever heat. Love. Understanding. *Forgiveness.*

He kept coming until he was standing before her, and even then, he did not pause. He reached out and he was touching her again, taking her chin with his fingers and holding her still.

She could feel the bluntness of his grip. The strength in him as he moved her head one way, then another, as if inspecting her. As if she was a horse he was considering purchasing.

Amalia found herself trembling as if she was exactly that much of a thoroughbred, when she knew—when the entire world knew, for that matter—that she was no such thing.

"Not so high and mighty today, are you, Princess?" came his voice. Just as she remembered it. Rough. Low and intent. She'd heard that voice in her ears as he'd danced with her in empty ballrooms here. As he'd moved above her in the bed they'd shared that summer, taking her innocence and giving her so much more in return. Lust. Longing. Love. A whole life. "Did I not tell you what would happen if you dared return?"

"Joaquin…" she whispered.

"Allow me to remind you." His green eyes glittered with a fury she had seen once before, on the day she'd left him. And this was no homecoming. Not the kind she'd imagined all these years. This was vengeance. "You destroyed me, Amalia. I promised you that if you ever gave me the opportunity, I would return the favor. And here you are. Humbled. Cast out. Slinking back to my island, tail between your legs, as I told you that you would."

"Joaquin," she tried again, though it seemed that every time she spoke his name, his grip on her tightened. Just enough to remind her. Of how commanding he was. How…bossy. How he had set the terms of their trysts and then executed them and she had melted, and burned, and happily done as he pleased.

Because it was what she pleased, too.

She pulled in a breath and fought for calm. And she wasn't sure she managed to get there—but the fact that she was capable of trying showed her how different

things were now. How different *she* was from the girl
she'd been five years ago, because she'd spent that time
training to become a queen. And queens could not allow
anything to rattle them.

Not even Joaquin Vargas.

Amalia found herself grateful for all those years
she'd thought wasted.

Because it was the best—and only—defense she
could imagine having against this man.

"I had no expectation that you would be here," she
managed to say now, because a defense might protect
her but it also seemed critical that he know she hadn't
come here for…this. "I intended to be a guest at this
hotel, nothing more. Just a regular guest. Not like last
time."

"I see the years have made you a liar." He tipped
her chin up, his eyes a green fire. And yet even if he
hated her now, her body couldn't tell the difference.
This fire was still a fire, and she burned for him the
way she always had. His mouth was merciless as he
brought it closer to hers and that, too, burned bright
and hot inside her. "But don't worry, Amalia. I will
deal with that, too."

And then he slammed his mouth to hers.

CHAPTER TWO

EVERYTHING INSIDE HIM was a roar.

Of triumph. Of need.

And that longing he had not been able to stamp out, despite five years of trying. Five years of assuring himself that there was nothing this woman had that he would ever need again, not after she'd left him the way she did.

She had eviscerated him and Joaquin Vargas never forgot a single slight.

He had made a career out of answering each and every one. All those who had laughed at his ambitions, growing up in and out of homelessness in Bilbao. Fighting for every scrap, until it occurred to him that what he was good at was the fight. Therefore, why not make the scraps bigger?

That was how he'd battled his way to his first million. Then several more millions. He'd been reveling in that accomplishment the summer Princess Amalia had wrecked him, then compounded that sin by leveling him when she'd left.

Unforgivable offenses, by his reckoning.

Joaquin had responded the only way he could. The only way he knew how. By exponentially increasing his wealth and holdings so that now he was one of the billionaires the world took such pleasure in claiming to hate.

He imagined he would hate billionaires too, were he still where he'd begun.

But in a world where there were billionaires, Joaquin had long ago decided that he might as well be one of them. Better that than be stepped on by someone else's billionaire shoe.

But all of the focus and fury that had defined his life and meteoric rise seemed to melt away from him, because he was kissing Amalia again. And she tasted the way he remembered. Like the lie he had believed for too long, that summer. Her soft, yielding lips. The little noise she made in the back of her throat.

Her taste, God help him. Innocent, when he knew better. Unutterably sweet, still.

At least this time around he was prepared.

Joaquin set her away from him, but didn't let go of her slender shoulders. More slender than he recalled, he thought, and then hated himself for entertaining even an inkling of the concern for her she certainly didn't deserve.

"I warned you not to come back here," he reminded her, his voice raw. "Or perhaps you were not paying such close attention, so focused were you on making certain I knew my place."

Her singular blue eyes were too wide, too bright. But it was her lips that caught his attention. He had always loved them swollen from his. Today was no exception.

It was harder than it should have been to focus on anything but that as his hunger for her stormed through him as if she had never betrayed him.

But he forced himself to study her closely, because he needed to remember that the woman he looked at now—elegant from head to toe, draped in cashmere with her hair swept up into something fussy—this was the real woman. This was the Princess she had chosen over him. The girl who'd captured his heart, dancing in the moonlight with her black hair all around her like a careless shadow—she was the dream. She was someone he'd made up.

And he'd paid the price for his fancy.

"You don't understand," Amalia said quietly.

And as he watched, she blinked a few times, then straightened. Her expression shifted from the hints he'd seen of her emotions to something opaque. She looked distant, yet calm, and he felt that as a kind of loss, because she was different now. She'd been so vibrant, so bright, that summer. The very hint of his disapproval had made her tear up.

Joaquin found he didn't like the evidence that she had grown while they'd been apart. For in his head, whenever he thought of her—and he did not like to admit how often he thought of her—she was still his unexpected princess. Perhaps crueler than he'd given her credit for at first, but then, she had been so young. Perhaps no longer the innocent he'd discovered here, sitting in the sun, eating fruits far less sweet than she was.

Beneath his hands he could feel the difference in her. She was bonier, perhaps. But stronger.

"What choice did I have?" she asked him now, sounding very nearly *serene*. An insult, surely, when he was nothing like serene himself. Not in her presence. That she could act otherwise was like salt against an open wound. "There was no possibility, ever, that the Crown Princess of Ile d'Montagne could have a relationship with you outside the privacy of this island. You must know this."

"Is this where you tell me that you had no say in this matter? I think we know that is another lie. We all have choices, Amalia. It is only that some of them are more pleasant than others."

He couldn't say he liked the way she smiled at him then. It was too sad, for one thing. An almost wry curve of her lips. While in her endless blue gaze, there was a certain knowledge he did not care to identify.

When, he could not help but recall, the girl he'd known would have looked at him with eyes filled with tears had he even obliquely suggested she might have lied to him. That was how open she'd been. A bright summer's day, always.

He still missed the heat of her, the endless clear blue. And he hated her for that weakness.

"You sound like a man who has had the pleasure of his own choices for most of his life." She inclined her head slightly, far too regal for his taste. "That sounds lovely. You will have to tell me what such a life entails. Because I find myself standing at a precipice. Behind me, a life of duty and obligation but it turns out, none of it was mine. And before me…who knows?"

None of this was going the way Joaquin had planned. The kiss burned within him, still. As if she was the one who had dealt him a punishing kiss, so that his lips might bear the stamp of it. When he had meant to do that to her.

He let go of her and stepped back, glad that the grand fountain in the center of the lobby made the tumbling noise it did, for he felt certain if it did not, he would have heard his own heart. It was beating far too fast.

When Joaquin had often thought that his enemies were right and he had nothing but ice water where his veins should have been.

"You seem to be missing your staff," she said when the silence grew between them. Proving that she no longer rushed to fill a moment of quiet, the way she had five years ago. Heedless, reckless. So eager to please. He had been braced for haughtiness from the woman who had a palace to make demands on her behalf. For peremptory orders and the kind of entitlement he had always despised. Instead, she had all but wriggled like a puppy every time he'd glanced in her direction. "If you've fallen on hard times, that was definitely not mentioned when I booked. Or in any of the papers that regularly print various takes on your hagiography."

"I cleared the island," he said gruffly.

As if it was an admission.

She smiled again, but it was as distant as the first. "Not on my account, I hope. I'm perfectly capable of hiding in plain sight. It's why I booked a villa, so that all anyone looking will see is a woman in a large sun hat, minding her own business."

"I'm afraid there are no villas available," he told her smoothly, getting his feet under him again here. At last. "If you wish to stay here, there will be…alternate arrangements."

He was glad he'd let go of her. Glad that he'd put some space between them. Because he had acted on instinct the moment she'd walked into the lobby. There had been no thought. No plan. He'd simply walked to her, put his hands on her, tasted her.

He did not regret those things. But now, reason could return. He could take this moment to truly get the measure of her.

Joaquin moved away from her, over toward the rough-hewn wall so he could lean against it and observe her as he'd intended to do from the start.

She was still, bar none, the most beautiful creature he had ever beheld. He'd seen pictures of the real Princess they'd unearthed off in America somewhere. She was lovely, certainly. Yet to his mind, that Amalia shined far brighter than her dusty old mausoleum of an assumed family had always been clear. He'd seen pictures of Queen Esme, with her regal nose and aristocratic chin, which was to say, not much of one. Amalia was etched in delicate lines, each and every one of them highlighting her perfection.

He told himself he was lucky this time. Because this time, he knew that each and every hint of delicacy in her bearing was a lie.

"Alternate arrangements?" she echoed lightly, looking almost entertained. "How mysterious."

As if this was some clever little cocktail party in that palace of hers, where every moment of biting repartee was rewarded.

When the truth was, she was in his house.

And they would play by his rules.

"I was in love with you," he told her, with bite. And all the fury of the past five years. He saw her jolt at that and thought, *Good.* But it was not nearly enough. "I would have given you the sun and the moon and the stars, had you but asked. Instead, you pulled rank. And now when I think of those things I felt, the memory leaves me nothing but shame."

He watched her face closely, looking for... But he wasn't sure what he wanted to find. Uneasiness? Regret?

He was Joaquin Vargas. He needed none of those things.

She gazed back at him, her expression carefully unreadable. Or almost unreadable. Her eyes were a shade too blue. And then, because he saw the darkness there, he looked for other tells. She was too still, perhaps. Her hands were in fists even though she tucked them against her body as she folded her arms over that wrap she wore, as if hugging it closer.

The years had taught her to hide. But he had always been talented at finding his way to hidden things. She stood little chance.

"I owe you an apology," she said, but her voice was so…unruffled. Joaquin wanted to rage. He wanted to shout. He wanted to…mess her up, or better still, watch her as she messed herself up. Instead, all she did was gaze at him, as if this was nothing but a tranquil bit of talk. Not important. Not the least bit meaningful. "I was young and overwhelmed. I have regretted being cruel to you every day since."

And Joaquin could not understand why this woman got to him the way she did. Still.

It was an outrage.

He had not anticipated the *pull* of her, like some kind of magnet. It had never crossed his mind that it would be like this. Not now, on the other side of half a decade.

When he would have said he'd long since moved on. He rarely came to Cap Morat. He had so many other properties, scattered across the globe, that one little island off the coast of Spain—the country that had tried to kill him and had nearly succeeded, way back when he was a kid—hardly appealed. He'd been so busy these intervening years, acquiring things. More money. More businesses. More line items for his various portfolios.

His own fortress that could never be torn down.

Still, when her reservation had come in, flagged because she had both security concerns and was clearly using a false name, he'd figured out who she was. And he'd known instantly how he would handle it.

Even though all this time had passed. Even though, if asked, he would have said that what he remembered from that summer here was the slight she'd administered. The cruelty she'd dealt him at the end, not because it had taken him out at the knees—though it had—but because he was not a man who took insults lying down. He had built an empire on that. For years he'd promised himself that should the opportunity arise, he would happily take revenge on this woman. The same way he made certain to take his pound of flesh from anyone who dared cross him.

It was part of what made him so formidable and so justly feared.

Her apology could not change that.

No matter how she tasted.

"I'm afraid I cannot accept your apology," he told her, thrusting his hands into the pockets of his trousers. The moment he did, he felt somehow more like himself. And less like that unhinged, lust-addled creature he became around her. Only her. He lounged there against the wall and regarded her coolly. "I do not believe you mean it."

"You are mistaken," Amalia said, but in that same way. As if nothing that happened here could possibly affect her, so offensively placid was she.

"I am very rarely mistaken." He bit off the words as if they were curses. "Though when it comes to you, I will confess, I am forever imagining you to be something other than what you are."

Her brows rose slightly. Only slightly. "Why am I certain that is not meant to be flattering?"

Joaquin could not remember her being quite so dry,

back then. But then, his memories were so physical. He remembered the cries she made when he thrust within her. How greedily she'd taken him. How wildly she'd come apart beneath his hands.

She'd been a princess then, but she had acted unlike any haughty noble he had ever encountered before. Maybe that was what struck him today. There was no hint of that heedless girl, reckless with wonder. There was only the Princess she'd become.

What a shame to have put in all that work and be cast out all the same, he thought.

Not with any sympathy.

"If all this is a precursor to you telling me that you will not permit me to stay at one of your properties, I understand," she told him, as if she was doing him a favor. "Though I'm not sure why you felt you needed to deliver that information with a kiss, instead of the customary email."

Neither was he, but he did not intend to share that with her.

"You can stay," Joaquin growled. "It is only that there are conditions."

Her blue eyes gleamed, as she drifted toward him, looking every inch the elegant blue blood she wasn't. Not really. That chignon, just so. The cashmere wrapped around her. The quietly elegant dress and understated heels he knew at a glance were Italian and likely made for her, personally.

"Let me guess, you intend to humble me in some way," she said, in that conversational manner she had, though her face gave nothing away.

He recognized it as a disarming tactic. Powerful women used it to charm and beguile—and he needed to remember that she had trained her whole life to be a queen. She knew all kinds of tricks. He forgot her power at his peril—and Joaquin had made a career out of knowing exactly who he was up against. It was only that he'd never wanted that to be different before.

Amalia was smiling again, that easy curve of her lips that did not match her steady blue gaze. "Your vast, incomparable male ego was bruised, and so you would take it out on me now. But you failed to consider a very important point, Joaquin."

"Unlikely."

Her smile deepened. "I have already been humbled. Everything I thought I was has been taken away from me. How do you think you can add to that?" She laughed, though it bore no resemblance to the laughter he recalled from their summer, all that sweet, spun gold. Cascading all over him like her hands on his skin or the brush of her hair over his body. "I've already been brought to my knees. Surely your little revenge fantasies are overkill to that."

"Not at all," he said softly. With intent. "My revenge fantasies are not metaphors, Princess. I want you on your actual knees."

She let out the sort of breath that might have been a gasp from a woman less in control of herself. In Amalia's case, her lips barely parted. It was hardly noticeable.

Unless, of course, a man happened to be paying as close attention as Joaquin was.

"You want me to kneel down in front of you? Right here?"

He really did. "For a start."

And as she stood there, staring back at him as if she was trying to size him up anew, Joaquin found that he was enjoying himself. The way he'd expected he would. Before that kiss he hadn't meant to indulge in.

Because whatever happened next, he'd already won. He had taken control of the situation. It was already a balm for the scars she'd left behind her.

Too much had been taken from him when he was a child. He'd vowed, as he grew, that no one would succeed in doing so again. Not when he was big enough. Not when he was strong enough. Not when he was rich enough.

And, because he was all three, he took such insults to heart. He kept the ledger, such as it was, and it felt fantastic to cross this one off his list.

Or maybe it was the way she was looking at him, as if she couldn't decide whether to flee or fling herself at him, that had him feeling that way. Either way, he liked it.

"I want to make sure that I'm understanding you," Amalia said in that same frosty way of hers.

He didn't like that she talked that way now, but he had every intention of messing that up, too. If she stayed. One thing he knew about Amalia was that she could not possibly remain frosty with him for long. Many things might have changed between them, but not that. He could feel that same chemistry the way he always did, lighting up the room they stood in. Sending off sparks that lodged themselves deep beneath his own skin.

Like it or not.

"You want there to be kneeling," she was saying, very slowly, as if encouraging him to hear what she was saying and correct himself. He did not, and her blue eyes narrowed slightly. "Because that will make you feel…better about yourself, somehow?"

"That very much depends on what you do when you're kneeling down there, Amalia," Joaquin murmured. "I feel certain you can figure something out."

"And what, pray tell, will I be getting out of this display?" she asked and laughed. Again, as if she thought this was a cocktail party. "I can understand what you might get out of it. I get the impression from all I've seen of you over the years that women do not habitually break up with you. If anything, they appear to trail about after you for years after your assignations, clinging to a pant leg if at all possible."

"I'm an excellent lover," Joaquin said. He lifted a shoulder. "But then, this you already know."

Her cheeks were pink, but she didn't shrink into herself. If anything, she stood taller. "Again, I understand the stick. What I'm not certain of here is the carrot. Is there one?"

"You tell me," he shot back, his tone almost lazy now. Because she wasn't running for the docks. She wasn't even walking away, cloaked in her rank and privilege, like the last time he'd seen her. He suspected that meant he'd won. "Everyone knows that your Queen did not boot you out the back door with nothing but the clothes on your back."

"You'd be surprised."

"Even if she did, there are any number of places you could have gone. I believe there are whole pockets of Europe that cater exclusively to deposed and discarded royalty. You came here. That sends a message, Amalia."

"I assumed your hotel would be filled with guests. And yes, I will admit it, I have a sentimental attachment to the only other period in my life when I was free to do as I pleased. It made sense to come here and book-end that." She matched his shrug with one of her own, looking cool and unruffled. It made his hands itch to dirty that up a bit. More than a bit. Because he did not care for how casually she said that when surely it was a huge admission. That she had relished her time here. That she was attached to the memory. When there was no part of any memory she could have of this island that did not involve him. "I'm sorry if you're making that more than it is."

"I'm not making it anything." Joaquin allowed himself a smile, and he doubted his was decorous. "I'm offering you a choice. You, who claim you never had a choice, can now exercise one. And so soon after leaving Ile d'Montagne. This is the gift I'm willing to give to you. Behold my graciousness."

"A gracious gift that requires kneeling," she said after a moment, but her cheeks seemed pinker. And there was that pulse in her neck, making a nuisance of itself. Telling him things her cool tone did not. Everything in him went tight and hot. "On what looks like a rather hard floor."

"Ah, Princess. If it wasn't a hard floor, what would you learn?"

Amalia laughed again. "I didn't realize that this was a learning opportunity. How silly of me. Because it does seem to be a bit more about humiliation, to the untutored eye."

"There are few things that teach a person more than humiliation," he replied, as if he was doing her a great kindness. And perhaps he was. "But all I have asked you to do is kneel. You are the one who finds that humiliating. Suggesting that what humiliates you is you, Amalia. Not me."

"Somehow," she said after a moment, pink roses on

her cheeks, but an assessing sort of look in her blue eyes, "I suspect that there's a bit more to it."

"You know me so well." Joaquin thought he saw her repress a little flinch at his sardonic tone. "It is simple enough. I will not take your deposit. I have no interest in being funded by that Queen of yours and her guilt money. If you'd like to stay here, Amalia, there was only one type of currency I will accept." He smiled even wider then, because here, in this moment, it felt better than he'd imagined. And he'd imagined it would feel spectacular. "Your body."

She stared at him for a moment, seemingly frozen solid save for a slight widening of her summer-blue eyes.

And he'd imagined this a thousand different ways. She would storm away in anger. She would slink away in shame. Either way, she would know the sting of being reduced to nothing more than a scratched itch. She, who had looked down her nose at him and told him he should have known better than to imagine the likes of him could ever mean anything to a future queen.

Better still, he would get to witness it.

But she didn't turn on one of her elegant heels and stalk toward the exit. Instead, her head canted slightly to one side. Her eyes narrowed, and if he wasn't mistaken, brightened.

"From princess to prostitute in one boat ride," she said softly. "That is quite a trajectory."

His pulse picked up at that, particularly in his sex, where it pounded like a drum. "Again, these are words you choose."

Surely she would gather herself up and walk away now. He couldn't wait.

But instead, while he gazed at her in expectation,

Amalia—until recently the Crown Princess of Ile d'Montagne—closed the distance between them. She swept the wrap she wore aside, dropped it between them, and while he watched, gracefully sank to her knees.

Again, everything in him…roared.

And this was far more intense than any piddling victory.

Joaquin felt stripped down, as if she'd cut straight through him when all she'd done was obey. The way she'd always done, that summer, because it had brought all of that wildfire pleasure to them both.

"Are you trying to call my bluff, Princess?" he managed to grit out, though he was having trouble focusing on anything but the need in him. Blistering hot, all-encompassing, and, if he wasn't careful, catastrophic.

"Not at all," she replied, looking up at him, a half smile on her perfect mouth and feminine mystery in her gaze. "I currently have the freedom to do anything I want. So why not do this?"

"This is what you want?" he challenged her, from between his teeth. "To debase yourself before me?"

"It's only debasement if I feel debased," she retorted, with a flash of something he could not read in her gaze.

Maybe he was too far gone to read it.

And then, as he stood there, every muscle in his body alight with the effort to keep himself in check, she leaned forward. She put her hands on his legs, then ran her palms up his thighs, and everything in him went from a roar to a howl.

Not just need, but a kind of bone-deep possessiveness he'd told himself, in these five years, he had only ever imagined.

She ran her hands up higher and tipped her head back as she found his belt.

And all he could see was that shining blue gaze and the way she pulled her bottom lip between her teeth. She worked the belt open, unzipped him, and then pulled him free.

Her hands around him like a celebration. A homecoming.

There was a breath. A moment. It was electric.

He still thought, *She will get up now. She will walk away. She will try to turn this to her advantage—*

But the advantage was all his, even if she thought she was taking control here.

Because Amalia, his princess, tipped herself forward, still holding his gaze, and sucked him in deep.

Just the way he'd taught her.

CHAPTER THREE

LATER, AMALIA WOULD likely think this through a bit more closely. Possibly beat herself up a little, because surely when a man vowed revenge, she shouldn't throw herself on her knees and take him in her mouth as if that was the only thing she'd ever wanted to do.

But she couldn't think about that now.

Because finally, *finally,* she had Joaquin in her mouth again, and she couldn't think of a single other thing she would rather do just now than this.

Having dreamed of this at a desperate fever pitch for five long years, she did not intend to waste a single second doing anything at all but enjoying it. Enjoying him.

The taste of him, salt and man, like the sea. The thick heat of him in her mouth and the thrill of it, to see if she could stretch her mouth that wide. To test herself against his relentless length. To feel that prickle of concern that this time, she might not be able to do it—until she did.

And she knew what he liked. He had taken such care to teach her, that long-ago summer. She dropped her hands from his thighs to clasp one wrist behind her back, circling it with her other hand, well aware of the picture that made for him. And she might have worried that even that had changed, but the moment she did it his hand came to her face. He smoothed his hand over her jaw, her temple, then over her hair. Then sank his fingers into her chignon, so that he was what held her head in place.

Right where he wanted her.

And already she trembled, because she knew what would come next. Memory seemed to twine with the moment, making her burn too hot, too quick. She concentrated on the stroke of her tongue against the warm steel of him and the way he began to move, thrusting gently in and out of her mouth.

And with every thrust, he increased his pace but held her still. He set the rhythm, surrounding her with all of that heat and control, so all she could do was deliver herself into his hands and surrender to the tumult of this. The rough, raw joy.

That was the paradox of Joaquin. That was what she'd battled with all these years, longing to go and find him again despite knowing she couldn't have him. There had been the freedom of this island that summer and she had loved not having to live with security forever within sight. But the real truth was that she'd never felt more free in all her life than when this man held her in his hands and brought them both all this pleasure, more intense and beautiful than anything else she had ever known.

Even though she had known that she could never love him in return, no matter how she felt inside. No matter what she wanted.

The only thing she had ever been allowed to love was Ile d'Montagne.

Amalia felt it again now, that tidal wave of sensation, so vivid and bright that it was hard not to squirm where she knelt. She pressed her thighs together, though it was never enough—not when he was near and she knew what he could make her feel. And even though this time, she had five years of longing built up inside her, she could only make the fire dance higher and higher—she couldn't find any relief.

Then again, maybe it wasn't relief she wanted. Not when everything inside her seemed wrapped tight around that same narrow column of flame and hunger, and only Joaquin could put it out.

Or make it burn on, brighter than before.

And still he thrust in with that ruthless command, then pulled out, filling her totally and then dragging himself back, so that both of them groaned.

She lost herself in the slickness, the taste, the glory of being his again. The heat of him inside her mouth and that hard hand on the side of her face, strong fingers in her hair. This was timeless, this taking. This giving. She could feel her body respond the way it always did, trembling closer and closer to that edge only he knew the contours of—

She heard him mutter one of his favorite curses. His grip tightened.

And it was only then, only when his thrusts grew jerkier, deeper, wilder and more exhilarating, that she unclasped her hands, and moved them to his hips.

So that when he spilled himself inside her mouth, Amalia shattered apart. Even as she drank him down.

Every last drop, then took her time licking him clean.

She remembered this view of him so well. She had seen it so many times. His head thrown back and abandoned, the green of his eyes hidden behind his sooty lashes.

That mouth of his that could bring so much pleasure, flattened out in sensual starkness as he took his own.

She had been the Crown Princess of Ile d'Montagne,

taught from a very young age of the power that was to be hers one day and what it meant. And yet she was not certain she had ever felt more powerful in her life than at moments like this, when she had rendered this powerful, masterful man as close to putty in her hands as he would ever be.

And now, she was nobody. Just a woman, kneeling before a man, while every nerve ending in her entire body shouted out its need and longing—because the pleasure she took in sending him spinning over the edge was only a pale echo of what it was like when he dedicated himself to the task of tearing her apart.

She remembered that all too well. Or maybe it was more accurate to say she longed for it.

And still, she felt newly dizzy with her own power here.

As nothing more than a woman who could do this to a man.

Joaquin opened his eyes and she was lost again in all that hard green. More brilliant than ever, just now, like an emerald fire bright enough to dim the Spanish sun. His gaze held hers for a long, fiery moment. Then his lashes, wasted on a man, concealed his gaze as he reached down and handled himself.

Amalia sat back on her heels, glad she'd thought to toss her wrap to the floor. It didn't disguise the stone beneath her or alter its hardness. It was like Joaquin, really. All that stone covered in softness, like a gift.

And surely there were things they should discuss. She could think of too many, right there off the top of her head, even while her heart clattered about inside her ribs and she was still battling the urge to squirm about and *do something* with all the sensation still storming about inside her.

Maybe this time, now that she was…herself, whoever that turned out to be, she could face him with honesty and openness. And somehow wash away the things she'd said to him five years ago so he would let her go.

She didn't have to put limits on how she enjoyed him now. She didn't have that ticking clock, counting down to the end of the summer and the resumption of her official duties. She could…simply sink into the marvel of the heat between them and see where it went. Wherever it went.

It felt like a new sort of freedom.

Assuming, of course, that this moment wasn't all he wanted from her.

Amalia rather thought he would dismiss her and prowl away, leaving her to marinate in how little he thought of her now. She braced herself for his cruelty—knowing full well she deserved it—

It was relief when instead of stepping away, putting distance between them, forcing some kind of conversation or merely offering a sneer as he left her, Joaquin only held out his hand.

Saying nothing, which, somehow, seemed louder to her than if he'd shouted.

And still, there were so many things she should have said then. It wasn't as if he'd been particularly kind to her today. Surely she should address that.

You were anything but kind to him, she reminded herself.

And anyway, she wasn't sure she had it in her to confront him. What did it matter what he said now or what she'd done back then? What mattered was this. This overbright, almost painfully intense connection between them. It had been there from the start. And right now, all she could seem to do was bask in the fact that the years hadn't dimmed it one bit.

So she took his hand.

More than that, she reveled in it as he tugged her up and onto her feet. The feel of his hand around hers once again. The grip she'd never expected to feel again. It was as if he was still holding her face, her head. Keeping her right where he wanted her.

Amalia was a little too invested in him wanting her. She accepted that. But then, the force of Joaquin's wanting could, she was reasonably certain, shift the stars in the sky to make the patterns he preferred. That was what it felt like.

As if, deep within her, she was only stars he rearranged at will.

For a moment they stood like that, their hands clasped together. He still leaned there against the stone wall, his green gaze as demanding on her as his hands had ever been.

She watched a new storm track across his face and held her breath, but then he moved. He tugged her along with him as he walked through the open stone lobby. He led her out the other side from the path she'd walked from the docks and her heart took up a kind of drumming, because she knew immediately where he was headed. Sure enough, they wound down away from the hotel, on a path marked PRIVATE. Down the stone stairs that ran along the cliffs and offered views of the sea, before winding around again to the owner's villa.

Though it was no airy villa built with tourists in mind. It had once been a dungeon, perched perilously close to the water line to give the prisoners something to think about.

Sometimes a man needs something to focus his at-

tention, Joaquin had said the first time he'd brought her here. Though he had been looking at her, not his handiwork. *And if it is not perilous, what is the point?*

Joaquin had transformed the old dungeon, a complicated maze of cells that let the sea in. She had laid with him here, on that altar of a bed in his stark bedroom, staring out at the sea that raged *just there.*

You could have had any one of the villas on the island be the owner's villa, surely, she had said. *Why would you choose a former jail?*

I am the orphan child of nobody at all, he had replied in a lazy voice that had not matched his words. *Nearly everyone I met predicted I would end up in prison. Or worse. The dungeon seems appropriate.*

Not that there was anything particularly dungeon-like about the home he'd built here, save its historic purpose. He had kept some of the details. The entrance, left intact, was a circular, medieval affair with bars everywhere. It had always made her laugh. Because it was all suitably intimidating, she'd thought then. It suited him, the fiercest man she'd ever met.

It still made her smile today, but that was more nostalgia than anything else. The door opened easily, a testament to the kind of money and attention he poured into every detail. No heaving and squeaking hinges here.

He ushered her inside, and everything was as she recalled it. Cool, stark whiteness everywhere, suggesting an airiness she felt certain none of the original inmates had ever felt. The stone was chilled and hinted of damp and was therefore strewn here and there with thick, richly colored rugs. There was art on the walls, most by identifiably famous artists. And instead of the thick stone walls that had once stood, every outward-facing wall was made of glass.

So that, depending on the tide, sometimes the ocean crashed right there against the walls.

It was still exhilarating, she found, as he led her from one room to the next as if he was on a mission. It was still overwhelming and exhilarating at once to be this close to the might and power of the water.

It still felt like him.

In his bedchamber, he whirled her into his arms, then backed her up. Amalia didn't know where they were headed and she didn't care. That, too, felt like a freedom. Because she was no longer the Crown Princess, duty-bound to put a stop to whatever happened with this man. She was no longer required to marry a man of Queen Esme's choosing, however little they might match her own inclinations.

She was no longer required to be anyone but herself, whoever that was.

Right now, all she knew was that she could not get enough of Joaquin Vargas. That he had tattooed himself upon her years ago, and if anything, the colors of that tattoo were brighter now than they had ever been then. As if time had made the mark upon her all the more vivid.

And only he could see it.

Her lips parted on a kind of gasp as her back came up against the thick stone wall at the far end of his bedchamber, hard and cold. Then he was leaning over her, a dangerous glint in his gaze and that storm in the green of his eyes.

And once more, Amalia thought that too many things were said between them, without a single word being passed.

This close, with the light from the sea and sky outside dancing over them, she found herself studying his face. The years had only made him more beautiful, more astonishingly, bracingly handsome. Maybe there were a few more crinkles beside his eyes. Maybe those sharp, sculpted lines of his face had been drawn by a heavier hand these days.

But he still made her heart flutter in her chest and her knees go soft, no matter what stone he felt she should kneel upon.

Going on instinct, and maybe not wanting to hear whatever he might say next—not now, not when she was lost on that wave of nostalgia and need—she reached up and began to trace the bold lines of his face with her own fingers. As if she intended to sculpt him herself. She followed the line of his brow, then the dark slash of his eyebrows. Down the length of that aquiline nose, then backtracking to trace this cheekbone, then that. Then she moved over that stark mouth of his, all the more sensual because she knew how he could use it.

Finally his jaw, so intensely masculine, making him look not so much like a fallen angel, but the sin that had preceded that fall.

He murmured something dark, too low to hear. And Amalia couldn't tell if she was sad she didn't quite grasp his words, or just as happy that they remained opaque. Either way, she didn't ask him to repeat himself.

And then, once more, he claimed her lips with his.

He kissed her, his hands propped on either side of her head. He held her there against that stone wall with only the seduction and steel of his mouth. His lips against hers, coaxing and castigating, as she lifted her hands to the marvel of his chest. He knew how to make her wild. He knew how to shift, at just the right moment, to make it all deeper. Hotter. To make her press up on her toes and push herself toward him, to tease and tempt her almost beyond reason.

Five years ago he had kissed her like this, on a moonless night beneath a whispering palm tree, and he had taught her what desire was.

And then he had taught her how to beg.

Then, better yet, what a thrill it was to get what she'd begged for.

When he finally pulled away now, Amalia was shaking. Joaquin's gaze was so dark it actually hurt. And she had no doubt at all that they were remembering that same kiss that had changed them both.

Forever, she thought.

There was torment in his gaze then, and she braced herself, because surely now would come a little bit of that cruelty he'd showed her earlier. Cruelty Amalia might know she deserved, but that wouldn't make it any easier to take.

But instead Joaquin only shook his head, then pushed himself away from the wall.

"Take off your clothes," he ordered her, his voice rough. "I wish to see all of you."

Amalia didn't hesitate. She instantly kicked off her shoes and reached for the side zipper on her dress.

And her own lack of hesitation answered a question for her that had lingered, all this time.

It had been the summer, she had told herself in the intervening years. It had been her youth and inexperience. He'd been the first man who had ever really caught Amalia's fancy, and that was why she'd been so abandoned with him. That was why she'd begged and knelt and obeyed his every sensual command.

She had tried her best to shame herself for her reactions to him as each year passed. She'd told herself that she had betrayed her people. That someday, Joaquin could easily hold that summer against her, telling all and sundry whatever salacious stories he liked that would undermine her position on the throne. How could she not have thought of that at the time? How could she have put herself in *so many* compromising positions?

Though she'd always known the answer to that. It was because she'd thought only of him. Only of Joaquin and the pleasure that burned on and on between them.

But even as Amalia had spent many a day lecturing herself for her trespasses, there had been a part of her that had never been cowed. The part of her that had always wanted him, no matter what happened. No matter what it cost her.

Even if it's the throne, that part had whispered sometimes, traitorously.

That was the part that haunted her dreams. Disturbing her sleep almost nightly, leaving her tossing and turning and waking up overheated, her whole body chaotic. She would lie there, panting, tears rolling down her cheeks, while too-hot images chased themselves in her head and weighed her down in her sheets.

She'd told herself for years that she'd built all this up in her head and made it—*him*—into something it wasn't. *Mountains out of molehills,* she would mutter at herself as she tried, and usually failed, to expel Joaquin from her head.

Especially when the Queen had talked strategic marriages.

But now she understood. It wasn't that Joaquin was himself the mountain, though he was certainly no molehill, either. It was this thing between them. This impossible compulsion. This *need.* That was the mountain, imposing and majestic and theirs to climb at will. She might have been young and foolish then, but she was neither of those things now. Twenty-five was only young when a person was aimless and didn't know what to do with their lives—not an ailment Amalia had suffered until recently.

And still, she wanted nothing at all but to please him.

Not because she felt subservient to him in any way.

But because the more she pleased him, the more it pleased her. Deep inside. Physically, yes, but it was so much more than merely physical.

And somehow, he had known that she needed that, right from the start. Amalia had spent her whole life in the service of others, but had never done so directly. On her knees. In his hands. She had never really understood true service until then. He'd given her that gift.

I don't know why I like to do these things, she'd whispered to him that summer. *I think it means something is broken in me.*

He'd been holding her in his lap in the chair across this very room, having picked up from where she'd knelt before him much as she'd done today. *You're looking at this the wrong way, I think,* he had said.

What other way could it possibly be looked at?

But even as she'd asked that question, she'd had her face cradled against his chest and could feel that same need coiling again inside her. Because it was never enough. No matter what they did, she wanted more. One look at Joaquin had opened up the floodgates inside her and she had doubted very much they could ever be closed again.

She'd been right. They had never closed.

But that summer, she hadn't wanted to think about such things. Because she'd known she would have to return to Ile d'Montagne. She'd known that whatever this was, whatever he'd tapped in her, she would have to shut it off again.

If she could.

You are worrying about what other people might think instead of what you think, he had told her, his chin on the top of her head, holding her there like they were puzzle pieces made to snap together just so. *I suggest you stop. There are no other people in this room,* cariño. *Here there is only you and me and how we feel. Nothing else matters.*

Over time, she'd told herself he'd only been saying that because it allowed him that power over her. But she knew better now. He didn't demand that power over her.

She craved it.

And so here, now, while the surf thundered outside and soaked the windows, Amalia indulged herself.

She didn't question the urges that raced through her, making her blood feel too hot in her veins. Today she was a new woman. Today she was whoever she wanted to be, so she leaned into these things she wanted. Having left her wrap on the floor in the lobby, she thought no more of it as she stood there before him and stripped off the armor she'd worn to leave the palace.

The perfect dress that showed her femininity without highlighting too many of her assets she kicked aside. The strand of quiet pearls she unwound from her neck and let fall. Then she stood before Joaquin wearing nothing but the lacy panties that hugged her hips and the bralette she wore because though her curves were not that exciting, it had been ingrained in her that a lady of stature did not wander about with her breasts uncontained like some common harlot.

But it turned out she might very well be a common

harlot, as she was, by virtue of the notably non-blue blood in her veins, common to the core.

She took her time pulling the bralette over her head. Then tugged the lacy shorts over her hips so she could shimmy then down her legs. Only when she was naked at last did she stand, find the green of his eyes again, and then unclip the hair he had messed up, but not undone, so that it tumbled down past her shoulders.

Joaquin's gaze ignited.

She felt as if the world was roaring out the pleasure of this, the tug of this unquenchable need, and only realized when he swept her up into his arms that Joaquin was the one making that sound. But then she realized that she was echoing it, there in the back of her throat. He carried her over to his bed and lay her out on the mattress, stripping off his own clothes in the kind of haste that indicated he was as swept up in this as she was.

That only made her glow brighter. Hotter.

And watching Joaquin undress himself was a pageant.

She made herself stay where he put her, so she could enjoy the show.

But it seemed as if she only got little glimpses of that flat abdomen, the ridges that climbed from it, and the magnificence of his chest. Because almost at once he was coming down to find her on the bed. To take her in his arms and roll them both around and around, until she was dizzy and giddy and lost, and his mouth was busy on her neck, her breasts.

She wrapped her legs around him and could feel the hardest part of him there against her inner thigh, a thick, long insistence she had already tasted so well.

Her mouth watered all over again.

Amalia thought then that she might die if he wasn't inside her. As quickly as possible.

It was possible she said that out loud.

He paused, reaching out to one of the tables beside the bed and quickly sheathing himself. Then he stretched her out beneath him, gathering her wrists in one hand and holding them up high over her head. She arched up against him, crossing her legs behind him once more, and despite five years of telling herself she would never repeat the shameful things she'd done in this bed, she was pleading with him again.

Begging him.

Again.

"Now, Joaquin. Please, now."

And she could feel the dark curve of his mouth as if he smiled like that inside her, even as she watched it change the shape of his mouth.

He teased her, because he could. He dragged the blunt head of himself through her heat, and laughed at the noises she made.

He made them both shudder.

And only when he was ready, only when he chose, did he lean down, gather her close, and then slam himself home.

Amalia broke into a thousand pieces immediately, digging her heels into the small of his back and holding on as she bucked and shook.

He waited, every part of him taut and tight. He held himself over her as if it took every bit of willpower he possessed to let her dissolve in his arms without joining in. He looked as if it was torture.

Only when she caught her breath did Joaquin begin to move.

And everything was wildfire once more.

Only this time, both of them burned.

His pace was impossible. And glorious.

And far, far better than the dreams that had kept her alive all this time.

All she could do was hold on as best as she was able, wrapping herself tight around him as he took them both on the wildest, most glorious ride of her life.

Her nails dug into his back. Her hips rose to meet his as if of their own accord. Her head was thrown back, she was sobbing out her joy, her need, her dark delight.

And in that moment, Amalia wouldn't have cared if the entire population of Ile d'Montagne was lined up at the foot of the bed, watching them.

Because this was beautiful. And she was entirely his.

It had been that way since the moment she'd laid eyes on him and neither time nor distance nor her role in a far-off kingdom had changed that one bit.

This time, when she shattered once more, she heard his cry as he came with her.

And she thought, as she spiraled off into nothing in his arms, that at least there was this.

Amalia might not be who she'd always believed she was, but there was still this. There was still Joaquin.

And somehow, some way, everything would be all right.

CHAPTER FOUR

Joaquin had miscalculated.

Grievously.

They spent the day in his bed—and all over the rest of the home he had abandoned when she had left him that summer. When the feast of her body could not sustain them any further, he had fixed them simple meals from the small kitchen he kept here, custom built for those times he did not wish to go to the trouble of walking all the way back to the main part of the hotel.

He had not thought that part through, either. He had spent a lot of time in this place while he was overseeing the renovation of the island. He had been new to wealth then and had wanted to keep an iron control over every aspect of the project. But he had not been that man in years. These days he preferred to control the many teams that did his bidding, not necessarily the projects he had them handle for him.

That was different. When it came to Amalia, however, he was as wholly invested as he had ever been.

He kept telling himself to snap out of it. But always, that same rush of desire would rise in him anew and they would end up back in his bed, learning each other all over again.

Now it was late. Outside the glass walls of the dungeon he had transformed into quiet elegance because it pleased him to know he could do such things, he stood by the window and watch the moon rise over the dance of the waves.

Behind him, the only living creature he had ever loved slept, her dark hair fanned out across the pillow and her cheeks flushed with the force of her dreams. All of him, he imagined. If they were anything like the ones he had of her more often than he liked to admit.

He did not have to look over his shoulder to confirm it. He knew the image would be burned into him forever.

Just like every other image, every other moment.

Joaquin had always intended to taste her again. He was not a man who believed in once-in-a-lifetime events—not he, who could so often dictate the course of both time and events. And lives, come to that.

He had not believed it was possible that he would never encounter her again, and the need to hasten that moment had burned in him. For years. He had liked the fire of it, because he'd been so certain it was hatred.

That it was what she deserved from him after her betrayal. He had taken a kind of pleasure in letting it grow, knowing that sooner or later, their paths would cross again. When they did, he would be ready.

This had seemed too good to be true.

First, that for all the haughtiness she had showed him at the end of that summer—all her talk of her station and what she owed her subjects—she was no princess, after all. He was a mongrel from the streets of Bilbao and yet he had as much right to the Ile d'Montagne throne as she did.

Joaquin knew all too well what it was like to be cast out, mocked and ridiculed, but no one had dared treat him in such a fashion in a long while. It was true that he had taken no small pleasure in the notion that she—so unprepared for these things, so insulated by a lifetime of imagining herself so high and mighty— must face them all the same.

Perhaps that made him as petty as he was sometimes accused of being. Though he noticed that those who called him such things were always the same people who reaped what they, themselves, had sown.

When he'd found that she actually dared return to Cap Morat, he had felt the way he often did when the world arranged itself to suit him. That all was as it should be. That all was right and good.

He had anticipated wanting her, for who would not want her? Amalia's beauty was exquisite and inarguable. Much had been made her whole life of the delicacy of her features, the stunning blue of her eyes, her innate grace.

All of which, it turned out, came courtesy of a cornfield. Not the royal heritage that was supposed to have produced it.

He had anticipated enjoying all of that, as he always had, because he had been captivated by her beauty once before. And enjoying more, perhaps, that all along, they'd been commoners together here. Despite her attempts to put him in his place.

Now the only difference between them was that he'd earned his money. Hers was a parting gift from the Queen—not her mother—who simply wanted the inconvenient farm girl she'd raised as her daughter and heir to go away. That tidbit had not made the papers yet, but it would. In the meantime, his sources had come through for him.

Joaquin had expected to enjoy that part, particularly. What he had not anticipated was the *punch* of her.

Even though he knew better this time. Even though he would never be so foolish as to love her again.

The attraction between them was outsize and astonishing, still. He hadn't expected the electricity of it to shock him the way it did. He hadn't expected that merely meeting her gaze would make him feel winded.

He had decided long ago that none of the things he'd thought he felt here, with her, were real. How could they be? He had lost her and he was Joaquin Vargas. He did not lose.

It had not occurred to him that she could be stripped of all the things that had made her who she was and yet still have her own power to spare.

Worse, that she would still have that same power over him.

When he had allowed no one else that kind of leverage. Ever.

Even so, he had expected it would work itself out. He had come to humble her, and he assumed it would be easily done. He would order her to kneel, she would refuse, and he would have the great pleasure of throwing her off his island.

Instead, she had knelt.

He was not sure that he had actually used the brain in his head between that moment and this. Indeed, he knew he had not.

So he stood still. He watched the moon and the sea. And he despaired of himself.

"You look appropriately ferocious for a man who lives in a dungeon half beneath the sea," came her silvery voice from his bed. "Even from behind."

Joaquin did not respond. Perhaps he could not. He heard a whisper of sound and then she came to stand beside him, wrapped up in the sheet from his bed. Making a sheet he had given little thought to, ever, look like the finest garment ever made to caress a woman's form. It looked as if it had been created to pour all over her like that, as if the moonlight had spun itself into silk.

"I'm going to be honest with you about something, though I probably shouldn't," she told him softly, as if this room had become a confessional.

Her gaze was directed out toward the sea, and his chest felt tight, because she looked almost...troubled. The frown he remembered but had not seen in years, in her press appearances or here today, had insinuated itself between her brows again. Her black hair tumbled down her back, looking anything but smooth. For a moment, it was like looking back through time.

Back to the meat of that summer, before she'd turned into a statue. Before she'd acted as if nothing about him or them concerned her at all. For a moment, he could see once more the bright chaos of the younger Amalia he'd known. Not the measured creature, the Crown Princess, who seemed to know too well that anything she said or did could be used against her.

It was unfair, he knew, when that was what he wanted from her. Anything and everything that he could use to do to her what she had done to him.

"Is honesty a factor here?" he asked, his voice hardly seeming like his own. He blamed the moon. "It was not before."

The moon he was busy blaming for his weakness had captured his attention, so he sensed her reproachful look more than saw it.

"I was nothing but honest with you, Joaquin. All summer long, and then at the end, too. Could I have tempered my words? Certainly, and I wish I had. But the message was still the same. There was no possibility that Queen Esme would permit any relationship between us. At the end of the day, what could possibly have prettied that up?"

Joaquin didn't want to touch that. Or maybe the real truth was, he wanted nothing but to touch it. To tear it apart with his fingers. To bellow out the five years' worth of wounded pride and all those other shattered things inside him he refused to accept were there.

He *refused.* "Was this the honesty you meant? I could do without it."

She turned, putting her back to the glass. Then she tipped her face toward him, still swaddled in that sheet, but he saw *her* there. Amalia, as deep in this as he was.

As he *had been,* he corrected himself.

"I had convinced myself that nothing could be as intense as that summer was," she told him, as if she was offering him a confession. And God knew he would take it, especially when her voice was so low, so raw. "I was wrong."

Joaquin looked down at her, though he knew it was dangerous. Her hair was tangled now, messy from his fingers. Just the way he liked it. Her lips were slightly swollen from his, and if he wasn't mistaken, the faint hint of his jaw was all over the tender skin of her neck.

This was how he liked her. Thoroughly debauched, and all his.

But none of this mattered. None of it was real.

"The intensity is the only reason I allowed you to return here," he told her, and even that felt like too much of an admission.

And he was staring down at her face. He could see her reaction.

She blinked, once. That was all.

And then the Amalia he remembered, the Amalia

he craved, disappeared as he looked at her. Her face smoothed out, and became serene.

Eerily serene, to his mind.

Something in him turned over at that, because surely that was a loss. Surely that was something less than honesty—though he doubted if she even knew how much she'd changed from that open girl back then, so filled with sunshine and wonder.

But he knew.

"Joaquin," she said, in a quiet voice that matched the sudden steadiness of her gaze. "I hope you know there was never a day—"

He moved then, sliding his palm over her mouth and holding it there as her eyes widened.

As blue as the sea behind her. And as treacherous.

He needed to remember that above all things.

Because he could not allow this. She had been the exception that proved the rule, and she'd proved herself unworthy of it. He had let her in. He had allowed her to see parts of him he hadn't known were there. He had never given anyone else that privilege.

And she had squandered it. It didn't matter why.

Joaquin could not go back there. He could not tolerate her inevitable betrayal once again.

He had grown up hard, but it had been his life. He had never cried about it. He had been far too busy digging himself out of the hole he'd found himself in by virtue of his birth. And it turned out that no matter what all the soft, well-fed wellness gurus liked to say, empires really could be built on spite.

Joaquin had built his that way, and happily. There had been nothing soft in him, ever, until he'd encountered a princess on his island.

She had made him *feel*. Then she had left him. He could not forgive it.

He would not.

Joaquin refused to entertain even the barest hint that they were headed in that direction again. If he could have dug out his heart with his own hands and gotten rid of it, he would have. He did not intend to risk it again.

This was about revenge and nothing more.

He could have moved his palm from her lips, but he didn't.

"There are only two things, maybe three, that I wish you to do with your mouth," he told her with a certain grimness that still didn't manage to cut that same desire for her that burned in him, always. "None of them involve talking."

He felt her smile there beneath his hand, and that did not help. She pulled her head back, so he could see that smile whether he wished to or not. And it did not exactly keep him focused on making this moment work to his advantage.

Because she might have changed in the years since he'd seen her. But she still looked at him as if he was a wondrous, magical creature when he knew otherwise.

"No one has ever spoken to me the way you do," she said, still smiling. Even her eyes were shining, bright enough to rival the path of the moon across the water. "I still don't understand why I like it so much. Or don't hate it the way I should. It was one thing when I was the Crown Princess and you could reduce me to nothing but a half-wild woman with a few dirty words. But now I really am nothing but a woman, and still. It has the same effect."

Joaquin couldn't listen to this. He couldn't engage with her in this way.

Allowing her to talk at all was the problem. He knew that. Because he wanted, still and always, to glut himself upon her. There was no changing that, apparently. There was no pretending otherwise.

But he saw no reason why he should risk *liking* her again. When he looked back, he could pinpoint that as the disaster that had precipitated all the rest. Liking Amalia had been the beginning and the end. When had he ever *liked* anyone?

His life had not lent itself to such luxuries. It had all been about extremes. Living by his wits on the streets, viewing others as marks or possible future marks as he'd set about getting out of Bilbao. And then teaching himself a rudimentary understanding of finance, mostly because he had once encountered a group of hotshot bankers in Madrid who had sneered at him and told him to get a job.

I'll take yours, he had replied.

And so he had. By virtue of buying everything that particular group of bankers had put their grubby fingers in, then firing each and every one of them. Simply because he could.

He had liked every step of the journey. He had liked how easy it was, once he put his mind to something, to make it happen. He had certainly liked firing the men who had thought themselves so much better than him on a city street.

But that was liking things he did. Not who he was.

Joaquin had never had friends. He had allies or enemies, with no in between. And well did he know that a friend one day was often an enemy the next.

He banked on it.

It had not been until Her Royal Highness Princess Amalia had gazed at him as if he was a sheer delight—

there on a patio he'd built in the sweet Spanish sun he'd always taken for granted—that he had discovered there was something else.

He hadn't understood it at first. What was this overwhelming compulsion he felt when he was near her? Not merely the urge for sex. He was used to that. He had always had healthy appetites.

It was only Amalia whose *company* he desired.

And look what it had got him.

He rubbed at his chest, annoyed that his heart still beat there. And worse, that he could feel it, as if it was a commentary on his behavior.

Joaquin could not allow this to happen again.

He would not.

"You were a virgin," he told her now, his voice dark. Almost as dark as the sea outside, gleaming beneath the moon. "You do not know the ways that men are with women."

And he could see the hint of a crease appear between her brows. He knew she would argue. Or say something that he would ignore in the moment and then spend the next eternity turning over and over in his head.

So he took her mouth instead.

And he wrested the sheet from her fingers, letting it pool at her feet, before lifting her up and wrapping her legs around him. Because surely, if he sank into her completely—if he indulged himself completely— he would burn this out, whatever this was.

This unwelcome poltergeist of sensation inside him that had never abated.

No matter how he had tried these last few years to blot her out as if she had never existed.

He carried her back to the bed and lowered them both down.

Her sighs were like music. Her taste was addictive.

But he'd already answered the question to his own satisfaction. She'd been a virgin that summer and he had been foolish. Neither of those things applied to this situation. Neither of those things were factors any longer.

He did not have to be careful with her. He could treat her as he had treated any woman, though he rarely allowed them more than a night. Perhaps a weekend, on rare occasions, usually because he needed a date for some or other event in some far-off locale. He always made certain the women he took with him knew where they stood.

If they didn't like his bluntness, he was always more than happy to find someone else.

Joaquin Vargas was known for his business decisions, ruthless and sometimes cruel. He treated women the same way.

And anyone else who happened into his orbit.

That was what he'd learned on the streets. That was how he'd survived.

This would be no different.

Having already made mistakes with her, he would not be so foolish as to repeat them. He would treat Amalia the way he treated any obsession he happened upon. He would give himself to it totally, knowing all the while that soon enough, his obsession would burn itself out.

Maybe then he could be free.

Of this. Of her.

And as he moved over her in the bed, sinking deep into her flesh, and losing himself in that glorious burn, he assured himself that was what he wanted.

Freedom above all else. Because nothing else that he had ever touched had lasted.

Only his freedom to do as he liked, then move on when he was done.

Soon enough, he would leave here again, and he would be free. But this time he would not carry her with him, forever lodged in his heart, in his sex, and too many dreams at night.

Joaquin told himself he was tired of being haunted.

So he set about vanquishing this particular ghost the only way he knew how.

CHAPTER FIVE

THE DAYS BLED one into the next. One week, then another.

It was tempting to imagine she had always been here on Cap Morat, in the shadow of the once mighty fortress. Amalia didn't have to try too hard to feel as if, maybe, she had sprung into life in the Spanish sun and the sweet sea breezes. That this was simply who she was, a creature of appetite and leisure, no end and no beginning.

One morning, she found herself wandering her favorite path. It was the one that wound around the perimeter of the island, ranging from down on rocky beaches to up on higher cliffs, every step offering stunning views. Either of the sea on all sides or of the hotel itself, standing tall on the highest part of the island. Amalia liked that there was nowhere she could go on the island without seeing the old fortress. As if it alone stood guard over her, keeping her past from catching up to her here.

It was a lovely notion.

Joaquin had allowed a skeleton staff back on the island. His half-underwater dungeon had an office suite and he retreated to it at odd hours, barricading himself in there to buy and sell and whatever else it was he did with such ferocity. But when he emerged, he did not always have the patience to make his own meals. It had not been more than two or three days before the kitchen and cleaning staff returned, along with few other key personnel to see to it that Joaquin had every last thing he desired at his fingertips.

Amalia greatly enjoyed being one of them.

She tipped her face up to the sun as she walked, happy that there was enough of a breeze off the ocean to keep her cool. She wore her sun hat, as planned, and periodically had to clamp it to the top of her head with a free hand to keep the wind from stealing it away.

Her whole life seemed to her now, here on this island, as if it had been a dream. Her childhood had been a dreary slog of lectures on responsibility, uncomfortable public events, and her mother's dire warnings about what could befall a young queen if she were not careful. Not that she had ever been given the opportunity to be anything *but* careful.

Then, a pop of color. A burst of light. Life, finally, came for her on this island. She had lived a lifetime that summer. And she'd known it while it was happening. Even then, she'd told herself to hold on tight to every scrap of color and sensation, for she would have to live on it all the rest of her days.

She really had done her duty the day she left here, walking away without looking back no matter how badly she'd wanted to and burying herself in her responsibilities once more.

And now here she was on this island once more. Slowly coming alive again.

Amalia didn't know what it meant long-term. If it meant anything at all. At some point, she was aware, she would have to engage with the world again. She would have to find something to do with herself. She was aware—Joaquin had informed her that the whole world was aware—that Esme had given her enough money that it was not necessary for her to do anything at all. She wanted to think of that as a gift, even a loving gift, but she knew Esme. She knew it was more complicated than that.

If Esme had her way, as Queen, her counterfeit daughter would disappear entirely. What Amalia thought Esme really wanted was to go back in time and not have this switched at birth situation happen in the first place. It was entirely possible Esme had discharged some of her ministers to look into time travel. But in the absence of that, what she'd likely prefer was that the stain that was Amalia—or, rather, the circumstances that had led to Amalia having been raised to imagine herself the daughter of the Queen of Ile d'Montagne—to fade from sight forever. Because the monarchy would go on, and Esme preferred that it do so with as little scandal as possible.

On the other hand, Amalia knew that Esme was genuinely fond of her. That despite everything, Esme likely wished that there was a way she could have kept the daughter she'd raised with her... But Esme was all about her throne, always. She would always put Ile d'Montagne first, even now.

She probably hoped that Amalia would continue to do the same. That she would choose a quiet life, far from the public eye, and live in a way that reflected well on the throne no matter where she ended up.

And there was a huge part of Amalia that wanted that, too. Because she hadn't stopped loving Ile d'Montagne, or the throne, or Esme, just because of a few blood tests. Still, even if she chose that route, if she lived the rest of her life in quiet, elegant virtue, there was still the question of where. And how.

Unfortunately, she didn't think she would be much good at doing nothing, however elegantly or virtuously, despite her time on the island. But here on Cap Morat, she wasn't doing *nothing,* exactly. She was luxuriating. She was engaging each and every one of her senses, immersing herself in the sensual banquet that never seemed to end.

She swam in the pools, as if testing them all to see which one might be her favorite, though she could never make up her mind. The one on the cliff with the infinity pool that made the horizon seem nearly *right there,* within reach? The soft, warmer pools clustered on one side of the hotel, some of them shaded, each and every one its own delight? How could anyone choose? There were also hot tubs at night. One set into the rocks outside Joaquin's dungeon villa, where the ocean waves would sometimes splash over into the pool set into the rocks, an exhilarating punch to combat the heat.

And that didn't begin to address the many beaches she could swim from, if she liked.

When she wasn't swimming, she wandered the island. She climbed up and down all the stone steps she could find, finding every nook and cranny she might have missed last time. And as she did these things, she took great care that when she found herself thinking in the usual endless cycles about Ile d'Montagne, Esme, and her true identity as a farm girl from Kansas, she stopped. She breathed a bit and remembered where she was. Then she tried to put it all out of her mind.

Not because she was hiding from it, but because there was nothing she could do to solve any of those problems here. Because most of those problems weren't her problems any longer, however strange that still was to her.

She swam. She walked. And now that the cook was back, she paused between these activities to eat. And eat. And eat. The cook, she knew, called her cuisine *European*. She took foods from any country that grabbed her fancy. Sometimes she combined it all. Sometimes it was identifiably the food of one country, or another.

And for the first time in her life, Amalia ate with total abandon. Because why should she care if her clothes fit her? Why should she worry for even one moment more about how she would look in photographs? The older she'd gotten, the more she'd fought to maintain a frame that was at least fifteen pounds slimmer than what she would consider her normal size, so that she would appear normal when photographed. It had simply been part of her job.

The part she was happiest to give up, she acknowledged now, while always having dessert. And then, afterward, she napped in the sun, or under an umbrella, dozing off in the afternoons and letting the sun and breeze do as they would.

All of the ways she occupied her time were soothing. And good for her, she thought. But what she did mostly, in and around the rest, was try her best to please Joaquin.

Some days he was harsh, his green eyes glittering and his mouth taut. On those days, there were rules. Tasks he set for her, knowing she would fail them, so that he could mete out his brand of starkly sensual punishment.

She loved every moment of it.

Other days, he was teasing, even playful. He would come and find her in the pools, or out somewhere on the island, and he would take her there. Sometimes he would pull her into a shadowed corner. Other times he would lay her out beside one of the pools, surging between her thighs right there in the open air, which she would never have allowed when she was still the Crown Princess.

But here, with him, she was someone new.

That long-ago summer, she realized now, he had been restrained. He had held himself back, keeping himself on a leash.

He was not doing that now.

Some days, he growled strict commands that she was to stay where she was, splayed out on his bed, only breaking for necessary reasons. And he would visit her, in between meetings, to please them both excessively.

Her head was so full of him—and every last nerve ending, and her skin, and possibly even her very bones—that a full month passed before Amalia bothered to pull out her mobile phone.

It was an unusually rainy day. Joaquin had stormed off to growl at his subordinates after taking out his mood all over her, deliciously. Amalia dashed up the stone path to the grand hotel lobby, where some thoughtful staff member had already lit the great fire. She curled up before it, and powered up her phone, tucking her bare feet beneath one of the blankets on the chair she'd chosen.

"Do you really want to do this?" she asked herself softly.

And the answer was no. She did not. She was perfectly happy as she was, cut off from the world. But it was a bliss born of ignorance. And she knew that sooner or later, she would have to face reality. Better on her own schedule, she thought.

Even then, while the lock screen of her phone filled with various messages, she held off from looking more closely at any of them. Just for a few moments more.

But an hour or so later, she had deleted all the messages from various so-called journalists. She had checked in with her secret social media presence, restricted only to a very few people she knew personally who were as averse to publicity as she was. And was touched to find that all of them had checked in to make certain she was well.

But what surprised her more was that there were three other messages, all voice mails.

One from Queen Esme, a frigid inquiry into her well-being.

Some might find that off-putting. But Amalia knew the Queen. And knew that for Esme, reaching out at all must have seemed an unforgivable lapse into sentimentality.

Amalia would hold on to that.

The second message was confusing. It was Delaney Clark, her replacement. Or, she countered as she thought that, the real her.

I would love to talk to you, if that isn't too strange, the other woman said. *It's nothing bad. I just know that you spent twenty-five years training for this job, so you're obviously the expert. I'd love to pick your brain.*

Amalia's finger had hovered over the delete button, and she'd urged herself to press it, but…hadn't.

She told herself she wanted no part of the palace, or anything to do with the real Crown Princess. Why would she go back there? Why would she involve herself in a life was no longer hers?

But she didn't delete the message.

The final message was one she was completely unprepared for.

Hello, came an older woman's voice. *This is Catherine Clark. I'm your... Well. I don't know what to call myself. But I want you to know that I knew. I knew when they brought me the wrong baby, and they told me I was imagining things. That I needed sleep. But I knew. I loved the daughter I raised. I love her still. And I don't need anything from you if you don't wish to give it. But I wanted you to know that... I love you, too. And I missed you when you were gone.*

She couldn't have said how long she sat there after hearing that message, her mobile forgotten in her lap as she stared off into the fire. That simple, quiet message had punched holes through her heart. She could feel it, suddenly filled with all those gaps, except other things flooded in, too.

All the memories she'd set aside or stamped out, because there was no point in wallowing in them.

They flashed through her now. Sobbing out her heart in her bedroom at the age of seven or eight, because once again the Queen had dismissed her for being too noisy. Too loud. Too frightfully common. She'd cried until her eyes were dry and her cheeks hurt from all the salt. And she'd wished, fervently, that she had somehow been adopted. Instead of imagining that she was secretly royalty, the way she understood some girls did, she had wished she could be regular. With a sweet mother who loved her, not a chilly queen who was forever harping on her every last act.

Another flash, sitting with a family when she was eighteen and on the cusp of her own schedule of solo public appearances. She and Esme had visited a family gathered around the bedside of their youngest daughter, who had been suffering from a terrible cancer. But none of them had seemed sad. They had been too busy making each other laugh, holding each other's hands, telling one another stories. They had been bright and connected and happy, even in the face of the unthinkable.

Esme and Amalia had sat silently in the back of the car that had ushered them home to the palace. Silent, because no one spoke until the Queen did, and Amalia knew by then it was never worth breaking protocol in Esme's presence. The whole way home Amalia had wondered what it would be like to have a family like that. Where what mattered was that they were together, no matter what.

And all this time, she'd had a real mother. Not a queen. A mother who had called her up, even though they were strangers to each other, just to tell her that she was loved.

She knew Esme would never do such a thing. It would not even occur to her.

If you ask them, a great many commoners have love and happiness, Esme had said once, when Amalia had dared to ask if Esme had loved her husband—supposedly Amalia's father—the late, lamented Jean Philippe, who had died not long after Amalia was born. *What we have is history. A legacy. The purpose of the throne to guide us in all things.*

Can't you have both? Amalia had asked. Too fervently.

Esme had looked at her almost pityingly. Amalia had been twelve and had been reading books she shouldn't, stealing them from the palace staff and inhaling them under the covers when no one was watching. But all those romantic paperbacks had given her courage. She didn't look away.

At twelve it had seemed a victory.

No, child, Esme had replied coolly. *It is but one of many choices you make in your life. No one can have everything. Only the foolish try.*

Thinking back now, Amalia thought that might have been the only time love had been discussed between them. At the time, she had been distraught, because she understood that Esme was telling her that her parents had never loved each other. But she'd also known that meant it was very unlikely that *she* would be permitted to marry for love, should she ever find it.

But Amalia couldn't imagine why she'd thought love was part of any royal picture, given the fact Esme had never said those words. Amalia hadn't expected she would. *I love you* would have been a weakness, and the Queen was focused solely on making certain her successor was strong and tough. And prepared, for anything and everything.

Love had nothing to do with it.

Yet now Amalia held in her hand a mobile phone that held a message that proved to her that from across the world, the woman who'd given birth to her had no fear at all of love. And no qualm about reaching out to share it.

She thought she ought to celebrate that. Instead, she felt shaken to her core.

And then, suddenly, it was as if the air changed around her. She glanced up, expecting to find the rain had cleared outside. But it was Joaquin who stood there.

He usually dressed for his meetings, always looking the part of the billionaire CEO he was on his various videoconferences. One day, to amuse himself during what he'd told her would be a particularly boring spate of meetings, he'd had her sit in his office with him, perched where he could see her. She had been completely naked. And from time to time he'd scribbled out directions for her. That she should touch herself this way. That she should move around that way. By the time he was finished with his meetings, Amalia was nearly sobbing with frustrated longing and hunger. And he had taken her right there, tossing her across his desk and slamming his way inside her at last. He had thrust once, then twice, before cursing and pulling out again to fumble a condom into place.

She'd been so ready for him that when he thrust home again, she'd screamed, then bucked out her pleasure against him while he sought his own lightning-fast release.

The memory alone made her breath catch.

Today he must have spent more time on the phone instead of a video. He wore a now soaking wet white button-down shirt, rolled up at the sleeves, and a pair of dark trousers that seemed to cling to every part of his thighs that she liked best.

"Have you been standing there long?" she asked.

Because there was something about the way he was looking at her. Almost as if he felt haunted.

"Not long," he replied in his gravelly way.

She remembered this from their first summer together. When she had become so attuned to him that she could feel his voice inside her, as if every syllable was a caress against her tender flesh.

Joaquin did not come closer. And Amalia stayed where she was, because she liked to look at him. And today he was wet from the rain, so that shirt clung to him the way she normally did. He looked like every fantasy she'd ever had.

She almost laughed. He *was* every fantasy she'd ever had.

"You look…sad." Joaquin bit off that last word as if it tasted bad.

Amalia glanced down at her mobile, then shook her head. "Not sad. Not really. I think my circumstances require an appropriate amount of introspection, that's all. And I'm new to the practice."

Outside, the rain picked up, beating down hard on the stones. It was so loud she thought it surely could have drowned them both out, had either one of them been speaking.

And still, somehow, the storm in Joaquin's gaze raged louder.

"Everything in my previous life was outward-facing," she told him, hardly knowing she meant to speak. It was the way he was looking at her with all of that green in his gaze. It made her feel reckless. "Whatever thoughts or feelings I might have had, about anything, needed to be locked away in service to my public persona. In case you wondered, I didn't get to pick that persona. The role was chosen for me and I was expected to fill it. The girl you met here five years ago was… not me. She was an anomaly. An escape from reality."

She saw his lips flatten at that. But he still said nothing, only stood there as if he had braced himself for a fight.

"I'm not complaining," she found herself continuing, though the idea of a *fight* made her blood move a little quicker. "Just a fact. My—Queen Esme is of the belief that while the monarchy holds all the power in Ile d'Montagne, there are also obligations incumbent upon those of us who hold—or held—those exalted positions. The public is owed access to us. Or not to *us,* as such, but these roles we play. She is also of the opinion that mystery is far better than exposure. I don't suppose this is something you would understand. I suspect you are always and ever you, no matter where you go."

She had found that exhilarating five years ago. He had been a force and she had been, perhaps, a little in awe of how *certain* he was. About everything.

Surely you must feel some hint of doubt, if only now and again, she had said once. They had been walking down by the water in one of the island's protected, rocky coves. It had been a hot day, but Joaquin had only seemed to burn brighter in all that sun.

He had held her hand in his, the heat between them always at a simmer. The look he'd sent her way had only set it to a boil. *For many years I could not afford doubt,* he had said. *Now that I can afford anything, I do not see its purpose.*

Amalia remembered thinking, *I wish I could walk through the world like that.* She supposed that when she'd left him that summer, that was what she'd tried to do.

Here, now, she watched his green gaze narrow, slightly. And he nodded. Once.

"And here's a little secret." Amalia pulled the blanket more firmly around her. "I liked playing that part. There might have been certain restrictions on my life, and I found those difficult at times, but the role of the Crown Princess? I enjoyed it. I knew that I could do real good and I worked hard to make sure that was at the center of everything I did. And I worked hard at the public persona, too. To always appear graceful. Compassionate. Pleasant, yet serious. To inhabit opposing extremes at all times, usually in heels, while always remaining just unknowable enough, because the people do not really want to know every last detail of the personification of their government, do they? It's not easy." She clutched the mobile in her hand. "And it turns out that all this time, it wasn't even my role to play. It would be strange if I wasn't thinking about it."

"They say you lived entirely for the crown." Joaquin sounded as if he was whispering, but that couldn't be true. Not when the rain was still coming down like that outside. It was only that his voice moved over her like a whisper, then into her like a caress. "That you bloomed with adulation and will wither away without it."

"Then I would deserve to wither away." She tipped her head to one side as she regarded him. "If that's the only thing I was, then I ought to be happy that it's turned out it was never my role to play. We're all just people at the end of the day. Aren't we?"

"There are different kinds of people." And again, she couldn't seem to look away from that green gaze of his, and how intensely he seemed to be watching her. As if he was looking for something in particular. "Most of them are weak."

Amalia didn't exactly laugh at that, though a puff of air escaped her lips. She lifted her hand to push her hair back from her face, and only then realized it was trembling. "Everyone knows your story. I don't think anyone can compete with it. Compared to you, there's nothing but weakness in this world."

"You say that, but I doubt very much you know what it means," he said, dark and yet layered through with too much fire. "You have never known what it is to be entirely alone, Princess. No one coming to save you. No one around to care. I could have died at any point during my childhood and no one would have noticed."

Amalia had never heard him put it quite like that before.

"I wasn't sad before." She wanted to whisper his

name. She wanted to touch him, comfort him. But she didn't dare do any of that. "But that makes me feel something a lot more than simply sad."

"There's nothing sad about it." He moved then, that rangy, almost rolling gait of his that made her think of how controlled he was. How ready, always, to attack. "Life is only ever about survival. My gift is that I have always known that. I did not learn it later, and to my detriment, like some."

"What you're talking about is *existence*," she said, with a quiet intensity that seemed to come from a new place inside her. "Living is something else. Living involves light, love. Anyone can *exist*. Most do. But it's only when you surrender to life that you get to be truly alive. And that's what matters."

Her words seemed to hang there in the grand lobby, buffeted this way and that by the rain outside and the cold wind that whipped through. By contrast, neither wind nor rain seemed to touch Joaquin at all as he moved toward her.

"And how would you know this?" Joaquin's voice was soft again, but she did not mistake that softness for weakness, not when she could feel the lash of his mockery just beneath it. "You, who have played a role that was not even yours all this time? Is that *alive,* do you think?"

But Amalia refused to be cowed by him. Not today. "I can't do anything about the life that I was told was mine, the one I tried to live as I was told I should." She lifted her chin, and somehow, holding tight to her mobile and knowing the message that waited for her there made her feel stronger. Brighter. "All I can do is make sure that the life I lead going forward is the life I want."

"You should know this by now, Amalia," he growled,

and he was standing over her then, his green eyes glittering. "No one ever, truly, gets what they want. Life is compromise—unless you win. And you, I think, were raised to believe you had already won, only to learn otherwise." He shrugged the way he did sometimes, as if nothing could matter. As if nothing ever had. "I do not think the life you have before you is going to be anything you wish."

The life before her that would not include him. He didn't say that, but that was what she heard. Loud and clear.

As if she was just one of his many women, clinging to his trouser leg. She was sure that was precisely how he wanted her to feel.

"I know my life will be exactly what I wish, actually," she shot back at him. "Because I'm not afraid of it. I don't have to conquer everything before me. I don't have to make certain that I win at all costs. The difference between you and me, Joaquin, is that I just want to be happy."

"No, Princess." That was twice he'd called her that today, and the sardonic way he said it made goose bumps roll down her neck. She didn't like it. But then, she supposed that was his point. He was doing this deliberately. So she decided, then and there, that she would die before she gave him the satisfaction of seeing how it got to her. "The difference between you and me is that I know happiness is a lie."

He reached down then and hauled her up and into his arms. The blanket fell off her, her phone clattered to the stone floor, and she didn't care. Because his mouth was on hers and his tongue was stroking deep, making her attempt at defiance seem silly.

When all she wanted was this.

All she really wanted was him.

He spun them around and carried her across the lobby, and she didn't understand what he was doing until she felt the rain fall all over them. Pounding down until they were both soaking wet.

Eventually he set her down on her feet, and a quick glance around showed her that they were out near one of the smaller pools, its surface agitated by the rain that kept coming and coming. Joaquin backed her up until she found the palm tree behind her and she held on as tight she could, her fingers slick against the bark.

He didn't stand on ceremony. It was like the storm all around them was in them, too. Joaquin worked the front of his trousers to free himself, and then he lifted her up, letting her arch back against the palm. Then he slid her down his body, thrusting deep within her.

And every time it felt better.

Every time, she thought there was no possible way the pleasure could be this intense. This beautiful.

And every time he proved her wrong.

She couldn't tell any longer where the storm was. Inside her, around her. Pounding on her head, pounding deep between her thighs.

Maybe they had been the storm all along.

When she arched up against him, sobbing out her joy into the rain, he let out a deep kind of roar. Then jerked himself out of her to finish on her belly.

Once again, he'd forgotten himself.

And she forgot everything.

"Careful," she warned, in a voice that didn't sound like hers. She sounded silly with lust. Half-mad with passion. Addled by him, again. "One of these days you're going to make me pregnant, and then you'll never be rid of me."

And it wasn't until her feet hit the ground with a jolt that she realized how badly Joaquin was taking that remark.

Because he was looking at her as if she'd betrayed him.

CHAPTER SIX

ONE MOMENT, HE'D been burning so hot he was surprised the rain didn't sizzle as it hit him.

And the next moment, he was chilled to the bone.

"Why are you looking at me like that?" Amalia asked, gazing at him like the impossible temptation she was. Soaking wet, wearing one of those gowns of hers that seemed to envelop her in far too much fabric, yet were almost too alluring to bear.

Out here, in all this rain, the fabric clung to her form, making her seem something more than simply beautiful. It was as if she became something else, something *more*. Some kind of myth, perhaps.

Thank the gods he didn't believe in such things.

"There will be no pregnancy, Amalia," he told her, and it was probably a good thing that she'd called out his shocking irresponsibility. It was certainly a good thing that she'd done it before he went too far. "Ever."

She stared at him as if he was suddenly far, far away. When Joaquin knew the truth. He was always that far away. He was always *other*. He was always surprised when people failed to recognize the fact that he was not civilized.

Not like they were.

Not like *she* was.

"They call me an orphan, but no one knows if that's true," he told her, the words seeming to come from deep inside him like so much rain. When he never spoke of these things. The stories told about him always glossed this part over. His *humble beginnings*. His childhood of *abject poverty*. Pretty ways to describe a life of grim desperation and too much terror. And he'd certainly never told Amalia much more than the broad strokes, because why would he want her to think of him like that? So weak and small? He felt overexposed already, but he couldn't seem to stop talking. "My parents could be alive right now for all I know or care. If they are, I'm certain they lost whatever humanity they possessed to the drugs and the drink long ago. Maybe they were taken by violence on the same streets where I was left to fend for myself. Whatever the reason, whatever happened to them, it does not take a genius to understand that I possess nothing in me that could ever make a good father."

"If we can only be what our parents were, then I fear we are all doomed," she said.

"I am happy to be doomed," he gritted out. "I thrive under such conditions. But I am not planning to pass it down."

She only stared back at him, clinging to the palm tree behind her as if it was the only thing tethering her to this earth. Joaquin did not choose to ask himself why he found that…a kind of grieving.

"I don't want your confidences," he told her, as harshly as he could. "I don't need you to tell me what it is to *be alive*. I thought I made myself clear, Amalia."

His intention was to devastate her. He wanted to, with a kind of greed that matched the lust he felt for her and made him feel the same intense shame—because surely that would get her to leave him. Because something had to break this fixation, this addiction, and he did not seem able to do it himself.

Surely if he crushed her, she would go.

And he could sink back into the life he'd made for himself, where he was not required to *feel* a damn thing.

He could see her pulse beating wildly in her throat. He could see the way she trembled, there in the rain.

But if he'd expected her to crumble, he was to be disappointed.

Instead, she wrapped her arms around her middle and studied him. Solemn and careful.

"I understand that you have a lot of anger about how things ended—" she began in the same way.

Joaquin let out a bark of laughter. "I was angry five years ago, certainly. But this is not anger, Amalia. This is revenge."

She blinked. "You're…taking revenge on me? And my punishment is…endless sex? Hot and cold running orgasms? Is this how you get back at all your enemies?"

He couldn't say he liked the way she put that.

Joaquin advanced upon her, well aware she did not cower. Instead, she stood taller. Still, he had to lean over her so he could run his hand along the side of her face, then grip her chin. He held her face there, and brought his down close, so they could be no mistake.

So that this moment could stand as an example of what was really happening here.

This moment that could have been a kiss, but wasn't.

Because this was no romance. This was what happened five years after the romance died—at her hands.

"I *loved* you," he threw at her, taking no care at all to ensure he didn't hurt her. He wanted his words to hurt. He wanted them to land the way they did, like bullets into her tender flesh. She jolted, and he liked that. "I would have given you anything at all. Anything and everything. I would have laid it all at your feet. But all you wanted to do was step on me."

She lifted her hand to his and he thought she would try to peel his fingers away from her chin—but if that was her aim, she seemed to get lost in it.

It reminded him of the first day she'd returned here. When she'd looked at him as if he was a ghost, but one she'd come all this way to find.

She was sopping wet now, soaked straight through, and he thought he should have been able to see through her, too. Not just the gown she wore, currently plastered to her every sweet curve, but *her*. He'd spent all this time peeling back her layers, learning how to make her scream, making her beg and cry out for gods who never came.

But he still couldn't read what he saw there in her endlessly blue gaze.

And he didn't see why she should be a mystery like the sea, when he could barely keep himself to the plan he'd made.

Maybe, a voice inside him suggested, *the mystery here is not her—as she meets your demands and shares herself in all possible ways, but you. Who do not.*

Joaquin didn't care for that thought at all.

"You like to make it sound as if it was my aim to hurt you all along," she said after a long, fraught moment while the rain came down in sheets all around them. "I think you know that's not so."

"What difference can it make? It is what happened."

"My hands were tied, Joaquin." He started to shake his head, but her gaze only seemed to grow steadier. "You will say that does not matter, but it does. I'm sure you would like to think that nothing on earth could have stopped you from doing what you liked back then. Or now. The reality is, there was nothing on earth that had any authority over you. There still isn't. I can't say the same."

"That is a weak argument, Amalia."

"I'm not talking about what I owed the Queen. I'm talking about the fact that my Queen was my mother."

She did pry his fingers from her face then. She held them away from her, though she didn't let go of him. Joaquin should have jerked his hand away. He told himself he meant to do it at any moment, but one moment became another, and he didn't.

He didn't care to ask himself why not.

"I think it might have been easier to defy a government," Amalia said in that same quiet, yet intense way. "A nameless, faceless body. But in my case, we were just talking about my mother. The only mother I had—and the only parent I had left. I had no wish to disappoint her."

He pulled his hand away from hers then, and moved back far enough that the rain could fall between them once more. And wondered what that must be like. To have a mother, or any parent, who cared that he existed—and who might therefore be disappointed in him. He couldn't make the notion take form inside him.

And he blamed her for that, too. "You can make all the excuses you want. I loved you and you left. Not exactly kindly. You can hardly be surprised that things are not the same now, all these years later."

"I'm not surprised at all."

Her shoulders straightened, that little tell of hers that told him she was slipping on that princess mantle once more, and he wanted to hate that. He wanted it to be evidence against her. But instead, he found he admired it—given how many titans of industry trembled before him, it was an enduring surprise that one tiny ex-princess seemed entirely unaffected.

Maybe not *entirely* unaffected, he revised in the next breath, when he took a closer look at the goose bumps running down her arms.

"I was only surprised that, having made it so clear how much you disdained me, you chose not only to come and greet me here on the island, but to stay," she was saying. "Then to clear the island of any other guests so we could reenact some of the best parts of our initial summer. If this is your revenge, Joaquin, it seems far too sweet."

He regarded her for much too long, and not for the first time, wondered how he had gotten himself into this situation. With this woman who could tie him into knots—and did, seemingly with precious little effort. When he was no pedigreed playboy like the titled fools Queen Esme had considered worthy of her daughter. He was Joaquin Vargas. He had faced down more so-called monsters this year than most people encountered in a lifetime. It was a sport. Sometimes he took a meeting for the express purpose of showing the self-aggrandizing heads of widely feted corporations how little he cared what they thought of him.

He had always been good at claiming the power in any situation.

And he had a flash of clarity then, slicing through the rain and deep into him. That was the trouble here. He kept confusing the issue. He kept letting her think he cared, and deeply. That was what she thought this intensity was.

Really, Joaquin should have anticipated that.

"How many lovers have you taken since that summer?" he asked her, almost idly.

And tamped down, hard, on the instant howling thing inside him that did not wish to know the answer to that question.

Amalia laughed. "Will you be sharing the number of your lovers in return?"

"I cannot possibly count that high," he replied coolly.

And she didn't flinch. Not exactly. Still, something changed, and in its wake, she looked rueful. "I knew that, of course. It's a funny thing, that love you claim you felt for me, isn't it, Joaquin? Because to the casual observer, it would appear that you expressed it by sleeping with every available woman in Europe. Be still my heart."

"But you never claimed to be in love," he reminded her, and his temper was a dangerous thing just then. It took every scrap of willpower he had to keep it within him. To make sure it didn't break those chains he kept wrapped tight around it. Because he shouldn't have had the faintest shred of temper in the first place. She had never told him that she loved him. No one had ever told him they loved him. He was the only fool who had uttered those words. "So I can only assume you slept with twice as many."

"My only lover was my duty to crown and country," Amalia replied, her blue eyes glinting in the rain. "Everything that happened here that summer was out of character in every way. An extraordinary departure from my actual life."

"And yet here you are again," he murmured. "When surely you should have headed straight home to your true motherland. Cornfields, as I understand it. As far as the eye can see."

He had never seen a cornfield. Yet Joaquin felt certain that the faint hint of derision he used when discussing them was warranted.

Amalia's blue gaze gleamed. "The only thing I know about Kansas is that it has tornadoes. The occasional witch. And farms that end up with ruby slippers, though I've never figured out what they do with all that magic afterward."

He didn't want to dwell on Hollywood nonsense. "All of this makes sense," he said instead. "You still place a virgin's importance on sex."

And he had meant that to insult her. But that didn't mean he liked it when the insult clearly landed.

When she looked as if he'd delivered an actual blow.

"In time, it will pass," he assured her, and he shouldn't have disliked his own words so much. Surely he should have exulted in telling her these truths. In setting her straight. "The more lovers you have, the more you will come to understand that sex is nothing more than a physical release."

She swallowed, hard. He watched her throat move. "And this is your revenge, then. Sexual exposure therapy."

He didn't mean to move closer to her again, then realized he'd done just that. This time he took her shoulders in his hands and drew her up on her toes.

Revenge, he reminded himself. *This is meant to be revenge.*

"I will do whatever it takes to conquer this," he growled at her. "I will not allow you to haunt me. We will stay here, you and I, until you cannot take it anymore and leave. Or until I feel as much when I touch you as I do in any random handshake."

She laughed at that. It was a wild, provoking laugh

and he thought she knew that, though she did nothing to stop it.

"How's that working out for you, Joaquin? Because it seems to me that if anything, this *handshake* of ours is only getting more intense."

He would have preferred it if she'd kept her unwelcome honesty to herself.

"It won't last," he bit out. "And even if it does last some little while, it's immaterial. Because there is nowhere for this to go. I won't be falling in love with you again. There will be no accidental pregnancies that link me to you forever. I rarely make mistakes, and when I do? I don't repeat them."

"Joaquin," she began.

He pulled her even closer, making sure that he could get his face even closer to hers, so that this was some kind of mockery of every kiss they'd shared so far. It almost felt the same. That intense, that passionate.

This close to unhinged.

"I won't pretend I don't enjoy this chemistry between us," he told her, almost touching her lips with his. "But the only thing I will ever want from you, Amalia, is your body. Do you understand me?"

"Perfectly," she threw back at him.

And for a moment, they both stayed as they were, her chest rising and falling as rapidly as his. Their breath seemed to saw through the air, disrupting the patter of the rain as it fell.

But it was far too much like all the other things they did when they were touching like this.

He uncurled his hands from her shoulders and stepped away, entirely too cognizant of the fact it was more difficult to do than it should have been.

Much more difficult.

Just as it was to turn on his heel and walk away from her.

He stomped down the path to his little dungeon and in all the time he'd stayed here, it had never felt more like the prison it had been than tonight. Joaquin resented the work he'd put into the place, because he wanted to slam the doors behind him, damn it, and yet they all were too smooth and closed too quietly.

In the bedroom, he stripped off his clothes and made his way into the grand shower enclosure and stood there, propping himself up against the wall as the water poured down all around him.

And he told himself he'd meant every word.

He had.

And still, everything in him leaped when the door to the shower opened some while later, when the steam had begun to billow around him.

Amalia stepped in, naked now. Her dark hair swirled around her, already wet. It seemed to call attention to her small, perfect breasts, and the indentation of her waist. He had spent a lot of time in this very shower with his hands splayed out over those hips, holding her sex to his lips so he could hear her cries echo off the tiles while he treated her like a dessert. He liked to prop her up against the shower wall, because he liked the way her fists dug into his hair as he held her up on his shoulders.

It was the only time he knelt before her. And that was fair enough, he assured himself. It was all about sex. That was what he'd told her, because it was true.

It wasn't that pleasuring her pleased him, deeply. It wasn't that sometimes, he thought the point of all of it was afterward, when she was limp and curled around him, sometimes right here on the shower floor.

It couldn't be the way she buried her face in his neck, the two of them simply clinging to each other while another bout of their endless passion wore itself out.

It had nothing to do with how he liked to carry her out of here after tasting her so thoroughly, so he could set her on the marble counter and take his time drying her off. Toweling every part of her body, then slicking her everywhere with the soft cream she preferred, so she smelled of night blooming flowers with a hint of spice.

And it was best all round that Joaquin did not permit himself to think about all the times he woke to find the two of them tangled up together in his bed, sleeping so close it was as if neither one of them could make it through the night unless they were touching in as many places as possible.

When he sometimes slept on the hard floors of his various residences, purely to remind himself where he came from. And to make sure he never forgot what real life was like without all the softness he now enjoyed.

Softness led to pain. Those were his earliest memories. He had learned either to keep from wanting anything—or to make sure he could buy the lot of it, so he never needed to worry about losing it.

He had veered from that course precisely once.

She closed the shower door behind her and looked at him, her eyes far too large.

"I keep trying to run you off," he growled at her. "But you won't go."

He shouldn't have said that, but she laughed it off anyway.

"Why should you be the only one using this chemistry of ours for your own ends?" she asked, lightly enough. Though he found he didn't quite believe it. Not when her gaze seemed far darker than that bright summer blue it normally was. "Maybe, Joaquin, I just want to use you for sex. Or is that not allowed?"

"It's entirely encouraged."

And as she moved closer to him, he caught her up, lifting her into the air so she could twine that marvelous body of hers around him. He slid her wet body down the length of his, then sighed a little when she opened one of her hands and showed him the condom she'd brought with her.

"So there can be no confusion," she whispered, and he couldn't tell if that was a challenge or a dig. When he shouldn't have cared either way.

He ripped the packet open with his teeth, and sheathed himself in an easy movement, then lowered her onto his sex.

And he'd told her she would get used to this, but he never did. The tight fit. The perfection of her body holding tight to his. The friction, the heat.

Joaquin took his sweet time lifting her up, then lowering her down. Again and again, until her head was tipped back, her eyes were closed, and she was not issuing challenges any longer.

She was chanting out his name.

He should have been jubilant, he thought later, after he carried her out into their bed and rededicated himself to the task of tearing them both apart. He should have been delighted that they were both on the same page.

And later, when she drifted off to sleep beside him once more, curled into his side as if this was something other than what it was, Joaquin lay awake and stared at the stone ceiling. Then out the glass wall where the sea surged and retreated, again and again.

She had just given him everything he claimed to

want. She hadn't fought him. She hadn't dissolved into tears, or begged him to change his mind.

Was that what he wanted? Was his true aim here no more and no less than to humble her? Was that really who he was?

Because a wise man would set that aside, when given assurances that both he and Amalia were on the same page. No emotions. No future. Just the delirious, delicious madness of the passion between them until it waned.

Surely that would be any day now, he told himself.

Any day at all.

Though perhaps he would have believed that more if he'd thought she really meant it. He found he didn't. He couldn't. He looked at her beside him, sleeping so peacefully, and couldn't ignore the way his heart thumped now.

Because maybe he was more sentimental than he liked to admit. Maybe he had fallen too hard for that artless girl he'd thought she was that first summer.

Some part of him had never believed the scornful Princess she'd become at the end.

And he knew his summer girl would never have agreed to an arrangement like this. She would have sobbed. Her heart would have been broken. She might never have told him that she loved him, but she hadn't had to. He'd known.

It had been in every glance, every smile. Every touch.

And she accepted, lying there, that he didn't like the possibility that none of that was happening now. It was fine if *he* did not fall in love. That was his goal.

But he didn't much care for the hollow feeling inside him at the notion that *she* didn't love *him,* either.

Joaquin found he didn't like it at all.

CHAPTER SEVEN

A FEW DAYS LATER, Amalia returned from a long late afternoon walk to find one of the few members of staff on
the island waiting for her at the top of the private path
that led to the dungeon villa.

"If you would like to change for dinner," the woman
said deferentially, "Señor Vargas waits for you on the
lower patio."

"Are you sure?" Amalia asked in surprise. Then
flushed a bit when the woman shot her a quizzical look.
She knew better than to make personal remarks to people who could not, by virtue of their position, respond in
kind. *Friendly does not mean friends,* Esme had drilled
into her. "I mean, of course. Thank you. I'll get there
as soon as I can."

She hurried down the path, pulling open the heavy
front door that always made her shiver a bit for those
who'd been locked up behind it, and half expected him
to be inside. No doubt laughing at whatever joke this
was, or waiting to pounce and examine her every last
facial expression to see if he could discern her actual
feelings. Then demolish them.

But the villa was empty. Amalia hurried through her
shower, realizing as she soaped herself up and rinsed
it all away that she couldn't recall the last time she'd

taken a shower by herself. Normally, it was only one more venue to experiment with all that *just sex* they were having.

After he'd left her in the rain the way he had, she had not faced the prospect he'd laid out before her with anything approaching equanimity.

On the contrary, she had cried.

A lot.

Her tears had been indistinguishable from the rain and she'd taken that as a kind of blessing. But she'd still slid all the way down to the base of that palm tree, cradled her head in her arms, and cried.

Because everything in her life had been taken away from her and it didn't matter whether she'd wanted those things or not. She'd spent twenty-five years believing they were hers.

Her mother being one of them.

And yet all the commentary—whether from so-called news sources, or the Queen's inner circle of courtiers and aides, or even Joaquin—all seemed to be in agreement on one thing. That this was all somehow her fault.

As if she, at three days old, had set out to usurp a throne located halfway across the planet.

As if, a voice had whispered inside her while the rain poured down, *your entire goal during your first summer here was to hurt Joaquin as much as you could.*

When the reality was, she had been so naive that it had never occurred to her to guard herself against him. She had fallen so fast and so hard that it had been all over in a single glance. And the only reason she'd managed to force herself to do what had to be done in the end was because she had been so besotted with Joaquin that she couldn't bear the thought of the alternative.

Which was Queen Esme doing what she could not.

She might have channeled her mother when she'd spoken to him, but she had still been far kinder to him than Esme would have been. Yet how could she explain that to him?

Amalia had been the Crown Princess of a pretty little island that most people treated as if it was a real-life fairy tale. No one would believe, ever, that she hadn't known what she was doing. That she hadn't been fully in control of everything that had happened here.

Deep down, she suspected Joaquin still thought that, too.

And that day in the rainstorm, the injustice of it all had left her heaving with sobs she usually kept locked away deep inside.

She'd cried and cried.

But then, eventually, the sobs had stopped.

Amalia had let the rain wash her face clean. She'd sat there, letting the storm pound into her, and she'd let go of the injustice. The unfairness.

Maybe, she'd whispered to herself, *this is what you deserve.*

Because she hadn't always been a good person, had she? She'd let her mother guide her too completely. Any enemy of Esme's had been an enemy of hers, that went without saying. Esme's opinions, on everything and anything, had been her guide. Even when she'd had the opportunity to act any way she pleased, in a situation Esme knew nothing about and could never know anything about, she'd defaulted to cruelty.

How could Amalia blame Joaquin for refusing to engage with her now when she'd treated him that way back then? Surely if she had half the heart she liked to pretend she did, she would not have been capable of saying the things she'd said to him then.

It didn't matter that she'd hurt herself, too.

Maybe what she really needed to accept was that she'd come here, not because she was after freedom. But because she needed forgiveness.

And maybe the only path to forgiveness available to her wasn't the one she wanted. Maybe she and Joaquin really would throw themselves headfirst into this passion until there was none left, and it would all dissolve into indifference.

Maybe, at the end of the day, that was the best version of forgiveness she was going to get.

That was why she'd gone to find him in the shower that day. That was why she'd simply accepted everything he'd said to her.

And in the days since, she hadn't attempted to provoke him. To poke or to prod for answers she liked, or to get him to admit that the intensity between them meant something. Because even if it did, he didn't want it to.

She supposed after the way she'd treated him, she deserved that, too.

Tonight, when she was out of the shower, she took her time with her toilette. She didn't often get the opportunity to dress here, and she'd missed it. Carelessly romping about in the Spanish sun was all very well, but she also liked the sultry lick of bold lipstick across her lips. The slick of mascara on her lashes.

Amalia knew he didn't like her chignon, so she gathered her hair up in something much looser and more inviting on the top of her head, letting tendrils fall where they would. Then she slipped into a shimmering column of a dress that she had bought on a whim but had never worn to any official function, because it was cut much too high on the thigh, and had no back to speak of.

Queen Esme would not have approved.

And only when Amalia approved of her reflection from every angle did she make her way back up the path. She crossed through the lobby, then headed down again on the other side of the old fortress, heading toward the patio that sat on a cliff out on the edge of the island, offering captivating views of the sea beyond.

They claimed Barcelona was visible on a clear day if conditions were right, though she'd never seen it. Then again, it was possible she'd never looked. She had always been far more focused on what was on the island than what might be around it.

She passed the patio where she'd met Joaquin for the first time, long ago, nestled far closer to the hotel. Seeing it made her smile as she kept going down the path, enjoying the soft evening air as she moved. The pathway was lit with small lanterns throwing off just enough light to make it from one to the next, leading her down a gentle slope toward the cliff's edge.

When she got there, Joaquin was waiting.

He, too, had dressed for the evening, and looked nothing short of commanding as he stood there at the rail at the edge of the cliffs. He was gazing at her as if he'd known the exact moment she would appear.

And as she crossed the patio to his side, Amalia couldn't help imagining what that look on his face might have meant, if they were other people…

As if she needed help to break her own heart.

"I'm surprised you wanted to eat together," she said when he took her hand in one of his and, astonishingly, lifted it to his lips. Her heart flipped over inside her chest, though she tried to ignore it. "I would have thought that doesn't go along with your…stated aims."

"You are here, are you not? I might as well enjoy your company."

But his tone was gruff. His eyes were too green. And something in her chest seem to clutch around the notion that this, somehow, was an apology.

The only one she was likely to get from this proud, hard man.

Amalia cautioned herself not to read too much into it as he led her over to a table that had been exultantly, meticulously prepared for an intimate party of two. It sat beneath a pretty canopy that blocked the breeze and any curious eyes from back at the fortress. Joaquin helped her into her seat, then took his own. And for a moment, she could confuse the odd butterflies in her stomach with the bustle of his staff around them as they poured out the wine, then served a first course, a small whimsy from the chef.

But when they melted off into the shadows again, she was left with Joaquin. And the sea. And the quiet all around them, as if this was the sort of date they'd indulged in that first summer, when sex had only been a part of what was happening between them.

That silly, fluttery reaction inside of her kept rolling around inside her, because this was the first time they had sat at a table like civilized adults since she'd arrived here. She understood that it was deliberate. Looking back, she should have known that from day one. He was keeping everything about sex and happenstance on purpose, when she knew perfectly well that he was capable of providing any experience that might take his fancy.

Five-star dining on a cliff above the sea on a whim, for example.

But somehow, even though she tried what was on the plate before her, she could hardly make sense of it. The only thing she could seem to concentrate on was the turmoil inside her.

Possibly because, here, dressed in the sort of armor she had always used to her advantage before, what was happening inside her seemed far more obvious. Because all the rest of the time they spent together, the only thing she could focus on was that greedy passion that she was certain was the ruin of her.

It had already ruined her. She'd known that for years already.

But she couldn't handle the way he seemed so content to sit there and *brood* at her.

"I think a lot these days about the sorts of things I take for granted that I never would have known if I'd stayed where I belonged," she said. For something to say that cut through all that dark green *brooding*. She waved her hand over the formal place setting before her. "Take something as simple as plates and utensils. I somehow think that place settings like this do not feature heavily on a Kansas farm." Amalia smiled as she said it. "Though in truth, I have no idea. For all I know, the woman who gave birth to me speaks of nothing, night and day, but appropriate table manners for all occasions."

"Table manners are nothing but a gateway," Joaquin said, as if he was handing down judgment.

He lounged there across from her, toying with his glass of wine, and his green eyes seemed to burn straight through her. "There's nothing the upper class enjoys more than the hoops it creates to keep upstarts and commoners out of its ranks."

"I tried a similar argument with one of my governesses when I was small." Amalia lifted her own wine to her lips to taste it, not at all surprised to find it was spectacular. "She was unmoved. And made me sit with a heavy book on my head to improve my posture while thinking about the error of my ways."

"I took a relatively high-class lover after I made my first fortune," Joaquin told her, as if this was the sort of thing they discussed all the time. So casual. So sophisticated. His *lovers*. She took a rather larger gulp of her wine. "She was a mistake for many reasons."

"Oh, by all means, enlighten me," Amalia replied as nonchalantly as possible, because she was certain this was some kind of a test. She had romantic feelings for him, as they had both agreed she wouldn't, and so, surely, she would react badly to details of his legions of other women. And in truth, it felt a lot like tearing off a scab to lean forward and smile encouragingly at him, as if what she really wanted was a close, personal tour through all the women he had loved before her.

She had to hope that *love* in this context was nothing but a euphemism. Not that it really made her feel all that much better to imagine Joaquin involved in the kind of wild, passionate acts they'd experienced together—but with someone else. With a great many someone elses.

But he was studying her face far too closely, and Amalia would throw herself off the cliff in front of them before she'd give him the satisfaction of seeing how this hurt her.

"She was like most of these high-class girls," he said with a certain casual disregard that set her teeth on edge. By design, she was certain. "You know how they are. Wholly unaware of how lucky they were to have been born into their position. Always so bored, for some reason, when the whole world is right there at their disposal. And, of course, deeply selfish in bed."

She had been prepared to be quietly outraged and outwardly impassive. But Amalia found herself frowning at him instead. "I don't think I know what that means."

His green eyes gleamed. "Do you not?"

"As you pointed out, so memorably, you are the only lover I've ever had. Am I selfish? Are you? How would I know?"

His gaze grew more intense and he leaned forward, reaching over to take her hand in his. And even that made her pulse leap. Even that made her body shiver into readiness, because she was so attuned to him now that all he needed to do was look at her in a certain way and she would simply *ignite*.

"One of the things that astonishes me about you, Princess, is that no matter your cruelty when it suits you, you are anything but selfish," he told her in that roughly stirring way of his. "Particularly in bed. And that is what many people do not understand. Good sex has nothing to do with tricks or positions. It is about pleasure. And a certain generosity of intent."

Amalia felt herself get warm. Everywhere. "I had no idea you were such a…master of the form."

She saw a flash of his teeth, that hint of a smile that made her feel almost embarrassingly giddy. "I think, Amalia, that you know very well that I am."

He let go of her hand to sit back in his chair again, still smiling while she turned pink all over. And stayed that warm, despite herself, when he kept telling his story.

"She was very boring, of course, this heiress," Joaquin said, as if that was obvious. As if heiresses in his experience were expected to be boring unless they proved themselves otherwise. "But useful. Like many of her ilk, her primary purpose in life was to irritate her father. And like most of them, she is now married to the tedious man her father chose for her, but only after having tortured her whole family with her terrible choices. Like me." He smiled, but this smile had more of a razor's edge. "She used me for her own ends. I used her for polish. Everyone likes a diamond in the rough, Amalia. But only because it is a diamond. It is not the rough that appeals."

"You seem so…unabashed," she replied, still warmer than she ought to have been, given the subject matter. "I was under the impression that most people at least *pretend* that the heart is what leads them."

"Some pay for school. Some have tutors." He shrugged. "I chose my lovers wisely."

"Not everyone can be so wise," she said, and realized she sounded far more wistful than she should have.

"Queen Esme did not make a list of marriageable suitors for you because she liked them." And there was that steel in his voice again, then. "Or because she thought you would. All of her choices were strategic, always. For the benefit of Ile d'Montagne, not you."

Amalia felt a bit less warm and pink, then. "Yes, but I was—"

"The heir to the kingdom. I am aware. I did not have the good fortune to be born so well situated." He didn't say that with his usual dark undercurrent. Perhaps that was progress. "I did not intend to allow myself to be locked out of anywhere I wished to go. Or anything I wished to do. If I have a secret weapon, as my enemies are so certain I do, it is this. As soon as I identify something I need to learn, I dedicate myself to learning it.

My adversaries will always think they have one upon me, with their fancy schools and their pedigrees and their silver spoon friendships from the cradle." Another shrug. "I certainly don't need to give them ammunition because I don't know which fork to use."

She mulled that over as the staff returned, taking away her untouched plate, and replacing it with another one, heaped with another demonstration of the chef's prowess. But still, she wasn't hungry. She watched instead as Joaquin picked up what was inarguably the correct fork, and dug in.

Really, she ought to do the same. "What happens when you've conquered all the things that need conquering," she asked him instead. "Do you even have a plan? Or are you simply trying to own as many things as it is possible to own before you die?"

"Only people who have never had to worry about money," Joaquin said, very quietly, "imagine that gathering it is not an end in itself."

"I suppose this is where, like all the lovers you had and disdain, I should apologize for the accident of my birth. Or rather, the proximity of my birth to that of the actual heir to the kingdom of Ile d'Montagne. An accident twice over, it seems."

"But that is the trouble with apologies, Amalia." She was caught, again, in that flash of impossible green. "Who is it that they really serve?"

He returned his attention to the meal before him as if he had merely commented on the weather. Amalia did the same, staring down at her plate and then eating the food there—also with the correct utensils—though she could not have said what it was.

Because what was clear to her, finally, was that there was no forgiveness to be found here. She suspected he might even know that was what she wanted. What was obvious to her, at last, was that he had no intention of providing it.

This was a man who had dated women he didn't like so he could learn *table manners*.

Really, what had she expected?

Amalia suddenly felt remarkably old, then. Exhausted, perhaps. Because she had loved him and lost him once, and that had changed her life. She had gone on as she always had, because that was what had been required of her.

But she had never been the same.

She had spent a lot less time wishing she could be normal, whatever that was. She had focused much more intently on living up to her mother's expectations, partly because she had known—even if Esme had not—that Amalia had already let her down. But also because she had left Joaquin to be what her mother expected her to be. She had left him, and badly, so that she could be the most perfect Crown Princess the island had ever seen.

Having lost so much, how could she possibly give the life she'd chosen anything but her all?

Now she'd lost that life, too. And she still couldn't have him. Not the way she wanted him. He would never forgive her. Never.

And Amalia did not think she had it in her to be nothing but a cautionary tale he would tell someday, about his *lovers*.

"This was not my finest idea," he said over coffee, when their meal was done. Done, though Amalia had hardly tasted a thing. "I'm too used to having you. Looking at you across a table is torture."

Because the only thing between them was sex, as far as he was concerned. Why couldn't she accept that?

Why did she keep imagining it could be different? Joaquin wasn't the problem. He had been perfectly clear.

She was the problem.

And even knowing that, she wanted him.

In any way she could have him.

"There are many kinds of torture," she said, which was perhaps unwise. She made herself smile when his dark brows rose. "Look at where we sleep every night. It's a wonder we can rest at all, with all the things that must have occurred within those walls. You do know they call it the Spanish Inquisition, do you not? That's for a reason."

He laughed, surprising her, when everything within her felt dire and fraught. "And here I thought you slept untroubled by anything. I blame myself. I must dedicate myself to tiring you out."

Sex, she thought again. *Always sex.*

It was really almost funny. Amalia had spent all those years dreaming of things like this each night. And now that she had him a thousand ways a day, she wanted…something else. Something more.

Not because the sex wasn't good. The trouble was that it was earth-shattering. Life-altering.

But he pretended it wasn't. He pretended it meant nothing.

When she could still remember too well how it had felt when he had openly adored her. When she had been so heedlessly, so recklessly in love with him and he had treated her as if she was rare and precious to him.

And there had been a little too much *nothing* in her life lately. Finding out she was nothing, for example. Then being treated like she was nothing by the entire world.

Now, this. More nothing.

Amalia wanted, more than anything, to be something. To be *someone.*

It didn't matter who. She just wanted to be *someone,* at last. And important in some small way to someone else.

And when she let herself think that, it seemed to take hold of her. It seemed to roll through her, marking her, shifting things around inside her. It made her understand, for better or worse, that it might be the one thing she wanted more than him.

"You're looking at me strangely," Joaquin said, and she wondered how long she'd been sitting like this. Staring at him and wishing things could be different. "It is as I thought. We are not meant to sit about making conversation, you and I. We have better things to do."

"What if I set you a challenge?" Amalia set her delicate coffee cup down, with a decisive click of the cup against its saucer. "Just a small challenge."

"To what end?" he asked, because he was always the businessman. He was all about angles and inroads, and the best possible way to get the most while giving very little.

She supposed she had always known that, too.

"There's no end, Joaquin."

She paused a moment, because she felt as if she was poised on a precipice, and not because this patio sat on the top of a cliff. Not because she could hear the sea against the rocks down below. But because of him.

He might think the time they'd spent together was a physical release, nothing more. Weeks upon weeks of it.

But she knew him. In ways she had never known another human being.

And she understood the world in a different way now, too. All the things she'd watched, or read, or heard talked about. All the ways that people interacted with each other, where sex infused everything. Looking forward to having it, wishing they had it, missing when they'd had it before. The world spun around and around the axis of sex, and it was impossible to think about it at all without realizing how profoundly it affected everyone who partook.

And yet men like Joaquin wanted to stand about and claim it meant nothing. That it was like going to the gym and getting a sweat going, if that.

Amalia fully comprehended that this was little more than a distancing attempt on his part. She even understood why. She had hurt him. He wanted to hurt her, and even better, keep from feeling anything for her again.

But she was here. She was taking part in all of this meaningless physical release with him. Joaquin might have thought that he could hide himself there. He couldn't.

The fact was, physical intimacy was intimacy whether he liked it or not.

Bodies couldn't keep up this kind of sustained connection without forming other connections, too. She wasn't as naive as she'd been when she was twenty, thanks to him. So she knew that just because it was intimacy—emotional as well as physical, after all this time—that didn't mean he was going to admit that they were having the relationship they were having.

It also didn't mean she was required to pretend they weren't.

"What if we didn't have sex?" She threw that out there with remarkable calm, when inside, she shook. "For a week. Or even a day. Just to see what happens."

He looked at her for a long moment. Too long. She saw a kind of knowledge in his green eyes that she didn't want to admit was there. As if he knew exactly why she was asking this question. And more, what it would mean to her if he agreed.

"Why would we do that?" Joaquin asked with a soft menace she desperately wanted to mistake for something else. But couldn't. "Sex is the only reason we are both here, Amalia. As well you know."

There was a finality to that. A certainty that she'd missed before. Or maybe she just hadn't been able to take it on board, too concerned with her own shortcomings. Too worried about whether or not he would ever forgive her.

He wouldn't. Because he didn't want to. And that was that.

At long last, Amalia let that settle in on her. She let it take root. And she had been through a whole gauntlet of discovery over the past few months. Mostly she'd discovered that she was nothing and nobody, despite having been raised to be a very specific somebody, fulfilling a very precise role.

This was different.

How could she willingly, knowingly subject herself to life without any hint of love when she was suddenly free to have any life she wanted? What was wrong with her that she *wanted* to stay here with a man who actively and only wanted, if not to hurt her, then to make certain she never, ever felt comfortable with him? A man who had made it clear in a thousand ways that because of what happened before, she could never deserve any better from him?

Why, after everything she'd gone through, was she signing up for this already long-lost battle?

I wanted you to know that I love you, too. And I

missed you when you were gone, Catherine Clark had said in that voice mail.

Across space and time, she was loved. As she was not loved here. And maybe it was time Amalia went and looked for love where it was offered.

It sounded so simple. Maybe all these games of princesses and billionaires had confused the issue. It was time for cornfields, ruby slippers, and the one person on this earth who didn't seem to have the slightest bit of trouble claiming she loved Amalia.

She didn't know why she'd waited so long.

"You don't have to do it, of course," she said now. She met his gaze and held it. She did not whimper. Or cry. "But I'm tired of sex, Joaquin. I'm tired of physical releases and nothing else." *And you,* she wanted to say, though she wasn't that brave. Because it wasn't precisely true. Like everything involving Joaquin, it was more complicated than that. "I'm going to Kansas."

CHAPTER EIGHT

AMALIA WANTED TO cry out something like *There's no place like home!* as she made her way along the country road, then carefully turned into what she hoped was the correct drive that would lead to the Clark farm.

She was in Kansas. And she had loved *The Wizard of Oz*. It would be lovely to think of herself as some kind of Dorothy, finally waking up to the place she truly belonged.

But it didn't feel like home. It felt alien and strange here, flat and unwelcoming.

Then again, that might have been her emotional reaction to leaving Cap Morat and Joaquin once again.

He had not made it easy.

The first thing he'd done was laugh.

You're tired of sex, are you? he'd asked her, still there at that table on the top of a cliff. *Shall we test that theory?*

And she would have liked to say that she had held steady. That she had stood firm in her resolve. That she had stalwartly refused to allow him to reduce her, once again, to nothing but that wildfire that forever burned between them. Nothing but lust and need, forever.

But she was not that strong.

She wanted him too much.

He had taken her there, right there on the table where she had barely tasted her food. But she tasted him. There was nothing better, nothing brighter. He'd swept what few dishes remained aside and made her scream out her need and her fury to the stars above.

Recklessly. Heedlessly.

He'd made her do it again and again.

I told you that you can leave whenever you like and I meant it, he had said, his mouth against her neck. *You are welcome to leave this island at first light, Amalia. I will call for a boat myself.*

She had waited, still splayed out beneath him, because she somehow did not trust this…helpful attitude on Joaquin's part.

Sure enough, his eyes blazed as he pinned her there beneath him with all that green. *But if you leave now, you can never return, Amalia. This is not a safe space for you.*

She'd sat up gingerly, as if she expected something to hurt, though nothing ever did. Maybe she wished it would. If it hurt, then maybe it would mean something after all. At the very least, maybe it would teach her a lesson she desperately needed to learn.

Thank you, she'd said, because it didn't hurt at all. Sensation swirled inside of her, the way it always did. She wanted him all over again, the way she feared she always would. *That has been perfectly clear for some time now.*

The next day, she expected him to intervene once again. To use her body against her, simply because he could, but he didn't. She woke alone in that bed beneath the high tide line to find her things packed. And even though that really did hurt, and the hurting was not better, she had decided to take that message at face value.

He really had called her a boat. She had taken it to Barcelona.

Once again, while leaving him and Cap Morat, she had not looked back. There was no need—she doubted she would ever get all the images of what she'd done there out of her head. And she already knew she took the ghost of him wherever she went.

Why bother looking back?

It had been simple enough to hire a plane once she reached Barcelona and fly herself to Kansas. Simple, but not easy. Because she had spent too long indulging her every whim on that island. She felt addicted to Joaquin, strung out on his touch, and it was worse this time. It had been bad enough after that first summer. But at least then she had been filled with purpose when she'd left him. She'd had her work to throw herself into, her role in the kingdom, a place in history. A future to work toward, like it or not.

Now all she had was the slender hope of *love,* of all things, from a woman she'd never really met—except as a newborn. In a place she would never have visited. As a stepping-stone to a future she still couldn't quite envision.

Amalia really did want, so desperately, to feel some sense of belonging here. To feel tugged back into the embrace of this land that had made her, but she didn't. She was grateful that Esme considered knowing how to drive a vehicle essential knowledge, because otherwise, she wasn't sure how she would have gone about hiring herself a car and drivers so far out in what seemed to be the middle of nowhere. Even so, driving felt treacherous out here where the flat land went on forever, so that the horizon seemed both impossibly far away and on top of her at the same time. The sky was too large here. The fields too secretive, somehow—though she suspected that was only because she couldn't identify all the crops she saw.

She eased the little hired car down the lane, wincing every time the dirt track gave way and the tires dropped down with a tooth-rattling jolt. But she'd checked and rechecked, and this was the address Catherine had given her.

Amalia had seen images like this her whole life. It was impossible to grow up anywhere, she imagined, without some notion of the American heartland stamped into her brain. Green stalks of corn. Golden wheat. Whatever the other crops she'd seen were, all in neat lines, rolling on forever. But it was one thing to watch a show. It was something else to find herself in the middle of it.

When she got to the end of the lane she was confronted with an actual American farmhouse to one side, an honest-to-God red barn straight ahead, and the fields of corn all around—hemming her in a bit, she thought. She hadn't really expected the corn to feel like a living wall. But Amalia blew out a breath and told herself that she was no coward.

Even if, at that exact moment, she felt the surely cowardly urge to turn the car around and drive away. As fast as possible.

She pushed open the car door, forced herself to climb out, then stood there, waiting for a sense of homecoming to sweep over her now that she'd arrived at the actual family home where she should have spent her childhood. To make it clear that she had made the right choice. To make all of this feel right.

But instead, she felt profoundly alone. There was only her beneath an endless blue sky above and the corn, watching her as she stood there, trying not to feel dizzy.

Despite herself, she missed Joaquin.

And Amalia hated herself for that weakness. How could she miss a man who didn't really want her? Or wanted her, but not in the way she needed him to? And yet even as she thought that, her body knew she was thinking about him and shivered with that same unutterable delight it always did.

Even here, a world apart from him after she'd left him *again,* she couldn't even work up a decent temper. She couldn't force herself to fall out of love with him, or want less from him, or stop feeling all of these things that would get her absolutely nowhere.

She just wanted him the way she always had. The way she supposed she always would.

And maybe someday, that would feel like less of a life sentence.

Because at the moment, she would have given anything to press her face into the crook of his neck, say nothing at all, and let herself believe that the way he held her could mean anything she wanted it to. That she was precious to him. That he would hold her forever. That what they were to each other meant more to him than a story he could tell over dinner one night.

Amalia jumped guiltily when she heard a noise. She turned to see an older woman step out from inside the farmhouse, letting the screen door slam shut behind her.

And she knew.

Maybe because there was no reason for any other woman to be staring at her like this, but she thought it was a little bit deeper than that. A little bit more.

This woman was her actual mother. And Amalia knew it. On sight.

After so much nothing, she had to admit that it felt like *something.*

She moved, jerkily, around the front of the car. Then she made herself walk across the yard toward the stranger. The stranger who was her mother.

Amalia hadn't known how a person was meant to dress to meet her mother for the first time. As an adult. She also hadn't known what a person wore on a farm. So she'd gone ahead and winged it, going for jeans and trainers and what she hoped was the sort of T-shirt that everybody wore. Instead of it being the kind of T-shirt that only people like her wore while swanning about, trying to seem *relatable,* which wasn't at all the same thing. That she was a fish out of water in every respect would be all too noticeable, she feared—

And worrying about her attire was a lot easier than worrying about all the rest of it.

But when she came to a stop just below the step the woman stood on, Catherine Clark, her *mother,* didn't appear to notice what Amalia was wearing. She was too busy staring at her.

At Amalia, as if she couldn't quite take her in.

As if Amalia was what mattered. As if she was the only thing that mattered.

"Here you are," her mother whispered. "Finally."

And it was possible they stood there for a lifetime. Maybe two, just gazing at each other. Both of them, Amalia was sure, were cataloguing the other's face. Looking for clues or possibly recognition. As if each of them was a treasure map.

And any other time, simply standing and staring at another person would have been awkward. Uncomfortable. But not today. Not with Catherine.

My mother, Amalia thought, in wonder.

It was only when Catherine came down from her step by the door, that Amalia even noticed that she'd reached out to grip Amalia's hand.

Had she been doing this all along? Amalia didn't know. But she found she didn't mind.

Just as she didn't mind when Catherine led her out into the fields, away from the farmhouse. Straight into the stalks that had seemed like a wall to her. It seemed to Amalia that they walked forever. The corn rose all around them and seemed to whisper as they passed, but Catherine kept walking until she reached a small clearing.

When she stopped, she smiled, and Amalia found herself smiling back. As if she couldn't help herself.

"When I was pregnant with you I used to come out here," the older woman told her. "I would lie down on the ground, put my hands on my belly, and tell you how your life was going to be. We couldn't see the whole sky but what we could see was blue and beautiful, and I wanted your life to feel that way. Endless possibilities, in or out of the cornfields." She smiled at Amalia fondly. So fondly that Amalia was taken back.

Because Esme didn't do *fondly*. And Amalia understood why. Esme hadn't been raising a daughter and hoping for the best. Esme had been preparing a ruler to take over the country she had dedicated her life to.

And still, on balance, Amalia found she quite liked *fondly*. She wanted to return the favor. She gripped her mother's hands and she smiled back.

"I have—I *had*—a good life," she said, because wasn't that what any woman would want to hear from the child she'd unwittingly given away? And the bonus was, it was true. Being away from that life for a little while had made that even more clear. "A very strange life, I suppose. But a good one. I know what people say about Queen Esme, and it's true that she can be quite formidable. But she loves me. And though I think she would never admit it, because she can't admit such things without appearing weak, this has all distressed her. Deeply." She squeezed Catherine's hands. "I have no complaints. The life I was brought up to lead was a good one. I loved my work. I adored my people. I loved the Queen, my mother. It wasn't always an easy life, but it was a good one. And now I get to do what very few people get to do in this life, and create an entirely new one."

She realized as she said these things that they, too, were true. That she had gotten lost in the things she'd given up and a man who couldn't love her. When all along, it had been a distraction from the real gift, which was this. Getting to stand here, looking into the eyes of the woman who'd carried her within her body. And knowing that whatever happened next, Amalia would be the one who chose it.

If that wasn't freedom, she didn't know what was.

"I can't pretend to understand the doings of queens and princesses," Catherine said after a moment. "But it brings me great joy to hear you did not suffer. And that these recent revelations have not wrecked you."

"They felt as if they might," Amalia admitted. And then, emboldened by the compassion in the other woman's gaze, continued. "I'll confess that I used to dream about having a normal life, but that didn't mean I actually wanted one."

"I understand," Catherine said, with a wry sort of smile. "There are few things on this earth more complicated than a wish granted."

Amalia supposed she would know, and better than most.

"But we are all so lucky now," she said, because she wanted to believe that. "Your daughter and I have two mothers each, just as you and the Queen each have two daughters. I suppose that makes us all family."

"And you and Delaney a kind of sisters." Catherine smiled. "For only the two of you can understand both what you've lost and what you've gained."

"This all sounds very wise and knowing and well-adjusted," Amalia said with a laugh. "I hope to fully believe all of it, someday."

Catherine's smile deepened. "I believe you will. And if I may offer a suggestion as you move from one life into a new one, as I myself have just done....?" At Amalia's questioning look she forged ahead. "When Delaney left for Ile d'Montagne, I left the farm as I'd wanted to do since her—since *your* father died before you were born. I thought I might sell it to the neighbors then, but as Delaney pointed out to me, the land is yours. You get to decide what to do with it. In the meantime, I've been building a life for myself in town. I would tell you I love it, though standing here, surrounded by so much history and so many memories, I feel the tug to return. Though I know I won't. My time here is done."

"If you have advice on how to bridge two worlds, I would love to hear it," Amalia whispered.

Catherine looked at her for a long moment, then beckoned toward the ground. Holding Amalia's hands, she took her time kneeling down. She sat for a moment, then lay back the way she'd told Amalia she'd done long ago. Then she waited while Amalia, who had not been raised to clamber about on the ground under any circumstances, did the same.

And perhaps it was foolish to feel a sense of liberation as she stretched out in the dirt, but she did. There would be no one to comment on what she was doing here. No one to take pictures of her in dirty jeans and a muddy T-shirt, then write snide headlines about it in the morning paper.

She could simply lie there, looking up at the perfect blue sky framed by the stalks of corn as they reached for the heavens.

It was peaceful here. Protected, yet isolated.

"I can see why you came here," Amalia said softly. Two black birds flew overhead, making rough, croaking noises at each other, as if they were agreeing. "Thank you for bringing me back here. With you."

Next to her, Catherine made a little sighing sound, then reached over and took Amalia's hand again.

"Love," she said, with the sort of gravity that lodged itself inside Amalia's chest. Right where it hurt. "Love is what matters, Amalia. The world will conspire against you. It will tell you that you must be practical. That you must contain it, hide it, make it palatable. But love is not meant to be hidden away. It is a gift, in any form. In every form. I lost your father before you were born, but I have loved him every day since. It's a *gift*." She squeezed Amalia's hand. "Whatever you do, you must do your best to never squander love, no matter where you find it."

And all told, Amalia spent two weeks in Kansas.

They stayed in the farmhouse, both of them, perhaps, needing to marinate in what could have been.

Catherine told her stories. Of her father, who she had loved so deeply. Of her grandmother, who, Catherine assured her, would have loved Amalia excessively and as far as Catherine was concerned, did so now from above. Amalia learned all about the Clark family, tracing them all the way back to when the first Clarks had left Ireland long ago. In return, she made her mother laugh and laugh with tales of palace protocol and the secret language of clothing choices, according to the ever-watchful press.

They would sit before the fire in the evening and exchange their stories. And at the end of each evening, Amalia would climb up the narrow stairs and find her way into a neat little bed, tucked up beneath the eaves. And dream about the life she might have had, right here in this pretty little place where life was simple—which wasn't to say undemanding. Because Catherine also told her why she'd decided to move off the farm. The demands of livestock, crops. The tether she had felt to this land, like it or not, through good years and bad, ups and downs, and everything in between.

But mostly, Catherine spoke of love. In different forms. The love she felt for the daughter she'd raised. The love she said she felt, here and now, for the daughter she'd carried. The love she felt for her own mother as a dutiful daughter who had not always agreed.

The love she felt for her husband, lost too soon and never forgotten.

When the two weeks were up and they agreed that it was time for Catherine to return to her new life in the aptly named town of Independence, Amalia knew that she would return. Often.

And not only because she'd decided not to sell the land.

She'd agreed to an arrangement with Catherine's closest neighbor, who would tend the land and the crops and claim all but a small percentage of any yield, thereby expanding his operation. Amalia also hired a caretaker for the farmhouse, the barn and the things that went with it—like the vegetable garden—because these things were what made the land a home. Delaney's home, she knew. The place where Delaney and Cayetano Arcieri had honeymooned, though that was hard to believe. Amalia could not imagine the ferocious warlord of Ile d'Montagne in *Kansas*.

But she could preserve the sweetness of this place for the children Delaney and Cayetano would certainly produce, all of them heirs to the Ile d'Montagne crown—and better yet, all of them grandchildren Catherine would claim as her own.

Making them their own kind of cobbled-together family after all. Amalia was happy to do her part.

And besides, she wanted the opportunity to lie in that cornfield again, and lose herself in the sky.

She left Kansas feeling far richer than when she'd arrived. And maybe that was why she took her mother's advice, like the dutiful daughter she'd always been to the Queen, and went to London.

In contrast to Kansas, all bright skies and sunny days this time of year, London was cold and damp. She wrapped herself up tight in the same wrap she had once thrown on a hard stone floor to kneel upon. Amalia fancied that if she concentrated, she could almost find Joaquin's scent clinging to the soft fabric, teasing her.

But then, his ghost had been with her the whole time she'd been out there in those fields. It was a place he had never been, and yet she'd been certain she heard his voice on the breeze. She slept alone, and yet she'd woken in the night—every night—convinced that she could turn over and find him lying there beside her.

One afternoon, while Catherine had napped, Amalia had walked out into the fields on her own. She'd let the stalks of corn whisper to her as she made her way along. She'd followed the directions of the bossy crows, undeterred by any scarecrow.

She'd found her mother's favorite spot and she'd stood there, her eyes shut tight, trying to feel as if she belonged here. With her feet in the Kansas dirt and her face to the Midwest sky.

As if, finally, she'd found her home.

But the only thing she felt there inside of her was Joaquin. So intently, so completely, that she'd jumped slightly where she stood, convinced that she could feel his hands upon her—

Yet when she opened her eyes and turned clear around the circle, she was alone.

Even now, in a sleek car crawling through traffic into Central London, she could hear Catherine's voice in her head the way she had that day. *Love. Love is a gift. You must not squander it.*

Amalia had heard all the things that Joaquin had said to her on the island. She knew that he'd meant them. And she might like to think, in the privacy of her own hopes and dreams, that he could not possibly remain this darkly furious with her if he did not feel *something*…

But if she knew anything in this life, it was that one person could not change another. Her own upbringing at the hands of one of the most stubborn women alive had taught her that. And besides, she'd spent five years trying to change her own mind. Her own heart.

All she could do was accept the gift that had been given to her, or not.

Amalia only needed to make certain that no matter what she did, she honored it. That she did not squander it. That she did not walk away from it, simply because it didn't look the way she thought it should.

She had dressed like the royal princess she no longer was today, though she'd left her hair down because he liked it. She had the car drop her off at the sleek office building in the city, where she knew he kept his offices instead of at his home. Amalia suspected she was far more likely to be able to talk her way past a receptionist than any domestic staff who were, in her experience, far more keen about protecting their employers' privacy.

And when she was ushered into Joaquin's office to find him sitting there, his green eyes glittering while all of London lay at his feet through the windows behind him, Amalia smiled.

"I told you what would happen if you left," Joaquin growled at her.

Which, she couldn't help but notice, wasn't the same thing as summoning security, having her thrown out, or having refused to allow her entry into his office in the first place.

She took that as an encouraging sign.

"London is *an* island," she said. "But it's not *your* island. Not just yet."

"Amalia," he began, in that commanding way of his.

And she told herself that this was love, not addiction. That this was freedom, because she'd chosen it this time. Maybe, she could admit in retrospect, she'd secretly hoped that Joaquin would turn up on the island when she'd returned to it. This time, she'd sought him out directly. It wasn't happenstance. It wasn't luck or coincidence.

It was love, she told herself. And maybe that was the real freedom.

So she unwound her wrap from around her shoulders, then dropped it to the floor as she'd done before, secure in the tinted windows that kept his staff from seeing in. Then she knelt down, smiled at this man she was sure loved her back no matter what he might say to the contrary, and proved it.

CHAPTER NINE

HE HAD WON.

The facts spoke for themselves. It was incontrovertible. Amalia had returned. And it was not lost on him that she had marched straight into his offices, given her name, and made no attempt to conceal her identity when she'd sought him out. That pleased him more than he chose to let on.

He'd won, damn it, and he lived to win.

Though for some reason, now that Amalia was back with him—if in London rather than Cap Morat, a pity only because it meant she wore more clothes—Joaquin could not access that sense of victory he knew he deserved to feel.

"What did you do today?" he asked her one night.

It was late. He had found himself impatient in the midst of closing a major deal, which was unusual for him. Those were the moments he lived for, normally. But nothing was normal these days. Not when he had Amalia living with him in his bright, modern Southwark penthouse, three floors overlooking the Thames that he rarely thought of at all while he was traveling, and now could hardly bear to leave.

He'd found her in the library he kept on the second level tonight and had joined her there, pouring himself a generous measure of Izarra before sitting on one of the notably uncomfortable midcentury armchairs near the gas fire that was made to look like an art installation, not a fire. Another decorator's touch he hadn't cared about enough to decline.

Something he hadn't explained to Amalia when he'd first brought her here. She had looked around, clearly wondering how the same man who could fashion himself something cozy in half-submerged cells could also live here, in this flat of planes and angles and architectural flourishes designed to be looked at, not lived in. For a man who was always at the office, it was nice to come home to a place that was especially created to make it clear that whoever lived here had both wealth and other homes.

But he knew that if he explained all this to Amalia, she would read things into it. He didn't want that.

Or he hadn't wanted that at first. Now he was less sure.

"I went shopping," she told him, looking offensively comfortable in the brutal chair she sat in. And she said it in tones of awe, as if she was confessing to taking up interstellar flight while he'd been pretending to pay attention in a contract negotiation. "It was the most astonishing thing. I simply…walked up and down Oxford Street. All on my own. I wore trainers like everybody else. No one recognized me. No even looked at me. I could have been anyone."

He swirled the liqueur around in his glass. "And this is a good thing?"

"I understand that you spent a considerable amount of time and effort becoming singular." Amalia's overtly blue gaze touched his. She did not touch the glass of Izarra he had set down on the angular table beside her.

She glanced at it now, but didn't pick it up. She looked into the fire instead. "But I'm headed in the opposite direction. I was always singular. And now I must learn how to blend. And I managed it, all on my own."

"Then, of course, you have my congratulations."

Even he could hear how dark he sounded. How ill tempered. And he couldn't have explained himself even if she'd asked—but then, that was the trouble, wasn't it? She wouldn't ask. She did not push him.

He could not complain. She was generous with her body, her time, her enthusiasm. She had come back to him and she had been like a ray of light. A beacon through the British gloom. As if she'd gone off to America only to return with the Spanish sun at her disposal.

Joaquin had basked in her.

But weeks had passed since she'd turned up in his office. Having never entertained a woman in his home before, Joaquin should have paused before moving this one straight in, but he hadn't. He told himself it was because he wanted access to her at his convenience, that was all. Besides, he truly did wish to see if that all-consuming hunger for her that had left him feeling so unbalanced and off-kilter on Cap Morat would continue to affect him here, where it was usually necessary that he go into his office each day.

He'd wanted to see if he could handle it in the real world of London as opposed to the fantasy of Cap Morat. That was the truth of things.

At first Amalia gave herself to him the way she always did. The way she always had. Fully, easily, generously. With that wildfire passion to match his own and that same near-desperation that never seemed to leave either one of them.

He had told her that the only thing between them

was sex, and the sex continued to be blisteringly hot, magnificent in every way. That didn't seem to change no matter what country they were in.

It was when they were out of bed that he found himself... Not quite unnerved. That was too strong a word. But he felt on edge. Because at first she had been so bright, but lately, he had begun to notice that she seemed dimmer. Quieter.

Though when he asked, she always smiled wide and told him she was fine. Then usually loved on him some more.

Why wasn't he satisfied with that? Had he not dreamed of this?

"It is like this library of yours," she was saying now, in that perfectly pleasant way she said everything. But he didn't believe the *pleasantness*. Not when he had watched summer ease away, out of her blue eyes, as one week bled into the next. He felt as if he was losing her when she was *right here*. It was maddening. "You take such pleasure in waving your lack of pedigree and education as a flag. This library tells a different tale."

Joaquin hadn't expected that. His heart, that useless, traitorous organ, began to clatter in his chest.

"I am merely aping my betters," he said quietly. But not without an edge to his voice that he couldn't seem to dispel. "Is that not the fantasy of the upper classes? That, given the opportunity, all of us peasants would try our best to fit in with them? If we could, that is."

"I can't speak to the psychology, Joaquin."

He was certain he did not mistake that faintly chiding note in her voice. But no matter how he studied that beautiful face of hers, he could not seem to crack the code. Amalia was too serene. Too distant. She'd come back to him a ghost in every way but one.

His need for her never eased. But he wanted *her*. Not this version of her who gave him everything he'd said he wanted, but was not the Amalia he craved—raw and undone and always so luminous, in bed and out.

Not the Amalia he still—

But he cut that off. With prejudice. He'd loved her once, yes. But that had been a long time ago. He knew better now.

That edginess in him had teeth. He took another pull from his drink.

"Let me hasten to assure you that I have no desire to impress snobby blue bloods," he told her. Perhaps more harshly than necessary.

"You're the one who keeps talking of performing intellectual feats for others, as if they might be grading you," she said, still sounding *pleasant*. She looked as if she were simply having the sort of conversation anyone might over a cocktail. And she looked engaged, too—not that serene armor she had used so well on the island. Why did it all leave him feeling as if she was that edginess within him, teeth too sharp? "But there are too many volumes in this room with cracked spines and well-worn pages for me to believe that you have not spent a significant amount of time educating yourself. Knowing you, I imagine it gives you pleasure to let these upper-class blue bloods you so disdain imagine that they are speaking of things you cannot understand. When, in fact, you do."

"Snobby, upper-class blue bloods like yourself, you mean."

She smiled, and that should have pleased him, surely. But it only made the disquiet in him worse. The way it did more and more these days. "But I am no such thing. I am made of hardy peasant stock and can trace my lineage all the way back to the potato famine in County Galway. So I am afraid, Joaquin, that you will have to take out these class preoccupations of yours on someone else."

And she might have seemed more and more a ghost to him by the day. Because he felt as if she was slipping away even when she right in front of him, though he could not point to anything she was doing to give him that impression. Just that the light she'd brought with her was fading—and how could he say such a preposterous thing?

He dealt in facts. Not feelings. Not *light*.

Still, there was one way he could reach her. He wasted no time standing from his uncomfortable chair, then going to pull her up out of hers.

"Shall I demonstrate these preoccupations, Princess?" he asked, his voice rough.

But she melted into him the way she always did.

And so he did his best to bring them both alive, right there on his library floor.

The days rolled by. He flew to Hong Kong. To New York. To Perth and back. And whether he took her with him or left her behind, it did not seem to matter. Nothing could make her glow again the way she had.

Not even him.

Telling himself that this was the sweetness of victory and he ought to enjoy it didn't help.

Nor did the notion he had, often, that she was *trying* to find her sparkle in there somewhere. Trying and failing.

One evening he wrapped up his meetings, then returned to the hotel he owned in Singapore. He found her in the private pool attached to the presidential suite, a sleek shape as she cut through the dark water, swimming laps with the skyline looking on.

Joaquin did not alert her to his presence. He stayed where he was, watching her move back and forth. And his heart ached inside him, making it entirely too clear to him that he was missing something. When he prided himself on never missing a thing.

Back and forth she went, slicing her way through the water, her black hair streaming out behind her like ink.

She stopped at one end and stayed there a moment, then two, her gaze out on the city. And when she turned around again, she started when she saw him standing there. But Joaquin found himself focusing on the puffiness of her eyes.

"Have you been crying?" he demanded.

The notion was unacceptable. It made the edginess in him scrape, hard.

"Why would you ask me that?" She lifted her fingers to her face and pressed, there above her cheekbones. "It must be the chlorine."

"Must it?"

Amalia looked at him for far too long, standing there in the water like some kind of selkie, his favorite myth. Yet this was not a moment for fantasy. Something about the blue of her gaze connected too hard to that ache inside him.

Like a blow.

For a moment Joaquin thought he might have swayed where he stood, but that was impossible. He did not *sway*.

She swam to the ladder nearest him, ducked her head back into the water, and smoothed back her hair. Then she rose and as she did, he realized that she was naked.

And he ceased noticing or caring if he swayed on his feet.

"What could I possibly have to cry about?" Amalia asked, her voice soft, but inarguably sultry.

And he thought, *She's using sex as a weapon.*

Just as he liked to do.

He wasn't sure he cared for it—but it was a weapon that worked.

On him as well as her.

And they had been back in London for some while when he remembered that night in Singapore again. The pool. Her eyes red from some emotion she chose not to share with him, when once she would have fought to keep her composure, only to tell him anyway. In one way or another.

Joaquin was astounded to find that he wanted her to tell him everything.

He had instituted nightly dinners and often found himself attempting to make conversation like he was... someone else. *Like you are as she was,* a voice in him liked to point out. *So desperate. So needy.*

But he refused to accept those things were true, so he dismissed them.

Tonight she had been waiting for him in the foyer when he'd come in from the office, dressed in what he knew she'd once considered her armor. All princess, no peasant.

Joaquin understood at once that she had decided to have a conversation with him. At last.

But he had no desire to talk, suddenly. Not if she felt she needed to wear armor to do it.

"I'm famished," he told her shortly.

And when she only smiled that damned smile at him, he'd stomped up the stairs, finding his way to the dining alcove he always preferred. Because it was a narrow stretch of bright wood on one side and glass on the other, and he could pretend that all of not-so-giddy London on the other side of that glass—from Blackfriars into the City—was just another ocean.

As indifferent, as inexhaustible.

But even a full belly could not make him feel easy about the way she looked at him, no hint of summer in her blue eyes.

"You clearly have something you wish to tell me," he bit out at the end of the meal, sitting back in his chair and trying not to look as if he was bracing himself. When he was. "That will make a change, I imagine, from all these weeks of silence."

Amalia frowned. "What silence do you mean? We speak all the time."

"Indeed we do. Of nothing consequential."

"Joaquin. You've made it very clear that intimacy of any kind is unacceptable to you. Or did I misunderstand?"

He could feel his jaw tighten. "You did not."

And, of course, she replied with that smile that went nowhere near her eyes. When once upon a time, it had transformed her whole face—and him, too.

But he knew of only one way to pry it from her lips, and she wanted to *talk* instead.

"I have excellent news," she told him, and he knew, instantly, that he would not agree with that description. "I have been in touch, cautiously, with Delaney Clark. The true Crown Princess, heiress to the Ile d'Montagne throne."

"I know who Delaney Clark is, Amalia."

She acknowledged that with the faintest inclination of her head, though gave no sign that she could hear his foul tone of voice. Which made him feel precisely how he did not wish to feel—like a grubby commoner who might ruin the fine lady's hem with his peasant fingers.

Not a feeling he had ever anticipated having in a flat last valued to the north of eight million quid. That he'd paid for in cash.

"I liked her during our single interaction back on the island," Amalia was telling him. "But it was hard to tell, really, what I felt about anything. That single interaction was a performance, and everything around it was…fraught. Anyway, after going to Kansas, it began to seem silly that she and I weren't some kind of resource to each other." Her lips twisted into something rueful. "She was the one who reached out, actually."

"That makes sense," Joaquin said, feeling his way to solid ground again. "It is far easier to step into the shoes of a farm girl than a princess."

She looked at him a moment or two too long. "Well. Precisely. I'm glad that was so obvious to her and to you, apparently. It had not occurred to me."

"Because you were the one who was demoted, Amalia." And he meant that kindly. Even his voice was softer, of its own accord. "Nobody has a roadmap for Cinderella stories in reverse."

And he could have sworn that Amalia looked… stricken, then. She swallowed, almost as if it hurt, and he waited while she took a sip from her wineglass.

Though he could admit that he was not saddened to see something—anything—on her face that was, if not the light he wanted, something different. Something that broke through her composure in the way he'd long thought only he could—and usually only in the bedroom.

"Delaney has offered me a position," she told him.

And of all the things he might have imagined Amalia wanted to say to him, none of them were that. "I beg your pardon?"

"She and Queen Esme wish to appoint me to a newly formed role. As a minister." And he watched, as if from a great distance, as she sat straighter in her chair. Squaring her shoulders the way she did when she was *working*. As if this conversation was a *job*. "Delaney needs someone who can prepare her for the role she must assume, but it must be someone she trusts. Someone without ambition, or the desire to sell her out to the tabloids. There is really only one person alive who fits the bill."

"Why should she trust you?" His voice dropped the temperature in the room by at least twenty degrees, which at least matched the chill within him then. "She is the reason you were cast out of the only home you have ever known."

"That is not exactly true." Amalia folded her hands in front of her. "Delaney is as much a victim of circumstance as I am. It was her husband who uncovered the truth about her parentage and mine. He is the one who went to Kansas to fetch her and put all of this into motion. She had nothing to do with it."

"Then you are either the most altruistic saint who has ever blessed this earth," he growled at her, "or a fool."

"Thank you," Amalia retorted, her voice clipped and her eyes ablaze—but at least that was light. "I appreciate your support, Joaquin. In this and all things."

And everything inside of him…imploded.

All that fire. All of these bleak weeks that he should have enjoyed to the fullest. The way she had haunted him across five years, and haunted him still, though she was right front of him.

The way she'd cried in a pool in Singapore and denied it, right to his face.

And all the while there was that ache inside him that he could not vanquish, no matter how he tried.

If he could have, he would have roared loud enough to shatter all the glass in this penthouse of his. In all of London, come to that.

Instead, he focused on Amalia.

On the way she watched him, too shrewdly, as if she knew every single thought that crossed his mind. As if she could feel all those things inside of him herself.

As if she knew, damn her, and was doing this anyway.

"I take it that this is not a remote position," he managed to bite out. "If you wish to leave me yet again, Amalia, I wish you would come out and say it."

"How?" she asked him, and he had never heard her use that tone before. It seemed to knock him over, though he knew he was upright. He was winded, and it took him a long moment—and a roaring in his ears—to understand why. It was the softness in her voice. It was the starkness of her gaze. It was as if he had never seen her before, not like this. Unadorned. Without her armor. "How do you think I ought to reach you, Joaquin? When you do not wish to be reached?"

He wanted that to be a slap. A fight. But it wasn't.

She was genuinely asking him these questions. As if her life depended on it—but she wasn't desperate. Not the way he remembered being when his life had been on the line. Too many times.

Not Amalia. She was showing him her softness. Her hope. With no apparent care for her own safety here.

He had never seen anything so reckless.

Joaquin pushed back from the table and stood up, in

a rush. As if he intended to do…something, but what was there to do? Flip his own table? Demand that she love him more than the palace that had expelled her when he had expressly forbidden it?

Order her to protect herself better? When he had just bemoaned her armor?

"You've been here for weeks," he threw at her instead. "*Weeks*. Do you really believe that is a privilege I grant to just anyone?"

"I know you don't," she replied, and he could see the torment in her gaze from across the table. He could feel inside his own chest, as if he was the one doing this to the both of them. "But then, this is my punishment, isn't it? This is what you wanted all along. To make me pay. To keep me close, as close to tethered to you as possible, while you give me nothing in return. So how should I reach you, Joaquin? Tell me what to do and I'll do it."

It would have been different if she'd thrown that at him in anger, clearly trying to hurt him. If she'd been fighting here. But she was only looking at him, her face vulnerable. Her gaze direct, and still too soft for his liking.

She was killing him.

"I have given you everything I know how to give," he hurled back at her.

And then felt as if she'd gut-punched him again, because that was a truth he had not so much as thought. Much less said out loud.

He had spent all these weeks focused on her. On watching her wither away before him. When perhaps the real issue had been him all along, because what she wanted from him he couldn't give. He didn't have it in him. He had been forged by harsh, cruel implements and what she was asking for was a kind of softness that wasn't in him.

It had all been taken from him, long ago.

"It isn't in me," he told her, though his voice was thick. "These things you want, I do not have them."

He saw sheer misery wash over her then, though she didn't look away. If anything, she sat straighter. Her blue eyes glittered, and he wanted to tell himself those weren't tears—but he knew better.

She was *killing* him.

"Do you love me, Joaquin?" she asked him.

It was as if the world stopped.

He felt it jolt and shudder.

And then, in the wake of that, everything seemed to buckle, crack, fall apart.

He buckled. He cracked. He fell apart—and yet he still stood there with the Thames behind him, the blue in her gaze all he could see.

How dare she ask him such a thing?

"I already loved you once, Amalia," he managed to grit out. "It was more than enough."

Amalia stood, then. And held herself so still, so precisely, that she reminded him of nothing so much as a blade. Even though he understood, on some level, that it was not in her nature to cut him.

Perhaps that only made it worse.

"You only love me in retrospect, Joaquin," she said, and she was not yelling. She did not sound cold or distant. She spoke quietly. *Softly,* damn her, and he would have preferred violence. Shattering glass, broken crockery. Proof that he was not the only one so blackened and hollowed out inside. "Only to justify your fury that I dared live up to the responsibilities I had before I met you. Only when it served you did you love me. Only when you could use it as one more weapon against me."

He wanted to shout, but managed to keep from it. He would never know how. "You have no idea what you're talking about."

Not because she was wrong. But because the way he had loved her before seemed like a daydream to him now. Because what he felt for her was not a summer, so quickly gone. It was an ocean. Challenging. Deep.

Eternal, something in him whispered, but he couldn't allow himself to catch hold of that.

"But I do." She spread her hands out before her, but he did not mistake this for a surrender. "I keep coming back to you, don't I? I keep trying. I keep thinking I can love you enough that it won't matter how you feel in return. I keep telling myself that if I manage to love you in the right way, it will make you feel the same. It will show you the way. But it won't. All it does is hurt."

He could still feel the buckling. The cracking. The world falling out from beneath him where he stood, and all of that was better than the pain in his chest. The pain in *him.*

"Why don't you just say that you don't like the life of an anonymous peasant?" he fired back at her. "That all your adventures in blending in on Oxford Street make you feel normal. Interchangeable. And Amalia Montaigne, once the celebrated Crown Princess of Ile d'Montagne, cannot abide it."

She shook her head at him, her gaze too bright, now. It almost made him crave the dimness. "You're making my point for me."

"If you leave me again, it will be the last time," he warned her, because that was all he had left. "It will be the end, Amalia. No matter how many times you kneel."

And maybe it was just the world turning again, that jolting feeling that rocked through him when all she did was gaze back at him.

So he could see the way her chest heaved, as if this was no easier on her.

That did not make him feel any better.

"If you have to threaten me to keep me," she said, very distinctly, as if she too could hear the noise in his head, "you don't love me. And I doubt you ever did."

He wanted to argue that. He wanted to shout down the building they stood in. But there was that starkness on her face and it was in him, too, and all he could do was stand there. Like he was made of stone.

Like he was that lonely fortress he had turned into a hotel, keeping watch on an island for invaders who never came.

And she was offering him a softness he could not abide. He would not. It was a weakness.

Surely how he felt right now proved that.

"Joaquin," she said, her voice thick now. And he could see that whatever haunted him, haunted her, too. "You don't love anything. And I fear if I stay, that emptiness will slowly chip away at me until I am as empty as you are."

And everything in him was a terrible din. An endless, brutal roar.

He wanted more than anything to fall to his knees for a change. To beg her to stay with him. To do whatever it took to keep her—

But that was not who he was. That was not the man who'd climbed his way out of literal gutters on the force of his will alone.

Joaquin Vargas dominated, he did not yield. Ask anyone.

"No one is making you stay here," he gritted out, though even his tongue felt bitter. "No one is forcing this emptiness upon you. By all means, Amalia. Leave if you want to leave. I will not stop you."

No matter how much he wanted to.

She let out the soft, rough noise of a small thing. Some kind of sob.

And Joaquin thought it likely ripped out what little heart remained in him.

But he didn't move. He didn't reach for her.

He certainly didn't *kneel*.

Amalia turned from him, her head high and her carriage sheer perfection, and began to walk away.

She stopped before she left the room and swayed a little herself, catching hold of the doorway with one hand. "Joaquin…"

As if, even now, she thought she could make him crumble. And the horror was, he wanted to.

The noises inside him were not small, but he did not wish to let her hear them. She had already seen far too much of him. If she hadn't, this would not be so painful. If she hadn't, he could have avoided all of this.

"Are you leaving me or aren't you?" he demanded, because that was what he had always done. Offend, not defend.

It had made him a billionaire.

Amalia let out another sound, more ragged this time. It was unbearable.

But she didn't wait to see his reaction. She didn't look back again. She tilted up her chin like he'd tried to hit her there, and walked away from him.

And he told himself, again and again, that this was another win. Another victory. Another feather in his cap, whatever that meant.

The reality was that he sat back down in his abandoned chair and wasn't sure he planned to get up again.

Amalia did not return. He heard the security system beep when she let herself out, and that was the end of it.

He stayed where he was for a long, long time, until he felt just about as empty as she told him he was.

But at least he'd won.

There was that, if nothing else.

Joaquin sat there for some time, telling himself it was enough.

CHAPTER TEN

BEING BACK IN Ile d'Montagne felt like an out-of-body experience.

Especially when Amalia was picked up at the private airfield by the same palace driver who had always picked her up. But then, instead of taking her to one of the private entrances as she'd expected, he delivered her to the front of the palace where anyone could see her arrival. See it and report it to the world.

Someone was making a statement.

Amalia had to adjust her approach to, well, everything in a flash. Because she'd been expecting that they'd sneak her in the side door, cutting down on the possibility of any photographic evidence of her presence. Since she was likely still considered to be an embarrassment. *Our Fake Princess* the papers had called her.

The senior aides had never looked at her the same way again.

It had never occurred to Amalia that the palace might *not* hide her.

But as the car slowed in front of the public entrance, all her training came back to her in a rush. As if she'd never been away. How to exit the car. How to walk, with perfect posture and a slightly inclined head, to indicate respect for the institution of the monarchy as well as her own quiet confidence. She had dressed for the palace in an understated dress and unobtrusively elegant cashmere cardigan, even if her heels were a trifle too exuberant for a person who could make no claim to the throne. She knew the courtiers would whisper amongst themselves and say she had aspirations above herself.

But the good news was, she didn't have to care what courtiers thought about anything any longer. Besides, they would say such things about her no matter what she wore.

She was ushered into the palace's grand foyer and expected to be marched off to some reception room or other, where she would wait to be given instructions. No doubt by some or other member of the senior staff—and likely someone she already knew. She was prepared to pretend she felt no shred of awkwardness whatsoever, because, it turned out, the moment she set foot inside this palace she knew exactly how to play her role.

Any role.

Because she had always been very good at this.

She stopped walking when she realized no one was escorting her, and more, someone appeared to be waiting for her. And Amalia was shocked when she realized that the person standing there beneath a chandelier that had inspired no fewer than seven separate well-known poems was none other than Delaney Clark.

"Well, thank God you're here," the other woman said in her warm American accent, which shouldn't have surprised Amalia at all. And yet it did. When was the last time there had been Americans in the palace? Had there *ever* been Americans in the palace? Having so recently been in Kansas herself, Amalia found she loved it. "I'm making a mess of everything."

"You shouldn't even be greeting me," Amalia said, in tacit agreement. "That's the sort of thing you have your staff take care of, if possible. Just so everyone remembers their place."

Delaney was wearing a similar outfit to Amalia's. Amalia thought they both recognized that similarity in the same moment. And as Delaney walked—too briskly, too energetically—toward Amalia, it was impossible not to notice how similar they looked, no matter what they happened to be wearing. They both had long black hair. They both had blue eyes. There were differences, of course. The shape of a nose, a chin. Amalia was taller. Delaney had a spate of freckles across her nose.

But they could easily have been sisters.

"I'm an American," Delaney said as she drew close, smiling. "The only places I'm aware of are geographic."

"Welcome to Europe," Amalia murmured. "We like a hierarchy."

Delaney came to a stop before her, dropping her smile. Her gaze became more intense. "I know how kind you were to my mother. I won't ever forget that."

Amalia smiled. "If you mean the Queen, I've spent a lifetime being kind to her. If you mean Catherine, well. She's actually my mother, too."

"I can't pretend to understand how hard this must have been for you," Delaney said, her blue eyes no less intense. "For me, everyone keeps going on and on about my change in fortune as if every moment should be a nonstop delight. I'm a Cinderella for the ages, apparently."

That reminded her of something. Amalia made herself smile, though thinking of Joaquin hurt. But then, trying not to think about him hurt, too.

It all hurt.

"Someone told me that I'm Cinderella in reverse," she told this woman who looked like her and who was now living her life. "And there are no stories for that."

Delaney's gaze turned shrewd. And Amalia remembered the first time she'd met this woman, in a press call that had been all about flashbulbs and fixed smiles. Even then, she'd liked her. Now, though, she liked her even more—maybe because she'd spent some time in that farmhouse. She'd sat on that much-loved couch in the living room and heard stories about people Delaney had known and loved.

They'd exchanged lives more than once already. How could they do anything *but* like each other?

"It seems you came to exactly the right place," Delaney was saying. "Because it looks like we have a lot of new stories to write, you and me."

Instead of summoning the servants to escort her to a guest suite, Delaney walked with her. And Amalia was so involved in pretending not to be overwhelmed by being back in the palace that it took her a moment to realize that they were walking directly to her old rooms.

"You can't be serious," she said when they stopped outside her old door. "These are the Crown Princess's rooms." She remembered herself. "They're yours, Your Royal Highness."

"Call me Delaney, please." And Delaney shrugged when Amalia stared at her instead of proceeding into her old rooms. "I don't actually stay in the palace." At Amalia's look of astonishment, she sighed. "My husband prefers to stay under a separate roof than the one the Queen enjoys."

"I see."

And Amalia did see. Of course Cayetano Arcieri, sworn enemy of the Montaigne family for the entirety of his life—a grudge he had inherited from untold generations in his very blood—would not lay his head down in the palace. Not until it was his.

"Did you choose the dower house?" she asked. "I've always thought it would be the best place to live. Near enough to the palace, yet also far enough away."

"This is why you are the only person in the world I can turn to for help," Delaney said then, her expression fierce and serious. "You already know everything I've had to learn on the fly."

And this felt weird. There was no getting around that. It *was* weird.

But still, Amalia knew—just as she had in London when Delaney had extended this offer—that this was where she belonged. She thought of Catherine and the cornfields, and even though it was in complete defiance of all known protocol, she reached out her hand and put it on Delaney's arm.

"I was very, very good at being the Crown Princess," she said softly. "And it will be my honor to make you even better."

And that was precisely what she set out to do.

She spent her first few days sitting down with Delaney—because Esme was unavailable, she was told each time she tried to see her—and her seethingly ferocious husband, who looked at Amalia with frank suspicion. Which she returned in kind.

"This is not my idea," he told her, seeming far too large and dangerous for the elegant dower house.

"I think we all know it wasn't mine," Amalia replied, princess smile in place. "Or I would be the one wearing the tiara."

"It was my idea," Delaney told him, with a private sort of smile. "And it's a good one."

Cayetano and Amalia, born and raised to be mortal enemies, were just going to have to learn how to deal with each other.

Amalia set up an office in the palace. She knew precisely which staff members she needed to ask to join her, and which ones she would allow nowhere near this particular enterprise.

"I think this means you're my chief of staff," Delaney said one day, sitting slouched in the corner of Amalia's new office, wearing clothing that would likely give Queen Esme the vapors if she were to see it. A T-shirt reading MIDWEST IS BEST and a pair of jeans that Amalia's former aides would have removed from her wardrobe and burned, without asking.

"The Crown Princess does not have a chief of staff," Amalia told her. "That sounds like something a common politician might require. You are a member of a royal family stretching back into antiquity." She smiled. "I believe you can call me your lady-in-waiting."

Delaney sighed. "That seems a very silly name for all the things you do."

Amalia eyed the true heir to the kingdom over the span of her desk. "Here's the thing about real power. It doesn't matter what it's called. All that matters is if you can wield it."

"I take it the lessons have begun," Delaney said with a laugh.

And every moment she wasn't in the palace or in the dower house on the grounds with Delaney, Amalia was exploring. She'd decided that she did not wish to live in the palace, and certainly not in the very same rooms were she'd been a different person. She was a private citizen now. And she might serve the crown yet again, but that didn't mean she wasn't permitted her own life as well.

Besides, she had lived on this island her entire life, yet knew it very little. She knew what their main city looked like from the safety of her motorcade. She'd visited any number of sites and toured them, but always in staid and formal arranged engagements.

Now she had the freedom, at last, to walk anywhere she liked. To do anything she pleased.

At first she worried that the citizens would respond badly to her presence, but it was the opposite. Everywhere she went, she was recognized, but that wasn't a bad thing. People stopped to talk to her. Many complimented her for going away with such grace.

"I think I might've had a tantrum or two, me," said one woman she met in the open-air market.

"I would bring the palace down," vowed another.

"I might have lit a match," Amalia replied, smiling. "But I stamped it out again."

After she'd been back on the island for a solid ten days, she had narrowed down her favorite spots and toured the various neighborhoods—on foot, not in a royal procession. She bought herself a lovely little cottage on the hillside, where she could look at the palace but also the sea beyond.

And if she stood there in the first place she'd ever owned, just for her, and looked for the hint of an island fortress on the horizon…she couldn't really blame herself. That was the good thing about a heart so thoroughly broken. Amalia doubted that any more damage could be done to it. Why not stare at the horizon? Why not cry herself to sleep?

It was just life. Her life, like it or not.

"You must be some kind of saint," sneered her least favorite paparazzo one morning.

Amalia liked to walk to work, because it gave her time to clear out the cobwebs of the dreams she had each night, all of them featuring Joaquin. She got to breathe in the air that smelled as she recalled it, salt and flowers. She got to be a part of the island instead of in it, yet apart from it. And she liked to tell herself, as she walked along, that this was what being alive was all about.

Feet moving. Heart aching. Breathing in deep, and still, enjoying it all in its own way.

"I hope I'm not a saint," she replied, smiling when she really did not feel like smiling at all. "Doesn't that usually involve horrid death?"

"Want to tell me what kind of person gets kicked out of the royal family only to come back and set herself up as an advisor to the very person who kicked her out?" He shook his head, the odious man. "I'll tell you what kind of person. A snake or a con."

"Believe what you like, Maurizio," she replied, with an airiness she was delighted to discover she actually felt. Because as little as she liked this man, she really didn't care what he said about her. It reflected badly on absolutely no one. He could think whatever he wanted about her. "You will anyway, and I'm sure your paper will love that."

Later that day, after preparing Delaney for a series of engagements that were deemed ceremonial but would actually be a test, Amalia ducked into a salon she knew was little used to make some notes.

And when she glanced up again, the Queen was there.

For a moment she could only stare. Then she remembered herself, and rose to her feet so that she could execute a proper curtsy. And not the one she'd used to greet her mother the first time she saw her each day, but the kind of curtsy she had not been called upon to give before. Deep and low, as befitting a commoner before a queen.

"I think that by rights you are an American," Esme said coolly. "And as such are not required to curtsy to anyone."

Amalia rose. "But I still think of you as my mother," she replied simply. "And I don't have it in me not to honor you."

She'd meant that to come out lightly. She wasn't prepared for the fact that *lightly* wasn't how it seemed to land. It hung there between them instead.

Then, as she watched, Queen Esme of Ile d'Montagne, who eschewed weakness in all its forms... looked very much as if there were tears in her eyes.

"I hope you know," the Queen said after a very long moment, and not in her usual ringing tones. "That is, I hope you understand..."

There was a time when Amalia would have leaped in to finish the sentence for her. To save her mother from anything, even what passed for her maternal duties. She didn't do that today. She was a new person, wasn't she?

So she waited.

"I only know how to care about one thing," Esme said stiffly, still with eyes far too bright. "This did not distress me overmuch, because I raised you to care deeply about the same thing. And I believed, for all these years, that whatever I lacked as a mother I would make up somehow as Queen. It never occurred to me that I could lose you, Amalia. I find what has happened…" She sighed. "It is unthinkable. I cannot fathom any part of it."

"Delaney will be a far better crown princess than I ever could be," Amalia said, and she knew she would have said that anyway. But she found she meant it as much when Delaney wasn't in the room as when she was. "And she's the rightful Princess besides. That matters."

"But she has gone and married an Arcieri," Esme said bitterly. Then she blew out a breath. "And she is not mine. Not the way you are."

The old Amalia would have been replete at this. For a woman who was in no way demonstrative, Esme might as well have taken up skywriting with those two small sentences that set years of her life aglow in retrospect.

But Amalia was not the person who had stuck away from this palace, under cover of night. She was the Amalia who had knelt upon stone and walked through fire. She was the Amalia who had found a kind of peace in a Kansas cornfield and who had looked a stranger in the face and known her instantly.

She was the Amalia who had lost the man she loved three times. And had no hope that anything could ever change that. Some fortresses could be renovated and made into luxury hotels. She'd seen that with her own eyes.

But others were like the old fortress she'd toured right here on Ile d'Montagne two days ago. Once used by the coastal dwellers to ward off the mountain rebels, it had been impregnable in its day. And now was nothing but a ruin, worn away by sand and sea and beaten down by the sun. It was good for nothing but atmospheric photographs.

Amalia knew too well what kind of fortress housed Joaquin's heart.

She knew too well what she had lost.

And somehow, that gave her the courage to look Esme in the eye.

"That Delaney is not yours is a good thing," she told the Queen she would always consider her mother. "I was too much yours. I would have married one of those milksop men you chose for me and obeyed you in all things. And that would suit you well, I'm sure, but only as long as you live."

"It is my intention to live for some time," Esme said sharply. "Especially now."

"Long live you," Amalia said, with a smile. "But no one lives forever, Your Majesty. Even you. And how would our plans have left the country? A weak king and a new queen too used to taking orders? I think in time you will find that Delaney will be a far better queen than I ever could have been."

Esme sniffed. "Maybe she could have been, if it weren't for the warlord."

"You know that he is right to want to unite the kingdom," Amalia said softly. "And he might not answer to you, but then, he listens to only one person on this earth. Luckily, she is your daughter. She will do great things."

The Queen looked over her shoulder, frowned, then shooed away whoever waited in the hall with the tiny flick of one finger. Then she returned her attention to Amalia.

"You did not take such liberties with me when you lived here."

"I did not dare," Amalia agreed. "Yet another reason I would have been an uninspired queen."

"Then you do not miss it?" Esme's voice was sharper

now. "Have you taken this role so that you can relive the glory that was once yours?"

Wasn't that what that toad of a paparazzo had suggested? He wouldn't be the first or the last, she knew.

"I will tell you a secret," Amalia said then. "Because you were my mother and you will always be my Queen." She waited for Esme to lean toward her, slightly. She did the same in reverse. Then she whispered, so no lurking courtiers could hear, "I don't miss being the Crown Princess at all. I much prefer telling Delaney exactly what she should do, and then retreating out of the spotlight into civilian life."

Esme took that in, a canny look in her blue eyes. Blue eyes that Amalia had always thought were like hers. But now, having spent so much time with Delaney, she could see that hers were an entirely different shade. More like the Balearic Sea, less like the calm waters of Ile d'Montagne's Royal Bay. She didn't know how to feel about that.

"And your sudden delight in civilian life and all its charms," the Queen said, as if she was musing. When Esme rarely mused. Commands were her preferred mode of address. "This would not have anything to do with your enthusiastic embrace of one, particular civilian, would it?"

Because, of course, Joaquin was everywhere she turned. Even in this conversation, where Amalia had not expected to find him.

"I suppose I should be horrified and outraged that you've had me watched," Amalia said after a moment. She shook her head. "But I find that instead I'm rather touched. That's as good as a love letter from you, Mother. Forgive me. I meant, *Your Majesty*."

Esme did not exactly unbend. There was a considering gleam in her gaze. "You are the only one I intend to forgive for familiarity of address," she said, with a slight inclination of her head, as if bestowing a gift. "But Amalia. Joaquin Vargas? He is unmanageable at best."

"Entirely so," Amalia agreed. She did not say, *And that's why I'm in love with him.*

But then, perhaps she didn't have to say that out loud.

"You may have been raised to be a princess you are not," Esme said, and Amalia thought she sounded almost...careful. "But that still means that you have one of the finest educations in the land. You're poised and graceful. And you're in possession of a considerable fortune that will, of course, only grow over time. You could have anyone at all, child. Must it truly be an uncivilized Spaniard who has not one respectful bone in his entire body?"

Amalia blew out a breath at that. "I appreciate the warning," she managed to say. "But this is all a bit embarrassingly after the fact. The choice was not mine to make."

When Esme only gazed back at her without seeming to understand, she felt her cheeks turn pink, and not in the happy way they did when Joaquin was near. This time it was straight embarrassment. "He doesn't want me."

She was proud of herself for saying that the way she did. A statement of fact, not laced through with self-pity, or any kind of whine. Amalia was proud that her voice didn't crack and that she didn't split wide open and bawl. That she could state an unpleasant truth like that, and still save her tears for the privacy of her own cottage.

When she was not under the gimlet gaze of a woman

who would never approve of Joaquin in the first place—and would certainly not approve of any mourning for him now he was gone.

Esme seemed to study her for a long, long while.

So long that Amalia's cheeks lost some of their embarrassed pink.

The Queen appeared to come to a decision. She drew herself up. "This is not something I would have told you if things had gone as planned," Esme said. "I would have had it cleaned up, swept away. I would have made certain you never knew."

When Amalia only stared at her, Queen Esme waved a regal hand in the direction of the salon's casement windows. "I think you may have underestimated how much your uncivilized Spaniard wants you, after all."

And even though her heart kicked into gear then, pounding at her, Amalia felt as if she was trapped in some kind of iron grip that made it impossible to move. It slowed her down as she turned and headed toward those windows, making her feel as if she was fighting her way through some kind of quicksand. All she could hear was the drum of her own heart in her ears. She struggled to put one foot in front of the other when what she wanted was to run.

This particular salon was set up in the front of the palace, looking down over the ceremonial forecourt and beyond it, the grand square where the public could gather and often did.

But today, though the square was teeming with its usual number of tourists, stalls, and bored teenagers, there was a bit of a crowd at the gates.

Because a man was there.

And Amalia's heart stopped in her chest, because the man was Joaquin.

Her Joaquin, here in Ile d'Montagne.

Her Joaquin, except it couldn't be, because *this* Joaquin was on his knees.

CHAPTER ELEVEN

Joaquin Vargas kneeled to nothing and no one.

But this was about Amalia.

And when it came to Amalia, there were no rules. There was only having her or not having her, and he had tried both. He'd had her without giving all of himself, which had resulted in not having her at all, which was worse.

The one thing he knew was that when all the usual things stopped working, it was time for innovation.

Innovation or surrender.

And he had come up with a thousand crazy schemes to bring her back to him. He could kidnap her. It was frowned upon in polite circles, but what did he care about such things as *polite circles*. But he still nixed that idea, because he thought Amalia wouldn't like it.

He was a remarkably wealthy man. He could hire his own army and storm the palace at Ile d'Montagne if it pleased him. But Amalia, again, was unlikely to support such an action.

Joaquin couldn't risk it.

Because she had left him in London and he had gone cold. Bitter. He had spent the first few days after her departure storming around his home and his office, verbally beheading anyone foolish enough to cross his path.

It had failed to make him feel the least bit better.

And at the strangest moments, he kept thinking of Amalia. Not in the usual ways that haunted his dreams, but in her two exquisite acts of surrender, both of which had completely disarmed him.

Both of them on her knees.

And both times, he had felt the same wonder as he gazed upon her.

Because he would have thought that kneeling down like that was an act so shameful, so subservient, that it should have made her tremble that she did it so gracefully. Beautifully, even. It should have made her seem less, somehow, in his eyes.

Except when she did it, it didn't seem like surrender.

More like its opposite.

Once that idea had taken hold, Joaquin hadn't been able to get it out of his mind. Like all his obsessions, save one, he knew that the only way to get rid of it was to immerse himself within it.

He hadn't known it was even possible to kneel down with no clear idea what might become of it. Even if he commanded them to bend, would his knees obey him?

He was Joaquin Vargas, who obeyed no one. He had built his entire identity on the fact that he alone walked alone. That he alone had always been alone.

That he was so powerful that the whole world ought to genuflect before him and often did, not the other way around.

But at some point, during another sleepless night in a cold and uncomfortable flat spanning three stories in a London that felt empty without one particular ex-princess, he faced the unpleasant, yet inescapable truth.

It was his pride that wanted power.

His heart simply wanted her.

Whatever it took. Whatever she needed.

Joaquin hadn't expected that he would argue his way into the palace. He hadn't been sure if they'd even let him into the country. But when they did, he delivered himself to that famous square out front that he'd seen on television too many times to count. Most of those times in the past five years, when he'd pretended not to be watching news reports from Ile d'Montagne, and yet had somehow caught every one.

Just for a glimpse of her.

He'd walked to the gates, ignored the guards, and knelt.

And he had convinced himself on the flight down from England that the moment he took to his knees he would feel better. He would feel whole. He would feel... whatever it was those smug holy people felt when they were finally living out their purpose.

He felt none of those things.

He absolutely hated every second of what could only be seen as groveling.

And Joaquin Vargas did not grovel.

But when the guards told him to move on, he was obliged to tell them that he refused.

"I am here for Amalia Montaigne," he told them, and let his voice ring out with authority and command. "I do not intend to move until I see her."

And there'd been no small part of him that was looking forward to the guards' reaction to that, hoping it would allow him to dust off some of his old street fighting skills. He could think of nothing he wanted more at that moment than to bash a few heads together.

But there were paparazzi around, which he'd anticipated. It was why he'd chosen this specific venue for his little display. It had taken them very little time to identify him, and the next thing he knew cameras were recording his every move—or lack of movement—and he was forced to stay right there, on his knees.

"Joaquin Vargas on his knees?" one of the paparazzi dared laugh at him.

"I take it you have not set eyes on Amalia," Joaquin replied, and the crowd laughed louder, with a smattering of applause thrown in.

And even as he said that he knew it would end up on front pages. Everywhere.

Some part of him welcomed that. Still, he was considering his options. Kidnap was looking better and better by the moment, especially when a few tourists ignored his death glare and took selfies right in front of him.

But then, finally, the grand front gates to the palace opened, right there before him.

And at last Amalia appeared.

Joaquin was vaguely aware she had not come alone. There were people behind her, possibly royal people, but he didn't care about them.

Because she was walking toward him, and suddenly, he knew that he could kneel forever. And would, if that was what it took.

"Joaquin," Amalia said, in that way she always said his name. As if she was counting her blessings each time she found it on her tongue. "Since when do you kneel?"

"Is that what you want?" He was not surprised to find his voice rough. And so he opened up his arms, wide, hiding nothing from her or anyone. "Is that what it will take?"

He saw her look around, as if taking in the crowd. But when she returned her gaze to his, she wasn't wearing that perfect princess smile any longer. He could see all the emotion in her blue eyes, stamped there for all to see.

It was all right there on her face.

And everything she was, everything inside her, everything *Amalia* burned so brightly there that he wanted to leap up and hide her from these jackals. From the world. From himself, certainly. He wanted to protect her if she wouldn't protect herself—

And in case the fact he was on his knees hadn't indicated to him what was happening here, that certainly did.

But he didn't have time to reel at that because she moved closer to him anyway, and then he took her hands in his. And then, as if they were all alone on Cap Morat once more, she dropped down to her knees before him.

"Now everyone will do it," Joaquin said, unable to be anything but sardonic when inside him, he could hardly keep track of that wildfire that surged through him. He wanted to call it lust. Need. Hunger.

But those were shallow words to describe what he felt.

They were also the least important part.

"I don't need you to humble yourself for me," Amalia whispered fiercely. "That's not who you are."

"I find nothing humbling in this," he told her, and was surprised to discover he meant that. "There is no weakness in surrender. You taught me that."

Amalia studied his face as if she'd never seen it before. "You know that I love you. But I love *you,* Joaquin. It's uncivilized. Unpredictable. Untamable. I don't need you to surrender anything. I don't want it."

"You shall have it all the same." He switched their hands, so that his were on the outside. He tugged her closer, so he could get her face close to his. The way he liked it.

"Don't do this," Amalia whispered. "It isn't fair. If you knew how hard it was to leave you—"

"But you made it look so easy, *cariño*. Every time."

Her eyes flashed. "It broke my heart. More every time. I doubt there is anything left. And if you think that you can—"

"Amalia," he interrupted her. "*Cariño.* I love you."

Amalia's eyes, the color of the sea, went blank. Her perfect lips fell open.

"I love you," Joaquin said again, with all the ruthlessness and tenacity that made him who he was. He could hear the murmurs all around them, and *I love you* floating on the breeze as it was repeated and repeated. *Good,* he thought. Because this was different from long ago, when he had murmured endearments in bed and then shouted out his *I love you* in outrage during that parting scene. This was better. "I love only you. I will never love anything or anyone *but* you. Not because you left me and so it is the only thing I can use as a weapon. Not as if loving you sometime in the past and losing you anyway is any kind of virtue. I suspect it makes me a damned fool three times over."

"Never," she whispered.

But he couldn't stop now. He bent his head to hers. "You make me imagine that this world is fair. That the life I have led and the things I have survived are the price I must pay to deserve you. And I believe that. I do. I would willingly pay them all over again."

And this time, his name sounded like a sob. That soft, small noise he hadn't thought he'd get to hear again. He wanted to hoard them all.

"I will not be satisfied with a summer when you were

twenty," he told her. "A few months five years later. Or not nearly enough weeks in a rainy London summer."

He lifted one hand to tug a tendril of her long black hair between his thumb and forefinger, then tucked the raw silk behind one ear. "I want them all. And I want all of you. No compartments. No rules. I want your body, but you know that. And Amalia, it isn't enough. I want your heart. I want your dreams. I want your hopes, your wishes, your mad ideas. I want to take your life and entwine it with my own, so that we are as close to one as two people can become."

"I want all of that," she whispered, and only then did he realize that her eyes had welled up with tears, and they were making tracks down her face. "You have no idea how much. But Joaquin, you don't want babies. And I want a family that no one can switch up on me. I want…" She took a deep breath. "I want everything, Joaquin. But you don't."

And a few months ago he would have agreed. Now he knew better.

He leaned his forehead against hers. "For you, my Amalia, I have learned how to be a man. You have taught me what it is to be human, and for that sin, I've broken your heart and blamed you for it. And still you kneel before me with tears in your eyes. Still you want me."

"In my whole life," she told him softly, so softly, when he knew he didn't deserve her softness, "I have wanted only you. The moment I was free of the palace, even if that wasn't what I had planned, I ran to you. I will always run to you."

"You will not have to," he vowed. "Because I will be right there beside you."

Her eyes overflowed again and this time he wiped away her tears.

"For you, I will become a husband," he vowed to her, there on his knees in the full light of day. "And a father. And you know who I am, Amalia. The gutters of Bilbao could not contain me. I have never accepted a single boundary that was ever drawn for me. Anything and everything I dreamed, I made real. And there is only one woman on this earth that I would ever consider marrying. Only one woman who I, on some level, must want to bear my child. For I have never been so careless. I never will be again."

Amalia was crying openly now, but this was not the red eyes in the pool in Singapore. He knew she might feel many things, but she was not sad. She was not a ghost. She was right here, in his arms, where she belonged.

"This must be a dream," she whispered. "I've had this dream."

"If it is indeed a dream," came another voice, "I'm very surprised to discover that I'm in it."

Joaquin glanced to the side and saw another black-haired, blue-eyed woman before him, though she could not hold a candle to Amalia. No matter the dangerous-looking man at her side.

Next to them stood Queen Esme in all her glory, and he anticipated that she would look at him as if he was something stuck to her shoe. But instead, the Queen nodded her head, as if bestowing her blessing, and even smiled.

And when he looked back to Amalia, she looked as full of wonder as she ever had that first summer. She looked bright and wild, the way she should.

"Marry me," he demanded, because he could do

nothing else. "Live with me, Amalia, and let us spend every moment we have together fully alive."

"Not merely existing," she whispered.

"Never," Joaquin promised. "Not as long as we draw breath."

And he waited there, on his knees before a palace, while the only princess he had ever loved gazed back at him.

He would wait forever.

And then, a smile breaking across her face, Amalia threw herself fully into his arms. Then she looped her arms around his neck, and kissed him.

As if, together, they'd written themselves a brand-new fairy tale. The one about a man like a wolf and the perfect princess who'd tamed him by not taming him at all, but loving him as he was, no matter how he snarled.

And then, together, they'd won.

Because there was only one way a story like that could ever be won.

With true love…and forever not far behind.

Joaquin couldn't wait.

CHAPTER TWELVE

QUEEN ESME INSISTED on throwing Amalia a wedding. She brought Catherine over from Kansas, and Amalia knew that both she and Delaney were equally taken aback and entertained by the way the two older women, each powerful in her own way, danced around each other—and yet seemed to like the dance.

"I guess we really are sisters, after a fashion," Amalia said after witnessing her two mothers laughing together, when she could not recall ever seeing the Queen laugh like that.

"Oh, this is definitely our family," Delaney agreed cheerfully. "There's no getting out of it now."

And so that was how Amalia Montaigne, no longer the Crown Princess of Ile d'Montagne, married the one true love of her life in the Royal Cathedral where she had been expected to marry a tedious bore at her mother's command.

This, she thought as she floated down the length of the church in a dress that had made both of her mothers teary, *is much better.*

Because it was Joaquin who waited for her at the head of the aisle, looking deliciously disreputable in his wedding clothes, his green eyes glinting all for her.

And when it was done, not one, but two mothers kissed her and hugged Joaquin, too.

Amalia supposed that all the papers the next day would try to outdo each other with their clever commentary—though the swords had been dulled by the world's delight in Joaquin's kneeling response to yet another vile paparazzo—but, in truth, she didn't care.

Because she and Joaquin returned once again to Cap Morat. Only this time, they stayed in the honeymoon suite there at the top of the fortress. And the sensual pull between them would always be a huge part of who they were, but this time, though they enjoyed each other as they always did, their hearts were unguarded. They were wide open.

And so they talked.

They took walks around the island together, hand in hand, and it was as if they'd talked like this forever. There was no subject too grand or too small. They told each other stories, they made each other laugh.

They got to know each other all over again, the way they had that first summer.

The way, Amalia thought, they always would.

And that was what they did.

They put love first, and when they did, love followed.

They left the island sometime later, but didn't discover that Amalia was pregnant until a month or so after that, when they were back on Ile d'Montagne. Joaquin, who liked her cottage but preferred more room to move around, had bought up the properties on both sides and was already meeting with architects to create the perfect home for them. One, he assured her, that would not be filled with refurbished jail cells or uncomfortable midcentury furniture. He could fly in and out of the island as easily as anywhere, and it was nothing to go back and forth to London as needed.

"You had better build a nursery," Amalia told him.

"I told you that I want children," he said, looking at her intently in a way that never failed to make her knees go weak. "Your children. I do not go back on promises, *mi cariño*."

"I never said you did. But we'll be needing that nursery," she told him. And slid her hands over her belly in case he'd missed her point. "In about eight months?"

She was somehow unsurprised when her husband reacted to this news by swinging her up into his arms, spinning her around, and then making sure she was well and truly pregnant by taking her right there on the cottage's small sofa.

Their son was born a month before Delaney gave birth to a black-haired, blue-eyed daughter, the new heir to the kingdom. She and Cayetano named the new Princess Catarina Amalia, in honor, Delaney said, of two of the finest women she had ever known.

In time, Amalia gave Joaquin three more sons, each one of them more delightfully disreputable than the last. And she was not the least bit surprised that her beloved, who had never wanted a child, was such a good father to his boys that it could still make her cry. And often did.

But it was not until the eldest Vargas boy, the extraordinarily stubborn and too-much-like-his-father Roderigo, married Princess Catarina that Amalia and Delaney stopped calling themselves sisters *after a fashion*.

Because they all became family in truth.

"And if I had to do it all over again," Amalia told her first royal grandchild, in the nursery of the palace where she had played herself, as a child, "I would not change a thing."

When she looked up, she found Joaquin standing there, watching her as he always did.

With love in his heart and written all over his face.

They had spent their life *alive,* and had fought to keep from squandering love along the way. They had treated their life, their love, and their happiness as gifts.

Because that was the way that *happy ever after* came true.

Every single day.

* * * * *

COMING SOON!

We really hope you enjoyed reading this book. If you're looking for more romance, be sure to head to the shops when new books are available on

Thursday 9th June